John Steele was born a
In 1995, at the age of tw
States and has since lived and worked on three continents,
including a thirteen-year spell in Japan. Among past jobs he has
been a drummer in a rock band, an illustrator, a truck driver
and a teacher of English. He now lives in England with his wife
and daughter. He began writing short stories, selling them to
North American magazines and fiction digests. He has published
three previous novels: *Ravenhill*, *Seven Skins* and *Dry River*, the
first of which was longlisted for a CWA Debut Dagger award.
John's books have been described as 'remarkable' by the *Sunday
Times*, 'dark and thrilling' by Claire McGowan, and 'spectacular'
by Tony Parsons. The *Irish Independent* called John 'a writer of
huge promise' and Gary Donnelly appointed him 'the undisputed
champion of the modern metropolitan thriller'.

RAT ISLAND

John Steele

SILVERTAIL BOOKS • *London*

For my dad. I could never repay what you did for me in life but I hope this goes some way.

And for the Bleecker Street crew of '95, John, Stan and especially Hugh. Part of me is still sinking beers with you on a rickety brownstone fire escape, and shooting the breeze in the cab of a truck with the South Bronx boys.

Cast Of Characters

THE COPS
ROYAL HONG KONG POLICE FORCE
Sergeant Callum Burke
Sergeant Bobby Ho
Sub-Divisional Inspector James Milburn

NEW YORK POLICE DEPARTMENT
Sergeant Mike O'Connell
Detective Georgie Ruiz
Detective Anton Galinski

DRUG ENFORCEMENT ADMINISTRATION
Special Agent Niku Mattila

*

THE CRIMINALS
NEW YORK IRISH
Paddy Doolan
Fintan Walsh
Jimmy Mulligan

NEW YORK CHINATOWN TONG
Sammy Ong
Mickey Chiu
Charlie Lin
Papa Ng

HONG KONG TRIAD
Tony Lau, Dragon Head (leader)
Pineapple Wong, fixer
Tse, 429 enforcer

*

THE CIVILIANS
Trinity/Nurse Löwin, Dominatrix
Johnny Johnson, employee, New World Movers
Willie Simmons, employee, New World Movers

New York City
1995

Chapter One

Callum Burke was late for the Chinese taxidermist's murder. He shoved a Camel between cracked lips and sparked his Zippo then leaned against the wall next to the subway entrance on 42nd. He lit the cigarette like a fuse. His watch read eight-twenty. A handsome drunk black guy in khaki pants and a busted-up jacket caught his eye and sauntered over, flexing and weaving through pedestrians like the booze in his system had liquefied his bones.

'Excuse me, man, you got thirty cents?' Alcohol fumes seeped through Callum's tobacco cloud.

'No, I don't have any change.'

'Thirty cents, man. I just need thirty cents for my bus to Chester.'

'Sorry. No change.'

'Alright. God loves you anyway, man.'

The drunk lurched off as a Latino girl in a PVC miniskirt with a sweet face and glazed eyes strolled up.

'Hey, baby. You all by yourself?'

'Just like the song.'

'You want some company? I got a half hour to spare.'

'Not tonight.'

A wired, scrawny white youth made a move after the girl tottered away.

'Hey, man, you got the time?' His voice was drowned by the stream of traffic heading to and from 8th Avenue. Callum cocked his head toward the youth as a siren howled from somewhere behind Port Authority.

The youth leaned closer. 'You got the time?'

Callum checked his watch. 'Uh, it's – '

'I got blow, speed, crack, H. What you need?'

'No, I'm good.'

'It's aaaaall good, man'

Callum pinched the bridge of his nose. A cop was standing on the corner fifteen feet away working hard not to notice the wicked business going down on his patch. The buildings of midtown rocketed skyward, swallowed by low rags of cloud oppressing the early evening bustle of the streets.

A tide of gossip, questions, information and bawdy profanity assaulted him. Before, in the other metropolis of Hong Kong, it had been just as raucous but most of it was Cantonese backwash, white noise he filtered out. Now it was rushing him, penetrating his skull and cannoning around in his head.

'Thirty cents, man? Port Authority's just across the street.'

The black man reappeared on his right, face bathed in yellow from a neon sign declaring, *In the day of trouble the Lord delivers him.*

'I told you already,' said Callum.

'Hey baby, you busy?'

'I'm fine.'

'You wanna' get high?'

'You wanna' fuck?'

'What time is it, brother?'

'Thirty cents?'

Callum dropped the spent smoke on the sidewalk and ground it out with his boot. He sparked up another and imagined himself through their eyes: the hustlers, the hookers and pushers. He looked younger than his twenty-nine years, despite the dark two-day growth on his face. A thatch of unruly black hair cut short and a nose skewed by a couple of prime shots in the ring. A wide mouth and a funny accent, maybe Irish but not like that comedy Top-O'-The-Mornin' brogue people put on for

4

St. Paddy's. Heavy black brows over affective hazel eyes that were tender or playful or flinty at the whim of his moods. Those eyes were his greatest tell.

The cop had crossed 42nd Street and disappeared downstream among the mass of citizens heading toward Penn Station on 8th Avenue. Callum took in the parking lot opposite, Port Authority Bus Terminal diagonal, the huge Camel mural across 8th to his right, and wondered how long he could live with this noise and fury.

Amid the chaos, a beautiful woman dragged a small child by the arm toward the subway entrance where Callum stood. Her hair was darker than shadow, her skin amber under the lights of the city, like she was sculpted from gemstone. She was East Asian but looked nothing like Irene Chu. Yet her face as she swept the child into her arms pulled Callum back to Hong Kong and his estranged wife. The child burrowed her head deep by her mother's neck and Callum felt the memory leave a cold crater in his chest as he thought of his daughter, how Tara would do the same. Tara's hands could barely meet as they encircled his neck back then. The mother and child passed him by on 42nd and disappeared down the steps to the subway and he felt a part of him descend with them.

Callum pulled hard on the cigarette. That was his problem – he always went hard. Drank too hard. Gambled too hard. Maybe he loved too hard, now that his family was gone. He'd blown it with them and almost blown it with his job.

And now he was in New York.

He'd been here once before, a short trip with Irene but that had been the Empire State Building, Central Park and museums. This, tonight, was low cloud crawling through midtown, the buildings monoliths scattered with pinpricks of light. Rain was close. He dropped his smoke.

He scratched his head. No one likes to watch a man murdered

but Callum couldn't duck this one, so might as well get it over with. It wasn't like he hadn't seen plenty of bodies. But this time, he'd watch the Chinese taxidermist's life snuffed out while he sat with a coffee and a cigarette. As he turned to enter the subway, he checked the change in his pocket and snorted.

Thirty cents.

*

Two hours later, and ninety minutes late, Callum stared at a dead TV screen in a hotel room downtown.

Sub-Divisional Inspector James Milburn said, 'Sergeant Burke, I'm less than impressed.'

Callum said, 'That's what happened, sir.'

He thought his boss looked tired. Perhaps he hadn't shaken off the jet lag of their flight across the Pacific, then the North American continent. The lanky Englishman was an Inspector in the Royal Hong Kong Police Force, and Callum's superior officer. Milburn straightened his Grenadier Guards regimental tie and blazer. He crossed his legs in an attempt to appear at ease but Callum knew he was wound tight tonight.

Despite recruiting Callum for the joint Hong Kong Police, NYPD, Drug Enforcement Administration task force of which they were now a part, Milburn was uncomfortable working with American law enforcement. He had tried to pass the buck of heading the New York-based Hong Kong Police team to a foul-mouthed Scotsman but had ultimately been saddled with in-country responsibility for Callum and his other colleague, fellow sergeant Bobby Ho. Now Bobby was standing by the mini-bar and the Americans were in the lobby calling their respective agencies before returning to the room.

The DEA had wanted to greet the Hong Kong policemen at 99 10th Avenue, their New York office. But they were swamped with guys on temporary assignment from Miami playing Crockett and Tubbs with the Colombians, so were forced to use Milburn's hotel room.

The NYPD and DEA had brought a VCR and some boxes of case files to the room earlier. A large photocopied sheet with shots of the major players in the case hung on a wall. A large book compiled of the same photos sat on the coffee table. The room was one of the smallest in a hotel wedged between a couple of soaring bastions of commerce in the lower Manhattan financial district.

Callum cleared his throat and said, 'I'll say again that I am sorry I'm late, Sir.'

But Callum wasn't sorry. He wasn't sorry that he'd given his last thirty cents to the drunk on 42nd Street for bus fare. He wasn't sorry that he'd had to go in search of an ATM, an endangered species in the Times Square vicinity, which seemed a catastrophic design flaw in the tourist heart of New York. Or that he'd taken the subway in the wrong direction and ended up hopping off at an elevated station somewhere north of Harlem. He'd jumped off the C Train back downtown at Canal Street and, deciding he was already late, dropped into a bar for a few steadying drinks.

Now he stood like a guilty teenager, taking shallow breaths and hoping the grown-ups wouldn't smell the booze. He caught Bobby Ho staring at him for a moment.

Ho was, like Callum, a Sergeant in the Royal Hong Kong Police, a Red Tab cop, so named because of his proficiency in English. He had a slight build and wore a polo shirt and jeans. As ever, he appeared quiet, observant and reserved. The Chinese cop looked away quickly and Callum's face lit up, his skin burning.

He knew he'd embarrassed Bobby, that Bobby would be squirming inside at watching Milburn fume. The discord would worry Ho – a bad omen for the business ahead.

Callum had worked with European, Chinese, Sikh and Pakistani officers in the RHKP and found them all the same. Some good, some bad, some very good at being bad. Bobby Ho was one of the good guys.

James Milburn spat, 'What the fuck do you think you're doing, Callum?'

Callum flinched. 'Sir, I got lost.'

'In a bloody shot glass. I could smell it from you when you walked in.'

'Sorry, Sir.'

'You're a sorry piece of work you useless bastard. It's your human failings rather than those as a policeman that concern me right now.'

Callum looked at the floor and glimpsed the book of criminal players they were in New York to bust open.

'I got lost,' he said again.

'You've been lost for months. You have to control your impulses, especially here. Especially now.'

'I don't want to be here.'

Callum stared at the tendons twitching in Milburn's long neck, the drawn skin an angry crimson.

Milburn said, 'It's a bit fucking late for that.' His tone, measured at first, shifted up through the gears. 'You bloody idiot. I could have kicked you out of the force for what you did back in HK. You could have done jail time. You're damn lucky to have hauled your head above water again. You're lucky to still have a job with RHKP, and you're well-fucking-lucky you were born in Ireland to have this opportunity come your way.'

Callum realised he was at attention and tried to relax back into his former whiskey-calm. His voice cracked.

'I believe there are other officers from back home you could have called on.'

'Murray is nearing retirement and Shaw is close to burn-out.

Mind you, they and your other compatriots haven't collected any charges in their careers.'

Possession of an Offensive Weapon. Assault Occasioning Actual Bodily Harm. Breaking a Triad foot soldier's jaw with a knuckle-duster in a Hong Kong bar fight after the hood had re-arranged a bar-girl's face.

If only the top brass knew that was the least of it.

Callum swallowed down a rush of whiskey bile. He thought of Tara, her huge eyes and small hands. He thought of Irene.

'You are representing the Royal Hong Kong Police Force,' said Milburn. 'You are representing the Crown colony. And you're representing me.'

An undertone of remorse seeped through the booze in Callum's bloodstream at that. He had been in a downward spiral for months and wasn't drunk enough to deny it. He had no desire to drag Milburn and Bobby down with him.

'This is a chance for you, Callum,' said Milburn. He sat on the edge of the hotel bed. 'It gives you purpose and keeps you away from Lau.'

Callum sobered a little at the mention of the *489 Shan Chu*, the Triad Leader – or Dragon Head – Tony Lau.

He bowed his head for a moment, took a breath and said, 'It won't happen again, Sir.'

Milburn frowned and nodded.

Callum saw Bobby Ho relax.

There was a knock on the hotel room door.

Bobby went stiff again.

*

Central District. Hong Kong.

David Chau clutched a carrier bag with both hands as he staggered along the jolting tram carriage past a teenager engrossed in her CD Walkman. He was breathing heavy, his bulk huge in the tight confines of the carriage, his gut grazing the shoulder of a petite old woman sitting in front of the teenager. A couple sitting two seats down glanced at Chau as he made his way toward them before staring out the window again. There were five other passengers, a young couple, two women in gym clothes and a businessman closer to the front of the car reading a newspaper. The businessman glanced at Chau and lowered his newspaper in a deliberate movement out of sight behind his seat-back.

The carriage bucked.

The businessman put his hand in his jacket and pulled something from inside, shielded by his torso. Chau staggered on toward the narrow, spiral steps to the lower deck of the tram, at the front of the car.

A still descended as Chau neared the businessman. The businessman's arms moved above the seat back, his unseen fingers working at something.

Or preparing something.

The muzzle flash of the Beretta M9 made a negative of David Chau's head. The old woman's hand twitched with each shot as two bullets drilled into Chau's skull above his left ear. Then she took a two-handed grip and fired three more rounds into his body as he dropped to the floor. The passengers screamed and leaped in their seats. The businessman threw his hands up, the wrapper of the pornographic magazine he'd been tearing open flying through the air.

The old woman stood for a moment over Chau's corpse, bouncing on the balls of her feet. Her cardigan was tangled in the elastic waist of her polyester pants revealing a leather holster tucked near the small of her back. She ripped off the headscarf and a wig. Then, head shaved to the bone, the killer turned and sprinted for the rear of the carriage and disappeared down the stairs. The carriage froze. A crease of white snow ran across the scene, like a well-worn fold in paper. Then the crease rolled upward as the video rewound and the murder played backward on the screen.

*

They stared at the VCR recording on the screen, David Chau back to his starting position in the tram carriage on the video tape: Callum, Milburn and Bobby Ho.

Now joined by DEA Special Agent Niku Mattila and Sergeant Mike O'Connell of NYPD Narcotics Manhattan North.

Milburn sat in a chair at the end of the bed, flanked on either side by the US cop and federal agent. Ho stood next to the TV screen. Callum next to him by the bed.

Milburn swallowed hard then said, 'You're the first people outside of the Hong Kong Police to see that video.'

O'Connell wiped his hands on his pants and leaned back in his chair. Callum thought the last time the New York cop had worn his suit Reagan was in office. Stocky with large, blunt features and a shock of black hair, O'Connell looked like someone had found the missing link in Queens and stuck him in the first thing came to hand on the Walmart sales rack.

The NYPD cop said, 'And so ends the rich tapestry of David Chau's fifty-seven years upon this earth, shot down by a midget Norman Bates on a toy train in British-Chinaland.'

Callum shot a look at Milburn, who offered a small smile to O'Connell. The tall, gaunt Englishman sat affecting an insouciant pose but his cool grey eyes had dropped a couple of degrees in temperature.

O'Connell gestured with his chin to the TV, perched on the unit housing the minibar and refrigerator.

'Your senior citizens got some anger issues over there,' he said.

Milburn rustled up a smile. 'Yes, and Mr. Chau was shot on the tram as it pulled into Arsenal Street. Such irony.'

'Your trams run on schedule, Inspector? 'Cause your men are lousy time-keepers.'

Callum felt a burn like the whiskey was aflame in his gut again.

'I thought I already told you what happened,' he said.

'And you're kidding, right?' said O'Connell. 'You're late because of some Good Samaritan bullshit? Thirty cents to a bum?'

O'Connell's foot was drumming a tattoo on the lush carpet. Callum held his temper in clenched fists dug deep in his jacket pockets.

DEA Special Agent Niku Mattila stood from his perch on the end of the bed. He was a big man with a quarterback build to O'Connell's squat bulk. While the New Yorker looked like a bum playing dress-up, Mattila wore his Armani like a Wall Street broker. The way he stroked his pencil mustache and pursed his lips, Callum figured he was calibrating every word before he spoke.

'Sergeant O'Connell has been building this case for some months, gentlemen,' said Mattila. He flashed a million dollar smile to match his thousand dollar single-breasted suit. 'But I'm sure he'd agree an hour or so isn't so long to wait to nail the bad guys.'

Callum knew Mattila had a lot riding on this. He was lead on the task force as the federal agent in the room. The DEA man was working hard to convey the right first impressions to the Hong Kong cops. The agent looked down at his jacket and pants and picked some troublesome lint off his knee.

Callum thought Mattila's manners would go far with Milburn. O'Connell was too direct. Strong coffee for the Englishman.

'If we could return to the tape,' said Mattila, gesturing to the TV screen. 'Inspector Milburn...'

Milburn folded his arms. 'Our geriatric killer is Danny Yuen. A street soldier for the 14K triads in the Wan Chai district of

Hong Kong. Twenty-eight but looks sixty. He has severely pock-marked skin and a drug habit. He developed quite the taste for no. 3 heroin: old and haggard before his time. Hence, most likely, he passed for an elderly person at a glance in the tram.'

'Hence,' said O'Connell, eyebrows raised.

'Sergeant Burke, you were an arresting officer when Danny Yuen was apprehended.' Milburn gave the proclamation of Callum's rank as much gravitas as he could.

'Yes, Sir,' he said.

Milburn nodded, grateful for the show of respect to his rank. O'Connell sniffed.

Mattila said, 'And was – uh – Sergeant Ho present at the arrest?'

'No,' said Milburn. Ho, stood by the TV, nodded, caught himself doing so and seemed to shrink a couple of inches.

Callum saw Mattila had glimpsed Bobby's discomfort. The DEA agent addressed Ho.

'Bobby, the killer, Danny Yuen, was arrested at his apartment in Hong Kong, right?'

Ho cleared his throat and said, 'Yes. He had the gun used in the killing in a plastic bag, along with a stash of *Red Chicken*: No. 3 heroin.'

'You figure the Triad gave him up.'

Bobby looked at James Milburn, confused by Mattila's question cloaked in a statement of fact.

'Yes,' said Callum, 'with an anonymous tip-off. Danny Yuen is a junkie and was out of favor. He probably carried out the murder for heroin, then the Triad rid themselves of their problem by giving him to us.'

Milburn said, 'And thus, shut down the murder enquiry. Yuen, terrified of the 14K, confessed and said David Chau was a random victim that he killed for cash to buy drugs. Yuen put it in writing that the murder was arbitrary.'

O'Connell said, 'Any cop could tell this was an assassination.'

'Sure,' said Callum, emboldened by the whiskey. 'The dead man, David Chau, worked for a business with some connections to the 14K Triad.'

'Stuffing dead shit,' said O'Connell.

Milburn said, 'As a taxidermist, yes.'

O'Connell laughed. 'Well, Mr Chau is ready for stuffing now, thanks to Danny Yuen and his Beretta.'

The Beretta, thought Callum. The fucking Beretta.

The murder weapon in the Hong Kong tram execution. Triad gunsmiths had fooled with the barrel to confuse ballistics, but Hong Kong Police could match the bullet casings found at the scene to the firing mechanism. A senior officer was having dinner with a DEA Hong Kong field office bigwig and mentioned the case. Turned out the casings also matched those found at the murder site of a federal informant 8,000 miles away on Pell Street, Manhattan. Same casings, same pistol.

The connection had raised flags.

It wasn't unusual for the Hong Kong Triads and US Tongs to share information, guns, even killers. They were known to facilitate murders on either side of the Pacific for one another, for a price. The theory floated that the gun had been passed from Chinatown thugs to Hong Kong Triads.

For some time information had been seeping in through Confidential Informants that the Hong Kong Triads had an interest in offloading large chunks of their business before the Communist Chinese Government took control of the territory in 1997. A major target was New York. There was a clear link between the Hong Kong 14K Triads and organized crime elements in a New York Chinatown Tong Association: the Hip Sing Tong. Hong Kong Triads had long been doing business with the US Chinese Tong Associations.

But not with Irish-Americans. Not until now. NYPD investigations had revealed the Chinese were interested in brokering a deal with an Irish mob in the city.

The Triads would provide heroin from Asia.

The US Tong would help bring it into the United States.

The Irish mob would distribute on New York streets.

Milburn had made a proposal to Callum: a chance to work abroad, get out of Hong Kong for a while and let the heat die down. And a shot at wiping the assault charges from his police record.

That was the deal-clincher.

And now here they were in a hotel room south of New York Chinatown plotting the downfall of Chinese and Irish-American organized crime.

Callum watched agent Niku Mattila lean back and cross his arms like an Ivy League professor mulling an academic quandary.

Mattila said, 'There are under a hundred Chinese speakers on the NYPD. The people in Chinatown can't or won't talk to law enforcement. The organized crime elements within the Chinatown Tong Association have the population terrified.'

He turned to Bobby Ho again.

'Which is why we appreciate Bobby here taking surveillance duties on Mott Street and working on the Title IIIs.'

Bobby Ho stiffened at the mention of his name. Callum knew he was gratified to have been entrusted with the responsibility of watching the Tong headquarters and listening in on the taps on Tong members' phones. He also knew Bobby, as the sole officer with the linguistic knowledge necessary to decipher and transcribe the taps, would carry the responsibility heavily on his shoulders.

'And Mr Burke,' said Mattila. 'Let's talk about your role in this investigation.'

A heaviness descended in Callum's gut. It took a moment in the last of the whisky glow for him to recognise it as a mixture of dread and resignation.

Then the phone rang.

Chapter Two

The guy with the rabbit stopped to check the beeper clipped to the belt of his Levis. The rabbit sat on the sidewalk, its leash slack. A couple of disinterested women in expensive-looking clothes stepped around it as they hurried toward 3rd Avenue. Probably on their way to dinner, thought Anton Galinski.

'You ever eaten one of those?' he said, picking at his finger-nails with a bronze key. 'Chomped on a rabbit, like Elmer Fudd always wanted?'

Georgie Ruiz squinted through the telephoto lens of the Canon and said, 'Looks like an American Chinchilla. Six-class breed for sure. And Bugs never got caught.'

'Since when are you a bunny expert?'

'As opposed to a pussy expert?'

'Fuck you.'

'Shit!'

A rat scampered from an alleyway in front of the rabbit on East 95th Street between 2nd and 3rd Avenues. The rat, similar in size, arched its back. Its jaws spread wide. The rabbit's owner looked down, yanked hard on the leash and ran for 2nd Avenue dragging the bunny in his wake.

'Jesus Christ,' said Galinski, 'speaking of pussies.'

Ruiz re-sighted on the doorway, atop a stoop, of the town-house midway along the street, and said, 'At least he's outdoors. Rest of the neighborhood's locked up for the night like the Black Panthers are gonna' march down 2nd.'

The NYPD Intelligence cops sat in a grey Toyota forty yards diagonal from the townhouse. Anton Galinski pictured all those socialite women locked up tight in all those Upper East Side apartments and how, in his head, they fell for the thirty-four-year-old Polish cop who knocked on the door canvassing for statements about some imaginary crime. Instead, that was, of ferrying VIPs around as a driver in the Intelligence Division like a glorified chauffeur. This here, now, was the shit. Stakeout. Real cop work. He was just self-aware enough to know there was some kind of hole in his life – that he'd never felt like a real cop in all his years in traffic and Intelligence – and that this was beginning to fill in the edges. Only problem was, his partner didn't seem so hyped for the work.

Ruiz had been cradling the Canon for twenty minutes in preparation for the appearance of Paddy Doolan, client of Nurse Löwin, a Vietnamese dominatrix despite her Germanic trade name. Galinski had wanted to bring the JVC but Ruiz refused. The camcorder's size would have been more difficult to manage and conceal, despite the gloom, and the image would have looked like shit on VHS in the low light anyway. So they sat in wait on the now empty street while the moneyed residents of this Upper East Side frontier, a few blocks from East Harlem, sat comfortably behind triple door bolts and pin tumblers and nightlatches and alarmed security systems. The Toyota was parked in front of a large apartment complex spanning the length of 95th between 2nd and 3rd while a regiment of imaculate brownstones lined the opposite side of the street, clean, straight and level in height as a movie star's teeth. Cars were parked avenue to avenue on the Brownstone side of the street. Galinski cleaned his nails with a key. It gave him something to do other than grovel to his partner.

Jesus, I hate when she's angry, he thought. Her face all seized up like she was having some kind of attack and she just shut down. She was two years his junior but came on like his mom when she was pissed. She gave him the silent treatment, too. He thought Latinos were supposed to love talk. Like that girl he was seeing last year, Regina. Great legs, nice smile but – *Mój Boże!* She never shut the hell up. Not Georgie Ruiz, though. If she was pissed, her eyebrows knit together and that Roman nose seemed to taper somehow like a sharp weapon, and her wide mouth shut tight narrowing her lips.

Georgina Ruiz was less than impressed that Galinski had pulled over to call his latest grad school bedmate, then got them snarled up in traffic. She had told Galinski to take FDR drive but his Polish bullheadedness had him stay on 3rd Avenue, and they'd run into collaterol from an accident a block over from Tramway Plaza, blocking the street like a clog in an artery. As a result, they'd missed surveilling Paddy Doolan entering the brownstone where Nurse Löwin plied her trade in pain.

Ruiz watched the street wondering how long it would be before she had to take a leak. She'd been on the way out the door in sneakers and those Wranglers Arthur called her mom jeans when little Sammy had dropped spaghetti sauce on her lap. So she'd had to switch to the Levis that were just a little tighter than last year, and then grabbed a coffee at One Police Plaza before picking up the car driving out. A stupid move because she'd probably have to piss soon and the coffee at the Puzzle Palace tasted like shit, anyway. She joined the NYPD over ten years ago. Now she was thirty-one. Arthur still said she was beautiful, still made her feel beautiful on those nights when the kids slept early and she wasn't exhausted after a shift. But she knew Isabella had added a couple of lines around her mouth, and Sammy etched a few more by her eyes. That was what kids did. But it was the eight years as a cop in east Harlem that gave her the most wrinkles. Then she'd transferred to Intelligence and the world didn't seem quite so out of control. Now she was back on the street on a task force with the feds and she wasn't sure she liked it.

She thought Galinski looked tired. Anton wasn't a bad-looking guy, nice blond hair, always tousled just right. He suited the tight black and grey check shirt and leather jacket combo tonight, had a good tight ass. But the dark semi-circles under his eyes looked like bruises on his pale skin. He should stop running after girls ten years younger than his thirty-four years and settle down.

A chopper buzzed somewhere over the East River, perhaps on its way to United Nations Plaza.

Galinski wiped the key on his thigh.

Ruiz tutted.

Galinski said, 'You hungry?'

Ruiz tutted again.

'You know what?' said Galinski, 'I get enough of this shit when I stay over at Cathy's place and I wanna' watch Monday night football. You want I should take a walk around the block, give some more room for your feminine indignation to stink up the car?'

Ruiz, oblivious, said, 'Does that guy look right to you?'

A man was closing the door of the brownstone housing Nurse Löwin's studio, checking the street looking east and west. A big guy, he wore a jacket over straight black jeans and rubbed his ass. Then he pulled the jacket over his crotch, took a couple of steps down the stoop and looked up at the front of the building.

'He look like he just got the shit paddled out of his ass and loved every minute?' she said.

'You figure he pulled the jacket down to cover a hard-on? He could be looking up at Nurse Ilsa-The-Wicked-Mistress-of-Yorkville's place.'

'You're shit at movie references, but yeah.'

Galinski said, 'So if he's had a butt-plug up his ass for the last hour, where the hell is Paddy Doolan?'

Ruiz gave Galinski a look could curdle cream. When she returned her gaze to the front of the building the man was standing at the foot of the stoop by a silver Porsche.

The crack of the gunshots was echoed by Galinski smacking his head off the passenger window of the Toyota. The man by the Porsche dropped.

Ruiz grabbed the radio and called in a 10-34 while Galinski yanked at his door handle. He fell from the car like spilt cargo, wrestling with his shoulder holster as he hit the concrete. The Glock came free and clattered on the sidewalk and he cursed as he heard another two shots. His hand felt hollow as he grabbed the pistol grip and struggled to a crouch.

Ruiz, her revolver in a two-handed grip, was backing behind the trunk of the Toyota muttering, '*Dios mío! Oh, Dios!*' She dropped to her left knee behind the car and sighted over the trunk, breathing hard. She could smell the dusty musk of the street, the reek of fuel from the Toyota's tailpipe. Her perception was razor sharp yet her mind was scrambled. The buildings opposite seemed to reel. She needed to slow the whirl of panic in her head. She was Georgina Ruiz, mother and wife.

And cop.

Ruiz yelled, 'Police! Show yourself and drop your weapon asshole!'

Galinski took up position at the front of the car. He used the hood to steady his shaking hands.

They knelt gasping for ten seconds that felt like minutes.

Galinski yelled, 'NYPD! Drop your fuckin' weapon and step into the street!'

They listened to the hushed moan of the city going about its business beyond the end of 95th street. Nothing moved.

'You call in a 10-34?' said Galinski.

'Yes.' Ruiz voice was a hiss.

'So where the fuck are the sirens?'

Ruiz edged past the taillights of the Toyota onto the street. She heard Galinski rasp something behind her but crept further across 95th, revolver pointed at the Porsche, legs moving in spite of her brain screaming for her to run back to cover. A curtain twitched to her left and she chanced a look, caught Galinski a couple of feet behind in her peripheral vision. He fanned left to get a wider view of the Porsche and stoop.

Before Ruiz's mind could fully register the fact, they were around the Porsche, the corpse revealed in degrees lying with its left foot trapped below the right knee, a dark halo of blood encircling the head.

Then Ruiz was cursing, hands on knees and Galinski was collapsing against the Porsche and fuck the forensics. The driver's door was open. No bullet casings on the sidewalk. Professional work with a revolver. A compact mirror attached to a short metal rod lay on the car's bucket seat. Asshole must have lain in the front seat, used the mirror to keep an eye on the stoop, then opened the door and shot the poor bastard on the sidewalk with half his head in the gutter.

A siren whined from a couple of blocks away. Ruiz was rocking with her hands on her knees, furious. They let the killer escape behind the cover of the parked cars when they couldn't have been more than twenty yards away.

When the first patrol car drew up on the street Galinski moved away from the Porsche and held up the shield on the chain around his neck. They'd declare their rank and bureau. There'd be the paperwork, the post-mortem on how the fuck a man was gunned down right in front of their eyes and the perpetrator escaped on foot from an empty street. But first, someone would have to make a call to the DEA.

*

Niku Mattila had gone, checking out the facts of a shooting uptown that had come through on the phone. He and O'Connell had been vague as to what was happening and Callum had willed James Milburn to push for details. Instead, the Inspector had sat watching the New York cop and federal agent confer by the en suite before Mattila excused himself.

Milburn had gone for a piss. O'Connell had stepped out of the room. Callum had grabbed a whiskey from the mini-bar. Bobby Ho had balked.

Callum downed the shot in one. O'Connell walked back in the room.

'Well, alright,' said O'Connell. 'Now daddy's out of the room, let's us kids have some fun.'

He gestured to the photocopied sheet tacked on the wall with the mugshots and surveillance photographs of the players they were here to take down.

On top, like the star on the Christmas tree: Tony Lau – 14K Triad Dragon Head. Callum had been avoiding looking at the shot. The last time he'd seen Lau in the flesh, the man had sworn to kill him. Lau had declared his blood vendetta, not with words, but with Triad hand signs. He would be in Hong Kong, picked up by the RHKP when the rest went down.

The first row of pictures below Lau were players from Lau's large faction of the 14K Triad. Some had sanctioned David Chau's murder on the Hong Kong tram.

The third row showed members of the Hip Sing Tong Association from New York Chinatown, including the leader, Sammy Ong, and his closest advisor, Papa Ng.

O'Connell pointed at Bobby Ho.

'These are the guys you'll be listening to. Some real-time taps, some recordings. We got a place for you on Mott Street to observe the Tong Headquarters, too. Stay well away from these psychos, though.'

He cocked a thumb at the row below. The Flying Dragons street gang from Chinatown, the Tong's homicidal muscle.

O'Connell tucked his thumbs in his belt, pushed out his chest and gave Callum a shit-eating grin as he cocked his head toward the bottom row of photographs as though revealing the prize on a gameshow.

'And these assholes are gonna' be your new best friends, Burke. Say hello to The Walsh Crew.'

Callum looked at the New York Irish mob. The leader, Fintan Walsh. Jimmy Mulligan, the right-hand man, and others. At the end of the row was Paddy Doolan.

O'Connell said, 'You boys ready to go to work?'

Callum scanned the pictures again. The crazy-paddy mugshots of the Irish. The hair-slicked, comic book sneers of the Flying Dragons street gang. The surveillance photographs of the Hip Sing Tong men.

Were someone to pin the cops' shots on the opposite wall, they'd follow the same order of importance, he thought. The feds at the top; then the NYPD and Milburn. Below them, Bobby Ho, vital for his language skills.

And at the bottom, Callum. His was the dirtiest, shit-end-of-the-stick deal in the whole game.

Callum knew to build a Federal racketeering RICO case in the US, law enforcement needed a lot of evidence. The DEA and NYPD team had already been working the case for months. Now Bobby Ho was in place to help transcribe the Tong wiretaps. But they needed more on the Irish crew. The Walsh outfit were the potential weak link. If the task force could build a solid racketeering case against the Irish, they'd have some insurance. While the biggest, head-in-the-clouds target was Tony Lau, the Dragon Head, the Triads were far too cautious – had too many resources with which to distance themselves from the heroin trail in New York.

The US Tong operated in a closed society. The hope was that Bobby Ho could accrue enough to prosecute but it was a huge ask.

But bust the Irish and prove a connection, and the task force could prosecute the Chinese through association. At least, that was the theory.

Paddy Doolan, last mugshot on the row of Walsh Crew photographs, was a hanger-on who grew up with the top men in the old neighborhood. He was erratic, a romantic, and a sucker for a pilgrim from the old country come to America to make his way. Callum would turn up, another Irishman trying his luck in the Big Apple, and hope Doolan would bite and take to him. Then, once undercover, Callum would push to get work with the Walsh crew and pray no one took a bite out of him with a .44.

His job would then be to gather more evidence on Walsh and his outfit. Evidence he might provide through testimony, material evidence and – God help him – recorded conversations. A fucking wire.

Milburn walked out of the bathroom.

'Bobby is a good policeman,' he said. 'He'll do you proud.'

Ho studied the carpet.

'We read your file,' said O'Connell, nodding at Bobby. 'You'll be a big help to our Chinatown operation.'

O'Connell turned to Callum.

'It's you I'm worried about.'

Callum said, 'Have you read my file?'

'That's why I'm worried. Where you're going, the chutzpah could be an asset, or it could get you killed.'

Milburn said, 'I'm not sure chutzpah, as you put it, is accurate.'

'Let's say balls then.'

Callum let Milburn talk. Least said, soonest mended, his mother used to say.

'When Callum joined us, he had a lot of anger after a stint in the Royal Ulster Constabulary. Lost a colleague, Jimmy Gilliland. But he loves the job and is popular among the men.'

O'Connell looked at Callum and said, 'How about your politics?'

Callum laughed. 'I don't follow,' he said.

'Are you doing all of this for Queen and Country, like a good Englishman?'

'I'm Irish.'

'But are you the right kind of Irish?'

'I was born on the island.'

'Irish-American father, but English mother. You ain't Irish Catholic.'

'Ah,' said Callum, 'I see.' He felt a craving for another drink but knew it would be a bad idea right now. The glass could end up in O'Connell's face.

'I don't,' said Milburn, 'see the relevance. He's got the accent, he was born there and, I hope to God, he can play the part.'

Callum said, 'Honestly, O'Connell, I couldn't give a fuck if you think your god's better than mine. My mother was a Protestant, my father a Catholic. All I hope is that whoever is up there, he's looking out for us all on this thing.'

The phone rang again.

'Sergeant O'Connell,' said Milburn, 'might I suggest you take that call.'

O'Connell smiled. 'I think I just might,' he said, picking up the room phone.

Milburn moved close to Callum and said, 'Don't let O'Connell wind you up. It's a test, most probably. Checking your temperament.'

And I almost failed, thought Callum. If the Walsh crew pushed his buttons, could he keep it together?

He said, 'My target, Paddy Doolan, has been in temporary accommodation for two months now but he won't stay there forever.'

'NYPD intelligence thinks he'll be gone in a few weeks,' said Milburn. 'Time is of the essence. You need to get close to him

25

ASAP. Once you're undercover, we'll meet up for briefings and NYPD will try to keep a loose eye on you when manpower permits.'

'Let's hope Doolan likes me.'

'Make him, Callum. A lot of people have pulled a lot of strings to put this operation together at such short notice. Now, Ho will take your passport and give you the replacement.'

Callum produced his passport from the inner pocket of his jacket and handed it over. Bobby Ho handed him a fake Irish passport two-handed as though proffering a gift.

O'Connell walked over and sat heavily in a chair at the foot of the bed. 'Mattila caught the two cops were there when the shooting went down.'

Callum said, 'What do we know about this new killing?'

'The victim's name is Solomon Dimitri Grundy, fifty-seven years old, white male, six-three and two hundred-fifty pounds. ID has him living in Brighton Beach. Little Odessa. The good news? Could be a Russian hitter.'

He folded his arms and shot a glance at Callum.

'The bad? Sol Grundy knew Paddy Doolan. Small world, huh?'

Callum shook his head.

'Ever heard of Murphy's Law?' he said.

' 'Course I have,' said O'Connell, all mock indignation. 'I'm as Irish as Paddy's Pig. Unlike some.'

He flashed a smile like he was sizing up where he'd sink his teeth into Callum first.

Callum didn't like it, the smile or the hit. He'd watched the Chau execution less than an hour ago and now a fresh body had turned up a few miles from where he sat. Like Bobby Ho would think, it was a bad omen. He just had to hope he could ride his luck – be that the luck of the Irish or the luck of the devil – and see this roll of the dice through.

He just prayed it wasn't his last.

Chapter Three

Tony Lau inhaled his Double Happiness cigarette, felt the smoke clog his hot throat and spat on the dirt. The Triad Dragon Head ground the butt out with the sole of his boot.

The man called Tse said, 'The heat is killing.'

Lau looked at the tin shack, the wretched dog sleeping under a gnarled tree, the black stain of ants swarming over the pig entrails in the dirt.

'This is no place for an initiation,' he said.

Beyond the shack lay the fields. Surrounded by huge, jungle encased hills, they were now bare of the neon oranges, rich purples, shocking pinks and blood reds which had carpeted the cultivated land last month. The poppy flowers had bloomed and the local tribe had lanced the pods, releasing the thick white sap – like nature's cum, thought Lau – within. The sap had congealed and the tribal families had returned to scrape the now curry-coloured sap from the pods and place it in wooden boxes around their necks. The opium crop was in.

'*Shan Chu* –Leader – I trust you had a comfortable trip to see us here in our modest, rural home.'

The general's voice was deep and strong, barrelling across the dirt road at the edge of the hill tribe village. It was the voice of a man who answered to no one but the gods themselves, whose daily bread was giving orders. The hill village, a collection of thatched long houses and rusted tin shacks holding back the vast sprawl of the jungle, was one of several under the protection of the Mong Tai Army and General Khun Sa was the all-powerful head of the fighting force of twenty-three thousand militia. Tanned and fit despite his sixty-one years, he strode up the slight incline flanked by three soldiers on either side, machine guns slung over their shoulders, in jungle combat fatigues.

'As always,' said Lau, 'the trip was a pleasure knowing I will see you at the end.'

The bone-jarring drive through Shan State from across the border in Thailand had been hellish as ever, the jungle reaching through the windows of their jeep and scratching their arms, pricking at their clothes. The thick vegetation was as lawless and unruly as the people of this north-eastern region of Myanmar.

This was Khun Sa's territory, a long way from Triad Hong Kong, and the man was over thirty years senior to Tony Lau. Lau had to strike a delicate balance between the proper level of respect and maintaining his own face as the Dragon Head, leader of his 14K Triad faction.

Khun Sa said, 'When is the last time you honored us with your presence, Leader?'

'Perhaps two years. Our *Cho Hai* made the trip last year, I believe.'

At the mention of his Triad *Cho Hai* fixer's title, Pineapple Wong brought up the rear with two young men. The fixer, Wong, a *Teo Chiu* Thai Triad, was smiling at the men as he pointed out buildings and people sitting in the shade around the village. The men nodded, eager. Wired. Frightened.

Pineapple Wong's sprout of spiked hair, the feature that gave him his nickname, was wilting in the blanket of heavy, wet heat. 'Leader. General,' he said in greeting.

Lau felt a prickle of satisfaction at the fixer addressing him first, further face on the general's turf.

The hill people were indoors or lounging in the shade. They had worked the poppy fields in early morning and evening through the harvest, avoiding the stifling oven of daytime. Lau wished the Triads could join them out of the sun but he wanted to take care of business and leave before nightfall. He didn't

28

trust the General quite enough to sleep under his roof, and there was a plush bed and Thai hooker waiting over the border.

But first there was a ceremony to complete and he didn't want to perform the initiation in front of the hill tribe or militia. This was Triad business.

'So, these are the new recruits' he said, studying the young men. They were Thai-Chinese like Pineapple and looked short and scrawny in comparison to the militia fighters. Their eyes were mad with anticipation and the narcotic they had taken to ease their fear at what lay ahead. They clutched envelopes containing their joining fees to become triad members.

Lau said, 'General, many thanks for permitting this Society business before our meeting. The shrine is ready and we will complete the initiation within the hour.'

'Very good,' said General Khun Sa. 'I will leave you to your blood and oaths.'

*

The incense scratched at their throats and seemed to stoke the wet furnace of jungle heat higher. That and the drone of insects, the birds calling, the tendrils of vines and tree roots made Tony Lau feel as though the jungle were wrapping him in its fetid breath ready to consume him.

He thought back to *then*: Kowloon Walled City. A winding network of filthy tunnels. Naked cables clogging the ceilings of the walkways. An altar. Paper banners. A *Heung Chu* incense master. Swords, street soldiers, chicken's blood. Nineteen-year-old Lau Waa-Ming initiated into a branch of the 14K Triad, first step on the long road to Dragon Head.

Now: mosquitoes, stagnant air, a small clearing in the jungle. A piece of paper with the Chinese character for *hung* surrounded by a triangle of heaven, earth and man. A small carving

29

of the deity, Kwan Ti on an upturned fruit crate as an altar. Three sticks of incense in a Coke bottle battling the rancid jungle stink. Sweat. Flies. The spicy reek of the Chinese-Thai recruits. A bottle of local liquor for the blood ceremony.

Tony Lau, as Dragon Head, was above the role of Incense Master but Pineapple Wong and the enforcer, Tse, lacked the seniority to perform the role in the initiation ceremony. So Lau had skipped the Buddhist and Taoist prayers. Tse and Wong had held Chinese handguns over the recruits' heads as they approached the altar, rather than swords. Lau had cleansed their sins by sloshing the wine in their faces rather than bathing them with water, and shortened the history recitation. He had lectured them on loyalty and brotherhood, and asked questions of the young men – would they be true to their brothers and society?

Would they spurn the police?

Then he walked to Tse and took his Type 77 semi-automatic, wiping the sweat-slick grip on a large frond. The recruits, kneeling in front of the makeshift altar, looked at the earth and waited. A bird shrieked under the jungle canopy.

Lau stepped to the altar, looked at the carving of Kwan Ti and turned to face the recruits. He tapped the first, a pock-marked youth of around eighteen, on the head. The youth raised his head and pushed out his pigeon chest. Lau placed the muzzle of the pistol on the recruit's chest.

He said, 'Which is stronger, the bullet or your heart?'

The saucer-eyed youth gazed back. The incessant insect-whine seemed to grow louder, engulfing them. Lau felt as though his head was swelling and a sharp stiletto of pain was settling behind his eyes. His finger was greasy on the trigger.

'My heart,' said the youth.

Lau ran through the thirty-six oaths like a mantra. His arm was trembling and his breath hot. He knew the kid didn't care about the recitation, that the young recruits cared only for money now. Tradition was facing extinction.

As it was with all things, he thought. In a hundred, two hundred years, who would remember this moment? Who would remember any of the men standing in this clearing?

'Recite the oath of loyalty and stand,' he said.

When it was done he turned to the second recruit kneeling to his left. This one was a year or two older, gaunt but good-looking. His eyes were clearer than when they met at the village. He had mastered his fear.

Lau said, 'Which is stronger, the bullet or your heart?'

'My heart.'

Lau pulled the trigger.

The trees erupted with the screams of birds, animals and the other youth as his compatriot folded in on himself to become another dead element of the jungle floor. Lau fired several more times. The shots were messy – he had been aiming for the recruit's eye and blew a hole in the cheek, then skull – but the bullets did their work. He gestured for Tse to bring the liquor and a pocketknife. The enforcer took a moment to acknowledge and Lau knew he was shocked that his Dragon Head had executed the youth himself.

The dead recruit was a DEA informer. He had been spotted with a field agent from their Chiang Mai office by a Triad-owned whore behind a drinks shack in her home village in northern Thailand. In accordance with expectations, Lau had put five more shots in the youth's head: through each eye, both ears and the mouth. The dead youth had seen, heard and said too much.

Another dog sent to Hell, thought Lau. Like the scum on the tram in Central. The fool, David Chau, had suspected the business at which he worked, a taxidermists in Causeway Bay, was involved in the heroin smuggling that generated millions. Chau had been right and had he approached the chemist who ran the

31

taxidermy business, he would have been employed in their work. Instead, he had stolen samples from the laboratory in the basement of the business, planning to pass them on to the police. So David Chau died on a tram in Central, gunned down by a junkie hitman almost as disposable as Chau himself.

Lau took the liquor bottle and passed the knife to the surviving youth. The kid fumbled the cut on the middle finger of his left hand and sliced into the fingernail. The enforcer, Tse, spat on the dirt and wiped his brow with a handkerchief. The recruit mixed the blood from his finger with the liquor in a wooden bowl and recited the mantra that he would bleed from the five holes if he betrayed the Society. The proof lay dead by his side. Then he drank the blood-liquor down in two desperate gulps. It was done. Six hours of tradition condensed to less than twenty minutes.

Fuck it, thought Lau, few of the new blood in the Society gave a shit about tradition so why should he? Their sacred paper was Hong Kong dollars.

But he knew he was fooling himself. There were some values that were as ingrained in his being as the Chinese blood in his veins. Values such as *xie dou*. Vendetta.

That was a code that blazed hotter in his soul than the incense burning near the traitor's corpse.

*

They gathered by the jeep like relatives waving off distant cousins.

General Khun Sa had made a tidy profit in the last couple of hours. Thirty million dollars. Lau had sat drinking tea with the opium warlord in a longhouse, negotiating supply from the poppy fields to a location in the northern Thai jungle. Half the delivery would be heroin refined in the general's jungle laboratories and half opium converted to morphine base which the

14K would refine themselves on fishing boats off the coast of Hong Kong. Khun Sa would transport the shipment via a mule train through the Shan States, the dense jungle canopy concealing the cargo from helicopters, his militia protecting it from bandits and rivals. The 14K's Thai operation would smuggle the morphine and heroin from the border to Bangkok and on to Hong Kong.

Tony Lau masked his relish with a comradely smile. The money to be made selling heroin on the streets would dwarf Khun Sa's payment.

'I appreciate you coming personally,' said the general. He gestured to a small track leading into a tangle of undergrowth and, with a hint of a bow said, 'Walk with me. Please.'

Lau returned the bow.

'Of course, General.'

Outnumbered and isolated, what choice did he have? Lau avoided his men's eyes.

As they walked, Khun Sa lit a cigar. He took a drag and exhaled, a cloud of pungent smoke rushing Tony Lau's face.

The general said, 'I have been in this business for decades. The Americans have tried to kill me. They put a bounty of two million dollars on my head. Rivals have come and gone and come again and yet here I am.'

He stared into the jungle as if something lay in wait for him there. Then he turned to Lau.

'Now I am under attack again. The new trade routes are reducing my importance in the opium business. The United Wa State Army challenge me militarily.'

In the heavy undergrowth the sounds of the village had been replaced by an unsettled quiet.

'People in my own organisation work against me, other Shan leaders turn from me. You didn't wonder why we met in this backwater, rather than Ho Mong or Ner Mone camp?'

'In this business, General, I find it best not to question certain decisions. We all operate on the fringe. Mobility is an asset.'

'Mobility is a challenge when you age, Lau *Sin Sang*.'

Lau kept his eyes on the track but felt a chill prickle on his neck despite the heat. He noted the use of the honorific with his name, absent when they spoke earlier.

Khun Sa said, 'I am in my sixth decade. I am a rich man. The Burmese have ambushed and accommodated me by turns through the years but now they want to assuage me. They are considering an offer. Official surrender in return for a quiet retirement. Lau *Sin Sang*, this may be the last time we meet, and it may be the last harvest with which our two organisations do business.'

'You have earned a quiet life, General.'

Lau and the 14K had suspected as much. The Americans, Hong Kong police and Thais had been working to disrupt Khun Sa's brokers and business associations. The Triad had already reached out to rival suppliers in the Golden Triangle. They had dealt with several informants in the past year. The dead recruit rotting in the jungle was the latest.

'That vermin at the initiation,' said the general. 'You, yourself, pulled the trigger?'

'Yes.'

How does he know? Thought Lau. Where had their watchers been?

Khun Sa said, 'With the utmost respect, be careful. A bullet is cheaper than a beer in the Golden Triangle. Any one of my men would have killed that rat. Your own enforcer, Tse, also. You are above such things. Your revered mentor and predecessor, Dragon Head Zhao *Sin Sang*, would agree, no?'

Lau understood. As a senior figure in the Society he didn't carry a weapon. It would be dishonourable and a loss of face to arm himself and be considered afraid.

He had wanted to establish his authority with Tse. But he had also wanted blood. The *xie dou* vendetta he held over the death of his predecessor, Dragon Head Zhao, had consumed him for a moment in the crushing heat. Zhao had been old but like a true father. The manner of his death still burned deep at times. The man responsible still laughed at Tony Lau in the small hours in his waking dreams.

'You are right, General,' he said, 'I understand.'

Khun Sa said, 'The scum you killed will never be found, of course. The weapon will lie in a jungle stream, rusting beyond use. But I urge you not to give the Americans any further reason to hate you.'

The general dropped the remains of his cigar on the dirt track and ground it with the heel of his boot.

'Enough,' he said, 'let's get back to your men. You must be tired and you have a bastard of a journey ahead.'

Tony Lau bowed in assent and the two men walked back toward the village with its tin shack, its gloomy peasants, and the wretched pig entrails in the dirt, now scattered and devoured by the furious swarm of ants.

Chapter Four

Callum knocked again. He heard a vicious cough and a voice thick with booze and sleep on the other side of the door called for him to enter. Itsic took the lead while he and Luciana brought up the rear carrying the buckets and cleaning utensils.

The room stank.

Son of a bitch, thought Callum.

Gabriel Muñoz always managed to have a shit in the bowl as the cleaning crew got to his suite. Never flushed. That could be some kind of gift, dropping a load on demand.

In the two weeks Callum had worked on the cleaning team in exchange for a bed in the Belleclaire Hotel on West 77th and Broadway, team leader Itsic had insisted on him paying his new-guy dues by cleaning the bathrooms. And in two weeks of cleaning toilets, Gabriel Muñoz had mastered the trick of stinking up the john just as Callum was knocking on the door. And the asshole *forgot* to flush. Every day.

Then, yesterday, Callum had been scrubbing the toilet bowl when he spotted a ball of plastic wedged behind the cistern and the wall. He gagged when he unfurled the plastic bag. Gabriel Muñoz had been shitting in a bag, waiting for the knock at the door, and emptying the contents in the toilet for Callum to deal with.

Now Itsic announced the cleaning team's arrival and offered a couple of pleasantries. Muñoz gave a grunt and glared at them. He stood in faded blue jeans and a white vest rubbing a forest of stubble on his jaw. Itsic emptied trash and dusted while Luciana concentrated on breathing through her delicate Spanish nose while hoovering. Callum flushed the john and swabbed the sink and bathtub then steeled himself and attacked the toilet. They worked in silence while Muñoz smoked a Lucky Strike. Finished outside, Itsic popped in the bathroom and whispered.

'518 next, Gabriel doesn't like us dragging our heels.'

'You guys go on, I'll be right there.'

Itsic went back to the bedroom as Callum spotted a roach scuttle below a cracked tile next to Muñoz's toiletry bag. You're in good company, he thought. He took a small clear Ziploc bag from his jeans pocket and eased the bag open, slipping the Ziploc inside between a can of deodorant and some razor blades. When he re-entered the bedroom Muñoz sat on his bed stubbing his smoke out in a mass grave of butts in a tin ashtray. The mound of tangled sheets on the bed was so thick a bum could have been sleeping inside. Muñoz was studying Luciana in her Bon Jovi t-shirt and denim skirt.

Luciana waited for Callum from the hallway. He could hear Itsic knocking on 518. Callum and Luciana left Gabriel Muñoz in his squalor and went next door.

They entered 518 when Callum said, 'Shit, I left my cigarettes in Gabriel's room.'

'Leave them,' said Itsic. 'I'll buy you another pack.'

'It'll take two seconds.'

Luciana said, 'You should listen to Itsic.'

'What are you afraid of?'

'I heard things about Gabriel.'

'He has some strange visitors,' said Itsic, 'and he doesn't like uninvited guests. You know this place. Hookers in half the rooms, needles on the stairs. Gabriel manages the hotel – you think he's an upright citizen? Stay away from him unless you're cleaning.'

Callum said, 'Two seconds,' and walked out to the corridor.

Muñoz opened his door on the first knock.

'What, not taking a dump?' said Callum.

'What you want?'

'I think I left my smokes in your bathroom. Can I come in?'

Gabriel Muñoz looked him up and down. He was a shade taller than Callum, his eyes deep-set in a caramel face. Wiry but the clear knot of his bicep twitched as he held the door. He nodded and stepped back, closing the door when Callum was inside.

'Must be tough,' said Muñoz, 'a cop cleaning up everyone's shit.'

'That, my friend, is the definition of being a police officer.'

'My definition, a cop *is* the shit.'

The Belleclaire manager sneered and walked to a desk strewn with papers as though someone had been throwing oversize confetti. He sat down to work on the accounts. The building was a grand façade on the Upper West Side, designed in 1903. The guidebooks wrote of Beaux Arts principles combined with Art Nouveau-Secessionist style. Writers and baseball stars had stayed in the vaunted rooms back in its heyday. What Let's Go and Lonely Planet failed to mention was, now half the property was owned by the hotel, the rest by a backpacker hostel chain and the building was a crumbling ruin inside. The walls were filthy, the rooms plagued with roaches and mice, the beds colonised by bugs. Many long-term residents were on welfare, doing their best to survive. Some were junkies, dealers and hookers. The stairwells reeked of crack smoke and desperation.

And presiding over all was the general manager, Gabriel Muñoz. Itsic and Luciana were right, thought Callum. Muñoz had plenty of dark characters in his contact book but the man himself was out of the drugs game. The residents might be getting high but not on his product thanks to a bullshit bust for possession back at Christmas, which threatened to send him down for an extended stretch due to two previous misdemeanors over the last six years. Enter the DEA. The Administration brokered a deal with Muñoz. His arrest and record on hold in exchange for enabling Callum's placement in the hotel, cleaning rooms for a bed. All to facilitate Callum meeting Paddy Doolan, Irish-American hood and, the task force hoped, point of entry to Fintan Walsh's mob.

Callum walked into the bathroom and called out, 'Hey Gabriel, what's this?'

Muñoz sauntered to the bathroom doorway with a studied apathy. He jerked his chin at Callum – what's up?

'What the hell is this?' said Callum pointing to the open toiletry bag and the Ziploc inside. Gabriel Muñoz peered into the bag.

'Fuck you, man! Don't you think about fuckin' me over like that!'

'I dip a finger in that white powder, what am I gonna' find?'

'Nothin' of mine!'

'See, that's the great thing about being a cop, Gabriel. I get to flush *mierda* like you away.'

'You can't do this, motherfucker. You need me to get you with your other Irish *maricón.*'

'I got a vice, same as everybody else, Gabe. For me, it's the horses. It's blighted my life, it has. Because no matter how far up you think you are, the odds will always cut you back down to size eventually.'

'Gambling is illegal in New York State, Officer.'

'Ach, Gabriel, this is just a friendly wager between friends. And the wager is this. Do you want to gamble that I won't torpedo this set-up and get you busted to Rikers? 'Cause there are plenty of other losers in hock to the law ready to rat to the cops in this city. Or do you want to play it safe and, next time my friends and I knock on your door, make sure the shitter is empty and smells like an East Side socialite's pussy on date night when her husband's out of town? Sweet, clean and inviting?' Callum put a hand on Muñoz's shoulder. 'No more shit in the john when I knock on your door.'

'That's it?'

'That's it. I don't care if you hang your ass out the window and manure the weeds nine floors below. Your bathroom is clean and odor-free tomorrow, forever and a day.'

Muñoz waited for a beat then sniffed and reset his posture to I-don't-give-a-fuck.

'Okay,' he said.

Callum pocketed the Ziploc and patted him on the cheek.

'See you tomorrow,' he said. 'Boss.'

When he rejoined Itsic and Luciana, he cursed. The Ziploc had leaked and he had baking soda piling up in his pocket.

*

'We slept under the tanks. We always parked up on a ridge, just out of sight of Hezbollah but sometimes we were so tired from the stress and the fighting that we'd forget to secure the handbrake, so we'd wake up with the Merkava rolling down the incline in the dark and have to run after it. It was a mess.'

Itsic smiled and took a drag on his cigarette.

He had the same skin color and wiry, ink-black hair as Gabriel Muñoz, a result of his Israeli parentage rather than Muñoz's Dominican heritage. But his eyes were hazel rather than the shark-black of the Dominican, his lips more generous than those of Muñoz.

Callum thought Itsic still had something of the military in his blood in how he tucked his jeans into combat boots and maintained the highest standards in the most menial of jobs. But the shirt and loose waistcoat, the addled mop of hair and the soft smile spoke of a different life, different aspirations. He had overstayed on a tourist visa in the hope of making a new life in SoHo. Once he found the right gallery, once his work began selling, he'd get the hell out of the Belleclaire and never look back. If you're going to dream, thought Callum, dream big.

'I dream of driving a car again,' said Luciana, 'never mind a tank.'

She checked through the aerosols in her empty bucket, ready to administer another cleaning to another room in the moldering majesty of the Upper West Side hotel.

This is like some kind of convoluted joke, thought Callum. Have you heard the one about the Israeli tank commander, the Spanish law graduate and the Hong Kong cop cleaning shitters in a doss house? The punchline was, neither of his companions had a clue he was a cop undercover. They thought he was no more than an Irish backpacker trying his luck in the Big Smoke.

'Once I get the green card, I can apply for a driving license again,' said Luciana.

She was twenty-four with a delicate frame and long hair scraped back from a flat forehead and tied with an elastic band. She was illegal too, and banking on her boyfriend, who had promised to arrive from Wisconsin soon, to whisk her away from the hotel. She would secure the treasured green card then buy a car, find a better-paid job and live the suburban sitcom lifestyle.

Itsic lifted his fist to the door of room 665, temporary residence of Paddy Doolan.

For the last seven days, as long as Callum had been on the cleaning team, Patrick Doolan – his shot at entry to the tight knit Irish Mob outfit – had been off the grid. A bit-player with connections to the main cast, Doolan was third generation Irish-American dating an Upper East Side dominatrix by the name of Nurse Löwin. Kicked out of his apartment by social services and the cops after a violent drinking binge, he was holed up in the Belleclaire until he found another place. At least, that was the intelligence the DEA and NYPD had gathered. Doolan had been AWOL all week.

The knock was huge in the empty corridor. No sound from the other side of the solid wood door.

Itsic tried again.

Nothing.

'Alright,' he said, 'we still got to clean the room, even if the occupant isn't there.' He began fiddling with his ring of room keys.

Callum was second in. He saw the backpack propped in the corner before he noticed the lock of fair hair snaking out from the sheets, the long worm of a body somewhere under the bedclothes.

Itsic said, 'Just here to clean the room, sir. We'll be out in a minute.'

The worm lay still, the hair unmoving.

Christ, thought Callum, what if he's dead?

He'd seen photographs of Doolan and the hair looked right, the sliver of it he could see. But it could be anyone under the sheets. Could be a woman.

They set to work. Callum listened for a voice of complaint at being woken by the team. He finished up in the bathroom and found the body in the bed unmoved.

'Aren't you going to hoover?' said Callum.

Itsic whispered, 'We might wake him up.'

'Gabriel won't be happy if he finds we didn't clean properly.'

'He won't like a pissed off guest complaining, either.'

Callum pointed at the bed.

'What does this guy want for his twenty-five bucks?'

The bastard tied one on last night, he thought. Drunk or high in the wee small hours and dead to the world at ten-thirty in the morning. A week of waiting and Doolan, if it was him, lay seven feet away oblivious to the two assholes debating sanitation policy.

Callum said, 'Got a smoke?' and sat on the end of the bed.

Itsic stared. What the hell was the Irishman doing?

He said, 'You got your own. Went back to Gabriel's room to pick them up.'

'Oh yeah. Got a light?'

Callum began rummaging in his pocket, the mattress springs complaining as he fidgeted. The sheets slipped toward the floor. Did the body move?

Itsic said, 'Christy, come on, man.'

Callum almost blew it. He was about to ask who the hell Christy was. Then he remembered Christy was Callum mark two. Christy Burns. The persona he'd live with for however long he was undercover, should that be the rest of his natural life. A dark cloud of fear edged into his mind and he chased it away and sprang from the mattress with a shout of triumph, a cheap plastic lighter in his hand.

Luciana flinched.

The body stirred with a thick groan.

'We need to move on,' hissed Itsic.

'Just one smoke. I'll light you.'

The lock of blond hair retracted under the sheets.

Come on, you sack of shit, thought Callum. Wake up.

'You know how long it takes to smoke a Camel?' he said, his voice almost frantic.

He didn't want to be here, didn't want to clean rooms, didn't want to do this job. But he'd fucked up in Hong Kong, he'd gotten himself in this position and now it seemed paramount that this asshole in the bed woke up. That this asshole was Paddy Doolan and that he made a connection with Callum Burke, now Christy Burns to all concerned. The faster he made a connection, the faster this whole operation would come to an end.

Calm down, he thought. Don't rush it.

Itsic, leaned close, 'You're gonna' wake this asshole up. Then this asshole is gonna' complain. Then Gabriel is gonna' complain, but not to you. You see what I'm saying here?'

'Listen, I'm tired. I walked from here to Battery Park City yes-

43

terday looking for work. Walked because I couldn't afford the subway. I spent my morning cleaning other people's shit.'

The lock of hair was back. From the corner of his eye, Callum watched it rise from under the cover until a pair of pale blue eyes appeared. Then a thin nose, open mouth and cheeks coated in a fine blond stubble.

'You know what,' said Callum, voice booming, 'I didn't come all the way from Ireland for this shit.'

The blue eyes searched the room and settled on the ranting Irishman in the center of the floor like a boxer bossing the ring. Luciana had retreated to the door holding her bucket in front like Red Riding Hood's basket. Itsic stepped forward. He looked at the man stirring in the bed. People like this guy who probably spent more in one night than Itsic made in a day's work.

The Israeli looked Callum in the eye and said, 'Fuck it. Light me up.'

They huddled, sparked the lighter and took a deep drag of their cigarettes. Luciana opened the window and sat on the inner ledge.

Callum said, 'You think when you've got your third exhibit in SoHo you're gonna' remember cleaning rooms and tiptoeing around sleeping guests?'

The blond hair had collapsed to neck-length around a slim face as the man in the bed sat up, rubbing his bare chest. An attractive face thought Callum, with a kind set to the mouth and a credulous, almost innocent quality to the spring-sky eyes. Probably still drunk. The face matched the file photos Mattila and O'Connell had shown him. Paddy Doolan in the flesh.

Itsic said, 'And you? Is Christy Burns gonna' be the next Irish immigrant millionaire in New York?'

Callum took a drag on his Camel. 'If I had a dollar for every one of us over here, I already would be.'

'Can I have one of those?'

The voice sounded like it was wading through mud but the man in the bed gestured to Itsic and Callum with his chin.

'Can I grab a smoke?' he said, voice clearer.

Itsic offered his Lucky Strikes, Callum his Camels.

Paddy Doolan swung his legs out of the bed to reveal a pair of gray boxer shorts and wiry legs covered in a light down of fair hair. He leaned his elbows on his knees for a moment, skin creasing over a tight stomach.

Come on, thought Callum, take one of mine.

Doolan was seized with a racking cough. He doubled over and looked like he was about to spit on the floor then eased his head back and reached toward Itisc.

'Better take one of those,' he said, 'don't think I can handle a Camel right now.'

He took a Lucky Strike from Itsic's pack and said, 'Thanks.'

'No problem,' said Itsic.

Callum said, 'Maybe I'll switch. You don't see Lucky Strikes back home.'

Doolan looked him over. He said, 'Do I know you?'

'Doubt it. I've only been in America for a few weeks. Unless you've seen me about the hotel.'

Paddy Doolan said, 'You been in this country a few weeks how come you're cleaning rooms in this shithole?'

'You know, arrived in New York, got carried away with the nightlife. Blew my cash and ended up doing this for a free bed. I finish up here before lunch then look for work in the city.'

'What kind of work?'

'Barman, waiter. Anything that pays cash in hand and makes tips.'

'You're Irish,' said the man. 'You legal?'

'For now. Got a three-month tourist visa but after that ...'

'Tourist visa. You supposed to be working?'

Callum looked Doolan in the eye and said 'What do you care?'

Doolan took a drag on his cigarette and peered at Callum through the gray-blue smoke like a veil across his face. His jaw tensed as though his brain was working on a memo to his mouth about what to say to this arrogant shithead standing in the middle of the room.

He said, 'Your friend called you Burns?' The words were slow and deliberate as though Doolan were punch drunk.

'That's right,' said Callum. 'Christy Burns.'

'Where you from?'

'Belfast.'

Doolan blew a smoke ring. 'Rough town,' he said.

'I think New York's got it beat.'

Itsic finished his smoke, grinding the butt out on the window ledge and flicking it outside. He made for the door and gestured to Luciana to follow then said, 'Sorry to disturb you. Christy, let's go.'

Callum took a long drag of tobacco, hoping to smother his anger. Now what? Would Doolan be here tomorrow? What if he moved out of the hotel before Callum got a better shot at making some kind of connection? Intelligence suggested the man was a dyed-in-the-wool Irish-American, a sucker for any sob story from the Emerald Isle. Had Callum overplayed the accent? Had he pissed the guy off with his attitude? Bollocks.

He walked to the window to toss his cigarette. As he leaned out and took in the smut-stained brickwork at the rear of the building trailing six floors to a small trash-covered courtyard, he heard the deliberate voice again.

'Listen, Christy. You don't wanna' be cleaning shit for a living. You don't wanna' be stayin' here, either.'

Itsic stood in the doorway and opened his mouth to hurry Callum out of the room but the deliberate voice took on an edge.

'Your friend'll catch up in a second.'

Doolan produced a cheap tin ashtray from under his bed and

crushed out his cigarette, his eyes never leaving the Israeli. Itsic looked at Callum then back to Doolan and nodded. He left the room with Luciana. Something warm spread up Callum's neck.

'What the fuck are you doing here?' said Doolan. 'There ain't no future in this.'

'I don't know anybody. I don't have a work visa.'

'Why don't you look around Woodside, or Riverdale, or Woodlawn?'

'I didn't come all the way here to live in an Irish town.'

Doolan nodded. 'I hear you,' he said. 'I'm staying here until I get some money is owed to me. I try not to sleep here too much, what with the bed bugs and all, been staying on couches on the West Side when I can. I got an apartment in the Village lined up for when that money turns up.'

He began rummaging through the tangle of sheets on the bed and found a crumpled pair of blue jeans. He checked the pockets, came up with a small creased card and reached out to Callum.

'You look pretty fit. This is a moving company on the Upper West Side. I do some work for them, moving people's stuff, office equipment, all kinds. You call them and say I told you to get in touch. My name's Paddy Doolan. Maybe you'll get some work, get out of here, find a decent place to stay.'

Callum took the card and looked at the embossed truck with an arrow on the side, the address and phone number, the company name. New World Movers.

He said, 'Thanks, I'll call when I got some change.'

Doolan rummaged again and came up with a few crumpled bills. He counted them in his deliberate way and said, 'Here you go, forty-seven bucks to get you started.'

'Thanks, man.'

'Paddy.'

'Thanks, Paddy.'

Callum tapped the card then put it in his pocket and walked to the door. He had one foot in the corridor when Doolan called after him.

'Hey, Christy, one other thing. I'm feeling better now I'm awake. I'll have one of those Camels after all.'

Chapter Five

'Heard about Sol, man.'

'Man, that's old news.'

'Cops any idea who did it?'

'Nah, he just another statistic.'

Callum watched the huddle of men as they stood on Columbus Avenue next to the open doors of the box-room. A short ramp led down to the doors below street level and the room piled high with book boxes, dish boxes, linen boxes. Stacked against the walls were the dollies on which the men would wheel wardrobes, couches and desks. The equipment of New World Movers. More men milled around on the sidewalk and three trucks were parked in front of the office, pissing off cab drivers as they battled their way down the four-lane avenue.

The men would be assigned to a crew with a foreman who doubled as a driver. They stood loose limbed, like their arms and legs were almost boneless. Their eyes were heavy-lidded, their movements slow but graceful. One wore earphones with an old Sony Walkman and moved his head to an inner beat. Callum walked over and stood a couple of feet away, ready for work.

He'd called the number on Doolan's card and spoken with a stressed sounding man called Bill who fobbed him off with a promise of work if a slot came up on a job. The man had been about to kill the call when Callum mentioned Paddy Doolan. The pitch of the voice rose an octave and Callum heard rustling papers and muttering. A minute later he had a promise of work and was told to come to the company offices on Columbus Avenue at eight next morning.

One of the men broke off from the huddle on the sidewalk and approached Callum.

'Hey, you new?'

'Yeah. How are you?'

They shook hands as the man chuckled. His palms were dry and calloused, his laugh deep and warm.

'I like your accent, man.'

'I'm Irish.'

'Like the Lucky Charms guy.'

'Right.'

The man introduced himself as J.J., Johnny Johnson.

'I'm Christy,' said Callum.

J.J. called two others over and they introduced themselves, Troy Jackson and Willie Simmons with the Walkman.

'My man here is from Ireland,' said J.J.

Troy said, 'You don't talk like Paddy.'

'He the real thing,' said Willie. 'Like Liam Neeson.'

Callum said, 'Are you guys from Manhattan?' He felt like the new kid at school. The answer came in unison.

'South Bronx.'

A short, bearded man with an impressive belly and powerful shoulders walked out the front door of the New World office holding a clipboard and took up position next to one of the trucks. He assigned the men standing around to various foremen. Troy went with a tall Australian sporting a crew cut. Willie joined an older looking Scot in a rugby shirt.

'J.J. and Christy, you're with Paddy.'

They walked to the last truck in the line where Paddy Doolan was stacking dollies in back. He wore a Gold's Gym t-shirt, jeans and boots, and a leather support belt. He jumped down from the back of the truck trailing the metal roller shutter with him and secured it.

'Okay gentlemen,' he said, 'let's go make some money, huh?'

The customer was late. Doolan had driven to the nearest McDonald's for McMuffins and coffee to kill time. J.J. had passed on the breakfast and disappeared for ten minutes.

Doolan had said, 'Buyin' beer.'

'Jesus Christ, it's before nine in the morning.'

'He needs a lift. You notice how he and the others were so slow back at the office? They ain't had their methadone.'

Doolan took a bite of egg and bacon and spoke through a mouthful of muffin.

'Some of the South Bronx guys are addicts. They get their methadone from the clinic, they can lift wardrobes on their own. They don't, they can't lift their pinky without a beer to start the day.'

'Huh, J.J.'s a junkie.'

'Oh no,' said Doolan. 'He's an addict. There's a difference. Guys like him or Willie, they're hooked, sure, but they got lovers and wives and kids and lives. They got apartments and they work when they can. You take a walk around Port Authority at four in the morning, you'll see a real junkie.'

Callum thought of busting the odd opium den in Kowloon, the emaciated men sprawled in the foul-smelling gloom, lives dissipating in the thick air with the heavy smoke.

Doolan said, 'You keep working these crews you're gonna' end up a foreman soon. The beard with the clipboard back at the office is Bill. He owns New World. He's a Connecticut Jew. You work well, you'll be a foreman and driver in no time.'

'I'm illegal, Paddy. I don't have a work visa or an American driving license.'

'You think Bill or any other business owner in New York gives a shit? Here's the deal: Bill don't trust other Americans, period. I did him a favor once so I get a pass but every other foreman and driver in New World is a European, Australian or Canadian and most of them are illegal. He sleeps easy at night because he thinks you got a funny accent, you're above reproach. You get paid in cash and his books look a lot more impressive into the bargain.' Doolan tore off another chunk of egg and bacon. 'Welcome to the United States of America.'

Callum raised his coffee in salute. They were parked by the 96th Street subway station, across Broadway from a glass and steel apartment building bossing a chocolate-colored brownstone next door.

Callum said, 'Who's Sol?'

Doolan looked at the brownstone across Broadway. He chewed on his breakfast for a couple of seconds. A rollerblader glided by in traffic holding a loose strap at the back of a beer truck. Doolan said, 'Sol's another Jew. Russian, lived out in Brighton Beach. He took care of the books for Bill. Why you askin'?'

Callum had seen the file. Solomon Dmitri Grundy had been a large man with thick-lensed glasses, and a close-shaved beard. His height had not helped distribute his girth as he had slim arms and legs but a huge belly and a scar where he'd had an appendectomy as a teenager. He had come to the United States with his parents when a child and spent all of his adult life in New York City. He never married and his parents had both passed. His brother died of a drug overdose in 1990. Detective notes revealed after interviews with acquaintances that Sol Grundy had been a shy man and a devotee of the Russian Orthodox Church. He attended The Church of the Mother Of God. No one had seemed to know he also attended sessions with his favorite dominatrix, Nurse Löwin.

Callum said, 'I heard J.J. and some of the other guys talking about him. Just interested. You know, if I'm gonna' do more work with youse I wanna' know who's who.'

Doolan said, 'What were they sayin'?'

'That something happened to him, I think. They mentioned the cops. Hey, sorry for bringing it up if it's a problem.'

Doolan kept his eyes turned toward the center island on Broadway and the brownstone beyond. There was a small pulse in his jaw. He put down his McMuffin and gripped the wheel. His knuckles were white.

The sounds of traffic seemed to fade out and all Callum could hear was a rushing in his ears. He jumped when J.J. opened the passenger door. The Bronx man climbed into the cab clutching a can in a brown paper bag. Doolan shot him an impatient look and started the engine.

'Our boy here thinks he's a New Yorker already,' said Doolan. His voice was slick with sarcasm. 'He's callin' us "youse" now.'

'*Youse* have never been to Belfast, have *youse*?' said Callum.

'Not yet.'

'So where do you think the fucking word comes from? We built half this fucking city for youse, after all.'

Doolan sat back in the driver's seat and fixed Callum with a pale blue stare. Callum met his eyes. He felt something kindle inside, snapping in his gut like when he entered the ring, gloves laced and ready.

J.J. took a slow sip of his beer.

Then he laughed, warm syrup filling the cab.

'You alright, Christy,' he said. 'You don't take none a' this man's shit.'

Doolan's eyes softened and his mouth cracked in a grin.

'You're a fiery Irish son of a bitch,' said Doolan. 'Yeah, you're alright.'

*

Paddy offered Callum a joint.

'No thanks.'

'You don't smoke?'

'Not in the morning.'

Doolan offered the smoke to J.J. who raised his palm, shook his head and took a swig of the dregs of his beer.

The client was over an hour late. They'd been parked up on a quiet street in Chelsea across from a row of red-brick town-houses. Like something from Peter Pan's London, thought Callum. The client lived in 416 and they'd been waiting to move a couch out of his apartment.

'Son of a bitch,' said Paddy. 'We get this thing down the stairs, we got to drive to storage in the Bronx before we make job two. Jesus Christ, there he is.'

A man in a disheveled suit with a trim brown beard was cross-ing the street waving at the truck. The crew clambered down from the cab and Doolan began chatting to the client. Callum and J.J. grabbed a couple of dollies, padded blankets and heavy masking tape from the back of the truck.

The apartment was a cramped space in the loft strewn with clothes, books and vinyl. A Persian rug lay in the center of the living area, the couch against one wall. A large antique walnut desk piled high with papers hogged a chunk of floor space. The client was an academic and had been held back by a troubled student in need of counselling on a doctorate paper. Callum and J.J. wrapped the corners of the couch with blankets and masking tape.

J.J. stomped on the edge of a dolly flipping it end up so he could grab it.

The academic's voice was nasal like it was channeled through a speaker in a subway car. 'Fabulous,' he said. 'Can you do any other tricks?'

J.J. stared like a bullied kid. He shook his head and wiped his nose with his sleeve. The academic looked away.

They upended the couch on the dollies and made to maneuver it out the door to the top of the stairs. Twenty minutes later it was still in the apartment. Doolan explained the couch was too big, the doorframe too small. The client's nasal whine pierced Paddy's attempts at reasoning.

'You can't move it?'

'Sorry, man, not today. It won't fit.'

'So take it apart.'

'We aren't paid for that.'

'You can forget about being paid, period,' said the client. 'I want to speak to your boss.'

J.J. shook his head with a heavy sadness and made for the stairs. He nodded for Callum to follow. Doolan's face flushed. Paper crinkled as he scrunched the job contract in his right hand, and he took a step toward the customer.

'The couch won't fit,' said Doolan. 'I'm gonna' go back to the office and tell Bill the situation and he'll take it from there.'

The academic glared and made a grab for the contract. Doolan seized him by the throat and shoved him backward into the couch. Couch and client toppled taking a standing lamp with them. The lamp clattered off the desk dropping a large paperweight hidden under a sheaf of papers. The floor shook when the client hit. The paperweight rolled under the desk. Doolan stood over the man.

'You fuck! You think you can put your hands on me?'

Callum looked at the doorway. J.J. was gone.

The client's eyes were red, his cheeks pale. His voice whined so high Callum expected feedback.

'My friend's wife is a lawyer. I'm gonna' call her and sue your ass.' He looked at Callum then back to Doolan. 'I'll call the cops.'

Doolan said, 'You touch your phone I'll beat the whiny-ass-bitch out of you.'

He bent down and yanked the cord from the upset lamp out

of the wall socket, then ripped it clean from the lamp. The client's mouth seized up and his cheeks went from pale to red. The first tears came.

He screeched, 'Call the police!'

The red eyes found Callum.

'Call the police!'

The cord slashed down on the man's legs. Doolan raised it and swung like he was wrangling a lasso and whipped the man again. It couldn't have hurt so much, thought Callum. But the effect was like electric shocks on the customer's skin. The screams were wild like a child with night terrors.

Callum grabbed at Doolan's shoulder. His fingers slipped off as Doolan brought the cord back to strike again. Doolan glanced back for a beat and Callum could see the red mist rising in those pale blue eyes, the skin drawn tight across the cheekbones colored crimson like war paint. If Doolan did real damage to this idiot he'd get locked up. Then the point of entry to the Walsh crew would be slammed shut, the operation dead before it had a chance to begin. But if Callum could turn the tables, take the initiative, Paddy might just come around and realize he had to protect the guy from the Old Country from the cops and get the hell out of here.

He clawed at Doolan's shoulder again, snatched at air but then found purchase. Callum put himself between the screaming man on the floor and Doolan.

He yelled, 'Call the cops? They'll be calling a fucking ambulance when I'm finished with you!'

He gave the client a kick in the thigh.

'You wanna' call the cops? You wanna' get me locked up? Maybe send me home? I'll make it worth your fucking while you whining wee shite!'

He threw another couple of kicks at the man. The client curled in a fetal ball.

Come on Doolan, he thought, close this down.

Callum took hold of the fallen lamp and raised it over his head ready to bring it down and wondered how he'd avoid doing real damage. The lamp had a long metal stand and he struggled with its weight. Christ, it was solid. Then the lamp was yanking him backward and he realized that Paddy Doolan was on the other end of it dragging him toward the door. Doolan got an arm around his neck and hauled him out of the apartment. He slid his arm around Callum's shoulders.

'Leave it,' he snapped. 'I got this. Go back to the truck. This guy won't call no one. He's got a twelve inch dildo fell off and rolled under his desk when I pushed him, and some of the papers came with it were polaroids would put Barely Legal to shame. This asshole's got a reputation to protect at whatever college he works.' He gave Callum a smile of encouragement that began in his clear blue eyes and rushed to a broad white grin.

Then Paddy Doolan turned and walked back into the apartment.

*

The second job was a cakewalk. A publicist moving from West Village to Brooklyn Heights. Callum made fifty-five dollars on the job and figured his accent got him the hundred dollar tip. There was a phone number from the publicist, too. She had a kind mouth and a small tattoo of a seahorse at the nape of her neck. It was a shame he'd never call.

J.J. jumped ship near Center Street once they crossed the Brooklyn Bridge back to Manhattan then Callum rode with Doolan up 10th Avenue toward the chain link gravel parking lot where they'd drop the truck on West 50th Street. He sat in silence drinking in the parade of stores, pedestrians, hawkers and loiterers, the throng thickening and buildings reaching higher into the yellow-tinged sky as they approached 42nd.

Doolan said, 'You okay?'

'Yeah, I'm okay.'

Paddy shook a couple of cigarettes from his pack one-handed onto the seat where J.J. had sat in the middle of the cab.

'Go ahead.'

Callum lit up, then lit Doolan.

'I'm sorry about this mornin',' said Doolan. 'First I took a shot at you with the *youse* thing, then I got a little salty with that faggot in Chelsea.'

'He deserved it. Wanker.'

'I like that. *Wanker*. Like jerk-off, right?'

'Yeah. Literally, in his case. You should've pocketed a couple of the photos before you left.'

Doolan blew a stream of smoke out the window.

'What makes you think I didn't?' He jammed the cigarette in his mouth and reached into his pocket, producing three polaroids. One featured a white, one a black and one an Asian girl. None looked a day over twenty-one.

'This guy's like fucking Benetton.'

Doolan laughed, dropping his cigarette on his lap.

'Shit!'

They drove another block with Doolan smacking out sparks on his thigh and stomping on the butt on the floor of the cab.

'You got a temper,' he said. 'Way you jumped in on that asshole. You got to control that.'

'He was gonna' call the cops.'

'About that.' Doolan put the truck in first and yelled at a cab that cut him off. 'I got kinda' pissed this morning when you asked me about Sol. What I said is true, Sol did the books for Bill but a week or two ago the cops turn up at New World and take Bill into the office. Turns out Sol was shot. I was on a long-haul job to Massachusetts, got stuck out in Martha's-fucking-Vineyard on a last minute job the night it happened. Poor bastard.'

'Dead?'

'Yeah.'

'Jesus.'

'Welcome to New York, huh?'

'Were you close?'

'No, I didn't see the guy much. It was probably a street robbery gone wrong or some shit. He was killed up near Harlem. Anyway, I don't like cops. You askin' about Sol made me think about cops and that put me in a bad mood, you know? Sorry.'

'I don't like them much either,' said Callum, 'they can be right bastards back home. I've had my problems with them, part of the reason I left. But you had the first client threatening to call them. That's why I started in on him. To shut him the fuck up.'

'I appreciate you helping out with that sleazy asshole and all, but I already saw the dildo, the pictures. I just wanted to kick his ass some before I closed him down. But we gotta' be careful.'

'You knew he wouldn't call the cops, to keep his reputation.'

'This time, yeah. But if they had turned up I might have spent a night in a cell and been put on some kind of bullshit assault charge. Not exactly the first time. It wasn't me I was worried about, Christy.'

Doolan put a hand on Callum's arm.

'It was you, man. You gotta' be careful. You're an illegal worker. If I didn't have something on that guy and the cops showed? Even you didn't touch him, you were on the first plane back to Ireland.'

Doolan turned right off 10th and onto 50th Street.

'And I don't want my new friend deported before I can buy him a drink and tie one on, huh? So let's park up and hit the Shannon for a couple drinks or ten.'

Chapter Six

Callum tapped the wheel to Tupac's Dear Mama and kept his eyes on the small bodega diagonal from the parked truck on the corner of 98th and Amsterdam Avenue. Willie and J.J. were inside buying smokes while Callum idled next to a dry cleaners eager to make a start on a job in north Queens. The faster they finished up the move, the earlier he could get over to Hoboken for a meet with Milburn. He'd been working three weeks for New World and, true to his word, Paddy Doolan had ensured Callum had got a gig as driver and foreman of a crew.

Willie and J.J. had missed their morning methadone and Callum was sure they were buying beers along with their smokes. He'd been against the stop but knew they'd be dead weight on the job if he didn't accommodate.

He'd never worked undercover. There weren't many opportunities for the white officers in Hong Kong but he'd heard stories of legendary Chinese Constables who'd worked Triad factions. Infiltration to the secret societies could take years as could building a prosecutable case. Those men were the eyes and ears of the force in Cantonese organized crime, men with seemingly infinite patience and unimaginable bravery. There were the few undercover agents who went rogue and lost sight of why they were running with a Triad in the first place. Corruption had long been a cancer among a minority within the HKPF. But the police who had infiltrated the Triads were a breed apart.

Now here Callum was, less than a month undercover and yet to be involved in anything criminal, sweating the rap on his cab door from a bored New York cop who might ask for ID and a driving license. He fiddled with the volume on the truck radio as Tupac finished and wondered how he'd live with it if he made it into the ranks of the Fintan Walsh crew. How much he might hate Paddy Doolan and the rest once he saw the work of the Irish Mob first hand.

How he'd sleep at night.

Or how much he might enjoy the rush.

The passenger door snapped open and Willie clambered in, earphones clamped in place, followed by a whistling J.J. They shuffled up on the seat each holding a brown paper bag from the bodega. Callum made to start the engine. They could sip their beers while he drove across the Triborough Bridge to Queens and fuck them if they spilled the shit in their laps.

'Yo Christy, give us a minute, man,' said J.J.

'We have to get going, lads. The client wants us by ten at the latest.'

'This won't take a second. You want a smoke?'

Willie produced a pack of Marlboros from his coat and slapped it against his palm to loosen the cigarettes inside while J.J. took two books of matches from his brown paper bag.

Recognizing a lost cause, Callum said, 'Go on, then.'

'Yeah, Christy. You alright.'

As Callum took the cigarette, J.J. spread a folded subway map on the dashboard. The books of matches displayed the legend "Angelica's Market" on the cover flap. Willie took one and opened it then pulled the matches up to reveal a small cellophane package of white powder.

'Fuck's sake!' said Callum.

'One second. One second.'

Willie opened and tapped the package onto the map. J.J. rolled two sheets from a small notepad they kept in the cab and dealt with his own package, tucked behind the matches in his book. He tapped his powder onto a magazine cover.

'You assholes!' said Callum. 'What the fuck is that? You know what happens if a cop sees you doing this? In the middle of Columbus-fucking-Avenue?'

Willie pulled off his earphones and shoved the rolled sheet of notepaper in his nostril, bent over the dashboard and snorted three times.

'It's done, it's done,' he said as J.J. followed suit.

They lit up smokes and sat back on the seat waiting for the high to start. Callum swore hard, lit his Marlboro with a plastic Mets lighter, turned the ignition and eased into traffic, pissing off a food truck in the process.

On foot, Manhattan swirled about the individual. In traffic it shunted, veered, cajoled and stuttered.

On the RFK over Randall's Island he spoke again.

'What was that shit? Cocaine?'

Willie laughed, a high squawk. 'We look like we from Tribeca? It was H, baby. Heroin.'

He and J.J. had begun the party five minutes after snorting. They'd become animated and loud. They talked about girls on the sidewalk, ridiculed a song on the radio, hooted along with another. When a newscast update in the ongoing soap opera of the O.J. Simpson trial came on they went into overdrive – 'Damn sheriffs is out a' the game, man. Jury dressin' in black? Kinda' shit is that? Jap in charge be racist, man.'

Callum concentrated on crossing the East River Suspension section of the bridge until they were past Astoria Park and into north Queens.

He said, 'You always go to the same place if you need to snort that shit?'

Willie said, 'Depends where we are, C. That store, Angelica's, is the closest to the office so it's easy.'

'How's the guy behind the counter know what you want?'

'We ask for a book of eighteen matches but a book usually got twenty. It's like a code, y'know? Hispanic guy knows what we want.'

'Hispanic?'

'Yeah, he got some cousin works as a manager in some hotel on West 77th, used to deal. One of his old connections gets the shit for this bodega guy.'

Was Gabriel Muñoz still connected to dope? Callum would drop that nugget about Angelica's with Mattila next time they met, make sure he was insulated.

'The Belleclaire Hotel? Shit, that's where I'm crashing.'

Willie sniffed, 'Small world, huh?'

'The bodega guy, is he Dominican? Puerto Rican?'

'Dominican, Puerto Rican, Mexican, I don't know. All look the same, y'know?'

Callum smiled. 'Like white guys, huh?'

J.J. laughed. 'No, Christy, white guys look mean. All angry and shit, all the time. Or maybe that's only when they be near a nigger.'

Callum said, 'You look in a mirror lately?' He shot the Bronx men a shit-eating grin with another smoke clenched between his teeth.

'Ah, you alright, Christy,' said Willie.

J.J.'s brow knit in furious sincerity. 'That's right, you okay, man.'

'I'm whiter than a used rubber,' said Callum.

Willie said, 'But you ain't *American* white. You Irish, come here and nobody gives a shit about you. You illegal – we ain't stupid, Christy. We know. You just shit, like us.'

'I'm honored.'

Callum turned into a street with an Italian bakery on the corner. Three old men sat at a table outside wrapped up against a late spring breeze. He could feel himself buzz like he was on something, like he'd been snorting in the cab back on Amsterdam too. It was Manhattan, speeding through his system, thrashing against the quieter, simpler streets of Queens.

63

It was like he was having a reaction to the decompression of the sister borough.

He made an effort to slow his driving and said, 'So how about Bill?'

'Bill be like any other white American,' said Willie. 'He don't trust a nigger so he don't have a single black driver or foreman on a crew. His Jew friend Sol was different, though. Used to look at us like we was like them starvin' Africans or somethin'. All sad eyed and shit.' Willie cleared his throat. 'Used to,' he said.

J.J. stared out the window.

'So, Sol was alright?' said Callum.

'He's six feet down in Cypress Hills now,' said Willie.

Callum dialed the truck radio to Elvis Duran's show on Z100. He said, 'You think it was a mugging gone wrong or what?'

'Dunno'. But rest in peace and all that shit.'

'Yeah,' said J.J. 'He could be a pain in the ass but he was a good person.'

'A pain in the ass how?'

'Sol's brother died a few years back. Some kinda' overdose, you know? He was on Wall Street. I heard bad coke or somethin'. Sol was real anti-dope after that. Used to check how we was doin' all the time. Nothin' heavy, just – "How you all doin' today?" But like he was real concerned.'

Callum said, 'Sounds like he was a decent guy.'

'Guess so,' said Willie. 'One thing I remember, first day Sol didn't show, two ugly-ass white guys turned up at the office.'

'Yeah? What did they look like, aside from ugly?'

'One of them had this real bad skin and a haircut like he was in grade school, with this old-school side partin'. Weird eyebrows, too: thin, like they was plucked. The other just looked scary, a big assshole with a busted nose and a bald spot and a beer gut.'

'Cops?'

64

J.J. smiled like he'd just figured out a joke.

'Not exactly.'

Callum turned down the radio.

'But the cops came to the office, right? Askin' about Sol?'

'Right. I heard Sol got shot outside some kinda' whorehouse. No surprise, he was a ugly motherfucker, wouldn't get no pussy for free.'

'Who'd you hear that from?'

'Heard Paddy talkin' to Bill. I was in the box-room, forgot my bandana and went back to get it. They was on the stairs that lead up to the office.' J.J. smiled and clapped Callum on the back. 'You don't need to worry, though. Cops ain't gonna' be interested in you, even if they come back. We know you're illegal. And you and Paddy was talkin' after he beat that asshole with the couch in Chelsea.'

'You hear a lot,' said Callum. 'Especially from Paddy.'

'Paddy,' said J.J., 'he alright, like you.'

'He's a white American.'

'Yeah, but we got the feelin' Paddy outside the system, you know?'

'That's right,' said Willie. 'Paddy's alright. For an American.'

*

The house was on a tree-lined residential street, all clapboard walk-ups and small shreds of lawn. Fords and Chryslers in the driveways wedged between each compact, sovereign home.

The customers were waging a civil war in ragged Arabic. Young, handsome and Middle Eastern, the man was gesticulating and barking at his partner. Some of their furniture was going into storage in Brooklyn. A dresser, an intricately carved chair, a cluster of boxes filled with clothes.

The woman matched the man's anger with an immaculate indifference. Callum thought she was beautiful. Skin the color of burnished gold in a white blouse and pale blue jeans, feet in leather loafers below legs so long they were almost lanky.

She looked nothing like Irene Chu but her spidery fingers and the arc of her arm, the tilt of her head, was an echo of his wife and times past in Hong Kong. The smooth brow, if a shade lighter, could have been Irene's as she lay naked beside him, the sheets kicked off the bed in the sweating heat, a fan working in the corner of their flat in Kowloon. He felt something stir at the memory, then fade.

The woman's partner glared and fired a parting volley of fierce Arabic. Again, Callum saw himself back in the flat in Kowloon, Tara already with one of Irene's relatives. He was raging against Irene. Raging at himself. Irene had said goodbye and the door had closed; a piece of his life shutting down.

Callum climbed up in the back of the truck and leaned hard on the dresser, wrapped in protective blankets. He took deep breaths through his nose and swallowed down the emptiness hollowing out his insides. His eyes began to fill and he whispered a curse, wiped at them, sniffed hard and caught the smell of dust and grime.

They drove to a storage facility in Brooklyn with the radio on to fill in the lengthening blanks in the conversation. It was hours since Willie and J.J. had got well on the junk and they dozed in the cab. A tinny drone came from Willie's earphones as the old cassette Walkman played. The woman followed in her BMW.

At the storage place Willie and J.J. worked like they were slogging through wet sand and Callum was sore and bitter by the end of the job. He left them griping by the chain link of the truck parking lot on West 50th and headed for 42nd Street Subway Station under a heavy sky the color of concrete.

By the time he walked into the Turkish coffee shop in Hoboken, wet from the spring rain, he felt like he had his own personal thundercloud over his head. The place had six Formica tables and a counter at the back of the room. Big ceiling-to-knee-high windows on the front. Too big for Callum's liking but at least the lighting was dim as the darkening sky outside. An old guy sat in the corner by the window with his hand down his pants.

'Here's our boy,' said O'Connell. 'How's life in the moving business?'

The New York cop had selected a table by the bathroom at the back of the shop. Callum sat down like he'd walked all the way from Brooklyn Heights.

'Where's Milburn?'

'With Ho. Your Chinese colleague was late calling in so your boss was concerned and wanted to meet him. And he gotta' report back to his bosses in Hong Kong. He thought I could run solo tonight, us being Celtic brothers and all.'

'Whereabouts were you born again?'

'Jersey City to an immigrant Irish father and third generation mom. You want a coffee?'

Callum went for a piss. He didn't like that O'Connell was running him like a confidential informant. It made him feel less like a cop. When he returned to the table he found a small cup of Turkish rocket fuel waiting. He sat with his back to the window then lit a cigarette and watched O'Connell purse his lips at the first flurry of smoke. Callum made sure to exhale in the cop's direction.

O'Connell said, 'You haven't called in a couple days.'

'I haven't had much to report.'

'So remind me where we are.'

'Previously on "Inside the Irish Mob". Paddy Doolan took me under his wing. I've been working on New World jobs. Doolan moved out of the Belleclaire Hotel and got himself an apartment on Bleecker Street. He's talked about sharing but nothing concrete so I'm going to his place after this to talk it over.'

O'Connell scratched his nose and squinted like a kid. He said, 'Love at first sight. What do you think of Doolan?'

Callum took a sip of the strong coffee. He stared at the inky liquid in the cup, rich in caffeine, and looked forward to getting some sleep sometime next week.

'He's where you thought he would be on the ladder in Walsh's Mob. Definitely low-level but connected. Seems a pretty garrulous guy.'

'In English.'

'Talkative. He's popular with the crews at New World, likes a drink, has a temper. You know he went off at that client last week. I can see why he's got a record for violence but I can also see why he hasn't done serious time. He's just a brawler.'

'Has he talked about Walsh?'

'Not a word. But I can feel he wants to trust me. We've been drinking a few times. I told him I hate police. I gave him the story: I got in trouble with the cops back home because I put one in hospital during a riot, ran to the States. We talk about women, sports, work. Boxing.'

He caught O'Connell staring at his broken nose.

Callum said, 'Doolan's started telling me a little about his family. His parents.'

'Have you reciprocated?'

'That's a big word.'

O'Connell bowed.

Callum said, 'Told him my parents passed and I have an estranged brother in Glasgow. The truth.'

They both drank. O'Connell looked past Callum out the window of the coffee shop. Callum watched the owner busy himself cleaning the counter.

He said, 'Did you know Sol Grundy's brother died because of drugs?'

'I read the Homicide reports. The DD5s.'

'Any angle on the dominatrix?'

'She was out that evening with friends. They back her story. Grundy came looking for her, found she wasn't there and got shot leaving her building. She came home to an episode of Law And Order outside her place and freaked. She cooperated fully with detectives.'

Callum said, 'Did you tell the guys on the case that Grundy worked for a business been swallowed up by an Irish mob outfit under investigation by the DEA?'

'Grundy's brother didn't die because of heroin.'

'Cocaine, right?'

O'Connell sat back in his chair.

'I think you got enough to worry about than to start directin' an NYPD murder investigation.'

Callum said, 'You know who the shooter is?'

'Take your pick: Irish, Chinese, even Russian. The Ivans out in Brighton done business with the Columbians before, could be they supplied the coke killed Grundy's brother. Old Sol tried to mobilize the community out there around Little Odessa. Stirred up a little shit in south Brooklyn.'

'And?'

'Fear and intimidation are a universal concept, Burke.'

Callum traced a circle on the tabletop. He steepled his fingers and looked into O'Connell's eyes.

'You don't want Homicide to solve Sol Grundy's murder because it endangers the RICO case. Maybe your career prospects.'

O'Connell uncrossed his arms and sat forward. Callum saw a slight flush under the cop's eyes like he was drunk. A bad drunk.

O'Connell said, 'When any New York City Police Department investigation, beyond what we are doin' here with Walsh and the Tongs, becomes any of your self-righteous fucking business I'll be sure to let your mongrel English-Irish ass know, fuckhead.'

The flush spread across O'Connell's face.

'You know what? Fuck you, you sanctimonious Hong Kong asshole. I reached out to Borough Command and yeah, sure, I put our needs first. The only way I see the NYPD catchin' the shooter is to bust Walsh and the Tongs. The only way that happens is through us. On a long shot the Russians did it, the hitter is probably out of the country by now. See, I don't think about my career, you Royal-colony-monkey-ass prick, or I wouldn't be scramblin' for overtime on a sergeant's pay. I think about shuttin' down the bad guys and puttin' motherfuckers like Walsh in jail.'

O'Connell stared at Callum for a beat, open-mouthed like he forgot what he was going to say next. Then his shoulders relaxed, the flush faded and he sat back again.

'Let me ask you something,' he said, 'you like being a cop?'

Callum said, 'Am I a cop? I mean, right now?'

'I read your file. I spoke to your boss. Milburn thinks you're a good officer with terrible judgment. He said you can't control your impulses. He worries that you might not be able to handle this. Should I worry? Or Mattila?'

Callum sat back like he was putting himself out reach of O'Connell's appraisal. 'I made a mistake in the past. I'm here now to do a job. Don't question my commitment and competence again.'

'Pretty big mistake. You broke the jaw of a Dragon Head's nephew with a set of brass knuckles, what I heard. Dragon Head Stanley Bamboo Zhao's nephew, to be exact. Then the old man, Zhao dies in a cheap whorehouse before he can save face for you punching the nephew by fucking you up. The nephew starts using and goes the same way as his uncle, dead from H. Bamboo Zhao's Deputy, Tony Lau, becomes the new Dragon Head and takes the whole thing very personally. So now you got old man Zhao keeping company with his ancestors and Tony Lau out for

70

blood. Big enough shit-storm for the HK police to fake a dishon-orable discharge and send you out of harm's way to New York. If that isn't a contradiction in terms.'

Callum leaned toward O'Connell, driving the cop's suspicions back at him.

'Stanley Bamboo Zhao died of an overdose of his own heroin,' he said. 'I was a good cop and made life difficult for Tony Lau in the past in Wan Chai: the man didn't need an excuse to try and get rid of me. You needed an Irishman to have a crack at infil-trating Fintan Walsh's outfit. Sometimes the stars align. So long as word doesn't get back to the Hong Kong triads that I'm here.'

O'Connell said, 'Well, while the Irish and Chinese might be doing business they're like oil and water. Intel has yet to catch a pasty face near a Chinatown Tong. The American side of Chinese organized crime is pretty autonomous anyway. Your man Lau is too busy in Burma and Thailand, or running his empire in Hong Kong, to make a New York visit.' He studied a fingernail. 'You're pretty insulated right now. And you got your boy Ho looking out for you down on Pell Street. One breath of Lau coming here and we'll reassess.'

Then there's Gabriel Muñoz, thought Callum. He gripped the rim of the table and felt his fingers go numb. He told O'Connell about the bodega, Muñoz's cousin, the possible drug connection. O'Connell listened, impassive, then told him he'd run it past Mattila.

'Asshole probably isn't pushing,' he said, 'just watching his 'cus makin' money from the sidelines. And if he is involved, he'll go down. Either way, we'll keep him clear of you.'

They finished their coffees and O'Connell ordered another. Callum was wired enough already. O'Connell went for a piss while they waited for his order and Callum checked the old guy, now asleep with his hands still in his pants.

Stanley Bamboo Zhao had been in a similar pose as Callum

had watched him die in a shabby block used by whores in Wan Chai, a sixteen-year-old girl crying nearby. He saw his shadow-self pull the sheets from the bed to wrap around the girl and usher her out of the door. Saw himself stand with his back to the door waiting. Waiting. He could smell the vomit and urine. Had Zhao been aware he was there? Had the Dragon Head been waiting, too: for him to act, to call for help, radio an ambulance. He thought of the narrow stairs down to the street, the stink of disinfectant. Then the clamor of Wan Chai, the uniformed men loading girls into the wagons, the snapping orders in Cantonese and bored looks of the pimps and muscle. All but Tony Lau, who had seen the body carried out of the brothel and looked at Callum with eyes like black razor slashes. Lau had raised his arm and arranged his fingers in a Triad hand sign. "Revenge".

It was part of why Callum had wanted his family out of Hong Kong. Part of why his wife and daughter had left the colony for The US. Another reason Callum had taken the offer of this job. Now Irene and Tara lived in Ohio. Cleveland might be five hundred miles away from New York but at least it was the same continent.

O'Connell came back and sat opposite with his coffee and crossed his arms.

He said, 'So why was Sol Grundy visiting the same dominatrix Paddy Doolan uses? And where was Paddy Doolan when Grundy was shot?'

'I don't know. I'm still establishing a relationship.'

'Well, you let me know when you're best buddies and make it soon.'

O'Connell sipped his coffee with raised eyebrows.

'The dominatrix,' said Callum. 'Could she be connected to the murder?'

'She was at a club when it went down, dancing with some girl-friends. Her friends back it up but if she's connected with Doolan, who knows?'

He scratched at his chin.

'We put a couple of devices in Doolan's apartment. Nothing intrusive. In a ventilation grate in his bedroom and behind the fan in the kitchen. Fitted them when he was out at New World. We'll listen in when you're there so try and get him talking shop when you're at Bleecker, okay?'

'He likes me. That doesn't mean we're best buddies and he'll share to that extent.'

'Thought you guys said mates; not buddies.'

'You guys?' said Callum.

'Brits. Irish Brits. Whatever.'

'You read my file. Didn't it mention my father? I'm part American.'

O'Connell drained his cup.

'Yeah, Protestant English mother, Catholic Irish-American father, born in Belfast. I might be from Jersey,' he said smacking his lips, 'but it's a damn good thing Paddy Doolan doesn't know you're less fucking Irish than me.'

Chapter Seven

The uniforms on the platform milled around the sheet next to the northbound track. West 4th Subway Station was oven-warm despite the cool, damp May night up at street level. The doors of the car wheezed shut at Callum's back and the A train re-started its clattering journey south.

He glimpsed a red beret, stained a deep brown, lying within the human cordon. A Guardian Angel slayed by a demon still roaming the city somewhere above. A man in black combat pants tucked in boots wearing a red bomber jacket and identical beret stood to the side talking with a cop.

Callum climbed the steps to the mezzanine. The cracked tiles by the exit to 6th Avenue, the painted iron rims on the buckled steps rubbed smooth and bare by thousands of New Yorkers ascending to the city above, made it look like the aftermath of some natural disaster. At least the station didn't smell of piss like so many others. A man slept on the street at the top of the steps. Other men in suits clutching umbrellas, women in party dresses, people in bar gear stepped around the body like the cops down in the station with the corpse. Callum soaked in the wet night, washing away thoughts of O'Connell across the Hudson in Hoboken.

He turned at the scratch and scuffle of something searching through some trash and saw a rat bolt for the chain link around the empty basketball court by the subway entrance. The streets were busy at nine p.m. The Brownstone strip of Bleecker Street was just off 6th Avenue. Callum turned off 6th at the green wedge of Minetta Triangle, a slice of benches and trees, onto Bleecker Street and its cafés, bars, clubs, pizza joints, comic book and CD stores, Korean groceries and tourist traps. Paddy Doolan's apartment building was a five-story townhouse, fire escapes zigzagging down its façade, peppered by window AC units. It sat across from a pretty brick building with a sign reading The Little Red Schoolhouse. Doolan's new place was on the second floor. Callum punched the buzzer by the building door as two men in evening gowns hurried by singing scales. The door buzzed and he pushed it open.

Tiled floor, bare walls with two wooden shower stalls to the left on the ground floor corridor. A TV mumbled somewhere in the far shadows. Callum climbed the stairs, hauling himself up with the wrought iron bannister until he reached the second floor. Doolan's door was to the right, the street-facing apartment on the floor. His knock was answered with a call to enter.

The door opened into a cramped kitchen. He saw wooden strips of wainscoting around the walls, chipped and stained. A window opposite looked onto the next building's wall a couple of feet away. Above the paneling, dirty cream painted walls. A small, flimsy-looking folding table sat in the center of the room and a small TV balanced on a radiator next to an open doorway on the left. The sink was next to the door of the apartment. A refrigerator stood next to another door standing open on the right of the kitchen. He stepped into the kitchen and leaned forward to look through the doorway on the left. A short corridor led to an open door and a toilet at the end. Boxes lined the left wall of the corridor with a single mattress laid across some crates stacked knee-high close to the kitchen. The floor was dirty linoleum.

'How you doin'?'

Callum turned at the voice and walked through the kitchen and into a bedroom with an empty fireplace with a phone on top and a mirror hanging above. A metal-frame bed was against the wall on the right. A dresser sat on the left of the door and an open window at the end of the bed looked over Bleecker, the fire escape out front framing part of the view. A man sat on a chair in the center of the bedroom, right ankle resting on left knee. His hair had a side parting through which Moses could have led the Israelites to safety. His face was soft like half-baked dough, the skin dimpled from too much razor burn. He wore a jacket over a checked shirt and black jeans with green Adidas sneakers. He looked at Callum with narrow eyes, eyebrows thin like he plucked them each morning.

Callum felt something cold tumble down his insides.

The face in the mugshot had been younger and thinner; the man in the surveillance photographs blurred, walking between parked cars. But it was him. Callum had seen Fintan Walsh in those images and more as he sat in briefings with O'Connell and Mattila. He knew of what the leader of the Irish Mob outfit was capable.

Walsh said, 'You got change for a fifty?'

Callum said, 'Who the fuck are you?'

Walsh leaned back in the chair and sniffed the air like he could smell roast dinner.

'Ah,' he said, 'music to my ears. Can I ask you a question?'

Glass smashed in the street outside and someone yelled.

'Don't you get so much fucking pussy with that accent?'

Callum took two steps to the bed and sat down. He said, 'What's with the fifty?'

Fintan Walsh gave an exaggerated quizzical stare.

'The fifty,' said Callum. 'You asked if I had change for a fifty.'

'Oh yeah.' Walsh began searching in his coat. 'Aren't you the Chinese guy?'

The coldness in Callum's insides dropped a couple of degrees.

Walsh said, 'You know? Chinese food. Delivery guy. Change for a fifty. Forget it, bad joke.'

A woman screamed in the street then laughed.

'Don't you wanna' know who I am?'

Callum said, 'I asked you that already.'

'Ask again. Nicely.'

'Who are you? Please?'

'Fintan Walsh. And you must be Christy Burns, Paddy Doolan's new buddy. Pleased to make your acquaintance.' He offered a hand.

Callum stayed put on the bed. He wanted this slow and steady. Not overconfident like he was holding some kind of hand, not too scared like he was folding from the start.

He said, 'Where's Paddy?'

'Mr. Doolan is uptown. Depending on the next five minutes or so you'll meet him or get the fuck out of New York, one way or the other. Now, take your clothes off.'

Callum sat forward on the bed with a creak. He made to speak.

'I ain't got time,' said Walsh, 'just strip.'

'Sorry but – '

'Strip.' The voice was weary but the hand that produced the S&W .38 snub nosed revolver from a pocket moved plenty quick. The gun rested on Walsh's knee.

'I'm the kinda' man carries one of these in a no-carry city and pulls it on a stranger, you better believe I'm the kinda' man that'll use it. Now take your clothes off so I can see your fucking cock.'

When he was naked Callum stood before Walsh, the lights of Bleecker painting his body scarlet and gold. He put his hands behind his head like he was under arrest and turned at the beckoning of Walsh rolling the revolver in a clockwise direction. The street went quiet for a moment and the silence in the room seemed to press in on his body before the sounds of people and a car horn blaring amplified his nakedness.

'You're in pretty good shape,' said Walsh. 'Put your clothes back on.'

Callum dressed.

'You scared?'

'Of course I'm scared,' said Callum. 'I've never had a gun pointed at me before.'

It was true. He had seen firearms in Hong Kong, discovered them in caches. The same in a brief, earlier stint in the RUC in Belfast. He'd seen the damage guns could wreak. A corpse washed up among the junks in Aberdeen in the Territories; his mate Jimmy, killed by a sniper's bullet in north Belfast. A Triad riddled with bullets in a car in Kowloon. But he'd never stood naked, facing a barrel, with searing pain, blood, shock and death just an ounce of pressure away.

'Alright,' said Walsh, 'as you may have guessed, your new friend Paddy Doolan got some dangerous acquaintances. Paddy is in a basement on the Upper West Side right now. He said you were alright. He thinks you could do some work for me so we're gonna' ride uptown and join Paddy and you're gonna' prove just how useful you might be. If you refuse, I'll pick up the phone and order my men to kill Paddy Doolan, chop him in pieces and throw him in the East River.'

Callum dressed and felt adrenaline course through his arms. He knew Walsh had to be bluffing – that the Irish mobster and Paddy Doolan were pretty tight – but he had to make a conscious effort not to rip the door off its hinges he was so wired. He rode the rush like he was surfing a breaker as he walked downstairs and onto Bleecker.

They were joined on the street by two men sitting on a bench nearby, one in a leather jacket, the other army surplus, both shopping from the extra-large rack. The men stood and flanked Callum. They walked and got in a car a block away.

*

Bobby Ho finished the steak with an appreciative nod. It was important that Inspector Milburn know he was grateful for his superior's generosity. He and Milburn were in a quiet restaurant near Wall Street with Agent Niku Mattila. Ho understood it was an indication of his importance to the operation – Milburn would never treat him to such a meal in Hong Kong – and, while the American food was larger in portion and heavier than he'd like, he recognized its significance.

Ho respected his superior officer. Milburn was fair, cold to British and Chinese alike, and dedicated to the force. He did not drink to excess in the ex-pat haunts, had never taken a bar-girl as a mistress and rarely lost his temper. The night he railed at Callum Burke in the hotel room a few weeks ago had been the first time Ho had seen the Inspector raise his voice in years.

There were those in the Hong Kong Police who resented the British officers, their lack of empathy for the Chinese PCs, their lack of effort in learning Cantonese. Some did speak the language, were fair to the Chinese staff and drove the localization policy forward with a nervous eye on 1997 and the handover. Some were getting out, some staying.

And there were Chinese Black Tab Constables in his station who disliked their fellow Red Tab colleagues because of their advanced grasp of English. He had caught looks on the job from several. It was immaterial to Ho. The job was the job and he would do it to the best of his ability, no matter who his commanding officer might be.

'Tell us about Phoenix Investments,' said Milburn.

'The Tong deposit almost every day in United Oriental Bank and branches of Maritime Midland around Chinatown. A company, Phoenix Investments, has also begun to make regular deposits. Previously, The DEA thought Phoenix was a Tong company but I believe it is a Triad operation. The money is being laundered through offshore accounts and deposited in New York. Standard Triad practice.'

Mattila said, 'This is with the full agreement of the Tong?'

'No, Sir.'

Ho enjoyed Mattila's presence as a child might enjoy the visit of an exotic uncle from a faraway land. The DEA Agent was open, gregarious, generous with his time and attention, and driven to the point of aggression. A typical American, thought Ho, and a breath of fresh air from Milburn's British reserve.

Mattila said, 'They aren't happy? How about Uncle Sammy?'

'Sammy Ong never discusses anything but family and domestic issues on his phone.'

Sammy Ong, venerable leader of the Hip Sing Tong. Advanced in years, slow and steady was Ong's way and it had served him well. Caution and acuity for protecting the Tong's secrets had seen him reign for over thirty years. His natural caution meant he refused to discuss Tong business on the phone, so Ho couldn't listen in on the Title III wiretap, live or recorded, by law. Only conversations pertinent to the investigation could be monitored. Ho could check occasionally to see if the conversation had changed to more relevant topics. It never did.

'However,' said Ho, 'Ong's right-hand-man, Papa Ng, has been drawn into discussing the deposits when talking to Charlie Lin or Mickey Chiu on their cell phones. And several other prominent businessmen in the Tong have discussed the deposits. They are concerned at the amount trickling in. Small enough not to trigger any financial investigations, regular enough to amass a large amount of capital.'

'Interesting,' said Mattila, 'this coming along when they are aligned with the Walsh crew. And if Papa isn't happy you can bet your ass Uncle Sammy isn't, either. Let's see where this goes with Phoenix Investments.'

Bobby Ho nodded. He had spent the last few weeks listening to hours of recorded conversations between various members of the Hip Sing Tong and sitting in a small room above a dumpling house on Pell Street watching the Tong offices, noting people he recognized from DEA photographs coming and going, and taking zoom shots.

'And the Flying Dragons?'

'I haven't seen any of the street gang at the Hip Sing offices.'

'Figures.'

Milburn said, 'Presumably, the Hip Sing prefer to keep their enforcers at arm's length. It would make political sense and maintain the veneer of respectability within Chinatown and beyond.'

Mattila nodded. 'When you contribute to the mayor's election campaign, you can't be seen to associate with street thieves and killers.'

'There are honest people in the Tong, Agent Mattila,' said Ho.

'How honest can you be when you play house with racketeers and drug peddlers?'

'I'd imagine,' said Milburn, 'it's much like your government or ours. Within the American Chinese Associations you get the crusaders, the honest people and the gangsters. But in politics – as in the case of the Tong – the dregs, rather than the cream, often rise to the top.'

Milburn rolled the stem of his wine glass between long fingers. Bobby Ho had often thought those fingers resembled the talon-like fingernails of some men in China, grown as an indicator of wealth and success.

The Englishman said, 'You know the history of the Tongs in America, Mattila. The translation of the word is *Town Hall*, after all.'

All three of them did. The Tong associations were established to protect the Chinese from American discrimination, intimidation, exploitation. But criminality flourished among the benevolent associations. Some within the very organizations established as guardians of the Chinese populace began to prey on their members and subjects.

Mattila smiled and took a gulp of his wine.

'Bobby, I meant no disrespect about the Tongs.'

'Please,' said Ho, embarrassed that he had been singled out for an apology before his superior officer at the table. 'No need.'

'So,' said Mattila, 'no mention of the Irish? Walsh or Doolan?'

Ho said, 'I'm not sure. They haven't mentioned any names and the only non-Chinese related group they discussed was the mayor's office regarding some kind of funding, and an Italian-American business group.'

'North of Canal Street I guess.'

'Yes, Agent Mattila,' said Ho – he couldn't bring himself to use Mattila's first name. 'However, I have heard mention of the Emerald Rat. They talk as though it's a restaurant but no such business exists in New York or Hong Kong. There has been a lot of talk of supplies. Food, spice, liquor.'

'Emerald could refer to Ireland,' said Milburn.

'Possibly.'

'And rat is a snitch or spy? Jesus,' said Mattila, 'you think they made Burke already? If so we got to get him out of there.'

Milburn said, 'I doubt Callum Burke is the reference.' He kept his eyes on his wine glass. 'I don't see how the Tong could be aware of his presence if he hasn't been given any insight into Walsh's criminal enterprises yet.'

'I have a theory,' said Ho. 'I read the file but can't remember: what is the date of Fintan Walsh's birthday?'

Mattila said, 'January 5th 1961.'

'It fits,' said Ho. He looked from a nodding Milburn to Niku Mattila, the DEA agent's brows knit in query. 'Fintan Walsh shares the same Chinese birth year as the Triad leader, Tony

Lau. They were both born between February 1960 and February 1961.'

'I don't follow' said Mattila, looking to Milburn for clarification.

'The Chinese Zodiac,' said Ho, emboldened. 'Lau and Walsh share the Rat as their zodiac. Walsh is Irish-American – Emerald. He was born in the Year of the Rat. Hence, the Emerald Rat.'

He looked at Milburn. The Englishman gave a small nod.

'Special Agent,' said Ho, 'I would like your permission to do something. I have been monitoring the Tong communications and am interested in workable connections. Would it be possible for Inspector Milburn and I to look at the phone records of the conversations I monitor? Perhaps there might be patterns that could help make sense of some of the communication.'

'LUDS and tolls,' said Mattila. He smiled. 'Yeah, I can set you up.'

LUDS and tolls, trolling through records to see if certain numbers come up with any frequency. List the numbers, throw them into databases like those of the DEA or FBI. Establish if any other law enforcement agencies are 'touching' the numbers.

'I'll need a court order, but the fact we got international calls back and forth from Hong Kong will help swing it.'

Bobby Ho said, 'Thank you.'

He was grateful to Mattila. And Milburn. His superior officer had deferred to him in making the request and given him the last word in thanking the DEA agent. Ho supposed it was the future for the Hong Kong Police after the handover in '97 but here and now, in New York, he saw the change in dynamic in his relationship with James Milburn. A softening of hierarchy, a recognition of his importance to the ongoing investigation.

He let the waiter clear his empty plate and took a long drink of his iced tea.

Chapter Eight

They drove around Columbus Circle. The car slowed to a crawl at a build-up of traffic where the avenue curved. A crowd of people stood in front of The Dublin House Bar on 79th, a man doubled over by the wall as he vomited. A couple of Hispanic women walked by and Walsh whistled through his teeth.

'Will you look at that Latin tail? Jesus, the sins I could commit but I wouldn't want to give Father McCusker a coronary in confession.'

They turned off Broadway at 96th Street and parked up a block away. Walsh walked out front, a man next to Callum and another at his rear. When they walked onto Broadway he saw the McDonald's opposite where he'd sat in the truck with Doolan. He looked up at the façade of the brownstone, the same building Paddy had stared at when Callum raised the topic of Sol Grundy as they ate breakfast in the truck. The brownstone seemed a darker shade of chocolate at night, the glass and steel building next door glinting in the city lights.

They walked down a narrow alley between the buildings to a service entrance. Walsh knocked and after a few seconds an older man, emaciated and gray like he hadn't been out of the basement in a decade, opened a metal door into the brownstone. They entered a cinder block corridor and followed the old man to a set of stairs down to a large laundry room.

Paddy Doolan sat in a corner in a metal chair with two men smoking by his side. They were laughing, passing around a forty-ounce bottle of Country Club.

Paddy said, 'Christy, you okay?'

'I don't know,' said Callum.

The air was thick and hot in the laundry room, and heavy with the scent of detergent.

Fintan Walsh snapped his fingers and one of his men, a thick-necked bullmastiff sweating in a leather jacket walked to a corner and brought another chair over for his boss to sit by a wall. Walsh pulled off his coat and adjusted his checked shirt before sitting.

'Alright,' he said. 'Alright.'

The old man hobbled out of sight back up the stairs while Walsh waved and another goon brought him the bottle of malt liquor.

'I thought only niggers and spics drank this shit now,' he said and took a swig. He raised his eyebrows. 'I tasted worse. Better than a hooker's piss, huh Paddy?'

Doolan smiled. He looked weary.

'Paddy and I grew up on this,' said Walsh, 'back in the old neighborhood. Hell's Kitchen. Then, the Kitchen was still Irish. Noonan and Featherstone were around, or their lackeys were. The rackets were Irish, the Longshoreman's was Irish, business was Irish. Now we got World-Fucking-Plaza on one side and empty tenements and bag ladies on the other. The old families are being pushed out block by block to clean the place up for the developers. You think the Mayor gives a shit? Giuliani's too busy having Bratton bust old men for pissing on the street corner to care about our people.'

Walsh took another slug of liquor.

'Look at the dagoes downtown. They're gonna' be lucky if they can hold onto three or four blocks once the chinks are finished. Chinatown been eating into Little Italy for years.' He pointed a thick finger at Callum. 'Those chinks, though. They're fucking smart.'

He put the bottle on the floor by his chair.

Callum said, 'Do you still live in Hell's Kitchen?'

'Christ no. There ain't nothing left for me there. We got some streets in the neighborhood, although the spics and city planners are moving in. But I live in Woodside now. Paddy here held on for as long as he could but the City sold his building, had him in that fleabag hotel you been cleaning as accommodation. Now he's living with the fags in the Village.'

Paddy looked to the stairs. Callum concentrated on keeping his Turkish coffee down. He could feel his t-shirt sucking at his back, the sweat turning his armpits slick. His legs felt hollow. Yet something inside made him watch Walsh, Doolan, the others with a cold indifference.

It was all off-kilter: he was afraid but not of these men.

He realized as the footsteps came to him from the stairs. It was the same fear as the walk to the ring, bending and stepping through the ropes, listening to the bay and snarl of the crowd before a fight. He was scared of his own weakness.

The old man hobbled forward with one of Walsh's muscle and a young man, maybe five years Callum's junior, in a pair of sweatpants and a 76ers basketball vest.

Walsh said, 'You still box a little, right?'

Callum said, 'It's been a while.'

'Well get your ass ready 'cause you're going ten rounds here and now with this firecracker.'

Callum took in the young man's arms, corded like rope. A thin mustache above generous lips, parted in fear and confusion. The vest hung loose on a tall, wiry frame. Hair slicked back from a low forehead and eyebrows marked by the slim white worm of a scar on the left.

Walsh said, 'Dylan here been doing some business on one of the streets we still run in The Kitchen.' He gestured to the man. 'What the fuck you wearing a Philadelphia basketball vest for in New York? You're fucking Puerto Rican anyway.'

The man looked down, dumb, at his 76ers vest.

'Saw a couple of your little chicas on the way up here,' said Walsh. 'Your women really got those natural curves, huh? Don't spend a lifetime eating fucking potatoes like Irish women. Tell you what, you beat my boy here? You and me gonna' go and bang a couple of them little Dominican chicks up in east Harlem, alright? You lose? They'll love you anyway. You're gonna' be a specialist at eatin' pussy without no fucking teeth.'

Dylan answered with a wild-eyed stare.

Callum felt a hunger in his gut. The man was scared. Scared like him. Like any boxer before a fight. Use it, he thought, focus. None of the pre-fight showboating. No crowd to influence judges. Just Fintan Walsh but what was the endgame? A job? Survival?

He heard Walsh laugh. He'd opened a book on the fight with the guys in the room, Doolan had put fifty bucks on 'the Irishman'.

Callum studied Dylan. The man looked around one-twenty pounds of muscle and bone. Lighter than Callum but probably faster with a longer reach. Fuck it. Let the other guy worry about him. He shrugged off his coat and loosened up, bounced on the balls of his feet. He'd never boxed bare-knuckle. The principal had to be the same, right? The low buzz of dread vibrating through your body like a bug trapped inside until you take the first hit. Then it's just like sparring. Defense. Punch. Move.

He was glad of his sneakers. Boots would have weighed him down. He jabbed the air but he was slow. He hadn't fought in months, hadn't sweated out a weight, hadn't trained for this. He was out of shape.

The men were laughing as the old man gestured for Callum and Dylan to face off in the center of the laundry room. A bearded goon was putting thirty on the Puerto Rican.

Callum said, 'Give me forty on this bum going down in the third.'

It was a stupid move, a brag to impress Walsh, and he staggered with the sharp jab. His cheek tingled and he lost his bearings for a second, enough for the Puerto Rican to follow up and hit him with a combination of body shots. He gasped for breath. His sides spasmed and he went small, pulling his arms in as the Puerto Ricans' punches jarred on his elbows.

Fuck him, let his knuckles smart.

Yeah, while I piss blood tonight.

His head filled with a low drone. He shoved the younger man, glimpsed him stumble as Callum bent double, cradled his right side. The man stayed upright and advanced while Callum was planting his feet. He knew he had to jab – the jab was the rangefinder. As he shot out a left the Puerto Rican hit him with another combination, three punches battering his shoulder, his forearm, his collarbone. The fourth cracked his right temple and the drone ratcheted up a notch. The Puerto Rican was fast. Comfortable with the violence.

Callum ducked, moved right under a shot, felt an arm slide over his t-shirt and bunch the material. He threw a combination at the younger man's stomach, hit his hip with the first shot but landed two on his left kidney and stepped back.

The Puerto Rican withdrew, his body cinched tight, a flicker in his eyes. Callum raised a hand and pulled his t-shirt over his head. The thick heat in the basement rushed in to smother his skin but he felt a freedom and watched the other fighter haul the 76ers vest over his head. The face of Christ gazed out from a sculpted chest, black on skin the color of toasted bread.

The man was lean as a greyhound, faster with combinations, easier in his movement. Callum needed to find a big shot. Feint, he thought. You look for that big shot early on, he'll know. Punch on the defensive, take some hits. The Puerto Rican's reach is longer. Get inside and nail the bastard.

Callum went at the man in a semi-crouch and walked straight

into a hard right. His head snapped back and he felt a rawness in his cheek. His eyes were clear, the nose untouched but his hands went to his face on reflex and his body took another combination, his guts churning, sides throbbing with waves of pain. That hard, pulsing ache that builds and saps at you and pulls you down.

Shit, he thought, the man was open on the right and I sleep-walked into it. Fucking kidneys are stinging. Lungs burning up with the bodyshots and this fucking heat.

But the fucker is relaxing his stance. Sees I'm hurt. Ready to come at me hard.

Callum saw Christ stare, baleful, from the man's chest, saw another tattoo on the left bicep, some kind of gang lettering. This fucker is fighting every day, he thought, fighting other hoods, assholes like Walsh. Cops.

He rolled his shoulders, felt his sides scream as he hunched.

Get out of the ring and on the street, he thought. Fight him dirty.

The man came on, ready to hit and move, to gnaw at him until his strength was gone. As he closed in Callum made a grab, almost lost him but dug in with what fingernails he had. He threw his head into the pinched face and felt something yield under his thick Irish skull. The man called out, the first word from either fighter, and thrashed in the clinch. Callum took an upright stance, a stance he'd seen a Russian sailor fight with back in Hong Kong, and drove two hard jabs into the Puerto Rican's nose. The eyes, already tearing, closed and he threw his shoulder behind the big right. His knuckles drove into the man's head above his right ear. He felt the stubbled hair scrape his fist, smelled the sour spice of sweat, the shock of the punch in his own wrist. The head snapped hard to the right and the man stumbled.

Callum stood over the man and went to work on the back of

the head, driving his fist down. He punched for the concrete floor, pummeling the Puerto Rican's head. He knew the man was taking it, that Callum couldn't do so much damage hammering at his skull. The Puerto Rican was a better boxer. Once he was ready, the man would throw another combination at Callum's body, cripple him and go to work.

But while the fighter's head was low, his eyes toward the floor, Callum moved to the side and drove his knee hard into the Puerto Rican's face. His jeans came away wet and the man dropped.

The Puerto Rican's hands came up in defense too late. Callum went slugger, pounding shots into the side of his head. The punches drove the man's hands aside and Callum's knuckles cracked off an eyebrow, the bone below the eye, the side of the busted nose. His fist was slick with blood, his own or the man's he didn't know. The Puerto Rican called out in Spanish and Callum drove his knee into the man's head again.

It was Paddy Doolan who grabbed him, his arms like a lover's embrace as he pulled him to his chest. Doolan's hand found the back of Callum's head and held him close.

'You did good,' said Paddy, 'You did good, Christy.'

Callum went limp. He let the buzzing in his ears fade and heard the men in the hot laundry room babble. When he turned, someone had lifted the Puerto Rican and was leading him to a metal chair, same type as Fintan Walsh's, in the far corner. There was blood on the floor. The old man was back and stood tutting.

'Yeah!' said Walsh. 'The fightin' Irish.'

He gestured for Callum to come stand in front of him. Doolan led him over and stood by his side.

'Paddy told me you fucked up a cop back in Belfast, that right?'

One of the men came over and handed a bottle of water and

his crumpled t-shirt to Callum. He took a long drink and wiped the t-shirt across his face. It came away red.

'Yeah. There was a riot,' he said. His words came in sharp gasps. 'I threw a couple of bottles, then got up close and landed a few punches and kicks on a riot shield. They tried to snatch me but my mates pulled me out. The riot was next to a factory. I got up on the roof and dropped a breeze block on top of one of the bastards. He dropped like a doll. Probably cracked his skull through the helmet.'

'Breeze block?' said Walsh. 'You wanna' say that again in English?'

'A concrete block. Anybody got a cigarette?'

Walsh offered a Marlboro and tossed him a lighter. He said, 'How you feel about that? You ever regret fucking the cop up?'

'Fuck him. They're all bastards. One less in the world is no tragedy.'

'And Dylan over there. You okay with handing him a beating?'

'I don't know him from Adam. Maybe he's an asshole, maybe he's a choirboy, it means nothing to me. Did I make money off my forty?' Callum lit his smoke and took a long drag.

Walsh and Doolan exchanged a look before Walsh sat back a little in the metal chair.

'Yeah, you made some money tonight,' he said, 'and I think you got a lot more coming. Go let Paddy buy you a couple of drinks. I'll see you again soon, Christy.'

Callum took another drag of his smoke and studied the glowing tip.

'One day on a moving job, Paddy pulled me out of beating an asshole client,' he said. 'Paddy was worried the guy would call the cops and I'd be deported back home. Now you have me fighting people and promising work I'm guessing doesn't need a social security number. What gives?'

Walsh smiled.

'Working with me ain't like kicking some random dickhead's ass. You got my whole outfit between you and the cops, and you'll make a lot more than fifty and tips. Now go let Paddy get you drunk, Christy Burns. I'll be in touch.'

Paddy Doolan took hold of Callum's elbow and led him to the stairs. As he put his foot on the first step, Callum stopped.

'Who's the guy? The Puerto Rican?' he said.

'Kid's a dealer,' said Doolan. 'Been working the wrong corners in Hell's Kitchen. The beating you just gave him's a lesson from our crew.'

'What's his full name? Dylan what?'

'I dunno' ... Acosta? Maybe? C'mon, let's get that drink.'

Behind them Fintan Walsh said, 'Looks like I'll be fuckin' those Latinas all on my own, Dylan.'

Chapter Nine

Number seven kept her eyes on the dancefloor. Unlike the others, she didn't seem glazed and indifferent with drugs and booze. Rather, she had the look of a penitent, stripped of her clothes, her sins displayed for all to see. Tony Lau took a sip of cheap vodka to dampen the warmth in his belly.

Nana Plaza in Bangkok was all he hated about Thailand. A courtyard bordered by strip clubs, bars and hotels renting rooms by the hour. Pineapple Wong, the Triad fixer, caught his Leader's look of disgust. He leaned close to be heard over the thunderous dance music, his breath hot in Tony Lau's ear.

'I understand your disgust, Leader. But this is the cost of doing business with the Thais. We endure their hospitality.'

Lau decided not to comment on the fact that Wong himself was a Thai. Nevertheless, the fixer was right. And the Thais had been good value. The Society had made hundreds of millions of dollars thanks to them transporting General Khun Sa's crop from the border to Bangkok for transportation to Hong Kong.

Pink and purple lights swirled around the Thai Tease Go-Go Club, girls in t-shirts, lingerie and high heels circulating among three tiers of booths facing the stage. Men leered and called and drank to summon the courage for a session with one of the bar-girls dancing on the stage in a hotel across the courtyard. Lau looked at the line of topless girls gyrating to the relentless throb of the music, numbers attached to bikini bottoms and panties.

He turned away and thought of the long line of indigenous tribal people, horses and donkeys, guarded by Khun Sa's militia, snaking through the Shan States toward the Thai border in the days after his meeting with the old warlord. Then *Teo Chiu*

Triads and local muscle would have smuggled the cargo across the border and south to Bangkok over a period of weeks. Truckloads mixed with a load of rice. Cargo hidden in tire rims or the transmission of trucks trundling along Route 1. He had spoken to a man who had driven with the morphine in airtight bags floating in the gas tank.

Lau's host, Spike Head Chan, sidled up and sat next to him on the u-shaped sofa in the booth facing the stage.

Lau had no desire for a girl tonight but no wish to cause Chan, his host, to lose face by refusing. Chan was in an ebullient mood. The Thai side of the operation had reaped a handsome reward for executing their mission in the chain that would take the narcotic to Hong Kong. The Thais would dine well for years to come. The 14K and US Tong accountants estimated they could charge at least $700 per gram in the major US markets such as Washington, Atlanta, Chicago. New York.

A girl in a Thai Tease Go-Go Club t-shirt approached. She looked older, perhaps in her mid-twenties. Some form of floor manager, thought Lau.

'You like anyone?' she said. She was more attractive than the others, thought Lau. There was an intelligence in her eyes, calculating how to appease his appetites and make some money. She might make a good Triad.

'You want drink?'

'Yes, okay, I want drink.'

'I like cocktail, okay?'

'Yes, okay.' He raised his arm to attract a waitress but the t-shirted girl put two manicured fingers on his wrist.

'You relax,' she said. 'I order.'

He watched her walk to the bar as though she were working a catwalk. Another girl passed their booth. Lau caught a glimpse of black eyes painted pink by the lights. The eyes turned their attention to the floor as the girl made her way back to the stage.

Number seven. The penitent. Lau stood and eased out of the booth. He caught the girl as she had her left stiletto heel on the first step to the stage.

'Please,' he said, 'may I buy you a drink?'

The girl stared for a moment and he realized he had broken club etiquette. The t-shirted girl appeared on his left.

'What you doing, sir? I thought you buy drink for me.'

'I do,' said Lau. 'Please, keep your cocktail. But I would like to buy this girl a drink, too.'

'She very new. Not experienced. She always dreaming, head in clouds. Talk about living in another country, living away from Thailand. She no happy here, think she too good for other Thais. I am better. We are good match, sir.'

'You are very pretty,' said Lau. 'Beautiful. But I like this girl very much.'

He gestured to the dancing girl who stood with one leg crossed over the other, eyes downcast again.

'Please, I will buy her many drinks. Okay?'

The t-shirted girl's voice was harder.

'She no drink. She dance. You want her time, you take her to hotel across Nana Plaza. She know the room and you pay for your time there. Okay, sir?'

He searched among the tiered booths. He found Wong as a purple strobe lit his shock of pineapple hair. Lau leaned across a scrawny girl cooing in the fixer's ear and told him he'd be taking some time with one of the dancing girls.

'Ah,' bellowed Wong, the alcohol storming his bloodstream now, 'we'll join you.'

Lau made to protest but caught himself. He had to maintain a sense of camaraderie with his subordinates, and the spirit of bawdy celebration that the *Teo Chiu* men would expect at the conclusion of major business. He fashioned a smile and they left the club together, Wong's companion sagging under his drunken weight as he staggered with an arm slung over her bony shoulders.

The hotel smelt of disinfectant and the faint scent of something burning. A couple of rangy Thais in jeans and soccer shirts nodded in the lobby. They climbed a staircase to the landing, the low pulse of dance music hammering at the walls from outside.

Wong lurched two doors down the bare corridor with his cackling girl in tow. Lau stood aside as girl-seven opened the door with the key provided by her t-shirted superior. The carpeted room was functional. A large bed, chest of drawers, bedside tables with lamps and a small cubicle to the left of the door with a toilet and shower. A window with venetian blinds leaked a luminous rainbow of neon from the street outside. The muted sounds of burping tuk-tuks and a piercing siren reminded them they were next to a busy thoroughfare.

'Please, you shower. Then me,' said the girl. They were the first words she'd spoken and Lau was surprised at the hoarse quality of her voice.

He nodded and stripped. As he washed, the girl sat on the toilet and pissed, and his face burned with embarrassment. He sat on the bed as she showered. Alone, he closed his eyes and sighed. He felt a solid weight descend on his shoulders and squeezed his eyes shut tighter as though he could drive the guilt out through his tear ducts. His wife would be sleeping now with their youngest child. The boy had not mastered his fear of the dark and slept in the room with his parents. His daughter would be dreaming in her bed, her shoulders rising and falling with each delicate breath as she slept.

He drove his family from his mind and fought down the hollow shame scouring his belly. He would see the priest upon his return to Hong Kong and cleanse his spirit. The sound of a fan drifted from the toilet-and-shower cubicle. He had chosen this girl because she was hesitant, perhaps ashamed. He felt a warmth kindle below his belly.

The girl stood in the doorway of the cubicle and he wondered how long she had watched him. She was naked. Her body was slim and angular.

She has accepted her fate for the next hour, thought Lau. He knew she didn't want him. He surprised himself as a desolate cold spread in his belly where he'd felt the warmth of desire.

The girl walked to him and took his hands then pulled him gently to his feet. She had him touch her narrow hips and moved against him. His mind reeled and he cursed himself. His failure to control his own body gnawed at his brain: his penis refused to react to the girl's touch.

Instead, the corpse of his mentor drifted into his mind. His Triad patriarch, Stanley Zhao – more of a parent than his blood father had ever been – carried from the entrance of a whorehouse in Wan Chai, Hong Kong Island. He wondered how the former Dragon Head, a man he had loved and respected like no other, could indulge in the pleasures of a prostitute so regularly for no more than lust. Perhaps when he, Tony Lau, reached such an advanced age as Zhao he would accept that a woman expected reward for giving her body to an old man.

Then he saw the face of Callum Burke in his mind's eye.

The Irishman had stood on the street watching him. He had paid no heed to the body of the great leader Zhao as it was loaded into the back of an ambulance. Tony Lau knew then that Burke had had a hand in the death. With Dragon Head Zhao's passing the policeman had wiped his slate clean. The people and lights had swirled and eddied around the cop and his expression had not changed as Lau found his own fingers make the symbol before conscious thought caught up.

Xie dou. Revenge.

'You no like me?'

He started when the girl spoke.

Lau said, 'I like you.'

He felt ashamed and wished they could speak in Cantonese.

'What is your name?' He knew the question was pointless and the girl would lie but he needed some way to identify her beyond a number.

'My name is Julia.'

'A nice name,' he said.

She looked at his flaccid penis.

'You not ready? Do you have a girlfriend?'

'A wife.'

'What do you do with your wife to get ready?'

'We kiss.'

'I cannot kiss. Only thing I not do.' She smiled, her small teeth painted red in a blink of neon through the slats of the blinds. 'But I can kiss down there.'

She descended with an easy grace and Lau wondered at the change in this "Julia" from the nervous girl-seven in the club to a practiced professional. He looked to the ceiling as he waited for her touch and breathed deep.

He could smell the disinfectant from the corridor. A musty scent from the carpet. Something like burnt brown sugar. Or was it strong, sweet coffee. His mind recognized the odor and did the math: the change in the girl, the fan in the cubicle; the sweet, burnt smell. She had smoked No. 3 heroin in the bathroom as he sat on the bed. Good quality too, the smell was relatively strong. He looked down at her and raised her chin. Now he could see the drug in her eyes, her lazy smile.

She held him in her left hand.

She said, 'You not like me.'

'You are very pretty,' said Lau, 'but not tonight.'

The girl rose from her kneeling position.

'I can talk. I studied English in a school in London once.' Julia smiled. 'It is my dream to visit Britain and Ireland. If I can make enough money here, I will go there to live.'

Britain, thought Lau. Ireland. Callum Burke was Irish. Callum Burke was a canker in his life.

The girl giggled and gave his cock a playful pat. He saw the feline aspect of her eyes, the joy of the drug coursing through her. They called smoking No. 3, Chasing the Dragon. He thought of his own Dragon: Dragon Head Stanley Zhao. He saw the girl's face painted red by the lights outside the window and thought of Callum Burke awash with neon on that Wan Chai street. The girl's smile was Burke's, mocking him like a *yaoguai* demon.

He didn't know how long the girl screamed. He didn't know how close he was to ending her as his hands closed on her windpipe and he straddled her on the floor. Or how long the two Thai security held him against the wall, the girl curled in the corner behind the bed, when Pineapple Wong stumbled into the room and snapped at them to release a senior member of the 14K Triad.

He didn't know how many times he had slaughtered Callum Burke in his mind. But he was sure, in his core, that the day of reckoning for the murdering bastard would come.

Chapter Ten

Callum climbed down from the cab like he was decades older than his twenty-nine years. The fight last week had been short but he was out of shape and the young Puerto Rican, Dylan Acosta, had worked his body hard. He should have taken an ice bath after leaving the basement on the Upper West Side but instead had sunk a couple of cubes in a couple of glasses of Bushmills that descended into an all-night drinking session with Paddy Doolan. A week later and he could still feel an ache in his kidneys.

Dylan Acosta. Callum had checked in with O'Connell and Milburn from payphones. Each time, he'd asked if Acosta had been seen around Hell's Kitchen and each time the answer had been no. Mattila had checked with contacts at the 15th and 18th precincts, claiming he had some intel on the guy from a CI, nothing concrete but enough that Mattila would like to get eyes on the man at a favorite watering hole or on Acosta's street. Nothing. Acosta's sister had called the 15th in a panic for three days running.

The Sol Grundy murder investigation was stalled. No ballistics to match and a clean crime scene.

One thing, Gabriel Muñoz was clean. Whatever his cousin was doing at Alicia's bodega, Muñoz wasn't involved. At least, in no way that the DEA could uncover.

Today's New World job had been an office move shifting cabinets and desks from midtown to a converted warehouse off Water Street at Seaport. He'd been with Willie and J.J.. Willie had had a fight with his girlfriend and downed a couple of 40 oz. bottles of malt liquor on top of his methadone. He got so drunk he dropped his Walkman and broke it. Callum told him he'd get it fixed for him at an electronics store.

Callum had come to understand a hierarchy within New World with Jimmy Mulligan at the top. Jimmy was the new Sol Grundy, Hell's Kitchen Irish rather than Brooklyn Jew. The moving company's owner, Bill, deferred to Jimmy on any decisions and had become a puppet ruler in his own kingdom.

And tomorrow Callum would take his backpack from the Belleclaire Hotel to Paddy Doolan's small apartment on Bleecker Street and spend his first night as Doolan's housemate.

He locked the truck and tossed the keys to the guard on the gate then lit up a Camel as he crossed 50th Street. He stood in front of a deli fighting the urge to buy a 40 oz. and working the Camel tip down to the filter before grinding it under his sneaker. People strode by, everyone in a rush. The afternoon was warm with a sweetness on top of the hot-rubber Subway smell seeping through a vent on the street. He wore a light coat that was too hot in the warmth of the day.

The fried chicken joint was empty when he entered despite the foot traffic outside and Callum smiled at the girl behind the counter reading a magazine article about Alanis Morisette.

'Hey,' he said, 'I'm gonna' buy a coffee but before that, you got a bathroom I could use? I'm kinda' desperate.'

The girl shot him a mouthful of teeth with a wad of gum wedged in the corner of her grin.

'I like your accent,' she said. 'You sound like the guy in the Lucky Charms commercial.'

'We're distant cousins. You got a bathroom sign over there, is it for customers?'

'Cute ones, sure.'

Callum winked. 'Thanks, I'll be back in a second for that coffee.'

He slipped through the door under the bathroom sign into a

narrow corridor with some boxes, cases of canned drinks and a mop and bucket propped against one wall. At the end of the corridor a door led out back of the building while another on the right had a hand-written bathroom sign. A staircase led upstairs next to the door and he climbed the steps.

At the top of the stairs he knocked on another door on a small landing.

The pipes of the building groaned. A cockroach made a run for cover by his foot.

'Come on, open up. That wee girl downstairs might wonder why it takes me ten minutes to do a piss.'

He heard a latch turn and locks click. The door opened and a pasty man in a Rangers cap, blue t-shirt and jeans beckoned him inside.

'You're Galinski, right?'

'Burke, yeah? I got it here. Just a second.'

Callum saw the intelligence cop rummage in a bag hanging from a hook on the wall. A woman was kneeling at the window peering through a telephoto lens at the truck lot opposite. Her hair was tied in a tight pony-tail, her sweat-shirt riding up her back, her legs tucked under her ass. Georgina Ruiz, he guessed. A blind was pulled over the window to just a couple of inches above the telephoto aimed at the truck parking lot. He doubted the two cops would find much of interest watching the old fart reading his newspaper in the small guard hut opposite.

Galinski gave him a Sony tape recorder.

'What the fuck is this?'

'It's to wear when you're with Doolan.'

'It's a fucking stack system.' He turned the recorder over and rolled his eyes. It bore a sticker with the words PROPERTY OF NYPD on. Someone had tried to peel it off and some of the sticker was torn.

Galinski glanced at the sticker.

'You can scrape it off,' he said.

'With what, a blowtorch? And where am I supposed to hide this on my body?'

'Use your imagination,' said Ruiz without turning around.

Callum said, 'I know your department are fucking me on this but I doubt it'll fit in my ass.'

She looked around and raised an eyebrow.

'Give Doolan's dominatrix a call. She'll help you out.'

He grinned at that. But when Galinski closed the door he looked at the Sony and his smile froze.

*

He had a piss and went back to the chicken place.

He shoved the recorder in his coat pocket and bought the coffee, catching sight of an open can of Pepsi and a half-eaten box of drumsticks behind the counter. Looked like a few more cans were sticking out of a pink Nike bag – the girl helping herself to a few perks while the boss was away?

Be careful helping yourself to the merchandise, he thought. New York's Finest are upstairs.

Or had she discovered someone was above? He had a sudden impulse to check.

She rolled the chewing gum across her teeth and impaled it with a canine.

Paranoid, Callum, he thought. He bid the girl goodbye and walked out of the place right into Paddy Doolan. He spilled coffee on the sidewalk.

'Hey Christy,' said Doolan, 'you coulda' bought me a Coke, I'da known you were in there.'

Callum paused a second felt like ten minutes then said, 'I needed a coffee. I'm beat.'

'It takes you that long to buy a coffee? I was at the lot five minutes before I crossed the street.'

'I needed a piss. The girl behind the counter let me use the john out back.'

A man with Einstein hair in a tattered check suit was reciting the declaration of independence over and over to a burly mustachioed man running a hot dog cart nearby.

'Poor bastard,' said Doolan. 'They been kickin' more people like him out of the mental wards and onto the streets. City's full of them.'

A young man in a leather jacket muttered an obscenity as he passed. Callum thought he was crazy or drunk until he saw the police car cruise by. Just another citizen showing their appreciation to the NYPD.

Doolan said, 'It's good you're here, I got an errand to run. You should come with me, this is important.' He nodded to the truck lot across the street and said, 'You drive. I just had a couple of beers and I don't need some asshole sideswiping me and calling the cops when I got booze in my system.'

*

Anton Galinski said, 'He's getting back in the truck. Shit.'

'Shit,' echoed Ruiz. 'If Doolan sees the recorder he's fried.'

'We gotta' call this in. Where's the car?'

'On 46th. We'll never make it on time to ghost him. Shit.'

Galinski got on the radio while Ruiz watched the truck pull out into late afternoon traffic with Callum driving.

'I called it in,' said Galinski. 'We got the truck's plate so we can track it.'

Ruiz looked older to Galinski. Her hair was scraped back revealing heavy eyes with dark sickles under each. Her mouth had become tighter, etching lines from her lips outward.

They grabbed their gear and locked the door on their way out. As they walked out back of the building and began jogging to their car Galinski said, 'You like him?'

'*Like* him? I don't know him. He's a cop and I don't want to see a cop go down.'

They reached the rental, and scrambled in. Ruiz took the driver's seat. She massaged the wheel for a second. Galinski'd never seen her like this on the job. Then again, they'd never been more than glorified chauffeurs for visiting dignitaries before now. But Ruiz was freaking him out with her tiredness and her fretting over Burke.

'It's sweet that you care,' he said. 'You'll be telling this guy Burke he's lookin' thin and feeding him burritos in no time.'

Georgie Ruiz put the car in gear. Her eyes flared. She shot him a look before pulling out into traffic and said, 'Screw you, you vodka swilling, sausage munchin' Polack.'

Anton Galinski smiled. Now that's more like it, he thought.

*

Callum made a left turn on 2nd Avenue and yelled at a blue Ford. Some band sang country blues rock on the radio and he listened to the words to tune out the wave of paranoia he was riding. Paddy Doolan slumped in the seat and put the soles of his boots on the dash. He'd ditched most of his coffee out the window. Now he turned the radio down.

'What's in your pocket?' said Doolan.

Callum felt a spike in his chest. It was dumb wearing a coat on a warm day like this, anyway. *Shit!*

'My what?' he said.

'Your pocket. It was kinda' hangin' outside the drugstore like there was somethin' heavy inside.'

'Really?'

'Yes,' said Doolan, slow like he was addressing an idiot. 'Really.'

Callum checked his mirrors. They were in Alphabet City and he was unsure of the neighborhood. The NYPD cassette recorder seemed to burn through his pocket into his skin.

Doolan took a drag on his cigarette.

'When I met you on 50th your hand kept going to that same pocket like there's something valuable in there. Or something secret.'

'Bullshit,' said Callum. He hoped Doolan didn't catch the waver in his voice. 'That's where I'm still hurtin' after my fight with Acosta.'

'One week on?' said Doolan. 'Kid musta' been eatin' his spinach.'

'We near this place?'

'Pull in here.' Doolan glanced down at Callum's coat pocket again but said nothing.

Callum parked in front of an old townhouse near the corner of East 5th Street and Avenue A. The sidewalk was cracked, chunks of asphalt scattered next to the curb. Debris crunched under the wheels of the truck. They jumped out of the cab on opposite sides and Paddy walked round to the driver's side on the sidewalk as Callum slammed the door. They stood for a second, Doolan checking out a couple of vagrants and a girl in a pink PVC mini-skirt with a life-sized snake tattooed down her right leg, Callum gazing up at the townhouse. It was tall and skinny and the walls looked buckled as though it hadn't been finished properly or the builders had to squeeze it so it would fit between its neighbors.

There was a stoop leading to a door with a smoked glass window. They walked up and Doolan pressed a buzzer and looked into a lens set in the wall. A clack signified the door was open and they walked into a small space like a cubicle with another painted door. There was a sound like a lock turning and the door opened inward. Callum could see it was reinforced steel behind the wood. Two big guys, one black, one white, stood behind the door. The walls were stripped of plaster in places to reveal the brittle wooden bones of the structure and music echoed from somewhere above.

Doolan had a hushed word with the muscle and beckoned for Callum to follow. He headed for a shabby granite staircase. A faint tang prophesied dark business on the floors above.

'Lemme' give you the tour,' said Doolan.

Upstairs the tang developed into the stinging reek of human sweat and piss and the stink of rotting garbage. This level was nothing but one long railroad flat, all the doors between rooms removed. Nothing on the cracked walls but ragged wounds in the plaster revealing more of the underlying structure. No furniture but a scattering of filthy couches and some blankets on the stained boards of the floor. It was like the inside of the building had been scoured by a tornado, thought Callum. Scattered figures lay in the garbage and their own bodily waste.

'This,' said Doolan, 'is a shooting gallery. You seen anything like this in Ireland?'

'No.'

Someone coughed up a lung and a small light flared in a corner.

'Some of these people are smoking like that pilgrim over there. Others are using pins: injecting with needles.'

'Hey!' A shout came from a tangle of bodies splayed on a rug in front of a couch. 'I ain't shootin' with no fags.'

Doolan leaned close to Callum.

'They think they'll get AIDS, they share with a faggot.' He offered Callum a smoke. 'Take it, it helps kill the smell.'

The smoke caught in Callum's throat, thickening the stench in the air.

'New York,' said Doolan. 'So good they named it twice.'

*

In a back room of the first floor Fintan Walsh sat in a checked shirt and jeans sipping a coffee when Callum and Doolan walked in.

'Hey, it's the Belfast Breezeblock. How you been since you went a couple rounds with our friend, Dylan?'

'Okay.'

'You want a drink?'

'I'm alright.'

'Might be hard to keep it down after the shit you saw upstairs, right?' He raised his coffee cup. 'Hell, everybody's got their drug of choice.'

Jimmy Mulligan sat at a desk behind Walsh tapping keys on a computer amid scattered printouts. He was a big man, hunched over the papers like an ogre from an old children's tale. Another door led into an alcove and Callum could see a shadow move within.

Walsh said, 'You did good last week. You end up in a basement with a load of men you don't know and beat some punk to a pulp. That takes some balls.'

Callum nodded, glancing at Mulligan's bald spot as the man bent to study some papers on the desktop. It was obvious Mulligan was one of the men J.J. from the Bronx had told him turned up at New World the first day Sol Grundy didn't come to work. Fintan Walsh with his thread-like brows and bad skin must have been the other.

'Paddy vouches for you. He says you're alright, that you're moving in with him. He's got a soft spot for strays from the Old Country but I need a little more convincing. Take your clothes off.'

The shadow in the alcove shifted.

Callum said, 'Didn't we do this already?'

'You sound more American by the day, son. It's good you're making an effort in our great nation. But I still need for you to take your clothes off. We gotta' make sure you're clean.'

Paddy Doolan offered Callum a reassuring smile. It came out more like grimace. One of the goons on the steel door stepped in the room.

Callum peeled off his coat slow. He could feel the weight in the pocket. He was so wired with paranoia he felt like tearing the clothes from his skin and screaming. His gut clenched and he saw himself from above, alone in this room with these dangerous men waiting for something bad to happen. He felt the sweat seeping from his skin, his breath quicken. He eased his arms from the coat so the weight in his pocket wouldn't fall and clatter on the floor. Then he folded the coat and placed it on a chair in the corner and stripped out of his t-shirt, jeans and boxers.

Walsh said, 'You know the routine. Turn around.'

Paddy laughed. 'You feel a draft, Fintan? Must be pretty cold in here.'

Callum forced a spirited, 'Fuck you.'

He stood naked while the bruiser, Paddy Doolan and Fintan Walsh studied the fading bruises on his side from the fight last week. After a minute Walsh motioned to the goon.

'Check his clothes.'

Callum stepped in front of the neat pile on the chair. It took all he had to make his legs move.

'You wanna' start fucking with my stuff, you have to go through me.'

Paddy said, 'Christy ... '

The goon said, 'You want a beatin', you got it.'

Callum let the madness of fear take him. He channeled crazy, tensed his body and yelled, 'I've been wearing those clothes all day on the job. What, you think I've got some kind of mic or whatever the cops use in the movies in there? Or are you gonna' plant some shit on me and have the cops arrest me here? Is the Puerto Rican dead and you want to fit me up for it? Am I a fall guy? I'll fucking have youse all before that happens!'

The goon spat a curse and Paddy Doolan grabbed the man's shoulder. The Irish accent, thought Callum, it's like a dog whistle. Soon as Paddy hears it his instinct is to protect.

Walsh clapped.

He laughed from somewhere deep and unguarded inside.

'Well, alright,' he said. 'You're alright, Christy. Maybe Paddy's right about you. You got that Irish in you, that's for sure. Alright Leo, back off. Paddy, relax. I seen you naked twice, Christy, and that's once more than some of the Latino chicks I bang. We're done with that.'

He slipped his right hand behind his back. It came back out with a Taurus model 85 revolver.

'Now, Mr. Burns from Belfast's fair city,' he said, 'bring your fucking clothes over here so I can go through the pockets.'

Chapter Eleven

The room seemed to shrink. Callum could sense his own fear leaching through his pores. The sound of Mulligan's chair creaking was a scream, the moan of a floorboard in the alcove a roar of complaint.

Paddy Doolan took a step toward him like he was approaching an untrustworthy dog.

'Come on, Christy. Give Fintan the clothes. Don't be takin' offence. We hate cops as much as you do, and they take an interest in what we do sometimes. We just got to be sure we can trust you.'

'How do I know I can trust you?'

'Because I haven't pulled this trigger yet,' said Walsh.

Callum knew he was too angry, that his terror made him furious. He lowered his voice.

'I've nothing to hide.'

Jimmy Mulligan's voice was chipped concrete and splintered Blackthorn.

'That ain't what your eyes are sayin'.'

He walked to the chair and lifted the clothes. He shot Callum a look of contempt and handed them over to Fintan Walsh.

Walsh took them and let the coat drop to the floor. It landed in a mess of folds cushioning the weight in the pocket. The keys for the truck fell on the floor. Walsh rifled the jeans while the muscle looked on.

They'd take their time with an undercover cop. Callum would never see his daughter or Irene again. He'd never eat pizza or drink beer or fuck again. It would be minutes into hours of searing, grinding pain followed by oblivion.

Walsh threw the jeans to Paddy Doolan and picked up the coat. He rummaged in the left pocket. The inside pocket. He weighed the coat and felt the imbalance on the right side. He looked up at Callum, his hand deep in the right coat pocket, then turned to Paddy Doolan.

Doolan said, 'What?'

'Exactly,' said Walsh. 'What the fuck is this?'

His hand emerged from the pocket holding the gray machine with a cassette tape inside. He held the Sony out like it was a bomb about to detonate.

Callum stared at the Sony, Willie Simmons's busted Walkman.

The NYPD minicassette recorder was out in the truck under the driver's seat, where he switched it with Willie's Walkman when he got out of the cab in front of the shooting gallery. Paddy had almost caught the switch when he walked around to Callum's side of the truck out front. Almost.

Paddy Doolan was laughing, saying the tape machine was Willie's Walkman. As adrenaline washed tension away, Callum tuned back in to the room and explained how he had acted the Good Samaritan when Simmons dropped the Walkman.

Walsh said, 'You're gonna' pay to fix this nigger's shit with your own money?'

'Hey,' said Paddy, 'Willie's alright.'

'Jesus, you too. I got a couple of social workers on my crew. Put your clothes back on, Christy. You're clean.'

Callum got dressed. He nodded, laughed, shoved the Walkman back in his pocket. He sat in a chair next to Paddy facing Walsh and watched the goon walk out and leave them with Mulligan and the shadow in the alcove. And he felt something flicker in his gut as he saw how the mobster-chieftain Walsh was including him alongside Paddy Doolan as a member of his Irish crew.

'Call it.'

'They say hold.'

'Hold? What am I, a fucking horse?'

'He can hear you on the radio.'

'He can kiss my round Latina ass, is what he can do.'

Ruiz didn't like the fact that DEA were calling the shots and Mattila was ordering her around. She didn't like the fact Callum Burke was inside an East Village shooting gallery with a voice recorder in his pocket and no back-up. Or the look of the big guy who had stood on the stoop of the shooting gallery for a smoke. The New York chapter of the Hell's Angels was a couple of blocks west and she knew some members would moonlight as muscle for various criminal concerns.

'This is wrong. Burke knows Doolan a few weeks and he takes him to a shooting gallery in Alphabet City? Why not ease him in with a couple of soft rackets – numbers, collecting protection dues?'

'I dunno',' said Galinski, his voice high with nerves. 'So they're fast friends. You know the Irish, all that clannish shit. Christ, we work with it enough in the Department.'

'It ain't right.'

'No, what ain't right is us working for the Intelligence Bureau and spending our days as fucking chauffeurs driving the French Delegate to the UN. This is a chance to do some real police work. We can be cops instead of fucking escorts so listen to what the man on the radio says and wait this out.'

They had parked a hundred yards or so from Burke's truck. Galinski played it tough but Ruiz knew he was worried, too. Ever since they'd seen Sol Grundy breathe his last on 95th Street they'd both been more on edge. Now Ruiz fretted that they were too obvious in this part of town. Two bums had already eyed them up as they sat in the car. Memories of the Tompkins Square Park riots in '88 lingered.

Ruiz said, 'How long has he been in there?'

'At a guess? Thirty, forty minutes. The Feds who tailed them from East 10th said they pulled up at the curb around five-twenty.'

'What's behind the building?'

'Garbage, trees, a dumpster. How the fuck should I know?'

'You're the super-street-cop, Gal. I been driving, didn't you check out the surroundings when we pulled into the area?'

'Jesus, am I glad I'm not one of your kids. You got problems coming when they're teenagers.'

'Yeah, 'cause Uncle Anton's gonna' want to date them, and I'm gonna' have to kick your sorry ass all the way back to Poland.'

'He's coming out.'

Burke came down the steps of the stoop with Paddy Doolan, Doolan slapping him on the back and laughing. Burke looked pale and drawn but he was in one piece and sucking on a cigarette.

Ruiz said, 'He looks like he aged a couple of years in a couple hours.'

They watched Doolan open the back of the truck and climb up to move some blankets and boxes to the sides of the cargo area. Then both men went back inside the building. Ruiz tapped the Buick's steering wheel. Galinski watched the truck in silence. Five minutes passed. A man in a dressing gown yelled something across the street at a young woman about his food stamps. Kids rode bikes toward Avenue B. A pigeon shit on the Buick's windshield.

Callum and Doolan reappeared and struggled down the steps with a wooden dresser looked like something from a production of Aladdin, a carved Arab or north African style arch covered with wire trellis work on one section. They loaded it into the back of the truck and wrapped it in blankets. While Doolan secured the furniture inside the truck with straps Burke walked to the cab. He fiddled under the driver's seat and clambered in. Then Doolan got in the passenger side.

Ruiz started the car as the truck pulled out into the street.

'He's okay,' said Galinski, 'we don't need to follow him. Doolan could make us.'

Ruiz ignored the remark and eased onto the street as the truck made a left onto Avenue A. She kept three car lengths back as they drove south for two blocks.

Just before the turn onto Houston Street Galinski called out. 'There!'

'What?'

'Something fell out of the driver's side window. Pull over.'

'I'll lose him.'

'He's undercover, he's supposed to be solo. Pull over or I'll open the door anyway.'

The truck disappeared into the stream of Houston traffic. Ruiz threw the wheel to the left as the cab behind blared its horn and drove past with a shout of, 'Asshole!'

Galinski hopped out of the rental and jogged to the corner. He bent, picked something up and walked back to the car.

He held up the Sony minicassette recorder, casing cracked, that Callum Burke had ditched out the window of the New World Movers truck.

*

They sat in a small room in the basement of the DEA building. Bobby Ho had brought a tape machine and listened to the recorded phone taps of Tong business. Sealing the worm was the term he'd heard Mattila use to refer to recording Title IIIs. Niku

Mattila had said some at the DEA thought the agency might be able to track cell phones for location in the future and, having seen the massive resources federal law enforcement in the US enjoyed, he wouldn't be surprised. He looked up at the pipes and cables running along the ceiling and had an image of massive earthworms burrowing through the bowels of the building.

James Milburn sat across the table with the phone records. They had gone through months of recordings by hand, taking the lion's share of work so Ho could continue monitoring the phone communications, both recorded and, when the Chinese cop could hide away in a surveillance room in Chinatown, live.

They had noted a couple of numbers that recurred with some frequency. One in Hong Kong, three in New York. The Hong Kong number, when cross-referenced with the HK Police, was a taxidermist and tanner based in Causeway Bay. The former employer of David Chau, shot to death on the tram in Central. HKPF had entered the number in their database in relation to the murder investigation.

Two of the New York numbers were lawyers who represented various Tong members. The third was a fashion design and production studio in SoHo, BOJ Garments.

Milburn had reached out to the DEA and FBI, and checked the NYPD NITRO database on the fashion studio number. He found a hit from five years ago. The NYPD and FBI had investigated the number in relation to an organized crime case. At that time, the number had been for a therapist who was supposedly treating Italian crime boss Vincent 'The Chin' Gigante in relation to mental illness. Law enforcement had suspected Gigante was using the therapist's office for mafia meetings, employing the confidentiality of patient privilege. Nothing was proven. The therapist closed for business last year and the building space had lain empty until two months ago when the fashion company moved into the premises.

'Bobby,' said Milburn.

'Yes, Sir.'

'This recurring number in SoHo, BOJ fashion studio. What was the business address again?'

Ho flicked through his notebook. His slim fingers felt slow and clumsy in his excitement at Milburn's interest.

'179 Grand Street, Sir.'

'A couple of blocks from the border of Chinatown. And they never changed the phone number.'

'Yes, Sir.'

Milburn stood and rocked on his heels, his hands behind his back. Ho had an image of the man on the deck of a warship like those old wooden battleships he had seen in paintings hung in the Inspector's office depicting the Battle of Trafalgar.

'Right,' said the Englishman, coming to some unknown conclusion, 'carry on, Bobby. I'm going to call on Sergeant O'Connell. Then let's see if you and I can't take a break from these salubrious surroundings and do a little leg work, shall we?'

He winked.

Bobby Ho flushed, smiled and went back to the job of listening in on New York's Chinese mafia.

*

Callum was back on 96th and Broadway, the building where Callum had fought Dylan Acosta in the basement. They stood next to the service elevator waiting for the super to turn up and give them access. Doolan was bouncing. He'd been gabbing constantly since they'd left Alphabet City. On the drive, Doolan had been distracted enough for Callum to grab the NYPD Sony and toss it out his window on the corner of Houston. Now he listened to Paddy gab about Walsh, about Christy Burns and the money they were going to make.

At the shooting gallery Walsh had welcomed Callum to the crew. There was a Mob of guys in Woodside, Queens, and a smattering from the old neighborhood in Hell's Kitchen, Manhattan. They had several rackets: some thieving courtesy of a continued representation in the Longshoreman's union, protection, gambling and – most lucrative of all – heroin.

Walsh had asked, 'You got any problems pushing drugs, Christy?'

Callum had pointed to the revolver in Walsh's hand.

'Like I can say no,' he said.

He thought he saw tumbleweed blow across the floor in the crushing silence. The shadow in the alcove moved.

'Yes,' he'd said. 'Yes, I'm fine with it, okay?'

Walsh and Mulligan had relaxed and they had all shaken hands. Then he and Paddy had picked up a dresser from the back of the entrance hall and put it in the truck before driving off.

Now the old super appeared on 96th with an agonized sigh and handed over a set of keys to Doolan, one of which unlocked the service elevator.

By the time the doors opened on the top floor, Doolan was a kid on the cusp of a candy store. He bounced on the spot with excitement. They emerged into a small service area with cleaning products, a storage room off to the right and a chair with a pile of American Heritage and New York Sportsman magazines. Doolan opened another door onto a rectangular space. The residents' building elevator was to the right, a closed metal door straight ahead.

Doolan rapped on the door and a slat drew back about head height.

'It's Paddy Doolan with a friend. I got a delivery for The Nurse.'

The slat closed, the door opened and a large man with a ruined face like a ploughed field, dressed in a black suit, stood aside and said, 'She's with a client.'

Callum and Paddy carried the dresser down a carpeted corridor with doors to left and right at equal intervals. The impression was of a hotel save for the hellish red lighting and black void at the end of the corridor where the lighting failed. And the occasional scream.

For a second Callum thought he might be dead and this was his own personal Hell. A howl on his left made him jump and Doolan laughed, his shoulders hunched, mouth a wide tear in his long face.

They stopped at the third door from the end of the corridor on the right. Doolan knocked. There was a sound like a moan spliced with a scream and then a clacking of heels. The door opened and a high school sweetheart smile lit up Doolan's face. A woman slipped out of the door. She was tall as Paddy's nose in her black stiletto platform boots. Her black hair was scraped back in a tight ponytail, a streak of orange fire running from temple to end. Her eyes were set in Cleopatra eyeshadow, her nose wide. She pursed her mouth, fattening already generous lips, gloss matching the red of her leather bodice.

The stereotypical Dragon Lady, thought Callum.

'Hey, Baby,' said Doolan, 'we got a delivery for you.'

The woman said, 'Baby, I'm working. You know that.' The accent was pure Brooklyn.

'Me too. Where should we leave this?'

The woman looked from Doolan to the dresser to Callum.

'This is Christy,' said Doolan, 'the guy I told you about.'

Callum nodded.

'Hey,' said the woman, 'good to meet you. Call me Trinity.'

'Not Nurse Löwin?'

She giggled, a high, clean sound in the dark surroundings.

'My real name is Trinh but Trinity is good. The Nurse thing just came from a German horror movie I dug.'

'The dresser?' said Doolan.

Trinity said, 'I got a client in here. Give me five minutes, I'll put him in the vacuum wrap. You can leave the delivery inside the door before I let him out again.'

'Who is it?'

'Benny.'

'Benny The Bug Man? Shit, make sure there ain't no roaches crawling around when we come in.'

Trinity leaned in and shared a deep, long kiss with Doolan. He cupped her ass and her hand dropped to his crotch. Then they separated and she slipped back inside the door.

Callum said, 'The Bug Man?'

'This guy, he's a construction worker. He brings insects in jars and lies on the floor, has Trinity release the bugs so they crawl all over him while she walks up and down his body in her heels.'

'Jesus.'

'Jesus ain't a member here, man.'

They stood in silence for a couple of seconds.

Callum said, 'I recognize this dresser.'

'Oh yeah?'

'I picked it up on a job in Queens. Arab husband and wife at each other's throats. Real beautiful lady. The dresser was one of the pieces we moved to storage in Brooklyn.'

'Sounds about right,' said Doolan.

'The woman was nice, didn't seem the type to be involved with Fintan's crew. Too classy, y'know.'

'She ain't. But her little brother is. He's into us for ten grand. To buy off his debt, she helped us out and donated her dresser to move some stuff for us.'

'What's inside?'

'Forty thousand dollars in white powder.'

'Shit.'

'Yeah. The shit those zombies in Alphabet City were shooting in their veins.'

Callum blew through his teeth. 'Does Trinity know?'

'She's okay with it, yeah.'

'Okay.'

'Okay.' Said Doolan. Then, 'What do you think of her?'

'She's nice.'

'She's the best thing ever happened to me. I was with this other girl, a fucking banshee from the Old Country. This bitch would take against me in her head and lock herself in the bedroom. Not open the door for three days then come out and drape herself all over me. Make-up sex was amazing, then rinse and repeat. It was fucking exhausting, Christy. Then I'm in some bar near the Village and there's Trinity. She's with some girlfriends, we get talking and next thing you know, we're together. The psycho I was living with found out and came after me with a bread knife.'

'What'd you do?'

'Ran like a bitch.' Doolan laughed. 'I ain't into hurtin' women, you know? Even in self-defense. So the Irish girl leaves me, and Trinity and me hook up. She works here two nights-a-week but it kinda' sucks. The mistresses here are like contract workers so they have to pay a percentage of their fee to the owners. I set her up with a loan in her own place on the Upper East Side so she can see private clients. East 95th. She can take the transverse right across the park.'

'Who owns this place?'

'Our crew owns the building. Trinity does a little work for us on the side.'

'It doesn't freak you out, her seeing all these other guys? The bondage stuff?'

'Whatever she does with them, it ain't sex.'

That's pretty relative, thought Callum.

He said, 'But she's gettin' off on it?'

'She's gettin' off on what she does, not who she's doin' it with. And, some days, it's just a job, you know?'

'Yeah, alright, that makes sense. Kind of.'

'She loves me,' said Doolan. 'She don't sleep with no one else, she don't date her clients – only me. And we don't do none of the bondage stuff, just go to the movies, eat, have a drink. She's unbelievably flexible, man.' Paddy allowed himself a smirk. 'She's like a contortionist. She could fold herself into this dresser, she wanted to. Incredible in bed.'

Callum raised his eyebows.

'Sometimes we go dancin' at Webster Hall,' said Paddy, 'you gotta' come with one of her friends. She's more loyal than any woman I've known. And don't let her size fool you, she's one strong lady.'

Callum chucked Doolan under the chin.

'Fuck you,' said Paddy, his voice warm like a straight scotch.

The door opened and Trinity hissed, 'No swearing, okay. I told you before, it cheapens the experience for the client.'

Paddy said, 'Sorry, baby.'

Callum said, 'Sorry, ma'am.'

'Alright boys, let's get this done.'

They carried the dresser into the room, a sparse space with a metal chain curtain at one end. A coffin was propped against one wall, a wooden cross on another. A pair of medieval-looking stocks were next to the door and a selection of leather whips and floggers hung by the coffin. A pile of crushed bugs had been swept to the corner. Suspended by straps in the center of the room was a human figure wrapped in rubber head-to-toe. A tube was inserted in the rubber located by the mouth and some form of artificial lung was pumping oxygen to the client inside the vacuum-sealed bodysuit.

Trinity crossed the room and Callum wondered how she could move so silently in stiletto heels on the tiled floor. She parted the chain curtain with a soft clinking sound and they left the dresser inside next to a pile of nipple clamps. Trinity put a finger to her lips as they padded for the door again. Next to the stocks, Doolan grabbed Trinity and they shared another deep kiss. Then Paddy broke the clinch and winked as she gave him a playful scowl and the rubber-wrapped figure began mumbling through its wrapping.

As the door closed behind them, Callum and Paddy heard Trinity bark, 'Quiet! You want I should crush you like your sad little bugs?'

Paddy Doolan looked at the closed door for a moment and slung an arm around Callum's shoulder.

'Alright, let's go,' he said. 'And what d'you say Christy, ain't she an angel?'

Chapter Twelve

Anton Galinski and Georgie Ruiz sat across the room from Niku Mattila and Mike O'Connell. James Milburn and Bobby Ho were on a sofa against the wall of the small office at DEA New York Division HQ on 10th Avenue. The walls displayed posters from Chinatown, Chinese scrolls, and a map of South East Asia with a doodle made by the DEA station chief for northern Thailand when in town on a visit.

All the cops were dead beat. The air outside had a pre-dawn bite and the sun would be clambering above Hudson Bay in less than an hour.

Mattila said, 'So our boy is wrapped up for the night.'

'Last we saw,' said Galinski, 'he was stumbling into the Belleclaire at 0400.'

'His last night there before he moves to Doolan's. And you tracked him with our guys?'

'DEA all the way. That okay with you?'

'Yeah,' said Mattila, 'and Alphabet City is far enough from the 5th to keep them out of it. You know how cops like to talk.'

O'Connell raised an eyebrow. 'And all cops are dirty?'

'That's not what I'm saying. But the 5th precinct is relatively quiet and one reason for that is Chinatown. You got Chinese on Chinese crime but the majority is never reported because people are too scared to call the cops, they don't trust the cops or they haven't got the English to understand the law here.'

'However,' said Milburn, 'we don't believe there's been much direct contact between Walsh's crew and the Tong as of yet, anyway. One or two people on either side but the Tong won't want to be seen to be dealing with Walsh at this stage and vice versa. Callum should be insulated from the Chinese side of the operation. He's probably fine.'

Ruiz said, 'Probably? And what happens if Burke winds up in a dumpster tonight?'

'At least we got the bagpipes in place already for his funeral,' said O'Connell.

Ruiz made to say something but Galinski placed his hand on her arm. She looked at him like he was her old man home late from the local dive bar and shrugged him off.

'Now,' said Mattila, 'on to the main order of business. Sammy Ong and the Hip Sing Tong.'

Ruiz rolled her eyes and said, 'The *main* order of business? We got a cop in – '

'Ruiz, I want you to understand something,' said Mattila. 'Fintan Walsh and his boys are cavemen. The Chinatown Tong and their Hong Kong associates in the Triads are the Blue Ribbon criminal syndicate in New York City. Forget the Five Families: they can't hold a candle to the Chinese. These guys have a network of family, honor, trust and obligation that's tougher to break into than any other organization I know. Also, they're intelligent, patient, loyal, disciplined and low-key.'

Ruiz said, 'So join up. None of this justifies you making Burke low priority.'

Milburn sat forward on his chair and crossed his legs.

'Callum Burke is well aware of everything the Agent has said, Detective Ruiz.'

He nodded to Bobby Ho.

Ho said, 'The Triads never break in interrogations. When they join their Society they are threatened again and again with terrible death if they betray their brothers. They may admit their guilt under questioning, but swear they acted alone. The Tongs would be similar.'

Mattila stood and moved to a map of Chinatown on the wall.

'We're going after the Hip Sing but there are other Tongs,' said Galinski, 'with other street gangs. Like the On Leong and the Ghost Shadows.'

'The Hip Sing are closer to the Hong Kong Triads. They're using Walsh and his crew. There are more working parts in their operation; more pressure points to hit.'

'Burke is not exactly a pawn,' said O'Connell. 'He can bust Walsh and his Mob, sure, but if he can prove there's a relationship between the Walsh Mob and Sammy Ong's Tong we can use the racketeering charge against Walsh to strengthen the RICO case against the Hip Sing. Prosecution through association.'

Ruiz said, 'We got it.'

Mattila said, 'And also – '

'We *got* it!'

Galinski was inspecting his nails. His face was a blank but Ruiz knew he was pissed by the pulse of his jaw as he clamped it shut. She knew he would be embarrassed by the lecture from Mattila and Milburn. Galinski was having a ball on this assignment.

Bobby Ho stood to report on the Title IIIs.

'There is much chat on the phones of a business endeavor,' he said. 'The Tong talk about the business as though it's a new restaurant, as we know. The terms used are often centered around food or food supplies. This can be confusing: Triads often refer to illegal immigrants as pigs; heroin or prostitutes as chicken.'

His face burned and he felt ridiculous. His English sounded absurdly formal and stilted to his own ears.

'Your guy in Hong Kong was shot, was a taxidermist,' said Galinski. 'Where does that fit in with the restaurant business?'

Milburn said, 'Not being an authority on taxidermy, I haven't the faintest idea. However, Bobby checked phone records related to the Title IIIs and found a number which received a persistent number of calls. I have discussed the matter with Sergeant O'Connell and he, Sergeant Ho and myself will visit the business.'

'What kind of business?' said Ruiz.

'Fashion design and production, BOJ Garments. It's only been in existence for a few months.'

'You want the guys to pick up a couple of nice dresses, Georgie?' said Galinski. 'Tired of wearin' the pants in your house?'

'Let's get back on point. Bobby?' said Mattila as Ruiz gave Galinski the finger.

Bobby Ho wiped a thread of sweat beside his eye and cleared his throat.

'There has been talk among the Hip Sing of a *kong su*, a negotiation. On some of the phone taps, Ong's colleagues have said the '*cousins*' are adamant they want to visit and talk over old times.'

O'Connell pinched the ridge of his nose. He'd been awake for over twenty-four hours and his wife would be pissed he hadn't called in. Declan had a piano recital to practice for and O'Connell was to drive him to the class later this morning. A goddamned piano recital. Why couldn't the kid be crazy about little league, for Christ's sake? Even soccer? He wanted to wind things up here and grab some fresh air.

He said, 'The 14K Triad are coming to New York for a meet?'

'No, this negotiation is on the phone for now, but Ong is talking about booking a flight to Hong Kong,' said Ho. 'The Hip Sing are planning to visit the Triad. The 14K may be trying to increase their direct influence in Chinatown and Sammy Ong is not happy. His closest ally and confidant, Papa Ng, has said as much on the phone tap. The deposits to the United Oriental by Phoenix Investments – we believe the 14K – have been increasing in frequency.'

'Increasing in frequency but not amounts or denominations,' said Mattila. 'Nothing to trigger a FinCEN investigation.'

Ruiz said, 'So the 14K are offloading cash abroad. Nerves about the handover in '97.' She looked at Bobby Ho. 'Are the Triad and Tong on a collision course or not?'

Ho shifted in his seat. For a moment he was ossified with nerves at the direct question. Then he saw Mattila give him a nod of encouragement.

'The Triad are much larger than the Tong internationally,' he said, 'but the Tong have control in Chinatown: for now. The street gang – the Flying Dragons – are thugs. The Tong do some good for the people so their influence is strong and Sammy Ong is a wise leader. His closest counsel, Papa Ng, is an idealistic man with some genuine desire to use the Tong for the good of the Chinese community. There is no great trouble with the rival On Leong Tong at present.'

Ho licked his lips.

'But they need the 14K Triad backing. The Triad has many more members spread through Hong Kong, Macau, Asia and elsewhere. The heroin which makes so much money for the Tong comes from the Triad. The illegal immigrants who work in Chinatown are brought to America by the Triad.'

Ruiz said, 'Sounds like neither side wants a war.'

'I think so.'

Milburn unfolded his angular frame.

'However,' he said, 'a coup d'état may be another matter.'

O'Connell yawned. 'Sammy Ong?'

'Possibly,' said Milburn. 'I'd suggest Bobby, while monitoring Hip Sing communications and keeping an eye on Pell Street and environs, listen for any signs of dissent within the Tong. Ong has, I believe, been leader for many years: age and seniority are highly revered among the Chinese, one of their many admirable qualities. But some of the American born Chinese – ABCs as they call themselves – or the Flying Dragons may be more candid should there be any anti-Ong sentiment. Ong's friend, Papa Ng, may be at risk, too.'

Bobby Ho nodded. The assembled cops stretched and rubbed red-raw eyes. In Hong Kong, it was already early evening and the tempo of life in Central, Wan Chai, Kowloon and beyond was shifting from the frantic commercial business of the day to the joys of drinking, eating, and the furtive pleasures that formed the bread-and-butter income of the Triad societies. And in New York, Callum Burke murmured in his bed through beer and whiskey addled dreams of brawls and women and junkies in filthy, broken down buildings before finally slipping into a deeper slumber to sleep the sleep of the dead.

Chapter Thirteen

Callum made it to Doolan's apartment in the late afternoon.

They sat out on the fire escape overlooking Bleecker and drank beer and watched the store signs and barfront neon blink awake. It was Thursday, close enough to the weekend for the street to fill up early with diners and drinkers. A harassed-looking father bought his kids slices at the small pizzeria across the street. In his mind, Callum had a flash of Tara playing on the beach. He washed it away with a Molson.

They'd barely touched on business last night, instead putting their backs into getting roaring drunk, so now Paddy gave Callum a brief breakdown of his role in Walsh's outfit.

'You keep doing the moving work. It's good cover for deliveries all over the city and keeps you busy and mobile during the day. You don't talk about what you saw last night or the work you do for Fintan: J.J. and Willie and the others don't have no idea what's behind the scenes at New World. The shit will be in furniture sometimes, others it could be in a box of cargo or somethin'. Some moves will be vanilla – no drugs at all. You also do some cash collections from stores and bars. Fintan liked how you handled yourself with the Acosta guy, thinks you'd be useful picking up payments from some of the businesses around The Kitchen. He might ask you to come out to Woodside once in a while to crack a head. You good with that?'

'If the head deserves it.'

'They will.'

Paddy took him to the roof so they could look over the city as night settled. The lowering light made silhouette castles of the brownstones with their water towers, and headstones of the downtown skyscrapers glimpsed between rooftop bric-a-brac in the distance. The twin towers of the World Trade Center stood like lightning rods stretching to the heavens.

'This'll be a great spot later in summer,' said Doolan, 'when the big thunder storms move in.'

Callum said, 'How can something so dirty and noisy and fucking chaotic be so beautiful?'

'You like it here, huh?'

'Yeah.' Callum took a pull on his bottle. 'Yeah, I think I do. At least right now.'

'How's it compare with the Old Country?'

'It doesn't. Chalk and cheese, y'know?'

'What, like night and day?'

'I suppose. Belfast is tiny in comparison, but you've got the Black Mountains, the Castlereagh Hills, the lough. You're in County Down and you're driving towards Castlereagh, or Craigantlet, to come down off those hills and there's this amber glow in the sky from the lights of the city, and you know you're almost home. All those people are down there in the Lagan Valley sleeping or talking or drinking or fucking. Or fighting. There's millions more people here but it doesn't seem as real somehow.'

Doolan studied his face.

Callum shrugged, cleared his throat.

'I dunno',' he said, self-conscious. 'Maybe it's the stars. There's no stars here. Too many lights.'

Same as Hong Kong, he thought. The night sky was a pale grey dome against the clouds on Hong Kong Island and Kowloon. He thought of the bay, the multi-colored light show of Wan Chai and Central reflecting on the water. He thought of Irene and Tara in Cleveland. When this was over he'd go to Ohio. See how the land lay.

'Anyway, home's where the heart is,' he said.

Doolan knocked back the dregs of his Miller.

'Your home got a lotta' problems, though,' he said. 'What with the English an' all.'

It took Callum a moment to realize Doolan was talking about Belfast.

'It surely does.'

'*Tiocfaidh ár lá*,' said Paddy, mangling the Irish language pronunciation. 'Our day will come, right?'

'Will it? I don't think anyone's gonna' win outright from that mess.' Callum thought of the body in north Belfast, crumpled like paper. He'd only seen the aftermath of the sniper attack but he knew that Jimmy had been at the gates of the police station waiting for some soldiers to file back in after a patrol. Jimmy had been his best friend, the brother of two younger sisters and the son of a quiet couple who still wept on occasion when the day was long and the memories stung hard.

Callum said, 'It'll take years, more than I have left, to see a solution. There might be an end to the violence someday but the problems won't go away.'

'Yeah. Our day will come,' said Doolan. He was talking to himself, smiling, like Callum hadn't said a word.

They stood in silence as the racket of the city clattered and swirled around them. A chopper flying over downtown, the honk and wail of a fire truck, the yell of someone on the street below.

'You grew up in Hell's Kitchen,' said Callum.

'Sure did. Fintan and a lot of the other guys moved out for Woodside, the Bronx. Even Staten Island. Not me. I love Manhattan, always have.'

Paddy looked south over the rooftops to the towering monuments of commerce by Battery Park, dwarfing the unseen Bowery in the distance. Dwarfing Chinatown.

'You got millions of people on this island. Millions more coming in every day to work, tourists, whatever. But it's like a village,' said Doolan. 'I see the same bum on 3rd Avenue around 29th street every time I drive that strip. Guy pushes a shopping cart and wears a flying hat, one of those old-time leather pilot's caps with the goggles. There's a kid in Washington Square Park plays chess on the tables. I go there with a coffee sometimes, early, before the day really starts, and there he is. Probably plays before school. There's a girl on 76th and Broadway looks like she works in the Barnes & Noble up there. Sexy librarian type, glasses, pleated skirt. She buys a dog and a drink from Gray's Papaya and sits on the center island in the middle of Broadway to eat. Sits there in the middle of all that traffic and dirt and fumes, and she spits a wad on the sidewalk when she's finished. Looks like your grade school teacher and she hawks up a loogie every fucking time. I used to watch her when I was staying in the Belleclaire.'

He scratched his ass.

'Then one night I make a delivery to Trinity at the bondage club and there she is, librarian girl. The room door's open, 'cause some of them like people watchin', and she's in a leather bikini and thigh boots beatin' some other naked chick with a whip. And she spits on the other girl, just like she spits on the sidewalk. That's Manhattan. It can look business-like and respectable, and pretty sexy, too, but inside it's hard and dark and it can be fucking mean.'

'And you love it.'

'I do. It's like that Irish psycho I was bangin' before Trinity. It's probably bad for me but at least it ain't never boring. I guess that's why I like Trinity so much. She works all that craziness out with other people and I get the soft, *good* part of her. But I know there's a crazy bitch inside.'

Callum laughed. 'That doesn't make any sense, Paddy. You make it sound like you love Trinity because she's an escape from all the craziness; but you love Manhattan for its craziness.'

'That's New York,' said Doolan. 'Nobody said it had to make any sense.'

They drank some more. Behind, through the rooftops, the top of the Empire State Building was lit purple and Callum imagined the tourists on the observation deck looking down on him and Paddy Doolan, oblivious of the Mob rackets, the Tongs, the lost and fucked up souls in Alphabet City.

He said, 'Where do the drugs come from, Paddy?'

'Does that matter?'

'I dunno'. No. I mean, maybe. Fuck, I dunno'. I never did anything like this before.'

'You told us you were okay with it.'

'I am,' said Callum. He took a swig of beer. 'It's just, I wondered where the drugs come from, you know? Is it the mafia or what?'

Doolan almost spat his drink over the edge of the roof on the bar-hoppers below.

'You'd haveta' find 'em first,' he laughed. 'They been kinda' quiet in Manhattan since Gotti went down, do most of their business in Brooklyn and Staten Island. Not that they don't make money: trucking, garbage unions. But they don't work with us.'

Paddy said, 'Listen. I like you, Christy. Some guy off the boat from the Old Country, come to the big city to make something of himself. I respect that, you're a fighter, a pioneer like the first Americans, you know.'

Callum thought it best not to mention the first Americans were Indians, like the Sinister on the NYPD badge.

'I took you under my roof, I vouched for you with Fintan and that ain't no small thing, alright? But follow my line, man. Don't ask no questions and do what you're told. You care about the origin of the beans for your morning joe? Or the dough for your pizza slice? So don't think about where the shit comes from or the poor bastards using. Your job, like everyone else in this city don't live in a cardboard box, is to make money and if that's on the back of someone else – shit – that's the New York City food chain, baby.'

Callum finished up his beer. He nodded and slapped Paddy on the shoulder.

'Alright, man. Let's get another beer and drink to the food chain.'

Doolan smiled. In the light from the surrounding city it looked a little broken.

'Sounds good,' he said, 'but not right now. There's somewhere we gotta' be.'

On his first night at the apartment it was Doolan's place, Doolan's rules. Still, Callum wasn't in the mood for surprises.

He and Paddy dumped the beers in the trash and left the apartment. They walked west and Callum talked shit about the Mets, the Yankees, how the Major League had lost a lot of faith with the fans after the strike. Then they were next to the Hudson, Jersey glittering like strings of fairy-lights across the water. They turned north and stopped in front of a hulking shell, some nineteenth-century industrial place fallen into disrepair. The street was empty but for traffic slipping by and the lights of a dive bar on the corner a block north. A siren blared to life somewhere distant.

Paddy Doolan stopped and fished a pack of Marlboro from his pocket.

'You want one?'

'No, I'm good.'

'Christy, you sure?'

Paddy's tone was dead serious.

Callum caught a shiver across his shoulders.

Doolan stepped close and took Callum's face in his hands.

'You're good people. You remember that. You're good people.'

'How many beers did you drink, Paddy?'

Doolan offered a smile but it came off like he was in pain.

'C'mon,' he said and walked around the corner of the derelict building.

Callum fought to keep his pulse down and voice even.

They came to a padlocked metal door with a peeling fire exit sign. Paddy pulled a ring of keys from his pocket and, squinting through the smoke from the Marlboro jammed between his teeth, matched one to the lock. The door gave with a groan and they stepped into darkness.

Rows of old wooden desks in an old manufacturing space. Cracked plaster walls. Something scuttling through debris by a baseboard.

City light seeped through high windows, enough to define the basics. It could have been a bank rather than a center of industry with its vaulted ceiling and decorative plasterwork.

'This was used by the longshoremen until a few years ago,' said Paddy. 'Now look at it. It's a fucking shame.'

Callum said, 'Time waits for no man.'

'Is that some kinda' Bible shit? 'Cause that's Fintan's bag. Not mine.'

A shot rang out and Callum started and crouched. He looked to Paddy and saw him hit, clutching his chest, the Marlboro gone. His features seemed to squeeze together in the middle like someone was scrunching his face up in a ball.

Callum hissed, 'Paddy!' He felt a spike of some strong and righteous emotion for Paddy Doolan.

Then something seemed to pop in Paddy's face and he bellowed with laughter. He clutched again at his chest, half howling, half coughing. Another shot rang out only this time it sounded like what it really was, a flat, hard handclap. The voice of Fintan Walsh cut through the stale air.

'You ladies gonna' join us or what?'

Paddy stretched and walked to Callum. He slapped his shoulder.

'Like I said, Christy, you're good people.'

Callum's face burned and his eyes screamed murder. He said, 'This place is fucking creepy.'

'Man, this is only the start of the ghost train.'

They walked around tables and a pile of chairs to a doorway where Walsh stood in a long, stained apron with his arms folded.

'What's with the butcher's apron?' said Callum.

'Call it a hobby.'

Callum said, 'An Irishman's wife walks into the butcher's and says "You've a sheep's head in the window"; the butcher says "Missus, that's a mirror".'

They laughed.

'That's cute,' said Walsh.

They passed through a smaller, darker space with lockers toppled like dominoes and followed a twisting corridor to a room with toilet stalls, a wall of sinks and two shower stalls. High windows offered pallid light. Jimmy Mulligan stood against the wall wearing another apron. A carryall was on the floor at his feet. Plastic sheeting covered part of the floor and another apron was hung on a hook by the door. Paddy Doolan grabbed it. As he tied it on, Mulligan opened the carryall and took out a machete, a large butcher knife and a hacksaw. There was a chemical smell with an undertone of something profane. A smell every cop knew.

Callum looked at Paddy and tried to read his expression but Doolan kept his eyes on the floor.

'Paddy?' said Callum.

'You don't answer to Paddy right now,' said Mulligan. His voice sounded like someone had gone to work on his vocal cords with the hacksaw. He'd lost a chunk of his left ear at some time and his drinker's nose was like a subway map gone mad, cluttered with busted veins.

Callum said, 'What is this?'

Mulligan pushed his bulk off the wall. Walsh raised a hand to stay him and said, 'You're doin' good, Christy – two for two. You did a job on the spic kid up on 96th, you were clean at the shooting gallery and made the dresser delivery to the freak-show on the Upper West Side.'

Callum caught Paddy flinch at the insult to Trinity.

Mulligan walked to a toilet stall and pushed the door open. The smell got stronger. It burned Callum's nostrils.

'Say hello to an old friend.'

Dylan Acosta was sat on the toilet. He was naked, his eyes black like a feeding shark. The gray and blue-green tie-dye of putrefaction stained his skin. He'd been shot in the head. His eyeballs had hemorrhaged.

Callum dry heaved, and his mouth filled up with acid spit. His head felt heavy and bloated like Acosta's dead gas-filled belly and he doubled over, his face burning.

'We got a friend runs a funeral parlor out in Queens kept this little gift fresh for you, Christy, but the chemicals can only work for so long,' Walsh said. 'So it's time to pop your cherry.'

Mulligan produced the machete and handed it to Callum. Then Paddy put a hand on his back and pushed him to the cubicle. Callum swallowed over and over. He wiped his eyes, the machete heavy in his hand, and straightened slow like an old man. Walsh began humming The Fields of Athenry. Callum latched onto the old song in his head, used it to drive everything else away. He looked at Paddy and nodded.

Paddy and Callum took an ankle each and pulled Acosta's corpse off the toilet. The head cracked on the floor tiles.

Paddy winked at Callum.

'Just like hauling furniture, right Christy?'

They dragged the corpse toward the showers. Callum thought of the millions of souls around him in New York and Jersey living their lives while he labored here in a circle of Hell. Walsh's voice built to a crescendo as he approached the chorus.

Callum glanced at Doolan and said, 'You done this before?'

'You get used to it.'

Paddy blinked a couple of times as he dragged the corpse.

'You sure?'

Walsh hit the chorus.

Callum snapped.

He jumped into The Star of the County Down full blast and sang like he was drunk, like he was raging against the world. He drowned the low lying fields of Athenry, smothered the maudlin wail. It was a challenge, County Down versus County Galway, a fuck you to Fintan Walsh and his quiet sadism. A fuck you to whatever this shit was – an initiation? Prelude to Callum's own execution? Walsh's sick joke?

And a fuck you to Jimmy Mulligan, now springing forward with eyes on fire, face stretched in a furious war-mask.

Paddy grabbed Mulligan. Acosta's leg slapped off the tiles and Callum rolled his shoulders, tensed his body, back in the ring in his head. He still sang as Walsh joined Doolan with Paddy, calming Mulligan. Mulligan struggled, spat obscenities, roared a threat. He eased off when Walsh put a hand on his face.

Then Walsh turned to Callum.

'Hey,' he said.

Callum was staring at Mulligan, still singing.

'Hey!'

Callum stopped. It was the first time he'd heard Walsh raise his voice.

Walsh said, 'What's your fuckin' problem?'

Callum felt his eyes filling up and ran his arm across his face.

'You drag me here, to a fuckin' horror show,' he said, 'you

stand there like you're working in a slaughterhouse with your knives and shit; you show me the body of some guy you had me fight last week: what, now I have to cut him up? And then what? You kill me? Somebody gonna' find me in the river next week in wee pieces? Like a fuckin' jigsaw?'

Callum was coming back to earth now, hitting hard like Acosta's dead skull on the tiles. He'd lost it. Let his fear make him mad, spiraled into a crazy-rage.

I'm a fucking cop, he thought. This isn't the first body I've seen, I didn't kill Acosta. Lean on Doolan, he's the friend in the room. I gotta' find myself, regain control. I'm a goddamn cop.

A picture of Tara swam into his mind, sitting on a swing. He tucked the image away like a photograph in a wallet, somewhere in his head, away from this madness.

He laughed. It came out harsh and high-pitched. The others stared.

'You aren't gonna' kill me?'

'What the fuck?' said Walsh, 'I just put you on the payroll. Paddy, what's wrong with this guy?'

Paddy snorted.

'Just a crazy mick, I guess.'

'I like crazy,' said Walsh, 'when it's channeled. You use that crazy in the right way? You'll do alright.'

He walked over and gave Callum a soft slap on the cheek.

'My people are from Monaghan so I don't give a shit,' he said, 'but Jimmy here is from Galway stock. You drowning out that song got him pissed.'

Mulligan was back against the wall with his arms folded. He looked at Callum like he knew something was off. There was a black malevolence in his eyes.

Callum said, 'Listen, Mr. Mulligan, I'm sorry. I didn't mean nothing and I'm sorry for offending you.'

Walsh grabbed the back of Callum's neck and gave it a squeeze.

'Alright,' he said, 'but drop the Mister bullshit. It's Jimmy and Fintan, okay? Now, let's do what we came here to do.'

*

Later, the smell clung to him like a cheap booze sweat after a big night out, soaked into his nostrils. It wouldn't budge no matter how much he tried to smoke it out with a pack of Camels. He lay on the mattress near the toilet in the apartment on Bleecker listening to Paddy snore through the door of the bedroom and saw snapshots in his mind's eye like flash bulbs popping on a crime scene. Mulligan's mug fierce with concentration, his deep-set eyes blinking through the thread of smoke from his cigarette. Walsh wiping his slick, gloved hands on his butcher's apron and lecturing how you got to remove the lungs of the corpse if you want it to sink in the river and not bob back up to the surface. Leering talk about some Latina actress called Lopez been on TV. Paddy's incessant chatter and wisecracks, his eyes wild, up to his elbows in blood. And the sounds: wet sounds, slapping sounds, the grate of tensile steel on bone.

When they were done and had wrapped the pieces of what had been Dylan Acosta in the plastic sheeting, Paddy and Callum had walked back through the still streets. Doolan's voice had seemed huge in the emptiness when he spoke.

'You did good, Christy.'

'You could've warned me, Paddy.'

'Now it's over, would you have wanted me to? I mean, would you have wanted to know that was coming?'

Callum had looked at Doolan, looked up to the sky wedged between the rooftops, and shook his head.

'It's Fintan's thing,' said Paddy. 'You want to be on his crew, you got to get your hands dirty. What we did back there was something you won't never forget, it's a kinda' bond.'

'I fought that guy a week ago. Did they shoot him as soon as we were out of that fucking basement?'

'Listen, Christy, you didn't kill Acosta: Acosta did. He knew he was dealin' on Fintan's turf. The beatin' you gave him was a warning. A couple of the guys drove the asshole home and rolled him out of the car onto the street. His mom found him. And you know what the stupid prick does? Hits the same fucking corner the next night, selling his dope. Only one way that was gonna' pan out.'

'But you gave me his head,' said Callum. 'The fucking head. I had to look him in his black eyes and take a hammer to his head.'

'Fintan's orders. Makes it more personal. Look, chances are, you're never gonna' kill anyone working for Fintan. This ain't a movie with bodies dropping every other day so furthest you'll go is giving someone a beatin'. Fintan's got guys for the stronger stuff.'

'Guys like Jimmy Mulligan?'

'Yeah, like Mulligan. But you need to see the consequences of what we do. You also need to get the teeth out of the body to fuck up identification. That's why you took the hammer to the guy. Anyways, let's go home and get some sleep. You'll feel better.'

So they had walked on and Callum had shoved his hands in his jeans pockets, and the fingers of his right hand had brushed the bullet fragment and the chipped molar he had dug out of Dylan Acosta's ruined face when the others were laughing and chatting.

And now Callum lay on the mattress and remembered, and thought of the bullet and tooth now in the coin pocket of his jeans. He remembered the hole he dug back in Hong Kong with his gambling. The hole he'd climbed out of with Stanley Bamboo Zhao's death. He remembered putting the bet on his own fight with Acosta. Callum had gambled and made money on beating the man. Now, he knew, he'd never place a bet again.

And he remembered one other thing Paddy Doolan had said when they were almost back at the apartment. He remembered how Paddy had muttered, almost to himself, how that wasn't right, though, that just wasn't right: how Fintan Walsh had called Trinity – his beautiful, precious Trinity – a goddamn freak show back in the abandoned longshoreman's building where they'd torn Dylan Acosta apart like a pack of wolves.

Chapter Fourteen

The boat pitched and rolled. Tony Lau flicked his cigarette over the starboard side of the fishing trawler into the waters of the South China Sea. He looked to the stern and saw, far distant, the lights of Port Shelter winking in the dark.

The surgical-style mask hung around his neck and he scratched at his throat where it tickled his skin. The odor of the chemical processes inside the trawler still hung in the air on deck despite the efforts of a stiff sea breeze and he regretted the cigarette. It had only served to clog his nose and mouth, thickening the rotting-garbage-stench of the refining process. The chemists were working below deck producing the heroin that would be sold in Hong Kong and Kowloon, and shipped abroad. The Number 3 H, the whitish-brown powder of 65-70% pure heroin so popular on the Triads' home turf; and the Number 4 H, to be injected by needle, impossible to smoke as it would evaporate. The chemists were well rewarded for their labors but they, too, struggled with the reek of the process. Lau had seen the small Buddhist shrine in the laboratory and the burning incense, an offering and attempt to combat the stench.

Once ready, the heroin would go through yet another chemical process. The taxidermy employer of David Chau, shot down on the Central tram, would be the final step in the chain to ready the narcotics for shipment to New York via Singapore and the Suez Canal.

The trawler was one of a fleet that had sailed from Thailand. It was registered to a Triad-owned company in Bangkok. No Thai trawler needed to file destination plans with the Thai maritime authorities and the company was no more than a telephone in an empty room. If the trawler was captured by naval or coastguard forces, it would be impossible to identify the true owner.

'Are you ill, Leader?' said the enforcer, Tse.

Lau smiled and dismissed the concern with a wave of his hand. Tse had become something of a personal bodyguard in the months since they had stood in General Khun Sa's village and signed off on the consignment of Shan States opium. Lau and his enforcer had founded a relationship of mutual respect. Tse offered his loyalty. He had come to realize that Tony Lau rewarded efficiency and competence, was a fair and just Dragon Head with plans for the future beyond the Communist takeover in two years, and would bring great success and wealth to those who proved themselves worthy.

Tony Lau had great love for his former Dragon Head, Father Zhao, but he could not deny there was a level of cronyism in the choice of personnel among the higher ranks of their Society. Lau had been forced to promote an imbecile named Hai to Deputy Leader. It would not do to pass over the most senior man for the post, and yet he knew Hai had reached his position thanks to his cousin's prominent role in another powerful society. Like a marriage of convenience, Lau's predecessor had favored the fool, Hai, in order to forge ties with their rivals.

But Lau had plans. Hai would serve a purpose for a short time only. Once the idiot had outlived his usefulness and been removed, Lau planned to give his enforcer the Deputy Leader position. He had indicated as much on occasion to Tse with oblique references. He had come to understand the enforcer was not easily swayed and gave due consideration to the traditions and values of the Society, dying qualities among the younger generation of Triad recruits.

One of those qualities was to ignore pain. The Leader could not be seen to let the discomfort of seasickness take a toll.

Lau said, 'I am fine, Tse. The strong, salt air is a shock after the pollution of Hong Kong, is it not? But bracing.'

'Yes, Deputy Leader. This pitching and rolling could be put to good use with a couple of young women.'

They laughed at the joke but Tse knew his Dragon Head only used other women when abroad like during the trip to Thailand.

'Are you happy with the operation?' he said.

'All seems well, yes,' Lau said. 'Thank you for accompanying me out here.'

'As always, it is my privilege, Leader. Perhaps you would like to offer a short prayer at the shrine before we go? It would surely be auspicious.'

Lau sighed.

'It would, Tse. But I don't believe I could summon the inner peace and devotion to the Buddha to do justice to my prayers in such a setting. Instead, I will visit the Hung Shing Temple tomorrow and speak with the priests. I appreciate your sentiments, however.'

Tse offered a bow. He knew his leader was a man of private faith who insisted on visiting the temples and shrines of the city alone in order to achieve the highest level of inner peace.

Lau decided, against his better judgement, to light up another cigarette.

'Come, let's have a final smoke out here before the launch back home.'

Tse offered a cigarette and lit it for his Dragon Head, then attended to himself. They stood in silence for a moment. The water lapped against the hull massaging the blistered wood and a jet passed overhead bound for the thrill-ride landing at Kai Tak airport.

Tse looked to the sky and said, 'It'll be sad, when they close Kai Tak.'

'All things must pass,' said Lau. 'The new airport will be miles out of the city.'

'The British will be gone by the time it's ready.'

'Yes. The British will be gone.'

'I sometimes think the Communists won't be so bad for business,' said Tse. 'After all, they need all the money they can get.'

Lau took a long drag on his cigarette and looked out to sea. Beyond the horizon lay Taiwan and the Philippines, and the vast Pacific. Then, finally, the United States of America. The Golden Mountain.

'Nevertheless,' he said, 'it is prudent to invest much of our funds in foreign projects.'

Tse nodded, finished his cigarette and threw it overboard.

'I have been scouting locations for the summit with the New York Tong,' he said. 'I found a hotel in Kowloon that seems suitable. Removed from much of the city, secure. I will provide the details for your approval, Leader.'

'Secure. Yes, security is of the utmost importance. Our American brethren have sadly inherited some of their adopted homeland's bombast.'

Now the 14K Triad's front company, Phoenix Investments, was buying property around Ong's territory, the Tong were beginning to sweat and express their concerns over Hong Kong encroachment. Yet the Tong relied on Hong Kong business, Hong Kong imports. Hong Kong heroin.

Tse said, 'I shall ensure The Tong leader enjoys the utmost safety while in our care.'

Lau tossed the remains of his smoke to the South China Sea.

'I have no doubt,' he said. He watched the dark waters swallow the glowing tip of the cigarette.

New York Tong leader Sammy Ong was an old man, shrewd but stubborn. He would never relinquish his territory, would use his police and political connections against any who came for him. The 14K Triad had slowly, methodically been flooding the Chinatown banks with their cash through the front company, Phoenix Investments, and had begun investing in New York Chinatown real estate. Through an unspoken law, the more businesses were housed in Triad buildings, the fewer from which the Tongs and their street gang could claim protection money. The more Triad capital in the banks, the more the financial institutions would favor Hong Kong money over that of the Tongs, and the less transparency they would afford the Hip Sing of Triad investments. A calibrated ploy to draw Ong out, to raise questions among those in his Tong regarding his power and suitability to lead – particularly among the young.

So now the Hip Sing Tong Leader would come to Lau to negotiate.

Lau smiled at the distant lights of the shore.

He and his enforcer began their lurching walk along the deck to the launch. They reached the small craft and climbed in. The pilot cast off and they began skipping across the waves toward the shore.

Tse leaned toward his Dragon Head and shouted above the engine.

'Perhaps this trip, on this boat, would be too much for Leader Ong.'

Lau said, 'Indeed.'

Tse leaned back in his seat, rolling with the motion of the launch, and said, 'We should respect those with the wisdom of age.'

Tony Lau nodded and folded his arms.

'My father always said,' he declared, 'a man must grow old and live long in order to see just how short life truly is.'

The lights of Port Shelter gave a wink of assent.

Chapter Fifteen

'That's it, I'm out.'

'How d'you figure?'

Callum spread his arms wide.

'I was party to the dismemberment of a body. The man had been executed. I got you evidence: a bullet and a tooth dug out of the corpse. I'll give testimony, the word of an undercover police officer. You put Walsh, Mulligan and Doolan away and it's game over.'

Mike O'Connell shrugged. He took a sip of Welch's and burped long and hard.

'That ain't the endgame here, Burke. We put the Irish away, where does that leave the Chinese? The DEA want the Tong, we all want the Triads and nobody wants you back in uniform.'

They stood in a derelict warehouse in Long Island City, Queens, next to an empty cargo crate. Callum kicked the crate. He stubbed a toe.

'I was involved in a criminal act. You have to pull me: it endangers your whole investigation.'

'No,' said O'Connell. He slammed the can of Welch's on the crate. It spat grape soda.

'What endangers my investigation is some whiny-assed bitch crying about how he's half-a-cop and got weak at the knees at the sight of a little blood.' He held up his hand and began folding down fingers with each point.

'You engaged in an unlicensed, bare-knuckle boxing fight and gambled on said fight; you were present in an establishment where people were buying and taking illegal narcotics; you were party to the dismemberment of a body, dead of a gunshot wound. The first two, you reported days after the fact. The last was day before yesterday. You withheld illegal activity from your handler, Burke. I can get you busted off this case and out of the Hong Kong Force, possibly prosecuted on criminal charges.'

Callum took a step forward and felt a flush of warmth at the nervous flutter of O'Connell's eyelids.

'Fuck you!' he said. 'I couldn't report to you because I was undercover and didn't have an opportunity to schedule a meet. And where the hell is Milburn?'

'Busy with Ho,' said O'Connell, 'I'm all you got.'

His spit flecked Callum's t-shirt. 'You pull this investigation, I'll fuck you so hard in the ass you'll never shit properly again.'

Callum balled his fists. 'You asshole. You can lock these guys up for life on a murder charge and you'll take a pass? What happens if they kill again? Can you live with that?'

O'Connell fished car keys out of his pocket.

'Come on,' he snapped.

*

They left the warehouse and climbed into a blue Ford Thunderbird rental. O'Connell drove south, the East River on their right. When they hit Dumbo, Brooklyn, he took the ramp onto the Brooklyn Bridge and drove across the river. The lights of Civic Center and the Financial District gleamed on the water and Sweet Jane came on the radio. For a moment, Callum loved New York.

Then they passed the squat bulk of One Police Plaza and the streets seemed to darken. City Hall was a haunted mansion, speckled with dim lights behind heavy curtains. Foley Square and the courthouses were like ruins on the deserted streets, as though time had preserved them as relics of a lost empire.

A block from Canal Street the neon kicked in, the signage like tracer fire stretching down the straight shot of Centre Street.

The Thunderbird took a couple of turns down narrow thorough-fares clogged with neon. The sidewalk shone with spilt water from produce stalls, and empty fish crates lay stacked next to hydrants. The streets were filled with Chinese strolling, brows-ing the late-opening stores, yelling and laughing and lining up outside dumpling or noodle joints. Callum felt something lurch inside. Something disconnecting. The scene outside the car was Kowloon or Hong Kong Island. Until you looked above the store fronts to the clutter of fire escapes clinging to New York brick. He wanted to hold his daughter, to lie with Irene. He wanted the real, the solid. Certainty.

'The On Leong Tong headquarters,' said O'Connell.

He pointed out the window to a large concrete building on the corner of Mott Street, all pillars and balconies with a dramatic, pagoda-style roof. They drove on, Callum more disorientated with each turn. O'Connell took it slow down Pell and jerked his thumb out the window at a plain five-story brick walk-up with a zig-zag fire escape on front.

'The Hip Sing outfit. Don't look like much, huh?'

More turns. More neon. Callum shifted in his seat. He imag-ined if he set foot outside the car he'd be grabbed, or catch a bullet, or spontaneously-fucking-combust. The fever-paranoia of the undercover.

O'Connell turned the Thunderbird onto the small side-street of Elizabeth. A couple of cop cars were parked at the curb and O'Connell pulled in twenty yards from a townhouse with green lanterns lit either side of the door.

Callum said, 'The Fifth Precinct?'

'The Fifth.'

'Are we going in for tea and biscuits?'

'Milk and cookies, man.'

Callum pulled a pack of cigarettes from his pocket.

'Don't smoke in here,' said O'Connell, 'I don't want to stink like an ashtray when I go home. I quit four years ago and my wife'll worry I started up again, she smells it on my clothes. I don't want my kids to smell it, either.'

'That's nice. You have a family, you have kids. You care about them. So a human being lurks in there somewhere.'

'Yeah, I care about them. So I'm sitting in a car with you in Chinatown and pulling overtime every chance I get. I finish a shift I go for a drink with Mattila, get home and flake out for a couple hours.' O'Connell sat back in the driver's seat and looked at the green lanterns on the precinct wall like cats' eyes reflecting light in the gloom. 'I love my family but I'm a dog – I love this shit, too. Running and gunning. Like Jimmy Solano.'

Callum rubbed his temple. He watched a couple of cops leave the precinct house.

'Alright, I'll bite,' he said, 'who's Jimmy Solano?'

'Manhattan South Narcotics guy two years back. Made a buy on Mulberry undercover, told the guys to hold the product while he went to get more cash; called in more cops and went to bust the dealers. They'd agreed to meet in a grocery store. Soon as he walked through the door they shot him. Two bullets, one in his carotid. He bled out before the responders could get him to the hospital.'

'If this is a pep talk, you're a bit wide of the mark.'

'I never worked with Jimmy, didn't know him. I don't know his wife and two sons. But I knew the grocery store owner who got his throat cut by the Flying Dragons for allowing their guys to get busted in his store. And the Flying Dragons are a street gang affiliated with?'

'The Hip Sing Tong.'

'Give that man a prize. Now, these guys,' – O'Connell pointed to the Fifth – 'knew the names behind the kids did the hit. City Hall knew the names but this community, man: it's locked up so fucking tight.'

Callum nodded.

'I hear you,' he said. 'Same in Kowloon. The dickheads pulling triggers are just the scum floating on the surface while the top guys are busy lunching with the great and the good. The number of times we had a murder or drugs charge where we knew a Dragon Head was the source of the crime, and had to suck it up while HKP brass shook hands on a rostrum with the bastard.'

O'Connell pulled the Thunderbird out on the street.

They drove in silence and listened to the city churn outside the windows. Streets became wider and brighter and O'Connell swung the car west. Past Penn Station, the strip of sex shops and peep shows and strip clubs began on 8th Avenue, stretching to 42nd Street. A couple of blocks over the street girls would be working the entrance to Lincoln Tunnel, catching the incoming traffic from Jersey.

The Thunderbird drove into a grid of brownstones, townhouses, tenements and decrepit building-shells. Callum began counting the bag ladies weaving through foot traffic making for Broadway. O'Connell parked up on west 50th and Callum felt a worm of paranoia gnaw at his gut. The New World Movers parking lot was a couple of blocks away.

O'Connell said, 'The One-Eight is that way, Midtown North Precinct. I knew a cop there, Brian Flannagan. Good Irish name for you. Brian followed a couple of guys into a building near Worldwide Plaza, just up 50th here, three years ago. They end up in the elevator together, close quarter gunfight. Brian gets shot four times and still manages to wound one of the guys. Any guesses where the shooters were from?'

'Fintan Walsh's crew.'

'Right. Walsh moved out to Woodside, Doolan has shacked up in The Village, but their poison is still running through Hell's Kitchen. The neighborhood is changing, sure. This Clinton bullshit, like renaming the area's gonna' wipe out the past. We got the uptown crowd moving in, the working class moving out: Black, Hispanic, Asian, Polish and honest to God Irish. But everybody remembers The Westies and everybody knows the remnants of Irish crime in Manhattan still lie in The Kitchen.'

Callum scratched his chin. It hid the tremble in his hand.

He said, 'They murdered Dylan Acosta for selling drugs on a corner somewhere around here.'

'That's a street corner pusher butchered but how many honest people have suffered because of these assholes? Paying protection, kids fucked up by drugs, bodies in the East River. And these are my people. The Irish, came here and carved something out of the shit end of the stick we were handed, fought for turf, fought for a foot in the door, political influence. We policed this city, built a chunk of it. The tourists come and drink in our bars. On Saint Paddy's Day, everybody in New York claims to be or wants to be Irish. We're still moving up – I don't want my kids to be cops. They're gonna' be white collar or doctors or some shit.'

O'Connell leaned in close and licked his lips.

'But every time Fintan Walsh pulls a move; every time some guy with a bodega has to hand over money to Walsh's crew just to stay in business, I'm fucking ashamed.'

'So put them away for Acosta's murder,' said Callum.

'I don't even know if I got them for murder. We can put them at a post-murder scene. You got a tooth and a bullet but you can be damn sure the gun it was fired from is at the bottom of the river right now.'

O'Connell put his finger to his chest.

'I want these motherfuckers for all of it. Murder, extortion, narcotics, rackets. And we get them for all of that – for the wider picture – we got a RICO case. We got a RICO case, we can pull the Chinese in. We prosecute them through association and parade the whole shit show in front of the press for the world to see.'

Callum laughed. It sounded like a crazy man's giggle.

'In the meantime,' he said, 'you have a dead undercover officer with no return address. Where are you gonna' send my body: Hong Kong? Belfast?'

He felt something cold between his shoulder blades at the truth of what he'd said. He envied O'Connell his surety. Irish. A New Yorker. An honest-to-God cop. Callum looked out the window at a bag lady pushing a shopping cart full of rags past a young man standing out front of a dive bar sucking from a bottle wrapped in a paper bag.

'I need a drink,' he said. He kept his eyes on the street.

*

A couple walked by Charles Schurz Park and ducked inside through the trees. The contoured lawns, paved walkways and stone features glowed in the city lights, deserted at night.

'What is this, Canada?' said the man. The couple linked arms and continued their walk along East End Avenue headed south. Headed away from Harlem.

Callum took a swig of beer. The paper bag around the can rustled in the quiet of the park, the low hum of white noise from the city barely audible in this corner of Yorkville on the Upper East Side. Mike O'Connell sat next to him on the lawn and sipped at a bottle of Snapple. Across the East River the lights strung along the Triborough Bridge shimmered through tree branches. Callum thought of driving the truck across the bridge weeks ago with Willie and J.J., snapping at the guys after they snorted heroin in the cab.

O'Connell glanced at the five empty beer cans on the grass and the drink in Callum's hand.

'We should get you back to The Village soon. Paddy Doolan might start wondering where you are.'

'He'll think I'm doing this,' said Callum raising his can, 'drinking somewhere. He won't wait up, trust me.'

Callum finished the beer and picked up a fresh can from a Morton Williams bag. O'Connell took it from him and slid it into a paper bag then scooped up the empties. Callum watched the cop clean up and pulled the ring on the next Labatt.

'I love this city,' he said.

'How much of that beer did you drink?'

'I'm serious. You can be anyone here. You can be a different person day-to-day.'

O'Connell took a sip of Snapple. 'Isn't everyone a different person day-to-day?'

Callum grabbed a cigarette from the pack next to him on the grass.

'But it's the melting pot, isn't it? I mean, I know that's bullshit and all. You got your areas where people cluster: Spanish Harlem, Chinatown, Little Italy, Brighton Beach. But still, most people probably have three or four bloodlines in the mix after all the years of immigration and whatnot.'

'*Whatnot*? What the hell is *whatnot*?'

Callum sparked up the cigarette. He took care to blow the smoke in a steady stream away from O'Connell.

'How about you?' said O'Connell. 'What're your bloodlines?'

'You read the file. I'm a mongrel. English and Protestant on my mother's side; my father, Irish-American and Catholic: that's a potent combination in Belfast. My grandfather was an Italian-American came to Belfast during WWII with the Army Rangers. He met a local girl and took her back to Boston. They married, had my dad and he came back as a young man to see Belfast and fell in love with my ma, who was studying at Queen's. I was born there.'

'So what, are you English, Irish? American now?'

'I'm Irish, Northern Irish, whatever you want to call it, but I never really fit. In the police back home, the RUC, one guy – my friend – in my station used to call me the irregular. Irregular Irishman. I used to laugh but it kinda' pissed me off. Then my friend was shot by a sniper.'

'That's hard, man.' O'Connell looked at Callum. His eyes were large and clear in the lights from the street.

Callum said, 'You know what I did? I ran away. Went to the funeral, drank for six months, fucked up on the job. I was gonna' get myself or one of the lads killed. We didn't have any support for that shit, just Bushmills and time. Then I saw some news report from Hong Kong on TV and thought that was my way out.' He took a drag on his smoke. 'So I ran away.'

He remembered the application process. Counting the days until he left the RUC, thinking there was still plenty of time for a car bomb or a mortar or a bullet to end his career early. He had stayed at a friend's place in London before flying out east, had spent the morning alone in the house before making his way to Heathrow, pacing the rooms whispering to himself. Weighing options, his insides getting colder, his body hollowing out: feeling more and more alone. But something had pushed him to take the train to the airport, to pass through immigration, to get on the flight.

He had felt a sharper, distilled shot of that same solitude in the basement when he fought Acosta; in the bathroom when he had cut the man up.

O'Connell said, 'And was Hong Kong your way out?'

Callum looked across the water to Queens but his head was back in the room in Wan Chai watching Stanley Bamboo Zhao choke up what was left of his life. The young prostitute watching Callum, Callum watching the Dragon Head turn his insides out as the heroin burned in his veins. He had felt nothing as he ushered the girl out of the room but he'd thought plenty. Thought how he'd busted Zhao's nephew's jaw. How the nephew had held the debt Callum had accrued on a string of losing bets with the 14K. How he'd let his anger at his own weakness and stupidity drive him to fuck with the younger Triad. He had thought how Zhao had paid Callum's debt in order to buy himself a tame cop on the Hong Kong Force. How Callum would have begun feeding information straight to Bamboo Zhao that week if the old man hadn't coughed up his last in that Wan Chai brothel.

And he'd thought, as he slipped on his gloves and eased the Dragon Head's contact book and pocket ledger from his jacket, how he had just acquired the only evidence of his gambling, his debts and his connections to the 14K faction from the corpse of the Triad'Dragon Head. The old man had been old school. He kept business personal. The paper trail began and ended with the books Callum placed in his uniform pockets. The 14K would know the truth – the nephew, Tony Lau and some others but the proof was in Callum's tunic pocket ready for burning. When he slipped out of the room the whore was crying softly in the corridor. He had to raise his voice above her sobs to call the ambulance.

Now the nephew was a dead junkie like Zhao, and Tony Lau was thousands of miles away.

He looked at Mike O'Connell and wondered what the cop would say if Callum spilled it all. What Milburn would do if he knew.

Callum took another drink.

'Hong Kong was Disneyland,' he said, 'it wasn't reality. A bunch of white police running a force of Chinese in China.'

'Like your buddy, Milburn?'

'He isn't the worst. One of the best, to be honest. He's learned some of the language, rates the Chinese officers, gives them respect. Milburn has a lot of time for Bobby Ho.'

O'Connell said, 'He's the most English thing I've seen since that stuttering prick, whatsisname? Hugh Grant.'

Callum hadn't heard. He was back in Hong Kong again in his early ex-pat days.

'It was crazy,' he said. 'Bar-girls, lots of drink, few if any consequences. There were good men there, plenty. But if you wanted, it was a time to let your baser instincts run wild.'

He smoked. O'Connell hadn't taken his eyes off him.

'I met Irene. We had our wee girl, Tara. Suddenly, everything was real again. It was like God just flipped the world over like a pancake. Everything looked the same but it was like I was split in two: half of me sleeping in my arms when I got home at night. You have kids. You know.'

'Yeah, I hear you.'

'And you want to do right by your family. You want the best for them and you hold yourself to these impossible fucking standards, you know? And a cop's salary ... well, you get it.'

'Damn straight I understand that part,' said O'Connell. His voice was soft and low.

A helicopter flew along the Queens shoreline across the river, a red light blinking on the nose cone. Callum threw his empty can, losing it in the gloom of the park before picking up the soft clatter of its landing on the paving somewhere to the right of the lawn.

O'Connell shook his head.

'I could bust you for that. Broken Windows policing, courtesy of the man in the big house over there.'

He cocked a thumb toward where Gracie Mansion, official residence of Mayor Rudolf Giuliani, sat near the northern boundary of the park.

'A slab of overtime in Central Booking downtown for me,' said O'Connell, 'and a couple hours for you in The Tombs. Might do your credibility some good with Walsh and his crew.'

Callum pulled the ring on another can.

'So if I go right here, I'm pissing on the Mayor's lawn?'

'You need a leak, you hide behind a tree. Last thing we need is a cop walking by sees you. Then I gotta' explain things and suddenly the 23rd Precinct is gossiping about some Irish meathead with an NYPD Fairy Godfather.'

'I'll spare you the indignity,' said Callum. He took a swig on the beer. It was starting to taste like shit. 'How powerful is the mayor?'

O'Connell shrugged.

'I guess he's the boss of the city. If this is the biggest and best city in the world, I guess Giuliani is the most important mayor out there. But let's face it, New York is one big pain in the ass. I wouldn't wanna' be responsible for it.'

'Is he the Mayor of Chinatown, too?'

'What, you're saying it's Sammy Ong?'

'Hong Kong's got a Governor. Right now it's a man called Patten. But in Tsim Sha Tsui or Mong Kok or Yuen Long, he's nothing. There, it's the Triad bosses. The Dragon Heads.'

'Like Old Man Bamboo Zhao, right?'

Callum lit another smoke. He looked east as he spoke, jabbing the air with his cigarette like he was lecturing Queens.

'Stanley Bamboo Zhao. You know why that oul' bastard had the nickname Bamboo? Ever been hit with a bamboo rod? It's fucking agony.' Callum took a long pull on the beer. 'He ran the gamut of Triad crime: Protection money, drugs, prostitution, smuggling, stolen goods. His organization snatched young girls off the street in poor areas. Then they systematically raped them and called it *stamping the merchandise*, can you believe that?'

O'Connell's eyes darkened as he leaned back in the shadow.

Callum sniffed and took another swig from his can.

'Any girl is gonna' feel like her world is over but the shame for a Chinese – you can't imagine. So the Triad forced the girls to work as prostitutes. They sold them to brothels and the price

160

became the girls' debt. They had to work it off but only ten percent of what they earned went to the debt. It could take at least ten years to work that off – can you comprehend what ten years of hooking does to a teenage girl?'

The air had become colder and O'Connell hunkered down into his coat. Callum swung his can in the air, spilling beer.

'Boys, too. The Triads sold weak ones to Southeast Asia, or to the Yakuza. They recruited the tougher boys. I ask you, O'Connell, how do you bust a brothel and wrap a blanket around a shivering thirteen-year-old, then go home to your little girl and play dolls and tea parties?'

O'Connell said, 'I dunno'.'

He looked at the dark lawn, awkward and self-conscious.

Callum was crying.

'Still,' said Callum, wiping his eyes, cigarette still wedged between his fingers, 'there's no difference in shoveling up what's left of a child after a bomb back in Belfast. It's the desecration of innocence.' He laughed hard and bitter. 'That's a mouthful after a slew of beers.'

Someone yelled on the street behind and the keen of a siren came to them from Harlem like the wail of a grieving mother.

'We should go,' said O'Connell. 'Go back to Doolan's apartment and sleep this off.'

Callum turned, his eyes raw in the light from the city, his cheeks lined with shining tear tracks, and looked at the New York cop. He had dropped his cigarette without realizing. A frown furrowed his forehead and he spoke with deliberation, desperate to get his message through, or not trusting O'Connell to understand.

'I just want to do something good, Mike,' he said. 'Something to make me believe I deserve my little girl. To prove myself to Irene.'

O'Connell made to stand. Callum grabbed his shoulder.

'We'll get Walsh and his crew. Then the Chinese. No more violence. No more drugs. No more kids. We'll get them together, Mike. Like the NYPD motto says.'

He wiped a thread of snot from his nose.

'Faithful unto death.'

Chapter Sixteen

Georgie Ruiz read through her notebook. Burke was still on the job but had point blank refused to wear a wire or recorder again after the close call at the shooting gallery. Mattila and O'Connell had agreed. Burke would update O'Connell at their meets and call in when needed, and Mattila would write up the Bi-Op reports. That left a lot hanging on Callum Burke's word but a cop's testimony still held weight in the criminal justice system. For now.

She and Galinski kept periodic watch on Burke. Weeks of ghosting him and Ruiz had written pages. Nothing compromising beyond breaking up a bar brawl, nothing embarrassing but for a cut on his face could have been the result of a fight.

If she were in Burke's shoes, Ruiz thought she wouldn't want to see the evidence of someone watching most of her public moves. She'd spoken to officers who'd been undercover, knew how paranoid the life could make you. And sometimes the voyeuristic side of the job made her feel a little dirty.

Many nights Burke went drinking with Paddy Doolan in bars around Greenwich Village or Times Square or the Upper West Side. Ruiz had written lists of stores Burke had visited with Doolan to collect protection money. They would enter, spend between five and fifteen minutes inside, then leave with smiles on their faces. Sometimes Doolan slipped an envelope into a pocket as they walked out the door. Delis, bodegas, laundromats, a cigar store. Most were on the West Side near midtown between 8th Avenue and the Hudson but there were a scattering of others. A convenience store by West 79th Street Subway, a pizza slice joint on West 70th; and a large brownstone on West

96th and Broadway she knew housed the S&M club where Doolan's girlfriend worked – the Nurse Löwin who Sol Grundy had visited the night he was shot down.

She kept the notes tucked in her pocket when not scribbling, tilting the book away from Galinski when writing – jealously guarding her observations. She recorded extraneous details: that Callum Burke had lost weight, that he looked stressed or angry or just burned out. At times he barked at his crews and chained cups of coffee. He was smoking more. He seemed at his worst when moving jobs took him to storage facilities in the outer boroughs.

She was too close, she knew.

Ruiz imagined Galinski laughing – 'What are you, his mama?'

But the man's psychological and emotional state would be crucial when the DA took the case to court and used his testimony. And on a deeper level, she couldn't comprehend the loneliness of Callum Burke's situation. She couldn't imagine being so far from home, from those she loved, alone among those animals. Walsh, Mulligan, and Doolan.

A name popped into her head, Joseph 'Joe' Petrosino. The only NYPD officer murdered on the job on foreign soil. Gunned down in Palermo in 1909 while investigating the Sicilian mafia. She hoped to God that Burke wouldn't become the answer to some macabre pop quiz question – Who was the only Hong Kong cop murdered in the United States?

*

The BOJ Fashion studio was SoHo chic – interior walls stripped back to brickwork, bare floors, and pretentious asshole in four-hundred dollar jeans and t-shirt that looked exactly like Levis and a Target top to Mike O'Connell.

'And you are a relatively new studio?' James Milburn asked the man.

'Relatively,' said the asshole, an emaciated thirty-year-old called Emile, sporting lensless glasses frames with lanky, shoulder-length black hair. His voice was a loud, nasal whine.

Emile clapped his hands together and bowed to Milburn. 'I'm sorry, you probably hear this all the time but I love your accent. I spent six months working in London and had the best time.'

'I'm gratified.'

They sat in a small side office off the main reception. The exposed brick wall behind Emile's desk sported a BOJ Garments logo; two walls were concrete and the fourth, facing onto the corridor, was glass. The business of designing and manufacturing the clothes went on elsewhere in the expansive space in lower SoHo.

'So, yes,' said Emile. 'We're a new face on the scene. It's one of the reasons we set up here rather than the Garment District. The rival houses are always spying on one another, head-hunting staff. It's savage.'

'Primal, I'm sure.'

'Even here, we lost one of our best people last month. Kevin Zuk. He just came in one day and said he'd quit at five o'clock.'

'Where'd he go?' said O'Connell.

'He wouldn't say but I have my suspicions. There's a big push at DKNY right now and they're spending like crazy. Their billboards are everywhere.'

'This space can't be cheap,' said O'Connell looking around.

'Sure, but we're far enough from Houston and close enough to Canal to shave a few dollars off the lease.'

'Excuse me,' said Ho. 'You design and produce clothing?'

'Exactly,' said Emile. 'We work in animal, vegetable and synthetic textiles from design to manufacture.'

O'Connell said, 'You been here a couple months. How come you haven't changed the phone number?'

'The old tenant moved out over a year ago but the building

owner maintained the number. It was easier for us to hit the ground running with a number already in place.'

'You don't think it's strange the building owner kept the number?'

'Maybe? I guess? But it was a selling point, you know.'

'And you never get calls for the old tenant?'

'Like I said, they moved out a while ago. I guess they hadn't been in business for months. It hasn't been a problem. We'll probably keep things as they are. Hey,' said Emile, leaning in and lowering his voice, 'you guys are cops: has there been a murder here or something?'

O'Connell said. 'Not yet.'

Milburn said, 'We are not investigating this business or address in particular. Another property on the block is being investigated for building violations. We simply need to speak to several other properties and tenants on the same street in order to present a case of wrongdoing by comparison when we take the offending parties to court. We don't require statements or any further action from you. We shall seek a conviction on testimony – ours.'

Emile was despondent, his dreams of a true-crime story for the Tribeca wine bars dead in the water. O'Connell was looking at Milburn with a raised eyebrow and the word *bullshit* written across his eyes.

'I would remind you,' said Milburn, 'that this is a conversation between yourself and three law enforcement officials. Should you share what we discuss in this room with anyone, you are open to arrest and prosecution under Case Confidentiality Violation Laws for the State of New York.'

O'Connell shifted in his seat at Milburn's cop-speak bull.

Emile brightened. This was sounding more salacious and exciting.

'You got it,' he said.

Milburn nodded and said, 'What was the building owner's name again?'

'Two-Six-Three Holdings.'

'How did you pay your lease?'

'BOJ Garments paid into the owner's corporate account. Give me a second to remember the bank.'

Emile took his glasses frames off and placed his thumb and forefinger on either side of his temple.

'Denise in accounts knows,' he said. 'No, wait, I got it. United Oriental Bank. You reminded me of the name, Detective.' Emile smiled at Bobby Ho. Then his features melted in horror.

'Oh my God,' he said, 'was that racist? *Oriental*? I'm so sorry!'

'No problem,' said Ho. 'You're sure it was United Oriental?'

'Absolutely. Is that important?'

'Not at all,' said O'Connell.

'Excuse me,' said Ho, 'you mentioned the textiles you work with, animal, vegetable and synthetic. Can you give us a list?'

Emile's eyes narrowed. 'Is this some kind of fire hazard issue?' he said.

'Just professional curiosity,' said Ho. 'My brother is a tailor in Hong Kong. He works with various materials too.'

Milburn gave Ho an appreciative glance. He knew the Chinese cop's brothers, all three, worked at the airport in customs, air traffic control, and security.

'Sure, I can do that,' said Emile. 'Give me a couple of minutes. It's just the usual, though. Cotton, silk, hemp, wool, leather. We even do some work on the leathers in-house.'

O'Connell said, 'Oh yeah, what does that involve?'

'Sometimes we have to soften the leathers in order to work with them. God, they can look so starved when we get them, depending on the supplier. We use fat liquors to re-grease. Sometimes for pull-up items, too. You know, proofing against the weather, creating surface effects and so on.'

Bobby Ho leaned forward.

He said, 'What is in these fats?'

'Fat liquors? Raw materials are oils like fish oils, claw oil, pig fat. Or palm oil, coconut fat, some waxes.'

'And alcohol?'

'Not our products. I know, the term is fat liquor and some brands have synthetic ingredients like fatty alcohol in, but we only use natural products.'

'Admirable,' said Milburn.

'Well,' said Emile, 'let me get you that list.'

'That would be great, thank you.'

Emile backed out the door and walked off down the corridor.

O'Connell said, 'Fat liquors.'

'Used in tanning,' said Milburn. 'Perhaps taxidermists would have some knowledge of the process.'

'Like your dead body on the Hong Kong tram.'

'David Chau,' said Ho.

They sat in silence, each walking through the facts and exploring possible connections. Triad owned Phoenix Investments leading to Two-Six-Three Holdings leading to BOJ Garments in SoHo but near Canal, right on the edge of Chinatown.

Fat Liquors, thought O'Connell, who'd have seen that coming? No doubt, being a cop threw more curveballs than Sandy Koufax. He could see the light in James Milburn and Bobby Ho's eyes. The shot of joy that you might have gained a couple of steps on the bad guys.

'You seen a lot of heroin smuggled through your turf in Hong Kong, right?' said O'Connell.

'Yes,' said Milburn. 'Wrapped in packages and hidden in fish, coffee shipments, even cow shit.'

'Mixed in baby powder,' said Ho, 'or rice.'

'I seen it dissolved in alcohol and bottled,' said O'Connell.

Ho said, 'Yes, heroin is soluble.'

Milburn said, 'And can be extracted later.'

Yep, thought O'Connell, we're on the yellow brick road. He took the shot.

'What if it could be dissolved in these fat liquors? I mean they're oil-based. Would that be a problem?'

'It wouldn't be easy,' said Milburn, 'but as my mother always said, nothing worth doing ever is. They must contain some acid and water as well as the oils.'

'So let's say for now that someone figured out a way to do it. What then?'

'If it can be extracted from booze,' said Ho, 'it can probably be extracted from fat liquor.'

'Perhaps by our missing tanner, Kevin Zuk,' said Milburn. 'So it's shipped over here as a tanning agent and extracted in New York for sale on the street.'

They sat quiet for another moment, weighing the likelihood and counter-arguments to the hypothesis forming.

'I gotta' take this to Mattila,' said O'Connell. 'The DEA got chemists we can consult on this. We should look into the build-ing owners, Two-Six-Three Holdings, too. They got an account in United Oriental: the bank – we figure – of choice for the 14K Triads.'

Ho said, 'Do you think this company is involved in anything illegal?'

'BOJ Garments? The only crime I see in this place is the price tag on the samples in their lobby. We can check them out, though.'

'Yes,' said Milburn. 'Strange story about this fellow Kevin Zuk, jumped ship last month.'

'Sure,' said O'Connell, 'although my guess? He couldn't stand our guy Emile's cologne.'

James Milburn allowed a wry smile.

Bobby Ho laughed.

*

Callum had picked up a beeper from a sullen Jimmy Mulligan at the New World office and then grabbed a breakfast sandwich. J.J. and Willie Simmons, methadone-free, had bought a consoling quart of Country Club each, sparking Dylan Acosta fight flashbacks in Callum's head. He watched the guys drink the cheap booze, joyless and methodical. He'd heard rumors among the crews that J.J. had been kicked out by his girlfriend.

The job had been a move in Jackson Heights. A Metro worker called Peter Carson, in deep with Walsh's bookies. Furniture to storage in Hunters Point. Storage probably meant drugs somewhere in the dressers or drawers. Storage meant an edge to Callum.

They drove to the storage place and lugged Carson's worldly possessions into the huge steel lockers, Callum guessing which piece held the narcotics. Then Callum's beeper went off.

'Fuck!'

The last job was a one-man vanilla – the phrase Doolan used for any move that was heroin-free. A couple in Woodside, Walsh territory. They were moving a couple of blocks from a house to an apartment and had rented their own truck but wanted help packing it, then unloading at the new address.

Shit! They were using their own truck. Callum would have to drop the New World truck at West 50th and take the 7 train back out to Queens.

Forty minutes later the 7 train crawled above ground on the Queens side of the East River and clanked past the Silvercup sign with the crazy bar-graph of the Manhattan skyline across the river. By the time it rolled into 61 St-Woodside station, Callum's mood was as foul as the weather. When he found the house it was much like Peter Carson's. The couple were in their late forties and offered him iced tea as soon as he got through the door. The wife busied herself inside while the husband and Callum packed the box truck and talked about the neighborhood. The husband, Phil, was third generation Irish-American, his wife, Samantha, a Jewess from San Francisco who moved to New York when the Sixties burned out. They had a daughter, Rhada, named by Samantha after a Hindu goddess, and were moving to an apartment to save on money after Radha's college tuition had cleaned them out three years ago.

When Callum and Phil went back in the house, Radha had arrived through the side door to help and was leaning against the worktop in the kitchen talking with Samantha. She was twenty-seven and had her mom's caramel skin and coal-black hair. Callum checked out her legs in her high-cut shorts and felt self-conscious in his stained work t-shirt and dirty jeans. Radha smiled and Samantha fussed around them, ushering everyone into the small living room where they sat on the floor and drank lemonade and ate small homemade cookies. Callum glanced at the windows, expecting to see Norman Rockwell set up with an easel. But he felt good, lighter than he had all day, maybe for weeks.

And he felt good about New York, and returned Radha's looks so her mom noticed and suggested they might like to go to the free black and white movie in Bryant Park next week. They finished up and, while Phil and Samantha packed the last of their belongings, Callum and Radha exchanged numbers.

'Might be nice,' said Radha. 'You like movies?'

'Sure. Are you really gonna' call me?'

'No,' she said, throwing him a casual smile and a toss of that sweet licorice hair, 'you're gonna' call me. Then we'll see.'

Callum felt sad when he saw their new home: an anonymous seven-story apartment block with sheer, featureless walls. Phil and Samantha, good people living decent, messy, loving lives and their reward for helping their daughter was a move from a small home crammed with memories to a soulless chunk of brick with the noise of the neighbors battering at the walls. While Fintan Walsh and Jimmy Mulligan and Paddy Doolan made more in a week than Phil could scrape together in a couple of months off the backs and toil and busted veins of others.

They finished the unload in an hour. Callum lost count of the jets flying over to land at LaGuardia Airport. When they were done Phil and Samantha pushed a roll of twenties in his palm.

'It's okay,' said Callum, 'the food and company was tip enough.'

'You take it,' said Phil. 'This city's our home but it can be a brutal place. You might need this sometime.'

'I have savings, really, but thank you for the kindness.'

Samantha gave him a serious look.

'Now you listen, Christy. Someday, you could have a child go to college and make you proud like us. And that costs, son. You aren't going to have the money to live that if you refuse help that's offered with the best of intentions. Take the tip and don't offend us.'

The serious look softened into a smile.

Callum took the cash. He thought of Tara. When this was over he would make damn sure he was a larger part of her life. He'd mend bridges with Irene. Life would be better.

Radha saw him out and they stood in front of the building looking at Doughboy Plaza, the WWI soldier statue perched on the small rise looking to the tall flagpole opposite. A 747 roared overhead.

'It was nice, you helping,' said Radha.

'It was nice, meeting you.'

'Yeah?'

'Yeah.'

She smiled and said, 'So, until next time?'

Irene flashed through his mind – he was still goddamned married – but he felt something with this woman standing in front of him right here and now. It felt like it could be the start of a journey, the kind he thought he might never have again. A shot at building something simple and strong and ... pure. Stupid? Maybe. Maybe Walsh and Mulligan and the rest were pushing all the wrong buttons and that made it seem somehow real important he see Radha again.

And O'Connell and Milburn would go crazy if he did. He couldn't start a relationship with a civilian in the middle of an undercover operation. But he couldn't stop wondering what it might feel like to lean in close and move his head and brush his lips against hers and ...

It took Callum a moment to realize his beeper was going off. Radha was still smiling. He could have stripped bare-ass and dived into those dark chocolate eyes.

He ignored the beeper.

She put her hand on his arm and let her fingers trail off his sleeve.

'Yo, man, you got the pink shirts?'

He was searching for something to say. Something to make her laugh and open a door for more next time. She took a step toward him and her smile got bigger as Callum stood there looking kind of helpless. She blushed a little and looked down at the sidewalk.

'Yo, man, the pink shirts.'

Radha hesitated and drew back some. Callum frowned.

'Yo, Romeo, the fuckin' pink shirts.'

He turned and saw a scrawny white guy standing behind him on the corner in a baggy t-shirt, loose denim shorts to his knees and Nike sneakers. His long hair looked like it hadn't been washed since Christmas and he had a crooked trail of track marks on his left arm.

'Listen, man,' said Callum, 'I don't know who you think I am, but I don't know what you're talking about.'

The man scratched his arm. 'Sure you do. I called the number, got redirected, and the dude said to come to Woodside Avenue and 56th Street. He said when I got here I should call and the dude would beep the guy with the shirts. So I used the call box across the street and heard your beeper go off.'

'Not me.'

'Sure it's you, I heard your beeper.'

'Walk on, man.'

'C'mon, man, I got the cash and I got the need. Gimme' a straw, huh?'

Callum stepped in close and spat, 'Walk the fuck on or you ain't gonna' be walking again.'

The scrawny guy stood dumb for a second.

Then he screeched, 'Yo, fuck you, man! I'm gonna' call Jimmy, gonna' get you fucked up! You costin' Jimmy business and me my good time, motherfucker!'

Callum turned back to Radha.

She was gone.

He stood for a second with no idea what to do or where to go. Then a red mist came down.

'You motherfucker!' he said, 'I'm gonna' fuck you up so bad, you motherfucker!'

The scrawny guy backed up. He stared, wild-eyed.

'I'll fuck you up so bad you won't have an arm to shoot up with! I'll break every one of your fuckin' fingers!'

The scrawny guy said, low, 'The cops man.'

An RMP patrol car slid to a stop across the street by the path up to the Doughboy statue. Two uniforms sat inside, looking at Callum and the guy. The cop on the passenger side clambered out and stood leaning against the radio car.

'Yeah,' said Callum, 'later, man.'

The scrawny guy nodded and sloped off down Woodside Avenue.

The cops kept eyes on Callum. He glanced at the brick apartment building and saw Radha in the lobby watching him from behind the glass door. She held herself tight and the look on her face was like a straight razor to his chest. He walked west on 56th sure in the knowledge he'd never see her again.

NYPD TRANSCRIPT (translation, Officer Bobby Ho [RHKPF])

TRANSCRIPT OF PHONE CONVERSATION BETWEEN MICKEY CHIU (HIP SING TONG) AND UNKNOWN MALE ON JUNE 19, 1995 AT 07:15 A.M.

RINGING

UNKNOWN: Hello?

CHIU: It's Mickey.

UNKNOWN: Are you okay? You sound funny.

CHIU: It's early for me. How are things with the family over there?

UNKNOWN: Fine. Father is looking forward to meeting his brother. When can we expect our American uncle to come?

CHIU: Another couple of months, perhaps. He has much business to attend to here. The Emerald Rat is a considerable investment, and risky in his eyes. He worries that the owner can't manage his staff effectively. They're less reliable than our own.

UNKNOWN: Of course. Father shares his concern. However, such will always be the case with foreign workers, but they know and understand the American clientele. That is why we have a family friend working with the new restaurant's owner. They have toured several of the new owner's other businesses already and are representing our interests in the venture. As such, they represent yours, too. We are, after all, family. However, if Uncle has strong concerns, perhaps he should

	consider an earlier visit with us. We can work together to allay his concerns.
CHIU:	I'll speak with him but he is very wise. Our family here will follow his wishes until such time as a younger member assumes his role.
UNKNOWN:	Of course.
CHIU:	With the business opening soon, when will we receive another order of produce? The staff are eager to serve our customers here in America and Chinese ingredients are our selling point. The quality of Asian produce is much superior.
UNKNOWN:	I will speak with Father.
CHIU:	Please apologize from us for causing him any inconvenience.
UNKNOWN:	Of course.
CHIU:	One more thing, Cousin. We are concerned about the rent for the new business. A lot of money is being invested in Chinatown. Of course, this is of great benefit to the community. However, much of this money is coming from Hong Kong. We, as an association, are concerned it will force some local concerns out of business. No doubt Uncle will discuss this when he meets Father but if there was any advice you might have for us, it would be much appreciated. We have a duty to protect the wellbeing of all Chinatown residents, you understand.
UNKNOWN:	I understand, cousin. The people of Chinatown are lucky to have such a benevolent organization work in their

	interest. I will mention your concerns to Father and see what he says.
CHIU:	Thank you, Cousin. Goodbye.
UNKNOWN:	Goodbye.

End of conversation

Chapter Seventeen

Callum said, 'Fuckin' Mulligan.'

Paddy said, 'How would he know you'd be outside with some piece of tail when he sent that asshole to you?'

'He wouldn't, he just wanted some junkie shithead to bug me. And the girl wasn't some piece of tail. She was nice.'

'It's not like you can afford a relationship with a chick right now, man.'

True enough, thought Callum, but he still felt denied. Like Mulligan had robbed him of an opportunity. He knew it was dumb but he held onto it – it helped with the job, gave him another reason to want to put these bastards away.

Paddy smiled then took a bite of his pizza slice. Callum didn't understand why he always ruined his pepperoni with that garlic powder shit they put on the condiments stands with the napkins and chili pepper flakes.

'That hump is fuckin' with me,' said Callum. He took a bite of his sausage slice.

'Keep your fuckin' voice down. You don't bad mouth Jimmy Mulligan, okay?'

'Why, is he the next Pope?'

'Mulligan goes way back to the old neighborhood with Fintan.'

'So do you.'

'Not like Mulligan.' Paddy picked at the rim of his paper plate, the slice drooping over the edge. 'Fintan's older than me, right? Jimmy Mulligan got a couple years on Fintan. He did some shit when he was a kid with The Westies: word is, he helped get rid of a couple of bodies with Mickey Featherstone and Jimmy Coonan, cut 'em up in an apartment and took some of the body parts out to the shoreline on his bicycle. On his fuckin' bicycle. What d'you think that does to someone at that age, huh?'

'That where Fintan got the idea for the shit we did with Acosta's body?'

'Could be. Mulligan went down for stealing some shit from a Duane Reade and went to Riker's for two years. Sixteen years old and he's in Riker's Island with killers, psychos, pushers, pimps and fuckin' perverts. You do the math, Christy. That shit's gonna' go two ways: you blow your own brains out or something twists up inside you, maybe snaps.'

'You scared of him?' Callum said through a mouthful of pizza.

'Damn right I'm scared of him. I got a record, sure, but the worst I done is break a couple noses in bar fights. Fintan don't take me that serious. He keeps me around 'cause I'm from the Kitchen, I do what I'm told and I'm loyal.' He tore a chunk off his pepperoni slice.

'You're smart, man,' said Callum. 'You brought me onboard, didn't you?' He balled up a napkin and threw it at Doolan's face.

Paddy laughed, 'You want me to go for three on the broken nose scorecard?'

They ate and drank grape soda, and looked out the big plate glass windows of the slice joint, watching the construction workers on the corner and the girls who came to the counter to order. The place was in midtown and traffic chugged by outside, the periodic blast of horns drifting in the door. It was a late summer afternoon and the heat in the city had lowered from raging oven to warm, damp blanket. Store owners still hosed down the sidewalk in front of their stores and a couple of cops stood in their light-blue short-sleeved shirts, fanning their faces with their caps and checking the foot traffic through mirror sunglasses.

Callum said, 'So tell me about the beeper again.'

Paddy explained that the crew had given a couple of phone numbers to regular customers, people with a major habit or guys who bought in blocks for their junkie friends. The numbers were for mobile phones in empty apartments on the West Side and switched untraceably to call forwarding. Someone on the end of the call gave the customer an address – often a street corner – and buzzed the dealer's beeper to let them know the customer was on the way. The dealers kept the heroin in doses called shirts, one-inch sections of plastic drinking straw heat-sealed at the ends. The dealers' could conceal the straws in their mouths or sleeves and flick them away at the first sign of cops to be recovered later or, worst case scenario, written off. The scrawny asshole who approached Callum had wanted pink shirts. Doses in pink colored straws.

'Jimmy Mulligan gave you the wrong beeper is all,' said Paddy.

'Jimmy Mulligan *says* he gave the wrong beeper,' said Callum.

And Jimmy Mulligan, Fintan Walsh and his crew, thought Callum, picked up the whole scam from the 14K Triad who did their street corner dealing with the exact same method.

It made him wonder just how close the Irish Mob and the Hong Kong end of the Chinese operation really were.

*

The click on the line was almost drowned by a firetruck rolling by St Patrick's Cathedral.

'*Wei.*'

Her voice was so small, so fragile among the maelstrom of midtown he thought it might crack on its way out of the receiver and sprinkle the word across the sidewalk.

'Hiya, Darlin',' said Callum.

Tara Burke said, 'Hi Daddy.'

He heard the excitement in her voice and his heart pulled a barrel roll.

'I was in a show, Daddy.'

'You were? That's amazing, what kind of show?'

'A spring show, at school.'

'A spring show? No way! What was your part in the show?'

'I was a flower.'

He saw her in his head, standing on the stage in some costume looking beautiful and awkward and cute and proud.

They talked some more and he could have punched himself at how blasé he'd been toward family life when he was with Tara and Irene. How he'd sat at home and shared his time with his daughter and his body with his wife, while his head and his heart had been wandering the streets, mulling over evidence and suspects, chomping at the bit until the next shift and he could get back out there again and chase bad men. Then how he'd lain awake fretting on his debts, promising himself one big wager – one big payday – to get clear.

Now he saw the quiet moments at home were the reality of life; or the raucous mornings when they'd yell from room to room, he'd cajole Tara to get ready, hash out the day's schedule with Irene, laugh over breakfast with his family and share the kisses and the goodbye waves for the day. The promises that they'd be together again that night.

Tonight he'd drink with Paddy Doolan and Trinity, and wake up in the morning feeling like he was just the kind of man he'd sworn never to be as a father.

He hung on Tara's every word on the line, read into every pause, every inflection of her voice. She was picking up an American accent thanks to life in Cleveland. Did she still miss him? Was he yet a vital part of her small, young life? Did she still love him? Then he heard her mother in the background, heard Tara plead, heard her admit – *It's Daddy.*

'You should have told me you were going to call.' Irene's voice was even. It was like the smallest thing could tip it into a screaming rage. Like she was straining for control. 'It's been well over a month since you called. Tara's been worried. She misses you.'

Callum said, 'I'm sorry, my life has been ... I'm kind of messed up – life is kind of messed up, right now. I just wanted to ... I needed to hear Tara's voice. Your voice.'

'Are you okay? You sound different.'

He felt an agonizing spark of hope in his chest. There was something in her voice that he hadn't heard for a long time.

He said, 'Yeah, I'm just lonely, you know. I want to see you.' He chanced it. 'I want to come home.'

The line went quiet. The city churned at his back.

A bike messenger yelled at a bus clipped him opposite St Patrick's.

Tara's voice was almost a whisper when she came back on the line.

'Bye, bye, Daddy.'

'Bye, Darlin',' he said, rushing the words, 'I love you Tara.'

'I love y – '

The line went dead.

*

They had a drink in The Wetlands Bar but quit after the tourist-photo-op drum-banging hippie crowd that hung out in Central Park weekends came in and started chanting. They stood on Hudson Street: Callum, Paddy, Trinity and a red-haired English girl called Sunrise with a stud in her nose and piercing in her navel.

'Where you wanna' go, baby?' said Paddy.

Trinity shrugged.

Callum said, 'I might call it a night.'

'Chinatown's nearby,' said Sunrise. 'We could go there.'

'Not tonight,' said Trinity, fast.

Callum gave her a look. She cocked her head and offered an awkward smile.

'I see enough Asians when I look in the mirror every day,' she said.

Paddy snapped his fingers and stuck his hand in the air.

'I got the perfect place,' he said. 'Let's grab a cab.'

*

'You kiddin' me?' said Callum.

Bill's Topless Bar was at 23rd and 6th Avenue. A counter ran along the wall on the left with a burly skin-headed bartender, a stage on the right with a bead-curtained door at each end, like a nudie-bar version of an airport baggage carousel. Tables and chairs sat in front of the stage on which three girls danced. They looked drugged or bored or both. A guy with a jaw like a cartoon superhero and eyes straight out of the Manson family gene pool sat in front of the stage, flicking his tongue in and out at a stupefied woman with chestnut-brown hair gyrating in a blue tasseled G-string.

Callum and the rest sat by the right of the stage.

'And what the fuck is this music?'

'What are you gonna' do?' said Paddy. 'Bill likes Garth Brooks.'

'The Thunder Rolls in a titty bar?'

'So take it up with Bill.'

'Where is he?'

'She's the pneumatic strawberry blond second from the left. Billie Granger, Strawberry Bill.'

Paddy lit a smoke and threw an arm around Trinity, who rested her head on his shoulder.

'Relax, Christy. I'm a regular. Fintan owns a stake in this place so the only money you spend is on tips for the girls. They're good people, man.'

They sat and drank and talked shit about O.J. and what was on TV and how much Trinity hated Hootie And The Blowfish.

The strippers rotated, three on stage at a time. Strawberry Bill took up position next to the bartender behind the counter. Paddy excused himself and went to catch up with her. Sunrise walked to the front of the stage.

Trinity studied Callum for a moment, poured him a beer from their second pitcher and said, 'You aren't very comfortable here, huh?'

They drank. Sunrise was giggling, talking to Manson-eyes. At the bar counter, Paddy began chatting with the bartender.

Trinity said, 'Paddy thinks you're good for him.'

'I'd say you fit that bill.'

'You'd be surprised. He's cute and considerate and he thinks he's crazy about me. But I learned to read people in my line of work. He doesn't want me so much as he just likes that he gets the side of me no one else does.'

Callum remembered Paddy telling him how flexible she could be and thoughts of her contorted into various bedroom positions swam through his head. He coughed and said, 'Can you read me?'

'I hardly know you.'

'We've met, what, four or five fuckin' times now?'

'When you talk like that, you sound like them.'

'Them?'

'Paddy, his scary friends. Walsh, Mulligan. You talk and swear like a New Yorker.'

'What did I sound like before?'

'You used different words, or you said things in a different way. It was like you were from the country or something. You seemed, I dunno', kinda' innocent.'

'And now.'

'Now, I think, you're trying to be something you aren't. You're faking it.'

He felt a shot of guilt in his spine and his face flushed hot. He threw the accusation back at her.

'You're the one scared of goin' to Chinatown.'

Her features switched in a heartbeat as though someone had thrown a strobe light over her face. Her eyes were venomous, lips drawn to show strong teeth. She looked about to take a chunk out of his throat. It took Callum a couple of seconds to realize he was staring and turn back to the beer on the table.

Paddy came back and grabbed his smokes from the table, kissed Trinity, winked at them and went back to the bar.

'Sorry,' said Trinity.

'It's okay,' said Callum, hands raised in supplication, 'it was just a joke. But I have to ask, *aren't* you fakin' it? I mean, you got Paddy all figured out, you don't see a future for the two of you. Shouldn't you cut him loose and save him some heartache later?'

'He's happy, I'm happy. That puts us ahead of the curve for most people. Until something better comes along, why end a good thing?'

Callum shrugged, lifted his glass and clinked Trinity's. Another pitcher arrived at the table. They looked back at the bar and Paddy gave them a wave.

Callum lit a Camel.

'You said I seemed innocent. So you know Fintan and Mulligan. You figure they aren't.'

'Jesus, I ain't that naïve, Christy. I am a dominatrix, don't forget.'

'How about Sol Grundy, did you know him?'

The music switched to a Black Crowes song and Callum nodded in approval. Trinity took a drink.

'Yeah, I knew Sol.'

'Look,' said Callum, 'nobody talks about this guy. But he's killed just before I start working at New World. It's weird, you know?'

'I know.' Trinity ran a finger along the edge of the table. 'He was shot in front of my place.'

'Shit.'

'Yeah. He was a client, one of the babies. These guys, they dress up like babies and I take care of them. Give them a pacifier, play with them, even put them down for a nap. It's an easy session and they're real gentle.' She frowned. 'I don't change diapers, though. Or breastfeed.'

'God forbid.'

'Sol came to see me to book a session, which isn't allowed, you know? I tell them they have to call, that they can't just turn up at my place anytime, unannounced. But he was nearby with friends I think, some kind of business dinner, and drank a little too much. He stopped by and the building super let him in, which he also shouldn't have done. Sol rang my doorbell. I was out with Paddy, a last minute thing for a friend's birthday. I wasn't at my building, Sol walked outside and someone killed him.'

Trinity took a drink.

'I came home, all these cops were in front of my place and I got scared, you know? You see more than two cops together, you know there's trouble. I told them I had to get home and they figured out who I was. Then a couple detectives interviewed me and that was that.'

She swept a lock of hair from her forehead.

'This city, sometimes it's just ... Manhattan is an island and it's this bubble, feels like a prison on the wrong day.'

'And you met Grundy's successor at New World, Jimmy Mulligan.'

'Through Paddy. We went to a party out in Queens just after Sol died, in some kind of social club. Maybe the Longshoremen's, I can't remember. Paddy was still living in that dump on the Upper West Side. Fintan Walsh was there, and Mulligan. We didn't really speak but I knew Walsh was buying into New World, and Mulligan was taking Sol's job.'

She levelled her gaze at Callum.

'And you gotta' be careful, Christy. I know Mulligan doesn't like you much. Not judging by how he looks at you.'

Callum said. 'You never saw us together. How would you know?'

Trinity tilted her head and gave him a sad look.

'Because he's standing in the doorway of this bar right now and his eyes are drilling a hole in your back, baby.'

Chapter Eighteen

'You shut it all down?'

O'Connell seemed to be straining to contain something explosive inside.

Mattila said, 'You're Goddamn right I did. I get intel on Walsh's criminal enterprise, I act on it. Burke feeds us the shooting gallery and protection marks, we shut the rackets down. We're law enforcement and I'm going to enforce the law.'

'You're a DEA action figure. What do you think Walsh and his crew are gonna' think when they realize the NYPD are squeezing them out of their protection racket, huh? On top of the Alphabet City shooting gallery getting raided? You don't think they might suspect a rat? And all roads lead to the new guy in the ranks, Burke.'

Bobby Ho looked at James Milburn. Milburn sat next to a window overlooking the Hudson and Ho, in the opposite corner, wished he could walk over and look out on the black river and empty his mind of the nightmare image of Callum Burke lying on an American street with a bullet-hole in his head, executed under suspicion by the Walsh crew. He knew Burke had a daughter.

Mattila stood to his full height.

'Now listen, O'Connell. I'll remind you I'm the designated O-One on this team.'

'You know well as I do, I'm O-Two because you got the Fed money and the smarts for the paperwork, but I know the neighborhoods. I got the street knowledge. And my knowledge tells me you keep interfering with Fintan Walsh's business before we got a stronger case, sooner or later Walsh is gonna' suspect a rat.

That means one murdered Irish-Hong Kong cop. So you better hope Walsh is still at the so-pissed-he'll-crack-a-few-heads stage. Otherwise, you got a dead undercover officer on your hands.'

Mattila swallowed hard and crossed his arms.

O'Connell dropped in a chair like he'd just been shot.

Bobby Ho tried to block the dark images from his mind.

And James Milburn sat silent by the window as the Hudson churned by below.

*

The cobbles were slick so Callum slipped when he got out of the Chrysler LeBaron. The Meatpacking District was empty at midnight. The underground club on the next block was closed for the night and the warehouses and butchers were silent. Corroded metal awning frames reached out from above shuttered loading bays. The abandoned elevated tracks of the old West Side Line crossed over the end of the street, an iron skeleton covered in birdshit and posters.

Callum took in the Marlboro Man, glaring down on the scene from a billboard on top of an empty chunk of industrial architecture opposite, as Paddy and Mulligan got out of the car.

Meatpacking District, he thought, near the Hudson Piers. Jesus, the DEA building's gotta' be no more than a couple of blocks away.

Mulligan had been calling around some of Paddy's favorite drinking spots looking for them both and hit pay dirt with Bill's Topless. Now he bid them follow with a jerk of his head. They walked past a phone booth covered with pornographic pictures and underneath the rusted tracks, emerging twenty yards short of 11th Avenue. A man stood smoking next to a brick wall covered with graffiti and a scratched metal door.

'Jimmy,' said the man.

'Donal.'

Donal nodded at Paddy and gave Callum a measured look before offering a hand.

'Christy,' said Callum.

When they did the rounds on the protection rackets, Paddy had explained to Callum that one of the crew, Donal Morris, had a cousin in Hoboken PD sleeping with a female officer from the 18th Precinct, the cops who policed Hell's Kitchen. Through Morris, Fintan Walsh paid off the cousin and his dirty-cop lover for information on the 18th's moves.

Mulligan gestured to the metal door.

Donal Morris said, 'I already unlocked it.'

They shoved at the door. It opened with a scream of protest.

Inside a couple of florescent lights flickered to life and revealed a stone floor and tiled walls. Long metal tables ran parallel the breadth of the room. A gutter lay at the foot of one wall and a rail ran around the periphery of the ceiling dotted with clusters of meat hooks. The hooks were stained a dark brown with rust and blood.

Callum tried to calm the artillery barrage of his heartbeat. Something was wrong and Mulligan had gone silent and sullen since grabbing Paddy and him from Bill's Topless. Mulligan had said this was on Fintan Walsh's orders, that they had urgent business to discuss. With Donal Morris on the scene, the business involved the 18th Precinct.

Callum studied Morris in the light. Tall with a bush of dirty fair hair and a long chin below a wide mouth and mean lips. His eyes were small blue stones set in deep sockets. He finished his cigarette and ground the butt under his boot.

Mulligan said, 'What the fuck happened?'

'She didn't hear nothin', I guess,' said Morris.

'When's the last time your cousin saw her?'

'Last night.'

'So did they exchange notes or play Scrabble or what?'

'He's my cousin, I don't wanna' know what he does in the bedroom with some lady cop.'

'Your cousin is a cop, too. You sure he ain't fuckin' with you?'

'Only person he's fuckin' is her, Jimmy. We're family.'

'What do we pay your cousin for, he can't warn us a crack-down is comin' with word from his girlfriend? We got cop cars parking up in front of the very stores we hit for protection. Blue shirts and shields going back to the delis and bodegas three, four times in a shift. Your cousin's squeeze didn't know this was comin'?' Mulligan popped a candy in his mouth. 'She gets a cut of what we pay, right?'

'That's the arrangement,' said Morris. 'My cousin, Roy, pays her from what I give him.'

'And he ain't holding out on her? Maybe she's tryin' to screw him 'cause he's holding back her cut.'

Donal Morris balked. 'No way, Jimmy. Roy is straight as a die.'

Paddy, standing a couple of feet from Callum, looked sick under the lights. His arms were limp at his sides, like a school-boy waiting to take his medicine from an irate teacher. He flinched when Mulligan called his name.

He said, 'Yeah, Jimmy.' His voice was weak as water.

'You and Jack Dempsey here been running the rackets.' Mulligan cocked a thumb at Callum. 'You sniff anything strange in the last coupla' weeks?'

'Nuthin', Jimmy.'

Mulligan turned to Callum and took a step.

'How about you?'

'I haven't been doing this long enough to know what's strange and what isn't.'

Mulligan spat on the floor and flashed his yellow teeth.

Callum felt a flash of hatred and tried for his impassive ringstaredown face. Too late. Mulligan's smile broadened at the murder in Callum's eyes. His ruined nose spread wide. The man got in close and looked Callum up and down.

'You turn up, the Alphabet City joint gets busted. Now it's the cops squeezing the West Side rackets. You'd almost think there's a rat in the house.'

'Hey, Jimmy – ' said Paddy.

'You shut the fuck up.' Mulligan pointed at Paddy but kept his eyes on Callum. 'You go back with Fintan so you're tolerated, Doolan. Don't give me a reason to lose my patience.'

'Least he still visits the old neighborhood,' said Callum. 'When's the last time you were west of Broadway?'

Mulligan's face went pale. He was still smiling but it was a rigor mortis grin now. 'What'd you say to me?'

'Paddy does the legwork with the Hell's Kitchen rackets. He deals with the suckers pay your fucking wages over there. Seems to me he deserves a little more respect.'

'Oh yeah?'

Mulligan's voice went tight and thin. Two veins formed a crooked V on his forehead and he stank of Bourbon and Old Spice. His hands dropped to his sides and Callum didn't like that they disappeared under the hem of his coat.

Paddy started bleating in the background and Donal Morris said he didn't need to see nothing messy. Callum filtered it out and heard Mulligan's hard breath and felt the heat from his body.

'I grew up in The Kitchen. Made my bones there,' said Mulligan. 'How dare you. How-fucking-dare you.'

'How *dare* you?' said Callum. 'What are you, my father?'

Mulligan stood inches away. His spit flecked Callum's cheek. He spoke like his whole body was straining at a leash.

'How – '

Paddy said, 'Jimmy, man, come on.'

' – fuckin' – '

Morris said, 'I don't wanna' get involved in nothing heavy, Jimmy.'

' – dare – '

Mulligan's arm came up from his side.

' – you!'

He shoved the barrel of a snub-nose Colt in Callum's temple. The metal was warm from Mulligan's body and the room tilted and Callum closed his eyes for a second to find balance. He swallowed and listened to the confused yells of Paddy and Morris. He opened his eyes and saw Jimmy Mulligan's face in close-up, bad teeth bared between cracked lips stretched thin. Callum wanted to close his eyes again, summon happy memories, die with something good as a last moment in this world. But instead he stared at Jimmy Mulligan like they were listening to the referee in the center-ring and the yells in the room were the crowd reaching fever pitch.

Mulligan grunted something then roared.

He walked over to Donal Morris in four strides and shot him five times. The report clattered off the metal tables and filled the space for a couple of seconds. Callum and Paddy went to their knees and Callum glimpsed Morris fold. He heard a soft thump as the body hit a table on the way down to the stone floor.

Then quiet.

The gunshot-roar faded so it felt like Callum had a thin layer of cotton wool in his right ear.

Mulligan gave an exasperated groan.

'Now look what you made me do.'

Paddy clambered to his feet. His hands shook.

'Jesus, Jimmy,' he said. 'You shot Donal Morris.'

Mulligan leaned on a table, the snub-nose in his right hand. 'It was supposed to be a beatin'. You and Burns were gonna' kick his ass 'cause the cousin let slip to Lee Doherty how he and

Donal were holdin' back the lady cop's cut. They was drinkin' at some bachelor party or somethin' out in Hoboken.'

'Doc Lee? The bag-man from Queens?'

Mulligan nodded. 'Doc was in a bar in Woodside and told Fintan. You and Burns were here to slap Donal around a little, give him a warning about skimmin' from the crew.'

Callum stood and looked at the body. The neck wound was still pumping a little blood.

'And the cops squeezin' the Kitchen protection racket?' said Paddy. 'Do we know what's happenin' there?'

Mulligan said, 'City Hall. We heard it's another clean up so's the uptown crowd can move in closer to Theater land and Fifth Avenue. Giuliani's zero tolerance bullshit.'

Irritated, Mulligan waved the Colt at Callum.

'You're gonna' clean this shit up,' he said. 'I still got a round in the chamber, asshole. Givin' me goddamned lip and makin' me lose my temper. You speak to me like that again, that's your ass lyin' on the floor.'

Callum began scratching his balls, keeping his body busy to hold off the shakes. His chest hurt like his heart kept ramming his ribcage and his legs were hollow. He didn't trust himself to speak.

Paddy said to Mulligan, 'Can we get some guys down here to help?'

'You two handle it. Look around for knives, choppers, machetes. Trash bags. You know the score.'

Mulligan shoved the snub-nose in his coat pocket and walked away. He popped a candy in his mouth as he opened the door to the street.

'Hey, I shot the guy in a butcher's,' he said, 'this is your lucky day, ladies.'

*

Mattila perched on the edge of the desk.

'I did it carefully and quietly,' he said, 'spread the word that the Mayor wants more police presence in Hell's Kitchen. The old story – ease more property development. Bring in the money. As far as the cops in the one-eight are concerned, it just so happens the increased patrols and liaison with local businesses are where Fintan Walsh collects protection.'

O'Connell looked at Mattila like a teacher who just discovered the slow kid in class had some smarts after all.

'That's not such a bad idea,' he said. 'You might just have pulled it out of the fire for Burke.'

James Milburn said, 'Nevertheless, it might be an idea for one of us to get over to Bleecker Street and keep an eye on Paddy Doolan's apartment. When Burke and Doolan are safely tucked up in bed, we can sleep easier.'

'Agreed,' said O'Connell. 'I'll sit on the place.'

'Before you go,' said Milburn, 'about Two-Six-Three Holdings?'

'Oh yeah, the fashion company building, right?' said Mattila. 'We checked it out. There are four companies in the building: your fashion company, two marketing companies and an art wholesaler. The other floors are empty. No connection between BOJ Garments and Two-Six-Three Holdings except the lease payment. However, Two-Six-Three Holdings is a subsidiary of ..?'

Bobby Ho almost raised his hand before he spoke.

'Phoenix Investments.'

'Correct.'

Milburn said, 'How about their relationship with the United Oriental Bank?'

'We got on to the Department of Treasury on that. Any money coming in is always in increments less than $9,000 so there's no mandate to trigger a FinCEN investigation. Best the Treasury can figure, someone in Hong Kong is moving money with computer-generated currency movements through dummy accounts in Asia and Europe. The last stop for the money before it hits the US is Zurich. By the time it reaches New York, the money is clean. No US laws have been broken.'

Milburn said, 'And that is probably only a portion of the cash.'

'How so?' said O'Connell.

'The underground Chinese banking system,' said Ho. 'Money changers, gold shops, trading companies. Many small businesses throughout Asia, and foreign Chinatowns.'

'How's that work?'

'Through the small businesses, smugglers establish letters of credit. Scrambled phone lines, couriers and a clandestine radio network transmit the transfer of funds.'

Milburn said, 'They can convert currency into gold or diamonds if necessary. All with virtually no record-keeping.'

O'Connell snorted. 'So how do they know how much is goin' where?'

'We,' said Ho, 'the Hong Kong Police Force, found a small piece of paper with a picture of an elephant on it. After investigation, we found the paper was a collection receipt for $3 million at a gold shop in Central District.'

'The system,' said Milburn, spreading his arms, 'is based on ethnic and historical trust. Kinship ties. Underground Chinese commercial interests.'

Mattila nodded. 'So we got a bank and a holdings company, backed by a Triad affiliated investment company, who look clean as a whistle on paper. The trail is cold. But we all know, Two-Six-Three Holdings is 14K. Now they are buying up property like the BOJ Garments building for Phoenix Investments. We know Chinatown prices are going through the roof. And we know the NYC Director Of Asian Affairs isn't too happy about us investigating a reputable Chinatown bank.'

O'Connell said, 'How about the fat liquors? Have your guys finished with their test tubes? Could the Triad dissolve the heroin and extract it later?'

'The DEA doesn't want to commit just yet but theoretically, yes,' said Mattila. 'We know Triad chemists can mask the origin of heroin by adding or subtracting chemical compounds from their product. We test a Burmese sample and it looks like it's Mexican. If it's possible to dissolve the drug in fat liquors, the Triads will have figured it out.'

They rose to their feet, checked watches and yawned. It was after 0100 and the building was quiet.

The picture of Callum Burke in Bobby Ho's head was no longer of a bullet-riddled corpse. Now he saw Burke in a bar drinking until dawn, maybe chatting with a buxom American woman or wheedling information out of the gangsters at the counter. Glamorous police work, like a Hollywood movie rather than the monotonous slog of surveillance, transcripts and Title IIIs.

Yes, he thought, Callum Burke was at this very minute in some New York nightspot living the debauched lifestyle of a free-spending, over-sexed American mobster.

Some men had all the luck.

Chapter Nineteen

Tony Lau drank his tea and felt sweat glue his shirt to his back despite the chill in the conditioned air. He looked through the gap in the center of the building that stood between his Hong Kong condominium and Kowloon Bay, and watched a small boat plough its way toward the Kowloon side.

The huge square hole in the building in front was a gate designed to allow the energy of a dragon to flow through the structure so the residents might avoid ill-fortune. No doubt the British sneered at such contrivances, or viewed them as quaint affectations. What would the Americans think? New York had no such concessions to nature or gods.

He sipped his tea as Deputy Leader Hai finished his report. The Society continued to funnel funds into the Chinatown banks in Manhattan and had acquired further properties. Sammy Ong was angered by the 14K investment but held his tongue due to caution and avarice. Test shipments continued to trickle into New York and the Irish-Americans were trialing their distribution with much success. Lau seethed at the mention of the Walsh organization. Callum Burke was Irish. Callum Burke had murdered Father Zhao. Callum Burke had fled Hong Kong and was, as far as Lau knew, still breathing. For some reason the Irish dog had been in his thoughts more and more of late.

All in good time. Patience was the key to revenge.

He said, 'Do we have any concerns with our friend in New York?'

Friend, he thought. Spy more like, and was a spy truly anyone's friend? The occupation required a conceited self-interest. They had people working openly with the Tong but their *friend* – their spy – was by definition deceitful.

'They continue to report to us on movements, Leader. The friend has attended several of the Walsh organization's places of business. Drug houses, offices, bars. They advise them on our interests as distinct from the Hip Sing Tong.'

'What are this spy's thoughts on the New York Police and their interference in Walsh's affairs? The drug house they shut down, and the protection rackets?'

'Acceptable loses, Leader. The Walsh organization is one of the few organized crime groups other than the Tongs left with concerns in Manhattan below Harlem. The Italians have been emasculated by the FBI, unlike the Hip Sing and the Walsh people. Our friend believes it is natural that the police will score the occasional victory against the Americans as their business is less self-contained than that of the Tong.'

Our *friend* is a duplicitous shit, thought Lau. But they had their uses.

Unlike Hai. The Deputy Leader was like a Wan Chai whore – he said the right things when in Tony Lau's presence but criticized and mocked behind closed doors. Lau knew his deputy opposed any move on the Tong and abhorred the prospect of direct business with Walsh and the Americans. He had continually compared Lau in the worst light to former Dragon Head Zhao. Particularly when in bed with his favorite bar-girl, who was a cunning and ambitious woman, happy to divulge Hai's whining to her friend – a voluptuous stripper who worked near the Central Mid-levels Escalator. Deputy Leader Hai's capricious mistress knew well that her friend and colleague was the sometime lover of Tony Lau's own personal enforcer, Tse. And so the chain of deception and treachery had led to Tony Lau himself and would end across the sea.

Hai continued.

'They say our proposed collaboration with Walsh is insulated from such concerns. The Walsh organization, and thus the police, have no knowledge of how or when the first sizeable shipment of heroin will enter the city. And the New York police as a whole have little interest in Chinatown at present.'

A golden light touched a window of a boat on the bay below and Lau shot a glance at his watch. It was almost four in the afternoon. He needed to bring Hai's report to a close. His guests would be here soon and he wanted a few moments to relax beforehand.

'Very well,' he said. 'Continue to deposit Phoenix funds in United Oriental and Chinatown Maritime Midland. Have Two-Six-Three Holdings buy the two properties listed in my latest report.'

Lau smiled at Hai.

'One more thing, Deputy Leader,' he said, 'I have received news that Sammy Ong will stop over in Japan before joining us for our conference. It seems the Hip Sing Leader wants to sample the volcanic waters.'

Lau walked to a sofa and sat.

'Ong has booked into a hot spring resort. It would be of great help if you could join him in Tokyo after his sojourn at the hot spring in order to give him a short tour of our concerns there.'

Hai's fixed expression of placid obedience slipped and Lau saw the small but vicious man within. He knew Hai had no love of the Japanese, often called them *rìběn gǒu*. It would stick in his craw to travel to Tokyo. But Ong had added the stopover to his itinerary and Lau would react to the move. His men would keep close company with the Tong leader while in Japan.

'Is the Hip Sing interested in our operations there?' said Hai.

'We will negotiate with Ong in Hong Kong. In any negotiation, we must start from a position of strength. The power and influence of Sammy Ong begins and ends in New York City while our businesses in Tokyo thrive and we continue to intimidate the yakuza in their own heartland. A demonstration of the breadth of our domain will set the tone for the arbitrations to come.'

The spark of anger in Hai's eyes reverted to deference.

'Of course, Leader.'

'That is all for today. I shall be at the Central office at 8 am tomorrow.'

Hai bowed and made much show of a slow and respectful exit. Lau stood again and finished his tea at the window. To left and right, other condominiums descended in rough tiers to the bay like a giant, shining Buddhist graveyard of marker stones.

On occasion he would trek out to the New Territories and climb the mountains, look at the islands sprawling across the South China Sea like a series of huge submerged beasts, their ridged spines showing above the waterline.

And in the distance, China.

Just two years until the handover.

Hong Kong would become a Chinese territory however much the people might believe – might know – they were distinct from the mainlanders. As insurance against Chinese interference, the 14K Triad would invest further in the US, in Paris, London, Rotterdam. New York.

Lau's wife was shopping in Central District and would be back in the early evening in time for the dinner Lau would cook. It was one of his most closely guarded secrets – that he cooked the evening meal. As Dragon Head he could not countenance the shame for him, the asides about his wife's failure in fulfilling her marital duties. Such a loss of face, no matter how small, how domestic, was a crack in his public façade and such a crack could lead to a shattering collapse if exploited by the right people. In this, as in much of life, the Society was politics.

He walked to the kitchen, enjoying the soft tickle of the carpeting in the living room under his bare feet and the sudden, cool austerity of the hardwood kitchen floor. He washed the teacup and set it to drain. He made some notes for a brief meeting with his enforcer, Tse in the morning. They would discuss Deputy Leader Hai, the Sammy Ong stopover in Japan and its associated timings.

There was a knock on the door.

He went to the small hallway and peered through the peep-hole before opening the door and bowing. The man was dressed in a long coat buttoned to his neck, despite the warmth of the afternoon. He smiled and bowed back. They exchanged pleasantries and a flush came to Lau's cheeks.

The deference he showed the guest, the clear dynamic of power in favour of the visitor, would have been an unthinkable shock to his men. The visitor slipped off his plain black loafers and they walked to the living room where tea was offered and refused. While the man took in the view, Lau carried a chair from the kitchen and set it next to the door to a corridor that led to the bedrooms and bathroom. He opened the door at an angle to the room and carried another chair to the corridor. The two chairs sat on either side of the door, screened from one another. Lau gestured and bowed for the man to sit on one, and his guest offered a small nod. The visitor unbuttoned his high necked coat and laid it on a sofa. His white collar was spotless. He sat.

Tony Lau edged around the man's knees and sat on the other side of the door.

Another secret, he thought. His rivals in the Triad world might see his devotion to a 'foreign' god as a weakness to be exploited. But he knew his secret faith was a personal strength, however shunned it might be by his men.

'Bless me father for I have sinned,' he said. He paused as he calculated how long had passed since his last confession and, in doing so, saw that he had forty minutes to complete confession, pray and say goodbye to the Catholic priest before his last guest arrived.

His last guest, the whore.

TRANSCRIPT OF CONVERSATION BETWEEN PATRICK
DOOLAN AND CALLUM BURKE AT 203 BLEECKER ST.
APT. 7, ON JULY 19, 1995 AT 07.56 P.M.

DOOLAN: We gotta' hit Delaney's tomorrow. Jimmy
wants us to pick up some cash and take it over
to the place near Jackson Heights.

BURKE: Delaney's is Fintan's neck of the woods. Why
can't Paulie Mooney do it?

DOOLAN: Paulie ain't around no more.

BURKE: Ain't around?

DOOLAN: No, not like that. Paulie's drinking in the
Parting Glass two weeks back and one of
Fintan's daughters walks in.

BURKE: Rose?

DOOLAN: Anne-Marie. She's got some kinda' message
for her pop and wants to leave it with Gerry.
You know Gerry, tends bar Saturdays. Gerry's
nervous havin' Anne-Marie around so he
brings her to that little cubby-hole by the far
end of the counter, where the public phone is.

BURKE: The place with the dirty pictures stuck on the
wall.

DOOLAN: Yeah. So Paulie sees Anne-Marie in there and
you know how she looks, so he walks over and
starts hittin' on her. He's fulla' Jamesons and
all horny and shit. So drunk he doesn't know
what he's doin'.

BURKE: He's fuckin' crazy.

DOOLAN: He's sure as shit sober now. Anyway, so Anne-
Marie, she's stuck in this booth and Paulie's
almost got his hands on her when Gerry comes
and kicks him on his ass. Anne-Marie runs out

204

	cryin' 'cause she's only fifteen and some 250 lb gorilla almost felt her up. Gerry has a couple guys take Paulie out back and knock him around some then puts him in a cab.
BURKE:	But that wasn't enough for Fintan.
DOOLAN:	Fuck, no. Paulie wakes up, can't remember what happened he was so drunk. It's Sunday so Fintan's at mass at Saint Sebastian's. Paulie figures he'll grab some breakfast at Kennedy's and read the papers. He's walkin' in the door of Kennedy's just as mass is getting out across the street.
BURKE:	Shit.
DOOLAN:	Yeah. So Fintan spies him and runs across Woodside Avenue and Paulie's like, "Hey, Fintan." Upshot is, Fintan marches him into Kennedy's and back to the kitchen and dips his balls in the fryer.
BURKE:	You're kiddin'?
DOOLAN:	Nope. Deep fried chicken balls.
BURKE:	I don't even wanna' think about what's in the mayo.
LAUGHING	
DOOLAN:	So Paulie got out of hospital and moved to his sister's place in Rhode Island. Poor bastard. Fintan was already pissed off anyway. Someone's been stealin' stuff from New World. Office shit like staplers and stuff. He figures it's gotta be the Bronx guys, sellin' it on to get well, maybe shovin' some stuff in their pockets when they go in to use the john in the mornings. And there's one thing Fintan hates, it's dishonesty.

BURKE: Okay. We better go to Delaney's tomorrow.
                    We have this fried food called battered
                    sausage back home and I don't wanna' find
                    my own junk on the menu.

                              *

TRANSCRIPT OF PHONE CONVERSATION BETWEEN
CHARLIE LIN (HIP SING TONG) AND FREDDIE WONG
(FLYING DRAGONS) ON JULY 15, 1995 AT 11.54 A.M

WONG: This isn't right. How long we got to put up
                    with this shit?
LIN: I know. We look like pussies.
WONG: To Hong Kong, too. Ever since Danny Yuen went
                    down for taking care of the rat on the Wan Chai
                    tram we been fucked by Hip Sing. They act like
                    bitches. Their banks are full of foreign money
                    and they're losing properties like it's Monopoly.
LIN: Maybe you shouldn't say so much on the
                    phone, man.
WONG: In case the cops are listening? Fuck the police.
                    Hey cops! How you doin'? You convicted any
                    Flying Dragons lately? No? Oh yeah, because
                    nobody in Chinatown trusts you assholes!
LIN: Come on, Freddie.
WONG: Fuck it. We can't dig for snakes (*NB. Traffic
                    in illegal immigrants*) right now because we
                    lost the empty buildings to keep the little
                    piggies (*NB. Smuggled aliens*) in. Even the
                    old men in the Association are suspending
                    some of the casinos.
LIN: I'm a young man in the Association, Freddie.

	Some of us are trying to make a difference but it takes time. You know how it is. The old men, the first generation, we have to show respect. The ABCs (*NB. American-born Chinese*) on the board have to shout to be heard.
WONG:	Yeah, well maybe you need to 'shout' a little louder. Maybe you need to 'shout' a message Mr. Ong will never forget.
LIN:	All in hand, brother. Be patient. Help is coming from Hong Kong. Just be patient.
WONG:	Patience don't pay the bills for The Flying Dragons.

*

TRANSCRIPT OF PHONE CONVERSATION BETWEEN
CHARLIE LIN (HIP SING TONG) AND FREDDIE WONG
(FLYING DRAGONS) ON JULY 26, 1995 AT 08:47 P.M.

RINGING

WONG:	Hello.
LIN:	Freddie.
WONG:	When is Mr. Ong going away? And Papa Ng?
LIN:	You aren't supposed to know about that yet.
WONG:	Everybody is hoping for it.
LIN:	Some of the old men aren't.
WONG:	The old men will fall into line behind whoever is in charge, especially if Ng is out of the picture. Come on, me and my boys are starving here.
LIN:	You got the stores on Canal. Work Brooklyn some more until this is done.
WONG:	The Ghost Shadows don't have to keep their

business in fuckin' Brooklyn. They laughing at us, Charlie. We're even losin' the tunnels, man. One of my boys liked this cute piggy (*NB. Illegal alien*) straight off the boat. He wanted to take her to a tunnel off Doyers for some fun. The fuckin' entrance is blocked because HK (*NB. Hong Kong a.k.a. 14K Triad*) bought the building.

LIN: Someone bought the building, you don't know who.

WONG: Come on, Charlie. Everyone in Chinatown sees what's happening. The On Leong sure as shit do. Word is, they and the Ghost Shadows are half laughin' their asses off, half pissin' their pants at the thought of HK makin a bigger play in Chinatown.

LIN: I have no idea what you're talking about.

WONG: Charlie, Don't –

LINE DISCONNECTED

End of conversation

*

TRANSCRIPT OF PHONE CONVERSATION BETWEEN CHARLIE LIN (HIP SING TONG) AND MICKEY CHIU (HIP SING TONG) ON JULY 26, 1995 AT 10.04 P.M.

LIN: Hello.

CHIU: Charlie, Hello.

LIN: Sorry to call so late, Mickey.

CHIU: It's fine, I'm just watching a movie and paused the tape. What can I help you with?

LIN:	I'm worried about Freddie Wong. He's making a lot of noise about business lately. He keeps asking about Father's trip and complaining about the foreign investment coming into the area. Trouble is, he's a lot less circumspect when he talks about it.
CHIU:	He's a kid. They all are.
LIN:	Nevertheless, we need to keep a lid on his side until things are settled.
CHIU:	Does he talk about the restaurant?
LIN:	The Emerald Rat? No. I'm not sure he even knows. That's business between ourselves and our foreign family for now.
CHIU:	Good. Alright, there's a little favor he can do for us on the Upper West Side. I'll discuss it with you tomorrow on Pell. That should keep him happy for a while.
LIN:	Thank you brother. Enjoy your movie.
CHIU:	Goodnight.

End of conversation

*

TRANSCRIPT OF CONVERSATION BETWEEN CALLUM BURKE AND PATRICK DOOLAN AT 203 BLEECKER ST. APT. 7, ON JULY 30, 1995 AT 09.18 P.M.

DOOLAN:	Why can't we sit on the fire escape?
BURKE:	It's raining.
DOOLAN:	So? We'll be dry with all the other shit above our floor. Remember those big storms I talked about? This is one of those, man. We sit out,

drink beer, watch the lightning and listen to the fire trucks. Why we gotta' drink inside? You got a hidden camera in here or something?

BURKE: What?

DOOLAN: A hidden camera. You recording me?

PAUSE

BURKE: What the fuck?

DOOLAN: You record this, get me drunk and do shit when I pass out, right? Record it and jack off later. Lemme' see, where's the lens?

BURKE: Fuck you! Fuck you and fuck off!

DOOLAN: Alright, alright. Jesus, calm down, Christy. It was just a joke.

BURKE: Well it isn't funny, asshole.

DOOLAN: Okay, okay. Here, have a beer and cool down.

PAUSE

DOOLAN: Sláinte.

BURKE: Cheers.

PAUSE

BURKE: Sorry I got so pissed.

DOOLAN: It's okay, man. This city winds everybody pretty tight.

BURKE: I just feel like I'm standing still, you know? I mean, I been helping you with the collections but that's dried up a little. I wanna' do more than lug dressers and wardrobes around the city. Beepers and phones? I want more, Paddy. Shit, Trinity sells the H from her dungeon. She's got more responsibility than me.

DOOLAN: You ain't Trinity.

BURKE: I get that but I want to move up in the crew. I

proved myself with Acosta, I been a good
worker. I played the strong-arm part with the
collections and never had to lay a finger on no
one. Maybe I pissed off Jimmy Mulligan,
maybe he pissed me off but I'm past that. I
don't think I ever offended Fintan except
singin' the wrong song when we were carving
up Acosta.

DOOLAN: Alright, I hear you.

BURKE: Donal Morris neither. I didn't complain when
            I got his brains all over my jeans when Jimmy
            shot him.

DOOLAN: Alright! Jesus, what are we, married?

BURKE: Now why are you getting pissed?

DOOLAN: Do you hear yourself? When you met me you
            was a potato eatin' mick straight off the boat.
            Rough around the edges but you was
            innocent, Christy. Now you're talkin' about H
            and rackets and carvin' up bodies like it's easy
            as takin' a shit.

BURKE: You know why I intimidated those poor
            bastards out of their profits on the West
            Side? Or ran H around the city? Or beat the
            shit out of Acosta?

DOOLAN: You didn't exactly beat the shit out of him. I
            mean he kinda' kicked your ass at first.

BURKE: I was tirin' him out. You never heard of rope-
            a-dope?

DOOLAN: Yeah, you tired him out by getting your ass
            kicked.

BURKE: I beat him, didn't I? You couldn't even beat
            your meat, Trinity didn't help you out. I was
            sayin' – what was I sayin'?

211

DOOLAN:	Why you did all the shit you did. Drugs around the city, all that.
BURKE:	Yeah. I did it 'cause of you. 'Cause you found me in that shithole hotel and gave me a shot. I was freaked but I did my best to prove to you I was worth it.
DOOLAN:	I'm sorry, Christy.
BURKE:	For what?
DOOLAN:	Draggin' you into all this. You ain't Jimmy or Fintan or me, man. You ain't Trinity. You're good. I can see it when I'm pickin' up the cash on the collections. You feel for those people handin' over their own money. For me, it's just another day on the job. You? I can see you feel it, man.
BURKE:	I don't regret any of it. You said it, Paddy. The New York food chain. I ain't the Christy I was at home. I wanna' keep movin' up that chain. You can trust me with anything. You can tell me who offed Sol Grundy, I won't breathe a word.
DOOLAN:	That's ancient history.
BURKE:	Whatever. I'll do you proud.
PAUSE	
DOOLAN:	Something big's comin'. Some kinda' partnership. You wanna' step up now, you're gonna' get in deep. You sure you want that?
BURKE:	What else am I gonna' do? My visa's expired. I can't get a proper job. What am I gonna' do back home? I want this, Paddy.
DOOLAN:	Yeah.
BURKE:	Don't look so sad, man. You changed my life. I want this.

PAUSE

DOOLAN: Alright. I'll talk to Fintan. Jimmy won't
wanna' give you the shot but Fintan likes you.

BURKE: Great! You won't regret it.

DOOLAN: *You* might, Christy.

BURKE: Come on, let's sit out and watch the lightning.
I can see it flash through the window. I hear a
fire truck already.

DOOLAN: Yeah, sure. Let's sit out and watch the storm
torch the city.

End of conversation

Chapter Twenty

Fintan Walsh was licking his finger and sifting through invoices in a Mexican place as Callum sat opposite. The layout was Texas or New Mexico cantina, barebones. There were tables on a linoleum floor, strip wooden walls and a long counter on one side with a couple of beer taps and not much else. The kitchen in the corner was mostly open, two men working the fryers and hotplates. A South American soccer match played on a TV behind the counter.

The eatery was on the corner next to the 61 St-Woodside IRT line station. Through the window, Callum could see the cars sliced in strips of light and shade on the street as the sun beat down through the metal structure. A gaggle of cops stood outside a store on 61st drinking coffee from paper cups. He counted five in all, an RMP parked up nearby.

He wanted to call Irene. Just to hear her talk. To get a couple of stories from Tara about what she'd been doing at school and flush away some of the corruption in his head after the last weeks.

The Donal Morris killing had hit him hard. Harder than cutting up Acosta. Callum had called Mike O'Connell, had pushed for the task force to move now, to grab Walsh and Doolan and Mulligan. No way, O'Connell had said. It was done, Donal Morris wasn't coming back and they needed more to connect the dots to the Chinese. Besides, O'Connell had laughed, casualties in a RICO investigation were well within the Feds wheelhouse, whether DEA, ATF or FBI. Plenty of informants had been plugged during cases, and plenty of informants had done the killing. There was a guy up in Boston with buckets of blood on his hands who'd been an FBI CI for years.

I'm gonna' drown in this shit, thought Callum. Christ, I'm still half-drunk from last night.

He'd volunteered to wear a device for this one. Not a Kell wire but this sit-down with Fintan Walsh could result in the kernel of evidence that opened up the entire RICO case, so he'd brought a recorder, the smallest and lightest available. Ninety degrees outside and muggy as a sauna and he was in an army surplus shirt instead of his customary tee so he could carry it in a pocket. It was taped to the shirt over his chest to stop the pocket sagging. At least he could wear the shirt open below his chest, show he wasn't strapped, but he buzzed paranoid on the booze-sweat staining his armpits, coating his face. He thought guilt was written in neon on his eyeballs.

He glanced at the kitchen. Did he catch a weird reflection on a metal refrigerator door? Like someone was standing just out of sight? Bullshit: undercover paranoia. He needed to straighten out.

But Callum's mind slung an image of the shadow in the back-room of the Alphabet City shooting gallery through his head. The strip search for a wire. What if Fintan had him strip again, searched his clothes and found a cop recorder this time?

Once Paddy set the time and day for his meet with Walsh and his pitch to go deeper in the crew, Callum had informed O'Connell. Mike wanted him clean, said they could worry about wires once he'd stepped up in Walsh's outfit. Ruiz and Galinski followed the play, told him they'd be across the street. Grab coffee in Marnie's or take some shirts into the laundromat. No, Callum had said, not enough. We need something on tape.

Walsh finished his paperwork and looked up, scratched his razor-burned chin.

Every tic, every movement, every glance screamed at Callum to run. That Walsh knew he was wired, was a cop. That he'd always known.

The drugs. The violence. The sleaze. The secrets. The lies. It all churned in Callum's guts, pricking his nerves, sharpening his perception, leaving him more strung-out than any drug.

So why are you here?

'Huh?'

'So why are you here? What d'you want, Christy?'

Fintan watched him with lidded eyes. His pencil-thin eyebrows were hiked up on his forehead.

'How's business?' said Callum.

'This one of those "how's things" questions where you're just bein' polite or do you really wanna' know?'

'Polite isn't one of my strong points. I'm interested.'

'Well, we're squeezed in Hell's Kitchen. The cops have increased patrols, it's harder to hit the stores for money but it ain't nothin' we can't get through. Problem is the 18th Precinct are throwin' some undercover shit at the street corner dealers, too. That's a bigger pain in the ass.'

He's layin' it out like he knows it's recorded, thought Callum. A voice in his head began jabbering, *Does he know and he's jerkin' me around?*

Fuck it, play it out.

Walsh toyed with the ballpoint wedged in the thick fingers of his right hand.

Is he weighin' up when to do it? When to kill me?

Walsh said, 'How's it goin', livin' with Paddy?'

'It's okay. We ain't exactly Matthau and Lemon.'

'I don't follow.'

'You don't watch many movies, huh?'

You're fucking this up. He isn't a cinephile. Calm down.

Walsh set the pen on the table.

'It's good,' said Callum. 'Paddy's good. New York is great.'

'Paddy says you wanna' talk to me about takin' on more responsibility. You know, me and Paddy go back.' Walsh leaned back in his chair and ordered a bottle of Jarritos lime soda. 'Have some chipolata steak. This place is incredible.'

'I'm good, thanks.'

Walsh called for another Jarritos and the Mexican owner brought it, nodding at Callum as he set the second soda on the table.

How much is this poor bastard paying to keep his restaurant here? Will he thank me if I put these animals away? Shit, I'll come back and order the full menu if I pull this off.

Walsh took a slug of soda and belched.

'So me and Paddy go back, in the old neighborhood. Paddy, he's always been kinda' soft, always needed someone to watch his back. I mean, he got his rough edges. You don't grow up in The Kitchen and not learn some street moves but he got a couple weaknesses me and Jimmy Mulligan don't share. First is, Paddy still believes in the basic good in people. The milk of human kindness and all that shit.'

'But you go to church across the street, right?' said Callum. 'God is great, love thy neighbor?'

'That's the beauty of bein' a Catholic, son. Everythin's open to interpretation. We got these old men in Rome decipherin' a book been written a couple thousand years ago. And they're smart. There's a lotta' money to be made here so they always leave a little wiggle room in case they gotta' tweak their story.'

'So Paddy has more love for his fellow man and that's a weakness?'

'Damn right,' said Walsh. 'Because it makes him gullible. People take advantage.'

Shit.

Walsh said, 'Take a drink of soda. Once you taste this you'll never want Coke again.'

Drink it and dive in. Brazen this out.

'It's good, yeah,' said Callum. 'So what, you think I'm takin' advantage of Paddy?'

'No,' Walsh picked up the pen again and began scratching a doodle on one of the papers in front of him. 'No, I don't. But I ain't so sure about that girlfriend of his. You're smarter than him: what do you think?'

'I think being trusting doesn't make him dumb.'

'But it makes him soft. Keep an eye on this Trinity chick, okay? You think she's some kinda' problem, you tell me.'

'Sure Fintan, sure.'

Walsh held the pen horizontal, a coarse finger and thumb clasping each end. He looked at it for a few seconds and his jaw clenched like he was ready to snap the plastic in two. Then he set the ballpoint down.

He said, 'Paddy's second weakness is, he can't let go of the past. He stayed on the West Side long after we outstayed our welcome. Giuliani wants to wipe that whole neighborhood clean and rebuild it. Why you think we got cops up our ass now? But Paddy clung to it like shit on a shoe and now he's holed up in The Village with the students and the fags 'cause he won't cross the river. Sure, we got some people live in The Kitchen still, soldiers. Cannon fodder. Like I could give a fuck about them. But Paddy? The boy just can't let Manhattan go when the place is lost to the rich, the niggers, the spics and the bums.'

Walsh took a drink.

'And the Chinese,' he said.

Christ! thought Callum, is he gonna' spill?

Walsh said, 'The Chinks are the future. You know how much a kilo of heroin costs in The Golden Triangle? Maybe $40,000. By the time it hits New York, you can sell it at $110,000 per ki.' He leaned forward and the table jolted. '*We* can sell it. The Tongs got Chinatown but they don't like dealing much north of Canal Street. So they sell wholesale to the Italians, the blacks, whoever so the shit gets sold all over. But times change, New York never stops, Christy. I heard the big boys wanna' move in from Hong Kong. Bruce Lee motherfuckers, the Triads. And they got bigger plans.'

He licked his lips, grabbed the Jarritos bottle and finished off the lime soda.

'We still got a street corner presence, we got New World to move merchandise in the five boroughs. We got a couple bondage clubs for a little distribution the vice cops can't bust so long as all's the freaks do is smack each other around, and nobody gets carried away and actually fucks someone. We still got some West Side muscle. We ain't confined to Jersey and Staten Island so these Hong Kong guys like us for a business arrangement more than the Italians. We got the longshoremen in Brooklyn, some union guys at La Guardia.'

'How about Harlem? The Bronx?'

'The Chinks are racist, man. They hate niggers. They won't work with those shitheads.'

'The Dominicans?'

'Too busy humpin' coke. Listen, what I said is true. City Hall got a hard-on for The Kitchen, bein' next to Broadway, midtown, the Actors-fuckin'-studio. I figure we got less than ten years to make our money with the Chinese before The Kitchen becomes Clinton and the Wall-Street-and-trust-fund-crowd are everywhere. Same goes for most of Manhattan. Giuliani wants to turn The City into Disneyland. We got to maximize the time left, man.'

He grinned.

He's unburdening, thought Callum. He scratched his chest and his hand brushed the pocket with the recorder.

The voice in his head whispered: *It's on tape.*

Callum said, 'Okay, that sounds great. But where do I fit in?'

'We talked about weaknesses, Christy. What are yours?'

I let a Hong Kong Mob Boss die to clear a gambling debt. I have a terror of dying before I can hold my little girl again, my estranged wife.

I'm the eternal optimist. I believe we'll see green-and-white ribbons on the World Cup trophy someday.'

'See, that's your problem right there. You're makin' a joke,' said Walsh. 'Your problem, Christy Burns, is you ain't no optimist because you don't have faith. You ain't a true believer.'

'You want me to go to church?'

'I want you to believe, son. Believe in me, in what I'm tryin' to do. This is America, not Ireland. You gotta' have a can-do spirit here.'

'So how can I prove I'm on board? You name it, I'll do it. I'll back the Mets for the World Series, you want me to.'

Walsh dropped the pen in mock exasperation. He leaned back in his chair, crossed his arms and said, 'I seen you angry. Like you coulda' popped me and Jimmy both when we took care of Acosta.'

It's on a reel in my head some nights, thought Callum.

'But I saw you committed,' Walsh said, 'I mean really driven, once. When you boxed that spic asshole before I plugged him. Man, that night I saw a fireball. I thought you could be a force of nature. Why d'you think we brought you in to carve the Puerto Rican asshole up? But you whined and bitched and moaned and picked a scrap with Jimmy.'

'Sorry I disappointed you, Fintan.'

'And you drank and worked the moving shit and you hit a slump, man. I can smell the booze on you now. And you come to me and you wanna' move up, you see why I got reservations.'

The inner voice coached Callum.

Don't panic, don't overplay.

'You said it, Fintan. I got some smarts. I want more. This city got a lot to offer but it takes money and I want – I need – to make more. You want me to prove myself, you tell me how.'

Fintan gave him a hard stare. He pinched his thin lips in his brutal fingers as breath whistled through his nose.

220

Then he said, 'You fight. Just like last time. Ten days from now. You sober up and you fight.'

'Fight who?'

'A two-time loser from Boston. Bobby Cooper. I got an event next week down in the Meatpacking District, bare-knuckle bouts. Six fights on the card, one with Cooper. Guy who was supposed to fight him ran out on me. You step in and fight Cooper, put him down and we'll see.'

'Who was due to fight?'

'Kenny Mooney.'

'Paulie Mooney's brother? Why'd he run out?'

'Don't be a smartass.'

'I'll do it.'

Walsh leaned close.

'I know you will.'

'What's the weight?'

'Cooper's a middleweight, carries about 165 lbs.'

'Okay, I'm around 162 right now.'

I'm fucked, thought Callum. Too much booze, too many cigarettes. But I'll fight. And I'll win because I have to or I'll bleed out on the goddamned floor.

'Cooper's also in hoc to his boss in Boston,' said Walsh. 'Likes the Red Sox, likes to bet. He's almost thirty grand deep with Dessie McGivern up there. This fight is his shot at diggin' himself out. They got a team of guys puttin' a spread on him to win. He takes it, he's clear. You beat him, McGivern puts a bullet in his head on the drive back to Boston and they find him ten years later in a landfill in Rhode Island. You put him down, it's like you're pullin' the trigger, Christy.' Walsh winked. 'That's the commitment I'm lookin' for.'

The voice in Callum's head hissed, *Clench your fist, stop the shakes.*

'You got it, Fintan. And then you introduce me to some people. Where's the fight?'

'I don't have a solid venue yet. There'll be a couple of Chinese there from Chinatown. After the fight we'll grab a couple drinks with them, I'll introduce you, we'll see what happens – if you beat Cooper. If you don't, we'll see about that, too.'

'I'll beat him, Fintan. I'll beat him so bad they'll have to shoot him when he's still out cold in the back of the car on I-84. I'll give this Cooper guy can-do spirit upside his fuckin' head.'

Chapter Twenty-one

Callum left the Mexican eatery and sparked up a smoke soon as his sneakers hit the sidewalk. Georgie Ruiz watched him from across the street and sipped her cheap coffee outside the deli on Roosevelt Avenue. She saw Fintan Walsh get to his feet through the cantina windows between hand-written flashcards taped to the glass: *Burritos – 2 for $4!! Free Tacos with every order!!* A waiter scuttled over to clear his table as Walsh turned back toward the kitchen and a figure emerged. Jeans and t-shirt, back in the shadows. Walsh walked to the figure and began a conversation.

Ruiz climbed into the driver's seat of the Honda rental parked on Roosevelt and spoke to Anton Galinski, sprawled in the back seat with a telephoto lens.

'Burke's going to take the 7 train back to Manhattan now. Jump out and catch it, hook up with him and check the recording.'

'What is this, Cagney and Lacey? When did you start ordering me around?'

Just once, thought Ruiz, just once it would be goddamned heaven if her partner did something without bitching or throwing out some snide remark.

'You can be the hot blond one, just follow Burke, okay? I'm gonna' ghost Walsh.'

'You're gonna' ghost him?' said Galinski. 'He lives a couple of blocks away.'

'So I'll save you the nightmare of the expressway takin' the car back. Callum's climbing the steps to the station, Ant. Come on, man.'

Galinski shifted in the seat and cleared his throat.

'You should take Burke,' he said. 'You might stand out too much with Walsh.'

Ruiz turned her body in the front seat to face him.

'Stand out?'

'We know from Burke he likes Latino women, right? He might notice you. I'm just another pasty-assed white guy but you're toward the stoppin'-traffic end of the scale. For *his* tastes, I mean, y'know?'

Ruiz felt a warmth in her neck and rubbed it below her hair, tied up in a loose ponytail, to stop it spreading to her cheeks. She looked back at the street and saw Burke halfway up the steps to the mezzanine hanging under the elevated tracks. He was finishing his cigarette before entering the station. She looked down so Galinski couldn't see her face in the rear-view and smirked.

'Maybe I should get a dye-job and then I can be the blond, huh?'

'Don't kid yourself,' said Galinski – Ruiz heard the smile in his voice, 'Lacey wasn't all that hot.'

*

Galinski waited for Walsh and played scenarios in his head. He busts Walsh and Mulligan in an old factory and saves a nubile redhead tied up in the corner, like some old pulp novel cover. He liberates Doolan's girlfriend, the bondage chick – Nurse watchamacallit – from her sick lifestyle and she crumples in his arms. He cracks the case and that new officer on the reception at the Puzzle Palace notices him and they make love until dawn. Or the chick in the DA's office. Or the Columbia senior moved in on his block.

Not Ruiz, though. She was smokin', sure, but it'd be like

banging your sister, Christ's sake. Her husband, Arthur, was a lucky man, no doubt. A woman like that – beautiful, great mom, honest to a fault – Georgie Ruiz would be the jackpot if they weren't partners. And if she wasn't married. And he didn't live at home with his mom. He knew he was an asshole when they worked together but it was the cop way and he *had* to ratchet that shit up because she was a woman. He couldn't be seen to give her an easy ride. It was for her own good.

And goddamn if it didn't rankle that she dug Burke. She'd never admit it, but it was there in her eyes, in her voice.

Shit!

The Buick slid by headed west on Roosevelt, Walsh driving and a figure hunched in the passenger seat. Baseball cap, sunglasses. Vague features.

Galinski scrambled into the front of the Honda and turned the key, slipped onto Roosevelt Avenue and moved through the gears. The Buick was a metallic blue Roadster, an uncommon color. He slapped the wheel and fought the urge to speed up. He was an idiot, getting lost in his high-school horn-dog fever dreams. Walsh's car had been following the tracks above. Roosevelt was a straight shot to Queens Boulevard. If he could catch them before the boulevard, he could tail them in the four-lane traffic. He muttered to himself.

'Metallic blue, metallic blue, metallic ... motherfucker! There you are.'

The Buick got caught at lights. Galinski stopped three cars back and settled in for the tail.

*

Ruiz stood by the doors of her train car and watched Queens slip by outside. She gazed down on the flat rectangles of stores and warehouses sat close to the elevated tracks, slathered in rust and

225

grime and graffiti. Further back from the tracks, she saw tenements crowding narrow streets fronting wide sidewalks.

Burke sat in the next car. She saw him sway in and out of view in the windows at the end of their respective cars. He sat staring at the floor, his legs spread wide.

A scrawny guy sitting behind Ruiz on the other side of the aisle had been muttering racial poison to himself and cackling about O.J. since 40th and Lowery Street. The six-foot-and-then-some black guy on the seat a couple of feet away studied the transit poetry posters above the windows and breathed deep. Ruiz half hoped he'd keep it together and avoid a scene she'd need to join, half hoped he'd kick the shit out of the scrawny guy before she could pull him off.

Both left the car at Court Square, the scrawny guy picking up his walking pace as the tall black guy followed him to the gate. Ruiz wondered if there were any cops around on 23rd Street below.

*

Galinski thought he'd lost the Buick Roadster when they joined the Brooklyn-Queens Expressway but traffic was snarled up for half a mile and he bullied his way lane-to-lane until he was four cars behind Walsh. They crawled for a time on the highest tier, Manhattan off to the right across the East River below a tobacco-stained pall. Traffic picked up speed and he almost lost the car again around Brooklyn Navy Yard but a couple of cop RMPs were cruising and Walsh slowed.

Their task force team was small and O'Connell or Mattila would take too long to reach him, but Galinski wished they had a couple of cars to leapfrog the Buick and take turns on the tail.

Still, this was the shit, he thought. This was what he signed up for. Once he drank and fucked his way through the mental fallout of the Grundy shooting, he'd been cruising on street-cop reverie, playing scenarios in his head: crouching behind a car while shots pinged off the hood, Georgie givin' him the save me stare before he returns fire and takes out the hitter; watching Walsh piss his pants when Anton-fucking-Galinski gives him the phonebook special in interrogation one.

He followed Walsh as the Buick exited the expressway near the Brooklyn Bridge and tailed him into Dumbo. They slipped down to street-level and he eased back on the gas and took it slow through empty cobbled streets over pot-holes and trash, giving Walsh plenty of space. The streets were deserted, the buildings cracked industrial shells, faded paint signs flaking on towering brick walls for long-lost enterprises: *Robinson & McKirgan's Butter-nut Bread, Ace Furniture Repairs and Fine Upholstery, Margoyle's Tonic. Margoyle*, he thought. Who the fuck got a name like Margoyle?

Galinski caught sight of the East River a couple of blocks away and saw the chunks of broken rock, twisted metal and piles of garbage on the Brooklyn shore. Since leaving the expressway he hadn't spotted another soul. City Hall might gut Hell's Kitchen for executive dollars but Dumbo was condemned to urban blight, far as Galinski could see.

The Buick turned right and Galinski parked up for a few seconds. It was tough to tail someone when you were the only other car on the streets and he hoped Walsh hadn't made him already. When he eased the Honda around the corner he glimpsed the Buick turn at the end of the street before the massive granite anchorage of the Manhattan Bridge. The tail-lights reflected red against the shadowed base and stopped.

Galinski parked and slipped out of the Honda. He winced with the click of the door shutting.

This is it, he thought, this is the shit.

But his heart pounded hard in a chest turned to ice. His hand went to his Glock in its hip holster and he remembered the clatter of the gun when he'd dropped it on the sidewalk the night Sol Grundy was shot. He started when he heard voices. Four: Walsh and three others. Fading, then growing louder with an echo. Accents. Laughter.

They're in the archway under the anchorage, thought Galinski.

He crept forward toward the darkness at the end of the street.

*

They ordered and took in the view of 10th Avenue through the windows. Ruiz opted for a sausage and egg sandwich with fries, Callum for a coffee. He wasn't comfortable. The Empire Diner was a Chelsea landmark, popular with the art crowd and exposed, even as they sat in the corner away from the windows.

'You should eat,' said Ruiz.

'I'll grab a slice later.'

'Come on, my treat.'

'I'm good.'

Callum felt a hot flush of shame when he snapped. Ruiz looked wounded for a second.

'Sorry,' he said.

He pulled the recorder out and held it under the table. When they finished up, he would walk north to the parking lot, pick up a truck and Johnny Johnson, and drive the hundred miles north to Hartford for a moving job. Mulligan had caught him on the beeper and told him about the job when Callum checked in on a payphone at Grand Central. He wondered if Walsh wasn't getting him out of the way so Fintan, Mulligan and Paddy could chew over the conversation with Walsh in the Mexican place.

Mike O'Connell walked into the Empire and sat next to Ruiz in the booth. He smelt of toothpaste and deodorant.

He said, 'What, you ordered without me?'

Ruiz said, 'He isn't eating.'

'I'll have a cheeseburger and you, buddy boy, need your strength so grab a bite,' said O'Connell. 'And you smell like a brewery.'

'Mom, Dad, I'm a grown up now. But you know what? Fuck it. I'll have steak and eggs. On your tab.'

'Hey, the Feds are picking up the bill. Let's grab some cheese-cake for desert.'

The waiter came over, took the new orders, gave them a way bigger smile than Callum's scowl deserved, and went back to the counter.

'I've got thirty minutes,' said Callum. 'Then I got a moving job to Connecticut.'

O'Connell lowered his voice. 'Loaded or vanilla?'

'Who knows? It's with J.J. and nobody's gonna' tell him.'

'You gotta' love the irony: the junkies from the Bronx bliss-fully unaware they're ferryin' H around the city. Walsh got a sense of humor, I'll give him that.'

'They're okay guys,' said Callum. 'They're just working like anyone else.'

He propped up a menu next to the sugar and brought the recorder out from under the table, concealed by the menu. It still had the tape stuck across the red light on its front.

It still had the tape running over the top of the recorder.

It still had the tape stuck over the microphone.

Callum's face burned. He felt he was sinking into his seat, dropping fast for a hard landing somewhere down below under the city.

Ruiz said, 'What's wrong?'

O'Connell looked from Callum's face to the recorder. His eyes hardened tougher than the polished steel tabletop.

'What'd you do?'

Callum peeled off the tape.

'Shit!' he said. 'Shit, I was nervous. Scared.'

He hit play.

They heard muffled noise. Unintelligible nonsense.

O'Connell turned red.

He said, 'You fuckin' mutt!'

Ruiz said, 'You got nothing?'

Callum shook his head and stared at the recorder.

O'Connell stood and went to the counter.

'Oh, Callum,' said Ruiz.

O'Connell sat down again with a waiter's pen and a pad of paper.

'Tell me what you talked about with Walsh now, before the last couple of brain cells you got left pop.'

*

Galinski hung back at the corner. The huge structure of the Manhattan Bridge threw massive shadows across the street. He'd heard four voices but there were five figures stood in a circle at the entrance to the archway under the anchorage around thirty yards away. Walsh, his companion on the car journey, and three others.

They spoke low and Galinski couldn't hear their words but the newcomers treated Walsh's companion with respect, their body language telegraphing subservience. He breathed slow and cursed in his head that he'd left the camera in the Honda. Not that he would have captured anyone's features but they would at least have a record of body types and height comparisons to Walsh. Galinski wondered what Ruiz was doing now.

Jesus Christ, he thought, I'm fucking alone here.

The scream made him jump and his shoulder hit a drainpipe. The sound was a thunder-crack in his head and he crouched small on the corner and put his hand on the Glock. He listened past the steam-hiss adrenaline rush in his head and heard shouting in Spanish. Galinski slipped the Glock out of the holster and fought back the sharp urge to piss. He squeezed the grip tight to stop his hands shaking.

I could slip back to the car and run like hell, he thought. It's not like anyone would know, Christ's sake. Go home later, talk with ma, drink a couple of cans. Catch the news: a body turned up under the Brooklyn side of the Manhattan Bridge on the late report. Drink more. Stew. Try to live with it.

But *you'll* know.

Fuck!

He knelt on one knee and peered around the corner again, the Glock held close to the ground.

Walsh was smoking, talking to the figure from the Buick. One of the other figures was on its knees now, hands clasped in an aspect of prayer and babbling. The other two figures stood over the kneeling man, hands by their sides just in front of the anchorage archway.

Whatever this is, thought Galinski, please let it pass. Fintan Walsh and whoever you are, let the poor sap on the ground walk out of here with a slap and a harsh word. He heard the swish of traffic above, hundreds of people passing to and from Brooklyn each minute just yards away. His radio was in the car. If he had it now he could call in a 10-13 and bring half the cops in the eight-four down here. Why hadn't he brought it?

Because I'm fucking terrified, he thought. My brain's gone to mush.

He could go back to the car – it was parked just down the street – call in and pray nothing went down until back-up arrived. Yeah, Ruiz would understand that.

He turned to go. A fire truck on the bridge above hit the siren and almost drowned the crackle of shots.

Galinski spat a curse and turned back to the anchorage.

Walsh and the Buick passenger were standing back from the others. The two standing figures were still aiming handguns at the kneeling man even as the corpse listed to the side and dropped in a heap on the asphalt. Galinski raised the Glock, yelled the words before his brain caught up to his throat.

'Policemotherfuckersputthefuckinggunsdownnow!'

The Buick figure grabbed Walsh and pulled at his sleeve.

'NYPDputthefuckinggunsdownanddon'tmove!'

There was a screech and three muzzle flashes. As the figures made for the darkness of the archway Galinski popped three shots back and took cover. He heard four more rounds fly at him and saw the wall opposite spit dust. He shot a look around the corner and saw Walsh and the Buick figure disappear into the dark. The other two stood at the archway entrance, guns raised and bodies leaning forward. Something small hung from the guns. Sandwich bags to catch cartridges. Galinski let out a breath and brought the Glock up, firing four shots, knowing they were wild but crazy-elated with the rush. The figures edged backward and fired a salvo then turned and ran into the black void under the anchorage. The cracks of gunfire seemed to follow them into the dark.

JesusChristJesusChristJesusChrist.

Galinski jolted at a truck horn on the road above and almost loosed off a shot at the sidewalk. He stared at the body across the street half-expecting it to stir, struggle to its feet and walk toward him. He knew the archway was an underpass and that Walsh, his companion and the shooters had probably run through and fled out the other side, but he couldn't follow. His legs itched with adrenaline but his feet would not move. After a full minute he decided to go to the car and grab the radio, call in the shooting and then check on the body.

Galinski ran back to the Honda.

He fumbled with the door handle, swore, grabbed the radio and fiddled with the channels, and fought the urge to piss again. He called in the 10-34 and made his way on feet that seemed to be floating above the sidewalk back to the anchorage.

Still just one dead guy lying on the asphalt.

Gun-in-hand, he crab-walked to the corpse. No shots, no yells. No bullet in his gut.

The body lay with its right arm twisted behind its back, eyes staring at the sky. No cartridges from the shooters thanks to the Sandwich bags. Professional. Galinski looked around and saw the building on the corner from where he'd traded shots. It had a huge faded advertising mural on the side from a bygone age, *L&H Stern Smoking Pipes and Holders*. He wondered for a second if the Sterns had been friends of the Margoyles way back.

Then Galinski walked behind a dumpster, opened his pants and took a long, loud piss. He laughed in a high-pitched giggle like a crazy man. Public urination, one of Giuliani's pet bug-bears.

Fuck Bratton and Rudy G., he thought, what're they gonna' do, arrest me?

Chapter Twenty-two

Two a.m. on the Bronx River Parkway and the truck crawled in traffic. The job had been simple and the customer tipped big. Despite the tip, J.J. had been lethargic and surly all night. Now he sat in the passenger seat in the cab and sipped malt liquor while Callum rolled a smoke and listened to Z100.

J.J. pointed at the radio and said, 'It's the Batman song, man. Can't go wrong with my man Bruce Wayne.'

'Can't go wrong with his girlfriend,' said Callum, 'Nicole Kidman, Jesus.'

'She too skinny.' J.J.'s head lolled on the seatback as Callum edged the truck forward in the gridlock. 'How you gonna' grab onto anything with that string-bean bitch? You need 'em plump if you wanna' hump, baby.'

'Don't start with this shit again, Johnny.'

'I'm serious, Christy. You come around my neighborhood I'll introduce you to Charlene. You climb in the sack with her, the cops'll list you a missing person.'

'I come around your neighborhood, no matter what I guess that's probably true.'

Johnny Johnson's neighborhood was only a mile or two's walk away in south Bronx but he didn't look like he could have mustered the energy to leave the truck.

Callum said, 'You got a Charlene waiting for you tonight, J.J.?'

'Not tonight. Just as well. I'm so tired I couldn't raise a pencil, never mind get my dick hard.'

He looked like shit. His eyes were red, his voice slow like the words were on a transatlantic line from his brain to his mouth. Callum had seen this before when some of the guys had missed their morning methadone.

'You sure you don't want to jump out somewhere? We're still in the Bronx.'

J.J. shrugged. 'Listen, Christy, don't be tellin' nobody but I ain't livin' at home right now.'

'What do you mean?'

'I lost my place. It's nothin'.'

'It's everything, Johnny. This isn't the kind of city where you want to sleep on the streets.'

'I ain't on the streets. Shut the fuck up, okay? I shouldna' told you.'

His face was like a sullen teenager. Callum shook his head and smiled.

'You're a crazy motherfucker, J.J.'

'Yeah, I'm a crazy motherfucker. Crazy motherfucker lost his motherfuckin' bed.'

'How about a shelter or something?'

'They kickin' people out of shelters, Christy. City don't have time for people can't pay their own way. It's okay though.'

'How the fuck is that okay?'

'I got a place to sleep. Inside, dry, not so cold if I don't find nowhere else by winter.'

'Legal?'

Now Johnny smiled.

'What,' said Callum, 'you breaking in somewhere at night?'

'I got a key.'

'You stole a key.'

J.J. feigned indignation. 'I ain't no gangster.'

'Where are you sleeping?'

'Ignorance is bliss, man.'

Callum changed gear as the tailback picked up speed. He had

a lot of time for Johnny but not a lot of space in his life for his shit right now.

'Just don't get caught,' he said.

He finished rolling the smoke and sparked up with an FDNY zippo. He rolled the window down. The night was mellow, the wet heat of the day tempered by the hour. He turned to offer to roll a cigarette for J.J. but the man had drifted off to sleep.

*

Ten hours earlier. Fried food smell clashing with O'Connell's deodorant. Prime steak like cardboard in Callum's mouth, eggs like rubber. Sick to his stomach at the recorder fuck-up but forcing the bites down.

O'Connell had decimated his meal. He tore mouthfuls from the burger like he was a lion ripping chunks from a kill.

Ruiz filled Callum in on Bobby Ho and James Milburn's investigation into BOJ Garments. The fashion company was clean but the connection was there between the building owner, Two-Six-Three Holdings, and Phoenix Investments. The theory of dissolving heroin in the tanning fat liquor was a real possibility. DEA had been on to US Customs; NYPD to Port Authority of New York and New Jersey. DEA had turned up a shipment of the tanning agent coming in to San Diego, another to Long Beach in the next month but nothing in New York. The Californian shipments were destined for the West Coast and Texas. US Customs would inspect the cargo at disembarkation and they'd track the cargo with the DEA once it hit US soil but both shipments, from Japan and Australia, looked legit.

The fashion house employee, Kevin Zuk, who quit BOJ Garments at short notice was a more promising avenue of investigation.

'Guess what Mr. Zuk did at BOJ?' Ruiz had said.

Callum had said, 'Leathers?'

'Wow, you should be a police officer.'

Mike O'Connell snorted at that one.

Ruiz ignored him. 'Turns out,' she said, 'he was an expert in treating the leathers for the manufacture of jackets, bags and wallets. He had a great working knowledge of ..?'

'Fat Liquors,' said Callum. 'Would he have had the skill to extract H from the solution?'

'Sarge?'

O'Connell said, 'I had a talk with his former manager, Emile.' He dropped the remains of his burger on his plate. 'Emile figures it was possible. One of the reasons Zuk worked with the material was he studied tanning in Wyoming, even spent six months in Sweden looking at their methods. He also took some kind of short course in chemistry last year, at the University of British Columbia.'

'He's Canadian?' said Callum.

'From Utah. Just studied up there.'

Callum sat back. 'Lot of Hong Kong Chinese emigrated to Vancouver in the eighties, and in the last couple of years. Big Cantonese population there. Big Chinatown. Some say it'll be the most Asian city in North America within a decade.'

'So he could have been recruited by the Triad?' said Ruiz. She looked skeptical.

'Right now, I wouldn't rule out the possibility they got their hooks in this guy, Zuk, and called in some kind of debt or whatever to work the H coming into New York.'

Ruiz raised an eyebrow, nodded and tucked a lock of hair behind her ear with a slender finger.

'You know,' she said, 'if this guy can work with the tanning liquids and the leather, could he soak the leather in the solution with the heroin and extract the drug from the goods later?'

'You mean coat a jacket or bag in heroin-laced liquors?' said Callum.

'Sure.'

Callum looked at a server pick up an order from the counter.

'Why not?' he said. 'If they can dissolve H in the liquors, they can soak the goods.'

Ruiz said, 'So maybe we should be looking at leather clothing, bags, accessories, too.'

Mike O'Connell took a slurp of coffee.

'Nice angle, Ruiz,' he said.

They sat in silence for a minute.

O'Connell broke the impasse with a muttered obscenity.

He said, 'We need the venue for your fight and that sly motherfucker Walsh won't tell you until the last minute. We gotta' keep ears on his phone.'

'Phones,' said Callum. 'He's got one for home, family, daily stuff. But I heard from Paddy yesterday he has a cell we don't have tapped. Only Mulligan and Paddy know about it in the crew. Them and a couple of women Walsh has been bangin' on the side. Paddy doesn't know the number. Walsh talks to someone else on that cell, someone other than Mulligan and the women. My guess is it's a player from the Hip Sing Tong. We get up on that phone, we can prove association.'

'But we don't have the number,' said Ruiz, 'and we can't get hold of it.'

Callum took a bite of steak smothered in yoke. He chewed and worked through Walsh's weaknesses in his mind. Just like a fight – adapt and overcome. Jab – the jab is the rangefinder. Probe until you find that weak spot, work the same point until you wear the other fighter down.

Ruiz said, 'I can get the number.'

Callum and O'Connell watched an idea bloom in her eyes, saw her face change. Her eyebrows knit, her lips pursed as her mouth tightened. Then she smiled.

'Walsh uses the number for extra-marital shenanigans,' she

said. 'Mrs. Walsh wouldn't be impressed if strange women kept callin' the house.'

Callum's brows arched as the penny dropped.

'And Fintan likes Latino ladies.'

'Right,' said Ruiz. 'Maybe I can have him notice me, he gives me the number and bang.'

'Let's hope not,' said O'Connell, 'but I get your point. Callum, where can we put 'em together?'

'Walsh uses a gym on Roosevelt Avenue.'

'Could be too obvious. Some woman turns up outta' the blue and starts hittin' on him among all the regulars.'

'So don't do it in the gym,' said Ruiz. 'Put someone in there workin' out to watch him. Set me up outside, let him get a good look at me and hope he bites. It's worth a shot.'

'He's gonna' need a real good look,' said Callum.

Ruiz took a sip of her drink and gave O'Connell and Callum a slow smile. Callum had an image of a lioness on the savannah stretched out and licking her lips, waiting for the gazelles to come by.

'Let's go shopping,' she said. 'We can put the feds money to good use. I have an idea how I might snare this sick son of a bitch.'

*

Callum flicked another spent cigarette out the cab window and pictured Georgie Ruiz at the table in the diner, hair piled up, eyes shining, skin the color of butterscotch. He could tell O'Connell liked her – liked her a lot more than her partner, Galinski.

They hit the on-ramp before he realized his mistake.

'What the fuck?' he said.

J.J. woke from his sleep and rolled his head to look out the passenger window. Cables whipped by as they crossed the

George Washington Bridge and left Manhattan behind. Callum worked through the truck's gears and cursed under his breath.

J.J. said, 'We headin' for Jersey, Christy.'

They were almost across the bridge now. Callum had followed I-95 and ended up getting sucked into the tangle of roads funneling traffic onto the huge suspension bridge leading to New Jersey across the Hudson.

'Jesus, I wanna' get to bed before sunrise,' he said.

J.J. giggled. 'Case you turn to dust?'

'Are you high? You're talking enough shit for it.'

'Why you think I been feelin' like shit all night? I couldn't get well. Just tired is all.'

Callum tensed as they came to the off-ramps. Now he'd have to hug the shore and drive down to the Lincoln Tunnel. It was past two-thirty.

'I picked you up at the office,' he said, 'how about your favorite Upper West Side neighborhood bodega? Eastman's right? Couldn't you grab a book of matches?'

J.J. scratched at his arm like he was trying to shed skin. The talk of heroin had him irritated and jumpy.

'I went by the place,' said J.J. 'Asshole wasn't there. It was his shift, he always works Thursday nights and if not, he leaves a sign in the window. But nothin', just some Asian guy behind the counter barely spoke fuckin' English. Yellow fuckin' peril, man. Leaving me sick all night.'

They drove in Jersey, Manhattan taunting Callum with its brilliance across the water.

'Asian?' he said. 'Like Chinese?'

'Weren't you listenin'? Yellow peril, Christy. A fuckin' chink.'

'Alright, alright.'

But it wasn't alright. Why were the Chinese in a bodega used to deal drugs by a Hispanic connection just blocks from New World Movers office? Did Fintan know about this?

They drove River Road, heading for the Lincoln Tunnel. It was the suburbs, all schools and quiet streets, just across the river from the flash bitch with her Empire State Building and Charging Bull and Fifth Avenue Tiffany's. And the darker side of her nature: the Bowery and Harlem and Alphabet City. Hell's Kitchen and Chinatown.

No, thought Callum, Walsh must have known about the Chinese move on Eastman's Bodega. The Hispanic operation was small but an irritation to a crew setting up business with the Tong. So close to the New World office, it was an affront like Dylan Acosta dealing on his corner in the Kitchen. Maybe the directive to cut the Dominicans off came from the Tong. They were more thorough than Walsh's crew, they were systematically purging Mulberry Street of the Italians and probably wanted a buffer zone around their new partners' base of operations. The dealer in the bodega was probably dead already.

And then there was the dealer's cousin, Gabriel Muñoz.

Callum swung the truck right to double back to the tunnel entrance. J.J. was humming a tune next to him, accompanying the radio.

If Walsh and the Tong knew about Muñoz, a former dealer in the family, they might consider the Belleclaire manager a threat. He could be next on the Walsh/Tong hit-list. Callum needed to find a payphone and have someone check the Belleclaire. Muñoz was an asshole but didn't deserve a bullet in the head. And what if the Chinese grabbed him and, to save his neck, he spilled on the undercover cop who holed up in his hotel to connect with Paddy Doolan?

Callum pulled up to the toll booth and patted his pockets for change, came up short and asked J.J. to help him out. He felt like shit after hearing Johnny was sleeping rough.

J.J. looked at him with red, morose eyes and handed over some coins.

'You know the worst of bein' a junkie?' he said. 'It ain't the cravin', or the hurt when you can't get well. It's the idea I'm goin' to Hell, Christy.'

'That's pretty Old Testament, Johnny.'

'My mama was a Baptist. Every Sunday out to church in Harlem with a Bible and a hymn book, and me in tow. I loved it. Got to see people I hadn't met up with all week, and everybody in their best clothes, like it was a kinda' party, you know?'

'Yeah,' said Callum. 'I know.'

'But when I got old enough the guilt kicked in.'

'Old enough for what?'

'Noticin' girls, sneakin' a smoke, playin' with my fuckin' self. You know – growin' up shit. Then everythin' that felt good seemed a ticket to the *other* place, feel me?'

'I feel you. Jesus Christ Almighty, I feel you.'

'So when I got on the drugs, and then they got on me – started ridin' me – I fucked everythin' up. You know, up to then the worst person I ever had in my life was my daddy, and that asshole didn't stick around past my ninth birthday. But when I started the drugs – I mean *really* started – suddenly, mama was cryin' 'cause of *me*.'

He rolled his head like he was trying to brush something off his shoulder with his skull.

'Shit,' he said.

'I get it, J.J. I mean, not really, but some people need an out from life.'

Callum remembered the moments when a bet came good, the fever on him when he placed the money. The world collapsing in degrees when each wager went bad and he got in deeper and deeper.

Callum could feel J.J.'s eyes drilling into him.

'I don't know if you're goin' to Hell, Johnny,' said Callum, 'but you're a prime specimen for redemption, brother.'

242

Then he gunned the truck into the black maw of the tunnel to descend below the river churning on toward Lady Liberty.

TRANSCRIPT OF PHONE CONVERSATION BETWEEN
CHARLIE LIN (HIP SING TONG) AND MICKEY CHIU (HIP
SING TONG) ON AUGUST 4, 1995 AT 08.03 A.M.

LIN:	Hello.
CHIU:	Good morning, Charlie.
LIN:	Did Freddie Wong take care of that business yesterday?
CHIU:	Yes. He left the trash in Brooklyn. There is some concern, however. Wong was interrupted by someone who appeared to be a green-jacket (*NB. Police Officer*).
LIN:	My god. Is he okay?
CHIU:	Yes, fine. The green-jacket found the trash, however.
LIN:	Should we consider firing Wong? After all, he botched the job and we have our professional reputation to consider. There are plenty who would be willing to replace him.
CHIU:	I understand your concern but I don't think we need to take such drastic measures yet. The Emerald Rat manager was there, as was our cousins' representative but both are fine. I think stability is our priority now. The day is so close.
LIN:	This is what happens when we spread our concerns beyond Chinatown.
CHIU:	Don't worry, Charlie. All will be well with the Emerald Rat, Leader Ong and our cousins. Enjoy your breakfast. I'll see you later this morning.

End of conversation

TRANSCRIPT OF PHONE CONVERSATION BETWEEN
CHARLIE LIN (HIP SING TONG) AND UNKNOWN MALE
ON AUGUST 5, 1995 AT 8.47 P.M

LIN:	Good morning, cousin. How is the weather?
UNKNOWN:	Hot and humid. We are all well, however. It is evening in New York, yes?
LIN:	Yes. I am calling to confirm our father's flight. He will leave JFK at 09.30 a.m. tomorrow.
UNKNOWN:	And he still has the stopover scheduled? How long will he stay in Tokyo? Has Papa Ng decided to accompany him?
LIN:	He will stay two nights in Japan. He wishes to refresh himself after the first leg of the journey before meeting his brother in Hong Kong. As we expected, Papa Ng will not travel. Age and health precludes it. Is our Uncle ready for Father's visit?
UNKNOWN:	Well prepared, yes. Our fathers will discuss the Emerald Rat and other business.
LIN:	We look forward to it. Our family has not been as united as we'd like in recent months but I believe this will be settled when our fathers conclude their business. Goodbye.
UNKNOWN:	Goodbye, cousin.

End of conversation

Chapter Twenty-three

The taxi pulled up on Pell Street and the older man emerged from the dim hallway. At five a.m. the sun was still toiling skyward to take position above the city of New York.

Bobby Ho stood in the filthy street opening to a basement diagonal to the Hip Sing Tong building and watched the Tong leader, Sammy Ong, clamber into the back seat of the cab with two other men. One he recognized as Thomas Chen, a senior member of the Tong in his late fifties. The other, Charlie Lin, was in his late thirties and one of the youngest of the senior Hip Sing members. Both treated Sammy Ong with great deference as they helped him into the taxi, then climbed in on either side of their leader.

He caught a glimpse of a wiry figure with a ducktail haircut standing in front of a darkened travel agency down the street. The hard, angular face of a recognized Flying Dragon gang member flared orange as his zippo caught a cigarette. Ho wondered how many other Flying Dragons members were on security detail for the Tong leader Sammy Ong's departure. Ho took a step down into the shadows.

A fourth man emerged from the doorway of the Tong headquarters and bowed deeply. He was dressed, like those in the taxi, in an immaculate suit and had a conservative haircut and rigid posture. Michael Chiu was second-in-command in the Hip Sing and would assume Sammy Ong's duties while the leader was away while taking his ultimate lead from Ong via phone. Ong's old friend and advisor, Papa Ng, would council Chiu, too.

The taxi pulled into the street, the headlights sweeping Bobby Ho's hiding place as the cab made for Mott Street and, ultimately, JFK Airport.

Sammy Ong was on his way to Hong Kong and a meet with the 14K. Michael Chiu took a deep breath and scanned the street.

Bobby Ho backed down the steps further into the darkness.

*

Down at the morgue an attendant was signing off on some paperwork on a couple of corpses. A male and female found in the Hudson River a couple of days ago. The bodies had suffered in the water but the cops had identified the man as one Gabriel Muñoz, manager of the Belleclaire Hotel on the Upper West Side. The woman's identity remained a mystery.

*

Milburn attacked his Taiwanese pork chops with relish while Bobby Ho worked on the blanket of sour pickles atop his bowl of rice. Niku Mattila sipped his tea. They were on Canal Street near Broadway on the western border of Chinatown, the restaurant basic with Formica tables, laminated menus, and colored paper lanterns hanging from the ceiling. A Buddhist calendar hung behind the counter and gold posters of Chinese folklore characters were dotted around the walls. Various lawyers and Government workers surrounded them, grabbing a bite a short walk from Foley Square, City Hall and the courthouses.

'He's gone,' said Bobby Ho. 'He left Pell Street at 0500 with Charles Lin and Thomas Chen.'

Niku Mattila said, 'Anything on the Title IIIs about Ong's itinerary?'

'Yes, Sir,' said Ho. 'Just that he will stopover in Tokyo for two nights before flying to Hong Kong. For refreshment.'

'Hookers and booze,' said O'Connell.

The cop sat next to Milburn and ran his fingers through hair that hadn't seen a brush in a couple of days. He was out of breath and had specks of dirt on his pants from passing-car splashes on the streets outside, scattered puddles left over from a pre-dawn rain shower.

Mattila set his tea cup down with much ceremony. He shot an apologetic look at Ho.

Oh god, thought the Hong Kong policeman, please don't bow.

'I must admit, I concur,' said Milburn. 'There has been some crossover in the past between the 14K and Japanese yakuza, particularly child prostitution and pornography, but nothing regarding heroin with Tony Lau's faction. I'd imagine there has been even less business between the Japanese and the Hip Sing Tong. Ong probably just wants to have some fun before the business in Hong Kong.'

O'Connell turned to Mattila. 'Can you use your Fed muscle and contact your office in Tokyo? Keep an eye on Sammy Ong and his men while he's there?'

'I'll make the call,' said Mattila. 'Your people can pick it up at the Hong Kong end, with our field agents there?'

'Yes. I'll check RHKPF are ready. We can filter communications through your New York office to ensure consistency.'

There was a brief discussion on the logistics of communication. Then Milburn went back to work on his Taiwanese pork chop while O'Connell accepted a cup of tea from Mattila. Bobby Ho returned to his pickles.

Mattila said, 'Still no leads on this Kevin Zuk, quit the fashion place in SoHo.'

'Chances are, he's in a lab in a tunnel somewhere under Doyers Street,' said O'Connell. 'I'm reaching out to a couple of guys I know in the Fifth. Good cops, they'll keep it discreet.'

They ate and drank in silence for a time.

'How is Callum?' said Mattila.

'He'd never wanna' say it,' said O'Connell, 'but better since Gabriel Muñoz turned up dead. It freaked him out, your tame dealer's cousin getting shot in front of Galinski like that. Now Muñoz been shot down and that loose end tied off, Burke sleeps a little easier.'

'Shame an innocent woman died with him.'

'Nothin' so innocent about her, she was in bed with that sack of shit. What worries me, Muñoz must have been dealin' again if he got snuffed. How come your guys didn't know?'

'We checked him out. He was clean. But these guys are like roaches: if they want to get back in the life, they'll find a way no matter what you do to stop them. Or maybe the killers followed the drug connection from the cousin and found it led to associates of Muñoz. Either way, he won't be our problem again.'

Mattila shot a look at Bobby Ho. He didn't want the Hong Kong cop to think him callous.

'There'll be an investigation, review of protocol and hard questions asked,' he said. 'We could learn a lot from the Marshalls on some of the finer points of protected sources.'

He brushed a thread off his arm.

O'Connell said, 'Georgie Ruiz thinks Callum's fragile and needs pulled sooner rather than later. But I think Burke's where he needs to be.'

Milburn said, 'So he's operationally sound.'

'Callum Burke is a driven man,' said O'Connell. 'He's scared, paranoid, and he's sweating his ass off to get in shape for his fight next week. But I've seen his type before. He's living right now, I mean really living. The NYPD got plenty of summons cops and God bless 'em, we need guys like that. But Burke is an attack dog, one of the 10% doing 90% of the heavy fuckin' lifting. He's riding the fear and rush of waking up every day praying he goes to sleep in one piece that night, but he's caught the sickness. He's hooked on the undercover work.'

'The fight,' said Mattila. 'I've been thinking, it could damage the case. You got a police officer engaging in illegal activity yet again: bare knuckle boxing. Not to mention the side book and the drugs could be circulating at the fight.' He frowned and said, 'The DEA cannot sanction a police officer engaging in such activity. And we don't even know where it'll be yet so we can't cover Burke on the night.'

O'Connell shot him a *don't-kid-a-kidder* smile. Then something clicked and his face dropped.

'You went to your fuckin' superior over this.' He leaned across the table and his voice dropped to an acid hiss. 'You never had one of your guys have a forced ingestion? Some dealer got a gun at their head, they gotta' snort the coke or shoot the H else they get a plaque on the memorial wall?'

Mattila shrugged. 'This is different, we have prior knowledge and it's too dangerous. First, we got a cop involved in a murder: Donal Morris down in the Meatpacking District. I know Jimmy Mulligan pulled the trigger but Burke helped dispose of the body – which has not been recovered – and, hell, I got to take some responsibility on that one stirring the whole Walsh crew nest. And now, we're putting him in the center of an illegal event surrounded by known violent criminals. We don't know where the event will be other than the say-so of a dangerous felon that it's somewhere south of 14th Street on the West Side. Something goes wrong and we can't pull Burke out in time to guarantee his safety.'

O'Connell said, 'His whole fuckin' life right now is an illegal event surrounded by bad guys. He sleeps in an apartment with a bad guy. Best/worst: he loses the fight and Walsh's favor/he wins and this Boston hood ends up in a Dumpster somewhere near Dorchester Bay.'

Niku Mattila stared at O'Connell. His lips parted in readiness for a reprimand but before he could speak, O'Connell waved him off.

'Christ, I'm only sayin' what we all thought at some point.'

O'Connell looked to Ho and Milburn. Milburn nodded. Ho looked at the tabletop.

O'Connell said, 'We pull Burke and he doesn't show for the fight, Doolan could get whacked, as his point of entry, so you can spin it that Burke is protecting life. You're the DE-fuckin'-A, Special Agent Mattila. Flex that federal muscle and play the system. Tell the Southern we'll take this across the river to the US Attorney's Eastern District if they don't play ball. They can go back to chasing Wall Street shysters while the Eastern takes the plaudits.'

O'Connell knew, too, that Burke could offset any involvement in criminal activity in the courtroom.

'Half the court case is personalities anyway – look at the shit show in California right now. You know what, I'll call it: O.J.'s gonna' walk.' He leaned across the table and said, 'Callum Burke is a father, an Irish cop putting his life in danger to prosecute American gangsters. He's a devoted family man desperate to re-connect with his wife and child. He's fucking catnip to a jury.'

Mattila studied his teacup for a moment then turned to Ho and Milburn in turn.

'You are in agreement to proceed, gentlemen?'

Spoken like a true politician, thought O'Connell.

The two Hong Kong cops assented.

'And the Title III on Walsh's cell phone?'

'Still on for tomorrow to get his number,' said O'Connell. 'Ruiz is putting her finest 42nd Street ensemble together for the operation. Listen, wait another few days, see what gives with the fight. The closer it gets, the more likely it is Walsh will give Burke the location. Chances are we'll get it once we get up on his cell.'

'If we get up on it,' said Mattila.

O'Connell grinned. Bobby Ho imagined him flashing the same smile when he locked some Harlem dealer up in the MCC.

Milburn said, 'Another few days.'

Ho nodded.

Mattila shrugged and looked at the floor. His shoulders slouched.

'Okay.'

O'Connell pushed his chair back from the table and stood with a grunt then studied the flecks of dirt on his legs.

'Shit,' he said, 'my wife's gonna' kill me when she sees these pants.'

*

Callum said, 'You're really eatin' that shit in front of me?'

'What, you wanna' slice of Sicilian white?' said Paddy through a mouthful of pizza.

'You asshole.'

'Relax, grab a beer'

'Fuck you.'

Paddy swallowed his slice and spread his arms – *I come in peace*.

'Another week. Then you kick this Boston guy's ass and we hit Kinsale's and tear it up.'

They sat eating in the Bleecker Street apartment's kitchen as roaches busied themselves in the corner by the sink and early evening shows played on the TV. Rain tapped at the window in the connecting bedroom.

Paddy let go a roaring belch and watched the Simpsons on the TV balanced on the radiator in the kitchen. Callum ate his porridge with methodical stoicism.

Paddy scratched his head.

'Fintan's goin' crazy at work.'

'Fintan works?'

'Ha-fuckin'-ha. At New World. You know the office shit was disappearin', staplers and Scotch tape? Now it's book boxes.'

Callum stretched. 'Maybe it's the rats.'

'I dunno',' said Paddy. 'It ain't like you can stick one of those boxes in your pocket.'

'Probably a crew out on jobs passing them off to sell somewhere. It doesn't take Sherlock Holmes to figure that out.'

Doolan paused with a slice at his mouth. His eyes narrowed. 'What, you a cop?'

Callum felt the color from his cheeks make a run for it out the door. He stared at Paddy skull-eyed.

Paddy snorted, laughing so hard he dropped pizza on the floor. Callum punched his arm.

'You fuckin' asshole.'

He sat back and watched Doolan in convulsions of laughter.

When Paddy calmed down he said, 'You scared, Christy? About the fight? I mean cut the bullshit. For real.'

Callum thought of the device in the apartment recording their chatter, imagined Ruiz or Galinski or O'Connell listening back to the recording.

He said, 'When you're training for a fight, you gotta' let the other guy worry about you. But for real? I'm nervous, yeah. And this guy, Cooper – he doesn't scare me, but the thought of what happens to him if I win does. That scares the hell outta' me.'

It did frighten him. He saw shades of himself in Cooper. Racking up higher and higher debt, sinking deeper and deeper in with the hoods who would one day extract payment in the most terrible way.

'Not *if* you win,' said Paddy, '*when* you win. You ain't just fightin' for yourself next week, man. You're fightin' for me.'

'Yeah, and I don't even know where? Has Fintan told you the venue?'

'Not yet.'

Paddy stood and hauled Callum to his feet. He threw his arms around him and pulled him close, slapping his back. Callum could smell tomato sauce and beer and tobacco. Doolan stepped back and kept his hands on Callum's shoulders. His eyes were wet in the light under the naked bulb hanging from the ceiling.

'I brought you in,' said Paddy. 'I vouched for you to get the sit down with Fintan and set this shit up. I don't know what angle he got on the side with this Cooper fight but you don't win, he ain't gonna' be happy. When he ain't happy, other people ain't happy, sometimes ever again.'

'Come on, Paddy. What's the worst that could happen? Jimmy Mulligan kicks my ass and I need a couple more ice baths.'

Paddy slapped him on the shoulder, wiped his eyes and dropped in his chair. Callum sat again.

They sat in silence. Commercials played on the TV.

Callum said, 'Shit, Paddy, you'll be okay. You and Fintan go back.'

'You're a good person, Christy, but you ain't stupid.' Paddy's eyes filled again and he grabbed another beer from the refrigerator, popped the cap and took a slug once he sat down.

He said, 'You ever faced up to a bully in school? There's always that kid who's bigger and knows it. The kid who lost his conscience somewhere along the way. Maybe he had it beaten out of him at home, or on the street, or he saw enough in his neighborhood to work out the bullshit they feed him in class is just that: bullshit. The honest people don't win. They fuckin' suffer. So this kid becomes a bully because he can roll other kids, or he can feel better about himself because at home he's a fuckin' punch-bag or worse. Or maybe because he hates the other kids for their weakness – or strength, dependin' on how you look at it. So this guy, he got another guy with him. This other guy, he's worse 'cause he's livin' off the brute force of the bully but he doesn't have the chops or the fuckin' brains to do it himself.'

Callum said, 'It doesn't take brains to be a bully, Paddy.'

'Call it cunning. Whatever. The bully is an asshole but the

other guy is just pathetic. He's a parasite. And the bully, he knows it. He knows, they ain't friends but he's got a guy can do the shitty work even the bully don't wanna' do. A fuckin' patsy.'

Paddy took a long draw on his beer. He swiped a thread of snot from under his nose with his wrist.

Callum leaned forward, pushing the porridge bowl aside. He reached out.

'Paddy – '

'Eat your fuckin' porridge, Christy. I'm goin' for another beer on Bleecker.'

'How about your pizza? You gonna' leave it here to taunt me?'

Paddy stood and made for the door.

'I ain't hungry no more,' he said, his voice thick. 'Let the fuckin' roaches eat it.'

He slipped out. Callum listened to his steps on the landing, the slap of sneakers descending the stone stairs. He imagined the final line of the transcript once NYPD had written up the recording from the hidden device, and went back to his porridge.

End of conversation.

Chapter Twenty-four

The day broke hot and wet, a pall of solid humidity hanging over the city, swallowing the tallest buildings and punishing the morning commuters. A typhoon was coming and Tony Lau looked to the sky from the tram as it crawled the fifty-degree slope to the summit of Victoria Peak on Hong Kong Island. Tourists took photos and stared at the towering shards of steel, concrete and metal rooted in the lower reaches of the mountain: the vast apartment buildings overlooking Kowloon Bay as it swarmed with small craft at the beginning of the working week.

It was a good location. There would be police officers at the top watching for trouble, ushering tourists back from precipitous falls, scanning the sightseers for pickpockets. A place to be noticed.

The Peak Tram labored into the upper terminus and he strode into the blazing August sun. His linen suit hung loose on his slim frame but still trapped the thirty-four degree heat close to his body. Looking across the bay, the mountains beyond urban Kowloon were reduced to waves of blue shadow through the heavy, wet summer haze clinging to the city. Lau's men, two bodyguards adept at violence cloaked in corporate suits, hung a couple of feet back, just as they had sat two rows behind him on the Peak Tram.

He checked his Rolex. Almost ten o'clock in the morning. Night in New York. 11.00 a.m. in Tokyo.

The Peak was alive with tourists. He spotted a couple of police standing near a photo-spot, a Chinese constable and a tanned Westerner. The Westerner caught Tony Lau's eye and paused for a moment, then spoke into his radio.

No doubting who the senior officer is, thought Lau. English bastards. Scots and Welsh, too.

Not forgetting the Irish.

He looked down from the peak to where he'd last seen Callum Burke standing on a Wan Chai street; where he'd seen Dragon Head Stanley Zhao dead under a sheet. He'd known then, looking at the guilt on Burke's face, but one of the girls in the establishment had confirmed that the Irish cop had entered the room while Zhao suffered his attack. She had waited outside the door when he shooed her from the room, and listened for the radio call for an ambulance. Nothing. The callous bastard had waited as a man died on the floor at his feet; as Burke's gambling debt had died with him.

The glint of sunlight on a tourist's camera lens brought him back to the present.

One of Lau's men carried a cell phone, waiting for the call.

Lau checked the Rolex again.

It was time.

*

Sammy Ong stripped in the small wooden room and thought of the Thai women with whom he had spent the night. He would shower in this changing room before entering the tub in the Japanese hot spring hotel. The women were washing upstairs in the hotel room before joining him in the private *onsen* pool of natural volcanic spring water. The pool was enclosed on three sides: two by a bamboo screen, the entrance to the changing room and shower on the other. Perched near a cliff edge on the Izu Peninsula, the open side overlooked Sagami Bay and Oshima Island.

Yesterday, Sammy Ong had met a driver at Narita Airport and headed for Kabuki Cho, the largest of many Tokyo entertainment districts riddled with organized crime-run sex shops, hostess bars and strip clubs. He had lunched with a representative of Tony Lau's 14K faction at a Triad-owned Chinese restaurant then been introduced to the Thai girls at a strip club upstairs. Charlie Lin had arranged for the girls to be taken to the hotel on rural Izu Peninsula for Ong's pleasure that night. Then Ong, Lin and Thomas Chen had driven out to the Port of Yokohama where the Ningbo cargo ship was moored. The ship would sail in two days, bound for New York. On board, 40 kilos of heroin would constitute a small percentage of the huge cargo.

Ong soaped his body, noting the folds of flesh where age continued to exact its toll. He counted liver spots and sighed.

Chen would be sitting in the bar at present. Lin had returned to Tokyo to make further travel arrangements for the flight to Hong Kong.

Ong rinsed off the suds.

The Tokyo-based Triads had given them a warm reception but Ong was no fool. The flow of foreign capital into Chinatown's banks, the acquisition of property, was a clear sign that Tony Lau wanted a greater say in Hip Sing business. Chinatown was finite in land and opportunity and Ong knew there were concerns among the Hong Kong Societies about the Chinese assuming control of the territory in 1997. Were they to expand in New York, the Hip Sing could be forced to contract. The negotiations of the next few days would be crucial.

The door opened and the Thai girls slipped in wearing Japanese *yukata* robes. They squeezed past him with much giggling, and through the sliding doorway of the changing room into the open air, trailing their fingernails along the bamboo screens before one of them dropped her robe at the edge of the pool sunk into the ground. She stood brazen in the hot August morning, her body the color of oolong tea, hair licorice-black and shining in the sun.

I am a lucky and foolish old man, thought Sammy Ong. He struggled to remember the girl's name from the booze-haze of last night's partying. Piti, he recalled. That was it.

He shuffled into the sunlight and sat slow and heavy on the edge of the pool. The other girl, Julia, walked behind him still wearing her robe. He had laughed when she told him her assumed name last night, at how innocently silly it seemed for a Thai whore. Julia.

While Piti slipped into the water, he heard the soft rustle of Julia's *yukata* falling to the ground behind him. He felt her body against his back, her small breasts brush his head. Piti bent and lifted him, flaccid, in her hand. She looked up at Julia and smiled.

*

Sunset Park, Brooklyn, was quiet as Sunday night eased toward the wee small hours of Monday morning. Papa Ng shuffled from the Chinese teahouse, one Cantonese business among many on a strip of restaurants, bars, travel agencies and beauty salons. Dubbed the Brooklyn Chinatown, the Hip Sing had several concerns in the area and the Flying Dragons cut the Tong in on a large slice of revenue from a couple of massage parlors and casinos they ran over a four block radius. Ng had enjoyed the Oolong and dumplings in the Golden Mountain Teahouse, even if he had to stomach the street gang representative who came to hand over the envelope of cash.

With shaved flanks and long, teased hair on top of his bullet-head, a sneer hitched to his mouth and the bare minimum of deference, the Flying Dragons "soldier" was the embodiment of all Ng detested in the youth gangs.

Papa Ng – so named because of a rumored sixteen prodigy in Hong Kong, New York and Toronto – abhorred violence. A frail man of seventy-eight years whose nature lent itself to his fatherly moniker, he understood the need for brute force but distanced himself whenever possible from those who applied it. He believed the Tong was of real benefit to the Chinese of New York and perceived the cash in his pocket to be the gains of victimless crime. If men wanted to gamble and screw their hard earned wages away so be it.

Ng opened the door of his Chrysler and collapsed into the driver's seat. He placed the envelope on the passenger seat and started the car. He pulled onto 8th Avenue and drove at a crawl. Turning west, he made for the Belt Parkway. He would cross the Brooklyn Bridge to Manhattan and cruise through Chinatown on his way north to his apartment on East 67th.

A block from the Parkway he caught the flashing light in his rear-view.

Cops in an unmarked car. Light on the dashboard.

Papa Ng sighed. He had been lectured before by some steroid-pumped police officer for driving too slowly. What the hell good were his tax dollars when the police force continually abused its power and left the real criminals unpunished?

He pulled over next to an auto shop by the parkway on-ramp.

The envelope of cash!

He grabbed at the cash and looked in his rear-view. Two cops were silhouetted by their dashboard light. Neither had opened their door.

Probably checking the plate, thought Ng. He shoved the cash under his seat and began fiddling with his license and registration as two uniformed cops got out of their car and approached.

The uniforms driving unmarked cars were probably part of some new initiative from Giuliani and Bratton, thought Ng. The Mayor and Commissioner would have been unimpressed with the sloppy look of these officers, one with shirt untucked on the right side, both smoking, strolling to the car with a disdainful insouciance. Ng began lowering the driver-side window.

The first cop stood back from the car with his hand on his gun, holstered by his hip. His face was bathed in shadow and cigarette smoke but Ng could see he was Asian. The second walked to the driver's door and leaned down to look in the window. Ng took in the shaved head above the ears, the lock of unruly, teased hair escaping from under the eight-pointed cap with the metal badge. He caught the sneer hitched to the mouth that broke into a serpent's smile as the Flying Dragons "soldier" from the Golden Mountain teahouse raised the revolver, cylindrical suppressor attached.

Papa Ng stared at the barrel of the gun. His face creased in rage.

'*Lan yeung!*' he said. '*Diu lei lo mo!*'

It was the first time in his life he had used such profanity, and the last phrase he ever spoke.

*

Sammy Ong clawed desperately at life but felt it slip away as the man entered the tub. He had felt the warm softness of the girl's breasts on his shoulders, followed by the sharp stab of a needle. The girl had stepped back as Ong had swung his arms and slipped, going under for a moment and gulping the scalding volcanic water into his lungs. When he resurfaced, the girls were standing either side of the tub with their backs pressed to the bamboo screens. He felt his body seize. His muscles revolted and he struggled for breath. Then a large man with a shock of spiked hair had entered. The man took Sammy Ong's head in his hands and forced him under the water again.

Ong's skin burned, his lungs filled, terror flooded all.

He wanted to fight but his limbs rebelled, paralysed by whatever drug the girl had injected in his neck. He saw the shape of the man above the water as his system shut down. His heart gave in and his lungs filled with water. Locked in his useless body, his brain died and he was no more.

Pineapple Wong stood back from the tub and watched the old man stare back from under the surface of the water. The girl, Julia, had done well. She had hit the old man clean with the shot of succinylcholine and, as promised by the chemists, the SUX – a neuromuscular paralytic drug – had shut down Sammy Ong's muscles, including the heart and those used for breathing.

In order to give the Japanese police an excuse to close the investigation, Wong had forced the old man under the water so his lungs would fill. The drug would metabolize into the by-products succinic acid and choline, normal to the body. The Japanese coroner would proclaim the cause of death to be a heart attack followed by drowning. Wong hadn't wanted to perform the hit but Dragon Head Lau's enforcer, Tse, was engaged in other business. Wong suspected Tse was being groomed for a higher position in the society.

The fact his Dragon Head wanted – trusted – Pineapple Wong to perform the deed indicated Pineapple himself could be in line for a promotion. And he would enjoy a night in Kabuki Cho with the girl, Piti, before flying back to Bangkok in the morning. The other girl, Julia, would fly first-class to London where she would be met at Heathrow Airport and driven to a Triad-bought house in Sussex where her aunt awaited.

A shame, thought the Teo Chiu Triad. The girl Julia stood by the bamboo screen, eyes closed as though in prayer, cheeks glistening with tears. There was something innocent about her that fired a crazy lust in Wong but the orders had come from Tony Lau himself: she was not to be molested.

He grunted to the girls to gather the old man's clothes in the changing room and composed in his head how he would report the successful killing to Hong Kong.

The homeless man found the body of Hong Kong Triad Deputy Leader Hai under a pile of cardboard in the concrete concourse by the West Exit of Shinjuku train station in central Tokyo. The 14K member subservient only to Tony Lau himself had been stabbed over forty times, his head almost severed. The killing occurred sometime in the early hours of the morning, the body left in the area around the station, renowned for vagrants. Hai's wallet was missing as were his shoes.

The Tokyo Metropolitan Police assumed a homeless person, or gang of such, had robbed the visiting Hong Kong business-man.

Tokyo Metropolitan Police officers began rounding up va-grants by the bus-load for interrogation at police headquarters. They worked in silence, comfortable in the knowledge they would pin the murder on a couple of the homeless, maintain their excellent crime clearance rates, and shut the Hong Kong consulate the hell up.

*

Papa Ng lay among the trees next to the auto-shop by the on-ramp to the Brooklyn Parkway until a dog-walker letting his Great Dane take a shit in the bushes investigated his pet's whining. Ng had six bullet holes in his face, neck and body. His car was parked a few feet away in front of the auto shop. The police checked out the vehicle. They found no envelope full of cash.

*

Hotel staff at the hot spring hotel on Izu Peninsula opened the private bathing space after three hours and several enquiries from other guests as to why the 'occupied' sign had been hanging on the door for so long. They found Sammy Ong naked in the tub. As they called the police and ambulance to collect the body, a newly-married couple from Yokohama declared they would be sure to stay at the hot spring resort of Beppu, rather than Izu, for their next long weekend break.

*

That brilliant morning on Victoria Peak, Tony Lau killed the call on his cell phone. There were plenty of witnesses to attest to him strolling Victoria Peak while Sammy Ong, Deputy Leader Hai and Papa Ng were liquidated on two continents.

Three deaths. It pleased him. Three was an auspicious number and the various Black Triad Societies shared the three-sided symbol. The union of heaven, earth and humanity.

Had he appeased his Christian God in heaven to some degree? The violence he visited upon the girl, Julia, in Bangkok, had weighed on him nights when his wife slept early. The girl was no lamb but she was an innocent in his *xie dou* – his blood revenge against Burke. Lau had felt a disconnect when his enforcer, Tse, had led her into his apartment.

Giving her a role in Ong's murder let her wash in the blood, giving her freedom to begin her life anew in the West. It offered Tony Lau some small measure of absolution.

He must now prepare for the conference with the new Hip Sing Tong Leader. The Leader had flown out of New York last night before Sammy Ong and Deputy Leader Hai were terminated. The new Tong boss would be leaving the Peninsula Hotel in Kowloon, ready to cross the bay and sit down with his Tong subordinate, Thomas Chen, and the top rank of the 14K Triad in a house near Repulse Bay. The new boss would require a formal appointment upon his return to New York, of course, but with the passing of Sammy Ong, as Deputy of the Chinatown Hip Sing, he must assume the role in the interim. He must assume the role in the negotiations of the next couple of days. And with Sammy Ong's closest ally and the eldest of the active Hip Sing members, Papa Ng, gunned down in Brooklyn, it was a formality that the new Tong Leader officially assume his role in the coming weeks.

The new boss of the Hip Sing Tong, Mickey Chiu.

Tony Lau gestured to his men to follow and strolled toward the Peak Tram terminus. He would make his way to Repulse Bay and meet his chief enforcer, Tse, for a short debrief before the Hip Sing negotiations. Tse would be tired, no doubt, but Lau was eager to hear of his brief trip to Tokyo. Of his flight out as bodyguard and companion of Deputy Leader Hai. Of his work with the Tokyo Triads butchering Hai in Shinjuku and dumping the body among the vagrants at the station. He wanted to discuss Tse's inauguration as new Deputy Leader of their faction of the 14K Triad in Hong Kong.

And, in the near future, New York City Chinatown.

Chapter Twenty-five

Callum brought the revolver down again and again. His arm shuddered with each impact. He swore as he battered the wooden grip.

'Consider this training,' said O'Connell.

Callum pointed at the cop with the butt of the Smith and Wesson.

'This was your bright idea,' he said, 'how about you do the donkey work.'

'You want a gun, you do what I say. And Mattila never knows. You're a deputized DEA Agent – that don't mean the Feds want a crazy-ass mick runnin' around New York with a firearm. This shit stays between you and me.'

'I'm a real mick now, huh?'

'Listen,' said O'Connell, 'those bastards Walsh or Doolan or Mulligan catch sight of that revolver, they'll recognise it as a cop gun. Glocks are out, too. So you break the grip, make another with a clothes hanger and tape and – hey presto! – you got a funny gun. Any two-bit dealer or Jersey bottom feeder could carry a piece of shit like that. It's a bad guy gun.'

'Piece of shit is right. A bent clothes hanger for a grip? So the story is I got it from some guy got it illegally?'

O'Connell wiped his mouth with a napkin and checked his pants for crumbs as he swallowed the last of his potato chips.

'Keep your cover story simple,' he said, 'and the gun still got chambers and a trigger, right? Long as it fires, what do you care?'

They sat in an empty DEA safe house out near LaGuardia airport listening to the same airplanes that roared over Walsh's home turf of Woodside come and go overhead. They'd talked about Mattila and his intent to veto the fight before O'Connell talked him down.

Callum was furious. He was shit scared day-in-day-out, sure, but the fight was his real 'in' to the drug business. It was worth it to see the fight through. It validated the months of fear and paranoia; it validated the man he'd been forced to become.

The big problem was that Walsh still hadn't told Paddy the venue for the fight and they weren't up on his private number. No venue, no place for the DEA and NYPD to target for surveillance. Each day passed without a definite fight venue, Callum got the sweats worse.

So he had asked for a gun. He knew it could be a liability, knew he might not have the chance to use it if things went to shit but the gun was a way to retake a little agency and O'Connell had scheduled this meet to hand it over. Callum would take it to the fight in his pocket in case something went south. O'Connell had brought a Ruger .357. Now Callum was smashing the handle against the edge of a metal sink.

'You got any candy?' said O'Connell. 'I'm still hungry.'

'There's a baby Ruth in my jacket pocket.'

O'Connell grabbed the bar and took a bite of chocolate. He watched as Callum battered the Ruger against the sink a couple more times.

He said, 'I heard Deputy Leader Hai's body is being held by the Japanese out in Tokyo.'

'Works for the Triad,' Callum said. 'Clean hits. He's killed in Tokyo while Sammy Ong dies at an outlying hotel: there's coincidence and then there's coincidence.'

'Factor Papa Ng executed in Brooklyn and you got a Chinese Night of the Long Knives, huh?'

'That'd be my guess. Someone in the Hip Sing made a play for the leadership of the Tong. Mickey Chiu travels to Hong Kong when his boss breathes his last, it doesn't take a jury at the LA Superior County Court to put two and two together.'

'And come up with a protest walk-out, fuckin' mugs,' said O'Connell. 'Oh yeah, I got the pictures.'

He pulled a series of photographs from his pocket of two bodies, a man and woman. He placed them on a table for Callum to study. Callum knew who was in the shots. But he sure as shit didn't want to see. He felt his skin itch and he wanted to bolt out the door and scream. Instead, he imagined downing a shot of Bushmills; savored the burn in his throat, the trickle of liquid fire as it seeped through his system, warming him. Calming him.

He looked at the pictures.

The torso's were bloated, the corpses' features horribly distorted.

O'Connell said, 'If I traced these I could sell them to the MOMA as an undiscovered Picasso.'

The man in the shots had matted black hair. Long, tangled locks fanned around the woman's head like dead plumage. Gabriel Muñoz and his lover, fished from the Hudson and laid out on the Jersey shore.

But Callum said, 'I don't know. It could be him but the features are so corrupted.'

'Tends to happen when you're shot six times in the face and dumped in the river.'

'And they were in garbage bags?'

'Yeah. Same garbage bags used at the Belleclaire. Coroner said they couldn't have been in the water more than a few hours. The gases in the bodies had them float to the surface and wash up on the shore. Sloppy work.'

'That's what worries me. It isn't like Walsh hasn't had plenty of practice at this shit.'

'We figure the Chinese did this. You saw the report.'

Callum had read the homicide detectives' notes. Witnesses in the Belleclaire said they heard Spanish and – maybe – some other language could have been Cantonese when the two victims were snatched. There was a series of snapping noises – probably shots fired with a suppressor. They saw a man with a Latino complexion and blood all over his face, and an unconscious young woman dragged from the room after the all the noise. The attackers wore jackets with hoods over their heads, faces hidden.

Callum looked hard at the photographs. Funny thing was, no matter how hard he reached for a memory of Muñoz alive and well, he just couldn't picture the man's face in his mind. Guilt, he guessed.

It wasn't like he led Muñoz to deal. It wasn't like he put the finger on the cousin for pushing H from the bodega. But it was another body in this investigation and Callum couldn't help feel somehow responsible. The male corpse was the right height for Muñoz, had the same kind of hair. The body was topless and shoeless but the skin had been discolored by the water and the face was all out of shape like a kid's drawing. The woman was in her underwear. She had also been shot in the face at close range, presumably at a different location after they had been snatched.

Their mouths were a mess. The teeth had been shattered by bullets and the remnants pulled out. Callum knew fingerprints had been destroyed thanks to degradation. There were DNA samples but they, too, were severely degraded by the water. It was going to take time for any results. The DEA had insisted the samples went to Virginia for PCR analysis.

'Fed pissing contest bullshit,' O'Connell had said. 'Could take 6 to 8 weeks. The guy's dead – it's the bad guys under investigation have to take priority.'

Now he said, 'Listen, it's Muñoz. He was snatched from the Belleclaire with a woman. Witnesses heard six shots and spoken Spanish. Muñoz's employer identified his body at the morgue.'

'How? Look at it,' said Callum.

'You're seein' photographs. The Belleclaire owner saw them for real. Poor bastard's probably still having nightmares. And Muñoz had his room key in his pocket, along with money in his wallet the DEA identified as cash they paid him for some information.'

Callum gave the revolver a crack on the edge of the sink.

'Yes!'

The Ruger's handle split. Callum began working at it, wedging the gun between his knees.

O'Connell changed the subject.

'Bobby Ho's been pulling long shifts, I mean real long, on the tapes. I told him to go get some sleep in his hotel room but he's napping at the office.'

Callum smiled. It was the typical work ethic of an honest, local Hong Kong cop.

'Milburn's helping out where he can,' said O'Connell. 'There's a lot of gossip around Sammy Ong's death in the Association. Sounds like a lot of members aren't buyin' the heart attack and drowning story but there ain't much anyone can do. Papa Ng was a big shock. The way he distanced himself from the darker side of the Tong, nobody expected him to go out in a hail of bullets. Tony Montana he ain't.'

Callum felt the revolver's grip give way. 'You know the 14K had to do the hits on Hai and Ong. The Hip Sing couldn't put that together in Tokyo.'

O'Connell finished his chocolate bar.

'You worried the 14K are getting closer? Some old face from Hong Kong might turn up in New York and make you?'

'You're damn right I'm worried. Why do you think I'm fucking around with this?'

Callum held up the gun.

O'Connell said, 'We're gonna' hit Walsh for his secret number in a couple hours.'

He put the candy bar wrapper in his pocket.

'You say Doolan is gonna' drive you to the fight in a New World truck,' he said. 'So, worst case scenario, we wire all of them in the lot on 50th the night before. There are maybe four, right? Then we can listen in on you in the cab and you can drop the address when you get there. We'll come runnin' and sit outside. If we can, we'll wire the Boston car while they're at the fight, too. Then we can pick them up on some bullshit traffic violation in case Cooper's gonna' buy it on the way home.'

'Tricky.'

'Damn straight. But not impossible.'

Callum set the gun on the table.

'You wanna' decide on the buzz word now in case I need to call you in on the night?' he said.

O'Connell leaned back and said, 'How about "shithead"?'

'Considering the assembled company, that phrase might see a lot of action. Oh bollocks.'

'You say "bollocks" in America, most people might think you're speaking a foreign language.'

'No, you're a bollocks. You got chocolate stains on you.'

'Shit!'

O'Connell sprang to his feet and began searching his pants. He muttered.

'Jesus, Marcie'll kill me. I can't do anything right at home these days. Jesus.'

Callum looked at the floor, at the ceiling.

He opened his mouth, closed it, opened it again.

He felt his face go hot.

Then he said, 'Mike, how come you're such a pussy when it comes to your family?'

'What'd you say?' O'Connell stopped searching his pants and took a step forward. 'What'd you say to me?'

'Look, I don't mean any offense, really, but you gave me the

Dirty Harry act from day one and then you piss your pants every time something comes up with your wife or kids.'

O'Connell looked at Callum like he was weighing options, maybe his chances.

Then he seemed to age a couple of years. His shoulders stooped and he brushed at his legs without enthusiasm. He looked at the floor when he spoke.

'Did you love your wife?' he said.

'She isn't dead.'

'You know what I mean. When you were married.'

'We still are. And what kinda' question is that?'

O'Connell looked up. He seemed to have a fresh clutch of lines around his eyes.

'No,' he said, 'I wouldn't wanna' answer that question from a cop either.'

He sat down and leaned back in the chair.

'I been married for twelve years. I got two kids. My wife, she's meticulous: plastic covers on the furniture and she dusts four times a day. She scolds the kids when they bring dirt into the house on their sneakers. Declan learns piano when he told me last week he really wants to play hockey. Lily wants a dog so bad but my wife won't have the hair on the carpets and couch.'

O'Connell stood and took the revolver from Callum. He weighed it in his hand.

'They're good kids, man. They understand and they do their best.'

'They understand?'

'They understand their mom is a cop's wife.'

Callum rubbed his hands on his sides. Tara had been too young to grasp what he did back in Hong Kong. She just knew mummy and daddy fought a lot.

O'Connell studied the revolver.

He said, 'This job makes you a real shit. You see people screamin'' and cryin' and fightin' and you see enough dead bodies and junkies, a part of you just closes off. Once you lose that part, it opens doors. Drinkin' too much, partyin' with women, whatever. You try to replace that part you lost with somethin'. I tried to keep my family in here.' He tapped his forehead with an index finger. 'I tried to think about them more but that's a tough balancing act because you start to see your kids at that child homicide crime scene, or your wife instead of the dead hooker in the taxi.'

He ran a finger up and down the barrel of the gun.

'Then one night, some asshole calls our house. I'm working and this guy tells Marcie I'm dead, I got shot at a drug bust gone wrong. She went crazy, man. She had to stay in hospital for a while and my cousin took the kids. Turns out the dickhead who called was on The Job, another cop at my precinct was pissed I collared a dealer he'd been chasin' for months. See, that's what this work can do to you.'

O'Connell shoved the gun in his pocket and motioned for Callum to pick up the broken handle.

'Marcie got out of hospital, she started the cleaning and the fussiness. I guess she has to fill a part she lost with that phone call. Anyway, she raises two kids on a cop's salary, doesn't bitch that we never get a real vacation, or time together without the kids, or when I pull overtime – which, like any cop, is more often than she'd like – and sleeps with a kitchen knife by the bedside when I'm workin' nights. Which, like any cop's wife, is way more than she'd like. So call me crazy, Burke, but I figure it's the least I can do to take my boy to his piano recitals and keep my fuckin' pants clean. Okay? Now let's go to my car. I got the stuff to make the new revolver grip in the trunk.'

Thoughts of a payphone, Tara's small voice and Irene lying with their daughter in an apartment in Cleveland flashed through Callum's mind. Had he lost that part of himself O'Connell mentioned? In Belfast, yes – there was a part of him died he'd never get back. Had he tried to fill the hole in his insides with drink? Some, yes. Women? No. Gambling? For sure. Then he'd lost another part of himself when he stood and watched Old Man Stanley Bamboo Zhao vomit his life away, and done nothing to help.

Then another corpse, Dylan Acosta, had helped him kick the gambling habit. For good, he hoped.

He thought, Every cloud ...

'Okay, Mike.' He said.

O'Connell said, 'Mikey.'

'What, are you that ten year-old kid in The Goonies?'

O'Connell sat back and crossed his arms, tilted his head and said, 'Hey, Burke, anyone ever tell you, you sound like the guy in the Lucky Charms commercial?'

'Fuck you.'

*

Three hours later O'Connell was parked up in a gray Dodge on Roosevelt Avenue across from the Woodside Sweat Shop Gym. Callum was by a grime-stained window above an Italian bakery overlooking the avenue, the El train tracks above. The finished funny gun revolver, constructed by O'Connell in the safe house, sat heavy in his pocket. Fintan Walsh was inside the gym, visible through the large glass windows fronting the street, on the free weights. Galinski was working a treadmill in the corner. The fittest in the team, he had drawn the short straw to work out while Walsh was inside and keep an eye on the target. O'Connell figured Galinski had some nervous energy to burn off after the shoot-out in Dumbo anyhow. The investigation into his shoot-out by the bridge anchorage had been fast-tracked thanks to Fed influence at One-PP. They needed him on the task force.

A couple of blocks away in a quiet street of two-floor walkups, Georgie Ruiz sat parked with Niku Mattila in a Ferrari seized by the DEA from a Philadelphia drug dealer, kitted out with new plates and driven to New York for the operation.

Callum imagined Ruiz in her skin-tight stretch miniskirt, loose blouse open to below her sternum and stiletto boots just past her ankle; hair scraped back to show off that knockout face. Ruiz made it look way less trashy than it should – the cop had class.

O'Connell had brought along police point-to-point radios. They'd gone to channel SP-TAC K so only the team could listen in on chatter – no RMP patrols or local cops could hear them. The team could hear NYPD radio chatter, however, so they'd know if patrols were in the area or 911 calls had come in for their location, a common distraction tactic of criminals if they made a surveillance team. Galinski would go to the window of the gym and stretch as a signal Fintan Walsh had gone to change.

In these moments, Callum Burke forgot the paranoia and fear. He was part of a unit with a clear objective: secure Walsh's private number for a Title III wiretap. He raised the radio.

'Be advised, target has gone to change. Galinski's in the window, K.'

'I see him, K,' said O'Connell.

Mattila said, 'Ruiz on the way, K.'

A minute later, the Ferrari crawled around the corner onto Roosevelt. The car revved, catching looks from passing pedestrians, and stalled in front of the gym. The driver's door opened and Ruiz stepped out, grabbing more looks than the precision Italian machine parked half up on the curb. She strolled around front of the car and opened the hood, propping it up, and stared inside. She had a radio with the incoming volume on mute taped by the engine out of sight, next to a small recording device.

'Alright, gentlemen,' she said, 'I'm in position, K.'

'I'll say,' said O'Connell.

Callum wondered what Mrs. Marcie O'Connell would make of the remark.

As Ruiz loitered a delivery truck pulled up and a tired-looking older man with flecks of gray in his wiry hair clambered out and made for a restaurant two doors down the sidewalk with a clipboard. A young man leaned out the cab window and looked back at Ruiz. He dropped from the cab like an alley cat in heat and strode over to the Ferrari.

O'Connell came over the channel.

'Be advised, Ruiz, you got horny Henry comin' up behind you, K.'

Callum heard the man speak over Ruiz's hidden radio.

'Hey ma'am, that's a fine machine you got there.'

Ruiz purred. 'You know it.'

'Shit, them lines ... I bet it goes real fast. Nought to sixty in what? Five seconds?'

'Faster than you can handle, baby. You don't got the power or stamina for a car like this.'

The old man with the clipboard exited the restaurant and saw his colleague flirting. He shot an exasperated look at the heavens.

On the radio Callum heard the young guy say, 'What say I reach under the hood and put my fingers to good use, see if I can't get that fine model running hot. See if I got the black in me to push it hard?'

O'Connell whispered, 'Ah shit.'

Fintan Walsh had walked out of the gym and caught sight of Ruiz talking to the young guy. He looked Ruiz up and down then stood watching her talk. His jaw was all but hanging open like a Looney Tune but his eyes were brick-hard staring at the young man flirting.

Callum heard Ruiz say, 'What say you run on and help pops over there, looks like your daddy's getting' antsy. 'Sides, I don't much care for chocolate.'

She shot a look at Walsh and said, loud, 'Vanilla's my flavour.'

The young guy spread his arms. 'Your loss, baby. There be a reason Africa's shaped like a boner and a sack, know what I'm sayin'?'

'Jesus, you're a regular Lord Byron.'

The young guy strolled back to the truck and began whining at the old man who started barking orders. Callum watched Fintan Walsh watch Georgie Ruiz. He knew Walsh was into her, thought maybe Walsh was afraid to move right now because he might show more than his hand.

Over the radio, O'Connell whispered, 'Alright, Ruiz, bend over the engine real slow.'

She hissed, 'What is this, phone sex?'

But she crossed one foot over the other and did as O'Connell asked, the skirt rising high enough to burn up on re-entry. Walsh strolled over.

A small sigh escaped Ruiz's lips then a moan.

Walsh cleared his throat.

'You in trouble?' he asked.

Ruiz stepped back from the engine, cocked a hip and placed her hands on the small of her back. Her blouse took the strain as she stuck her chest out.

She said, 'I don't know, am I?'

Cheesy. Just right for Walsh, whose idea of a courtship came from the Debbie Does Ditmars playbook.

He squared his shoulders and set his gym bag by the hubcap. He stood on the sidewalk at a right angle to Ruiz, standing in front of the Ferrari by the curb on Roosevelt.

'You want I should take a look?' he said.

'Yeah.' Ruiz stretched the vowels until they almost snapped. At the same time, she leaned back over the engine in slow motion, giving Walsh an eyeful of the midnight blue brassiere under her blouse. Callum saw Walsh lick his lips.

'You take a real good, long look,' said Ruiz.

They stood at the car talking like the script of a cheap porno. Walsh fiddled with the engine and Callum knew that, like him, O'Connell and Mattila would be sweating the possibility of Walsh finding the listening device or recorder. They were well hidden but if he looked too hard he could catch a glimpse.

The conversation dried up for a moment. Walsh would be desperate to impress, thought Callum, but had probably never seen the inner workings of a Ferrari. He'd be looking it over, checking every part. Checking enough to, just maybe, see the device.

He heard Walsh's voice go low.

'What's that?'

Something cold took a dive in Callum's gut.

Walsh leaned over the engine, trying to look further into the area behind the fender and headlights. The area where they'd secured the listening device.

Ruiz said, 'Hey!'

The young man from the delivery truck was back and grabbed Ruiz ass. Then he slipped his hand around her waist and pulled her close.

He said, 'You gonna' introduce me to your pops?' and nodded toward Walsh.

Walsh sprang back from the engine like he was an attack dog on a chain that ran out of length. Callum saw the rage build in his face, zero to sixty in a couple of seconds. He couldn't take his eyes away from the impending carnage, knew O'Connell would let things play out but hoped Mattila didn't have sight on the situation. The DEA agent was likely to step in somehow and blow the sting rather than risk Joe Public taking a few lumps.

The young guy had Ruiz close, her back to his chest, and was laughing as she wriggled against him to free herself. The old guy stood at the truck yelling for his partner to get his ass over there so they could make more deliveries. Walsh stepped around the front of the car. Callum could hear the young guy blabbering, Ruiz telling him to leave her alone. Walsh's silence.

Then a scream.

The young guy took a step back and went soft at the knees. Walsh hesitated. Ruiz turned and for a second Callum thought she was holding hands with the young guy. Then he saw the angle of the guy's hand to his fingers, saw Ruiz grip. He heard her speak.

'You want me to let go of your fingers?'

'Uh-huh.' The young guy's voice was shrill with pain.

'Alright, you pop those back in when you get back in your truck. Now get the fuck out of here, you hear me?'

'Uh-huh, uh-huh.'

She let go of the guy's hands and he stepped back again, almost got taken out by a passing Buick. He ran over to the truck in a crouch, the old man shaking his head as he clambered back in the cab.

Walsh watched as the truck pulled out into Roosevelt traffic. He stepped back onto the sidewalk and looked at Ruiz.

She shot a playful look back at him.

'Where you from?' he said.

'Washington Heights.'

'No, I mean … I mean, you know, your family.'

'Dominican.'

'Yeah, you got that sass, for sure.'

'You like that?'

'Yeah, I like that.'

Walsh stepped a couple of feet away from Ruiz. Callum saw him suck in his gut. Ruiz looked at him for a second then said, 'Wait a minute, you ain't Italian, are you? I had some issues in the past with Italians.'

'No, baby. I'm Irish through and through.'

'*Madre de dios*, you Irish boys? You'll leave your wives for me.'

Walsh grinned. His chin jutted forward.

'You don't have to worry none on that score, I ain't married.'

'So, what's that ring on your finger?'

'She's deceased. I wear it to heal the pain.'

Walsh's grin got wider.

Ruiz looked him up and down. She tapped her stiletto on the asphalt, then seemed to come to a decision.

'My name's Maria.'

'Fintan.'

'Okay, Fintan, I'm gonna' call someone to tow my car and take a cab to my mother's but thanks for your help.'

'No problem. I gotta' meet someone but you might wanna' take a look behind the fender. I think something got wedged in there. Maybe something from the engine.'

Callum felt that cold plunge in his insides again. He willed Walsh not to take another look.

Ruiz let down her hair and Walsh stared as it tumbled down the sides of her face and settled above her chest. She pulled it around one side of her neck, straining her blouse on the left and flashing midnight blue lingerie.

'So, you got a number, Fintan?'

'Yeah,' said Walsh. 'Yeah, I got a number.'

Ruiz walked around the car headlights and on to the sidewalk then opened the door of the Ferrari, leaned in and across the seat. Walsh stood back to get a look and went scarlet staring at her ass. She eased herself back out of the car. She held a pen and a menu for a pizza delivery joint in Washington Heights.

'You wanna' write your number down?' said Ruiz.

'Yeah,' said Walsh with a smile would put the big bad wolf to shame. 'Yeah, I do.'

He leaned on the roof of the Ferrari. When he finished, Ruiz read out the number. Callum imagined O'Connell's smile, Mattila punching the air. It had to be the target number.

Ruiz smiled and nodded. She lowered the hood and locked the Ferrari, got lucky hailing a cab straight away. When she made to climb in, Walsh said, 'Hey, Maria, you got a number?'

'Sure I do. 38-23-47.'

She blew Walsh a kiss then gave him a number they set up yesterday that would go to voicemail and, finally, a DEA agent who would act as 'Maria's' disapproving mother. Ruiz closed the taxi door and the cab drove east toward Hunter's Point and the Queensboro Bridge.

Fintan Walsh picked up his gym bag, shook his head and smiled as he watched it go.

Chapter Twenty-six

''38-23-47? Classy lady.'

'Yeah,' Paddy laughed. 'You know, she ain't answerin' her phone? Fintan thinks she might be blowin' him off.'

It was the day before the fight.

They sat out on the apartment fire escape. Callum looked across Bleecker at the Little Red School House. The sounds of the city seemed to settle in the air around them as they sat under a late summer sun. The sweltering heat of the last couple of months had eased. It was two o'clock and the children were inside the school opposite. Callum could see a small face peer through a first floor window. He closed his eyes for a couple of seconds and held tight to an image of Tara in a summer dress holding his hand on one of the islands in his head. The picture began to fade like an old Polaroid in an album and he frowned. Not enough pictures in that album; not enough memories.

When he opened his eyes the child in the window was gone.

'Tell you what,' said Paddy, 'you got all day tomorrow before the fight. Let's go out tonight.'

Callum started to protest but Paddy cut him off.

'No booze for you. Just a night out. Webster Hall. Couple of hours in the club, I bring Trinity with one of her friends – relax, not Sunrise – and who knows?'

'Are you crazy? You even know where the fight is yet?'

'Not yet, man. Fintan plays it close to his chest for fight nights. But listen, that mug Bobby Cooper gotta' work security in a social club tonight and a half-shift in a canning plant tomorrow before he drives down here. Half the guys fightin' tomorrow are workin' security in some bar tonight. So, tonight you don't drink but maybe you get lucky. You can be home by twelve if you want. Shit, you're still smokin' despite your fuckin' training. I'll call Trinity, set it up.'

'I need rest, conditioning.'

'You need to get out, man. It'll energize you before you fight.'

'No, Paddy, come on.'

'I'll go call Trinity.'

'Paddy – '

'I'll call Trinity.'

Paddy climbed through the open window into the apartment.

Callum scanned the street below. He needed to call in with O'Connell and see if the Walsh phone tap had revealed the fight venue. He needed some quiet time to settle his nerves.

He laughed. Quiet time. In Manhattan. Who was he kidding?

And it was best to stick close to Paddy. If he went out and Callum stayed home he'd be chewing his nails and watching re-runs, achieving nothing. What if Paddy somehow got word of the fight venue while at Webster Hall? What if another player came along and Callum missed some crucial intelligence?

It was plain and simple. He had to come along.

Callum set his tomato juice on the iron slats of the fire escape, lit up a smoke, and said, 'Shit.'

*

Niku Mattila shook his head. He sat across the desk from O'Connell and Milburn, Ho standing behind the others' chairs, in the office in the DEA building. He glanced out the window at the Hudson. The day had consented to provide a glorious back-drop of early September sunshine to light the scene.

'You don't understand,' he said. 'I want to be patient but I'm taking pressure from above on this. You still don't have an address for the fight and it's tomorrow night – how're you going to protect Burke with backup if you don't know where he is? If he doesn't have an address by tomorrow afternoon, we get him out and mop the players up at their homes.'

'Are you fuckin' crazy?' said, O'Connell. 'You do that, there's no guarantee anyone's at home. Best I can see, Walsh and Mulligan spend as little time with their families as they can. What happened to you givin' us more time?'

'Shit rolls downhill and I'm starting to smell pretty bad, Sergeant. The fact is, I can't endanger Burke's life any further. This is the deal, and it comes from Arlington and New York City Hall. If you do get a definitive address for the gathering, Burke will go to the fight venue under the pretence of fighting. He will wear a wire and give us the word, and we will bust every player in attendance before he steps in the ring. We got Walsh's crew on narcotics and murder, extortion, illegal gambling: there is a RICO racketeering case there, no question. We got several senior Tong on wiretaps and by association under the RICO statute. We bring them in and sweat them for the drug shipment and a route to the Triad. I'd say that's a significant finger in the dyke.'

'Bobby,' said Milburn.

Ho cleared his throat and said, 'We think you should see this.'

He rummaged in a small backpack and produced some papers, sliding them across the table to Mattila. The DEA Agent read the usual details of a Title III transcript, one of Ho's translations. A conversation between Charlie Lin and Mickey Chiu. There were a few lines of platitudes. Lin and Chiu discussed the arrangements for Sammy Ong's funeral tomorrow.

| LIN: | It will be a sober affair, no doubt. Freddie Wong is eager to attend. |
| CHIU: | On the periphery of the procession is acceptable. There will be members of the Fifth |

	Precinct there; City Hall. We don't need Freddie Wong mixing with a Precinct Captain or the Mayor's secretary.
LIN:	And the Emerald Rat?
CHIU:	Yes. I have been speaking with the manager on the phone and they will send a representative.

Mattila looked up from the page.

'Walsh is sending someone to Sammy Ong's funeral.'

O'Connell nodded and said, 'The old man's already been cremated but they're having a procession in Chinatown tomorrow morning. We got Walsh and Mulligan talking about it too, on Walsh's cell. You wanna' pull Burke right at the moment when the pieces are coming together.'

Mattila shook his head.

'Too many elements in play that could compromise him.'

Milburn crossed his legs, banging his knee on the desk.

'If you would read on,' he said.

Mattila turned back to the paper. After a half page he read:

LIN:	Are you looking forward to tomorrow evening?
CHIU:	It isn't The Garden but, yes, I enjoy a fight.
LIN:	A little bloody for my taste.
CHIU:	Most of America thinks we're all raised to fight like Jackie Chan, Charlie. The likes of Freddie Wong trade on that kind of misconception.
LIN:	Two men beating hell out of each other for sport is not my idea of an evening's entertainment. I've never understood the attraction of boxing.

CHIU:	The Irish love it. Think of tomorrow night as cultural exchange and cementing of business. Instead of dinner and drinks, a night of fights. And the Emerald Rat have a new employee they'd like us to see. He'll be on the roster. If we like him, they'd like us to consider using him at Red Hook the night after.
LIN:	Is that wise? We meet him one night and the next he's receiving supplies for the new business.
CHIU:	He's been working for the Rat for some time, they know him and trust him.
LIN:	Do we trust them?
CHIU:	It's a little late for that.

'My God,' said Mattila. 'Red Hook Docks. It's a shipment.'

O'Connell smiled. 'Damn straight,' he said.

'And they're discussing Burke.'

'Gotta' be.'

'We need to get on to Customs,' said Mattila, 'Port Authority, FDA, see what's coming into Red Hook night after tomorrow.'

'On it,' said O'Connell. 'So far, it looks like there's nothing in the way of chemicals, emulsions or liquids coming in. No clothing either, or bags. Course, we could have been working off of false theories.'

'Indeed,' said Milburn. 'There are toys in the cargo, Chinese manufactured. Building materials, some car accessories. We're still working through the itineraries.'

Ho said, 'At least we know the place.'

Niku Mattila pinched the bridge of his nose hard then rolled his head a little.

'Do we have Walsh discussing this on a phone?'

'No,' said O'Connell, 'but you gotta' see, we're at the crux of the investigation here.'

'You still don't know the fight venue. He would have to be strapped.'

'No wire, he gotta' be naked as the day he was born. He can't fight if he's strapped. If Doolan's got the venue by then, Burke will tell me. We're still on Walsh's phone. He's gotta' drop an address for the fight sometime.'

'And we can protect his opponent, Cooper, if he loses?'

'We pull the car over on its way out of New York, some bull-shit traffic violation, and hold him.'

'The fight is still illegal.'

'Burke's being coerced into it,' said O'Connell. 'In court, seventy percent of a jury's decision is probably down to presentation and personality, and Callum Burke's gonna' present a hell of a lot better than Fintan Walsh or Mickey Chiu. He's a fuckin' martyr.'

At least that's how the DA would spin events.

Mattila inspected his fingernails. He glanced at Milburn and Ho, then held O'Connell's gaze for a few seconds. He saw a street-hardened, ruthless and efficient New York cop with a callous, embittered core. Shit-head probably tied one on and beat his wife and kids of an evening, he thought. He decided to place all responsibility on O'Connell, in his own mind at least, and felt a weight lift.

'Sergeant Michael O'Connell, you're a hard bastard. We'll let it play.'

O'Connell flashed him a grin.

'Whatever it takes, Special Agent, whatever it takes.'

Chapter Twenty-seven

Two Europeans argued with a doorman at Webster Hall over the no-baseball cap policy and Trinity tutted three-back in the line.

'Fuckin' Frenchies,' said Luna, American-Caribbean with a Colgate smile, lips that begged to be kissed and an attitude bigger than her Foxy Brown afro. Paddy grunted.

'I think they're German,' said Callum.

Twenty minutes later, Callum's party were inside. They by-passed the smaller dancefloor moving to Ini Kamoze and hit the main hall. The space was thronged, ringed by a balcony and a huge projection of The Shining at one end of the hall. Girls in stripper outfits gyrated in metal cages hung from the ceiling over the dancefloor. Jane's Addiction played, strobes strafed the crowd and Callum almost tripped over a couple dry humping on the floor.

A clutch of young East Asians, maybe Chinese, were dancing nearby and caught Trinity's eye. She threw a few shapes, her body moving like there was something off-kilter. She looked like a girl possessed and her fingers twisted in tortured, arthritic patterns. Callum remembered Paddy bragging about her flexibility.

The young Asians moved off. Callum made an effort with Luna but her face was a series of still frames in the strobe, flickering from indifference to anger to disdain.

'I gotta' take a piss!' he yelled in her ear.

Downstairs in the bathroom, someone snorted powder off the top of the urinal. Moans came from a stall. A transvestite staff member with six-inch fingernails sold candy and condoms next to the sinks. Callum felt the room tilt like he was on a ship in rough seas and walked out of the bathroom and stood leaning against the wall of the corridor. A beautiful woman in a leather mini-skirt come over and laid a hand on his arm.

'You okay?' she said.

He looked at her face and smiled with gratitude. Ruiz had her hair braided and wore a simple blouse on top. She was stunning.

'You alright?' she said.

'Yeah, I'm okay.'

'We were up on the phones and heard Doolan arranging tonight. And we got the fight venue from Walsh's cell, Callum! 66 Little West 12th Street in the Meatpacking District. We'll be right outside when you fight tomorrow night.'

Ruiz's hand slipped down his arm and held his hand in hers for a moment.

Callum nodded. He felt something cold and tight inside. Somehow knowing the venue made the fight more real.

Ruiz gave him a look like she could read his mind.

'We're ghosting you,' she said. 'You're not alone.'

'Thanks.'

She leaned in close and breathed in his ear.

'You're sweatin' like crazy. You wanna' go, we can walk out together like you picked me up. Take some edge off.'

He brought his lips close to her ear and felt her tense.

'I'm just wound a little tight. I'll sit down and take a minute. Doolan is upstairs with his girlfriend and another female, Luna Robinson.'

'About the fight,' said Ruiz, 'Bobby Ho heard over the phones that a couple of Tong guys will be there like Walsh said. Ho heard there's a shipment of H coming in to Red Hook the night after the fight: that's when we make some busts. We'll get them all the next night.'

Callum sagged. He put a hand against the wall and threw his head back. It was almost over.

'Take care okay?' said Ruiz. She put her hand on his chest then walked toward the ladies' bathroom.

Callum went looking for Paddy and found another bar, smaller and thick with the smell of weed. There were movie-theater-style bucket seats against a wall and he got a soda from the bar and collapsed into one.

Shit! He felt sick with fear.

He'd left the funny gun and bullets wedged under his mattress in the apartment on Bleecker. Just as well, he thought, the way he felt right now he might pull it and fire a couple of rounds at the ceiling to let off some steam. He just wanted to stop for a second and let the world churn on without him. He sat and listened to reggae and closed his eyes.

Something brushed his knee and he opened his eyes again.

A Chinese-looking girl in a knee-length dress with a split up to her hipbone stood over him with a joint in her spidery fingers. Was she one of the group who had danced nearby him, Paddy, Trinity and Luna upstairs? He had no idea. She could have been twenty-two or forty in the low light and fug of smoke. She leaned forward and placed her hands on his thighs, keeping the burning tip of the joint away from his legs.

She said, 'Hi.'

'Hi.'

'You alone?'

'For now.'

She smiled and he saw she had a lipstick stain on one of her front teeth. Her eyes narrowed to black fissures in her angular face.

'You want to blowback?'

Callum feigned ignorance.

'I don't know what that is.'

'I take a smoke then I blow it back into your mouth. You just open your lips, close your eyes and wait.' Her voice dropped as she leaned in and whispered in his ear. 'That sound good?'

Callum got tingles in his shoulders. He felt he'd start shaking if he stood up.

'Sure,' he said. He was too tired to argue or feint and, what the hell? One hit of weed wasn't gonna' kill anyone. If he lost to Boston Bobby, the guy would clean his slate of gambling debt and the shipment would still come in the night after. He knew O'Connell wanted Callum to meet the Chinatown people, to bring that extra juice to the case, but you never knew when you stepped in the ring.

I hope I do goddamn lose, thought Callum with a spite born of fear.

The woman sat and shifted on his knee and came closer and her face darkened in the shadows as her lips almost touched his. She giggled and tilted her head like she was moving in for a kiss and Callum thought of Radha in front of her folk's place in Queens, thought of Irene, and he wondered if he felt this was all wrong because it was too easy, or because his record with women was so bad.

The reggae pounded around the room, ricocheting off the walls. The world was swelling and fading into a mish-mash of beats and echoes. He closed his eyes, waiting for the woman's touch and took a second to register her yelp.

Trinity stood next to her, a clump of hair in her fist, her arm tense as she yanked at the woman's bob, snapping her neck back. Cut glass cheekbones exposed to the light, the woman's mouth stretched tight in pain. Callum saw the delicate lattice of tendons in her exposed neck – he half expected Trinity to pull a knife and slit her throat. Trinity leaned close to the woman and whispered something into her ear like a lover. The woman's eyes glinted as they slid in Trinity's direction. She cried out when Trinity yanked harder on her hair. Trinity leaned close, licked the woman's ear, slow and gentle, and pulled her from Callum's lap by the hair.

She let go and the woman stared at her for a moment, her hair a mess at the back, her shoulders hunched. She looked closer to forty now and pulled her skirt down a little, smoothed her hair at the back and walked off through the crowd, glancing back once before leaving the room.

Trinity said, 'You okay?'

'Yeah, I'm fine.'

'She'd be a great client. I shoulda' taken her number.'

'What just happened?' said Callum. 'She was cute.'

'She was a skank. I've seen her before around here. She'll fool around a little but she's got a pill somewhere. Slips it in your drink, gets you fucked up and then leads you outside. Then some guys already marked you in here, roll you and you wake up in an alley less the contents of your pockets. You're welcome.'

Callum looked at her long, cruel fingers and small, sharp incisors as she smiled in the orange light of the club. She was a small animal but a predator, not prey. Maybe someone already spiked my drink, he thought. I feel pretty fucked up.

'You don't look so good,' said Trinity.

She dropped in a squat next to him and put a hand on his arm.

Callum said, 'Where's Paddy?'

'Upstairs with Luna.'

'Can you tell Paddy I stepped outside for some air? I need some space, you know?'

'Sure, I'll tell him.'

He stood like an old man and started when she took his hand in hers. She stroked his face with the other and led his mouth close to hers.

'Take care,' she said and kissed him deep, her tongue slow in his mouth. She took his hand and placed it on her ass. He opened an eye, trying to figure out what the hell was happening and caught her dark eyes half open, watching him.

The kiss broke.

Callum hunched to get close to her face.

He said, 'Tell Paddy.'

*

Outside the night was warm and sweet. Callum walked to the corner of East 11th and 4th Avenue and leaned against the wall, tilting his head back so his crown touched the pillar of the US Mail building. He toyed with the idea of a smoke but his chest and head felt thick after the weed-choked bar and a hint of the day's humidity lingered over the city. He wondered if Ruiz or Galinski knew he'd left Webster.

Callum had felt a spike of fear when Ruiz told him they had the fight venue. He'd have to take his lumps. The old mantras ran across his mind: *let the other guy worry about you; just the two fighters in the ring; he's feeling what you are; he's only human; he's scared.*

He was beat but Trinity had sent a jolt of energy through him when she pulled his hand close. He hadn't tagged her as the picket-fence-type but the sudden shift through the gears – a stroke of the arm to foreplay – had taken him unawares. Where did it come from? They'd been out before and never a flirtatious word, never mind swapping spit. Christ, he was tired. He needed sleep.

It was almost eleven-thirty. A few people wandered by between nightspots and a raggedy old man bedded down across the street.

Taxis sat waiting at a signal for the green light and it was after a passing RMP cop car sounded a couple of whoops to move a yellow cab that the uniformed cops walked up to Callum. Two Asian officers, one with his hands holding his duty belt, another with sinewy arms like bald chicken wings in his powder blue short sleeves, his right hand on his nightstick. Neither wore his eight-pointed cap and chicken wings had thick, unkempt hair creeping over his collar.

Both looked Chinese.

'You been in Webster Hall?' said the first, his head bobbing and shoulders hunched. He came across like a goofy freshman playing at cop.

'Yes, Officer,' said Callum. 'Just came outside for some fresh air.'

Goofy cop said, 'Did you speak with a Chinese lookin' lady in one of the bars inside?'

Callum felt a cold unease scurry across his mind.

He said, 'Yeah, she kinda' came on to me.'

'We need you to come to the precinct with us.'

The hairs on Callum's arms shot straight up.

'Sorry officer, what's the problem?'

Chicken wings said, 'We've received a complaint you assaulted the lady inside.'

His voice was high and tight. He kept rubbing the nightstick with his fingers.

Callum felt a crazy-scared-rage seize his gut. He took a step forward.

'That's bullshit! She comes over to me out of nowhere and offers me weed!'

'You took illegal narcotics?'

'No! She tried to give me weed and a friend told her to get lost.'

Goofy cop said, 'And where is this friend now?'

'She's in the club. You come in with me and we can find her. She'll explain everything.'

Chicken wings spoke up. He rushed his words like he was reciting a script and he was worried he'd forget his lines.

'It'd be better if you come with us, sir. We just need to be seen to act on this, you know? She probably felt pissed you turned her down or something, made a complaint to get back at you. It won't come to nothing, just come along to the precinct.'

'And if I don't wanna' come?'

Goofy cop's right hand went to the grip of his revolver and stayed there, the palm resting on the wood.

He didn't look so goofy anymore.

'I think you need to calm down. Just come to the precinct. You'll be home before the club empties, okay?'

Callum looked past the cop at the avenue. He couldn't see their car.

Chicken wings looked at his partner. The other cop kept his hand on his gun.

'Just come with us.'

Callum checked Chicken Wings' shirt collar brass for his precinct number. Five.

'Where's your precinct?'

'Jut co ...'

'Which precinct are you guys from,' said Callum. He shifted weight and glanced at the .38 revolver in its holster. 'How far is it?'

Chicken wings spoke, his voice even tighter like someone had him in a chokehold.

'The Fifth Precinct, Okay?'

'Chinatown? You're a little far from home, don't you think?'

'The lady made the complaint lives off Canal Street; and it ain't for you to ask the questions, alright. Just come with us.'

Callum's brain was in a screaming match with his body to stay calm.

'How far is Chinatown from here?' he said. 'Maybe twenty blocks? Where's your RMP?'

The cop rubbed the grip of his revolver with his palm. His eyes stayed on Callum but the lids were flickering.

Callum said, 'The Regular Marked Patrol. Your car.'

'How do you know what it's called?'

'I dated a girl had a brother was a cop.'

Chicken wings eased the nightstick out of his duty belt a couple of inches.

'It's a block over on 3rd. Now let's go.'

'Fuck,' said Callum, 'you!'

The two cops looked at one another. Traffic stopped and piled up at the signals on the corner behind them.

Callum said, 'RMP stands for *Radio Mobile* Patrol, fuckwit. And the Fifth wouldn't answer a complaint up here, they'd refer it to the local precinct. And you sure as shit ain't cops so get the fuck out of here.'

His heart pounded like the beat in the club and he started walking toward the people milling outside Webster. His legs almost shook, adrenaline pumping, threatening to take over and send him into a mad sprint. The fake cops moved with him but Goofy had taken his hand from the revolver and reached out for him like he was calming a wild animal.

'Just relax, okay? Take it easy.'

The howl of a siren rushed up the street like a blast wave from an explosion. Callum jumped and turned to see an RMP pull up next to a cluster of staggering bodies. Two men were entangled, a woman grabbing at one while another woman stood by crying and a man drank from a paper cup watching the drunken street fight. Two cops jumped from the car and began grappling with the brawlers. Callum praised the Lord for alcohol then turned back to the Chinese-looking fake cops. The wide sidewalk was empty but for a crumpled New York Post wedged against a doorframe and Callum's shadow, stretched and warped like a dream-version of himself.

The fake cops were gone.

Chapter Twenty-eight

Next morning, Callum rose with the sun. Despite lack of sleep he swung his legs sharply from the box mattress in the cramped corridor of the apartment and slung on some clothes. He padded on bare feet to the kitchen and listened at the door to Paddy's bedroom. He heard the low snore of Paddy and a small moan from Trinity.

He had gone straight home after the fake cops disappeared last night and sat out on the fire escape for an hour chain-smoking to calm his shakes. Then he'd gone to a phone on the street and called Mattila's office. No one picked up and O'Connell's number went straight to a message. Callum had forced himself to bed.

He slid the funny gun and shells out from the mattress. He wrapped them in a plastic bag and wedged it under his armpit then stepped out into the building hallway and slipped his sneakers on. He took the stairs to the roof.

Looking across the bric-a-brac rooftops of Greenwich Village and SoHo, he saw the World Trade Center defined black by the sunrise, like two bars of a giant prison cell. West of the financial skyscrapers sat the Meatpacking District. Tonight Callum would face a man he'd never met on a concrete floor on Little West 12th and beat hell out of him. He offered a short prayer that he'd see the sun rise again tomorrow.

He set the gun on the roof, lit up a cigarette and watched the dawn light coat the city in gradients like an advancing tide.

The fake cops had to be Flying Dragons. Too young and sloppy to be Hip Sing. Were they working with the girl in the club? Or were they taking an early look at him for the Tong before tonight? Would they have driven him to Chinatown and stripped him for a wire like Walsh on their first meeting? Did Fintan Walsh know they'd be outside the club? Was that why Paddy had dragged him to Webster Hall in the first place?

Whatever was happening, it wasn't in the script. He'd call O'Connell, then confront Paddy and Fintan about the Chinese fake cops, see what they had to say.

Callum picked up the gun and walked to a water tank next to the small brick structure housing the stairs to the roof. He opened the tank lid and set the gun and bullets, wrapped in the plastic bag, inside.

He finished the smoke and tasted the morning air, not yet pregnant with carbon monoxide and air-conditioning shit and the fumes of millions of people on an island just over two miles across at its widest point.

Paddy Doolan had a job this morning and would leave the apartment in an hour or so, but Callum decided to head for midtown and call the DEA office, let the team know about last night. He could pass his early morning departure off as a training run should Paddy ask. He took the stairs down to Bleecker and turned onto 6th Avenue.

He walked north then east. At Penn Station the strip of sex shops, peep shows and strip joints began, leading to 42nd Street. Stripped of its night-neon sass the Deuce looked dirty and tired and used up.

Just like me, he thought.

*

He called in to the DEA office from a payphone across from the Maine Monument at the southwestern corner of Central Park. Traffic swirled around Columbus Circle on his right. A man sipped a coffee from the regulation blue paper Anthora cup reading a newspaper by a hotdog cart.

The phone rang. No one picked up.

He tried O'Connell's cell.

O'Connell didn't pick up.

It was a little before 0930 and the chorus of Manhattan horns and sirens was building to the first of several daily crescendos.

Callum tried the numbers again.

Nothing.

Where the fuck were they?

The man reading the newspaper looked up. He stared at Callum. Then the man looked at a guy standing twenty yards from the phone-stand. Not checking his watch or hailing a cab or reading a map. Just standing.

Who the fuck just stands there on a midtown Manhattan street at this time of the morning? Did the asshole just nod at newspaper guy? Why isn't that guy eating a frank if he's standing by a hotdog stand?

Callum set the phone back in its cradle.

This was crazy. They're just two random guys standing on the street. He was losing it. But he moved off anyway. All the promises that the team would be there tonight, would back him up, and no one was answering the damn phone.

0935.

The fight was at 2130: twelve hours away.

Callum thought of the revolver wrapped in the bag in the rooftop tank with its makeshift grip of glue, tape, wire and elastic bands. He couldn't take it into the ring tonight. What fucking good was it?

He looked at the two men. Neither had moved. It looked like the newspaper guy hadn't turned the page in five minutes.

He decided to get out of there.

*

299

He cut across Central Park instead. He emerged onto 5th Avenue at the Met and wandered north. He checked for the two men he'd seen back at Columbus. For someone following him. All looked clear.

A couple of runners, a man and woman, darted out of the park from the reservoir. He decided to follow them to occupy his mind. He'd stop at another payphone and call in again. The runners cut into the Upper East Side, jogging past townhouses and fashion-model-slim trees. They crossed Park and Lexington Avenues, and cut north for a block. Then east again toward 2nd Avenue, choked with traffic and a hot, churning pall of fumes. They threaded their way across and on down 95th street. Callum followed. Then he slowed and stopped.

He was looking at Trinity's building.

The sidewalk in front was scrubbed clean where Sol Grundy had bled out on that night when Callum had begun his life of state-sponsored crime. How many people had walked over the spot where Grundy died, how many birds had shit on it, dogs pissed, rats scampered? Who remembered Grundy but for a handful of friends and relatives out in Brighton Beach?

'Hey, Irish, you spying on me?'

He almost called out in surprise. Trinity stood behind him, watching him watch her place. She wore the same short skirt, stiletto leather ankle boots and short, tight t-shirt from Webster Hall.

'Hi,' said Callum. 'You got me.'

Trinity gave him a smile didn't match her eyes.

'What're you doin' here, Christy?'

She took a couple of steps and stopped inches away from him.

He thought of last night and remembered the slope of her ass again, the smooth sweep of her skin. She never looked this hot before, he thought. Am I losing it? She said in Bill's strip joint I changed. Maybe she was right. Maybe the lie of being one of Walsh's hoods had seeped through to reality.

'You know,' he said, 'I really have no idea.'

Trinity tilted her head. Her eyes narrowed and Callum couldn't decide if she was amused or pissed. He thought of her yanking the woman back by the hair last night, how her lips pulled back from her small teeth like a shark.

He laughed. 'I was out for a jog before the fight tonight. I ran into the park and I saw this couple break off from laps of the reservoir and I just started following them. I don't know why. To make the run more interesting, maybe. And they ran down here and I realized I was outside your place.'

Callum smiled and Trinity made a small purring noise that spiked something hot in his belly.

'See,' she said, 'that's the Christy I met first time. Kinda' shy, kinda' awkward. I liked that Christy a lot.'

She stretched and Callum had an image of a feral cat limbering up.

Something was off, he thought. Trinity sounded like a Valley girl playing gangster's moll. She looked him up and down like she was measuring him for a coffin.

'So,' said Callum, 'what're you doing?'

'Going home. I live here.'

Dumb, thought Callum, goddamned dumb. He was beat. He had nothing.

Trinity put a long fingernail on his chest. It felt sharp through his t-shirt.

'You don't fool me,' she said. 'I know what you're up to.'

Callum stood sweating under the morning sun and blinked, waiting for the hammer to drop.

'I saw your face last night. I *felt* you when you touched me.'

Trinity walked around him and took a couple of steps up her stoop then sat and crossed her legs.

'It's okay, baby, I like you, too. I wouldn't have kissed you if I didn't, wouldn't let you put your hand there.'

301

She leaned back and put her elbows on the steps, her long fingers dangling.

'Look,' she said, 'I'm not one for lines so I'll put it real simple. Come upstairs and I'll give you a couple of pills and fuck your brains out.'

'What about Paddy?' Callum asked.

'That asshole fell asleep dry humping last night. He's gone off like overripe fruit in July.'

Again the tough-girl talk, thought Callum. She'd been tough as nails in Webster last night, that was for sure.

He looked up at the building, at the windows on her floor.

Did something move behind the drapes?

Goddamn paranoia, thought Callum.

Trinity stood, smoothed her skirt down and said, 'Don't look so scared, Christy, I won't treat you like a client.'

She shrugged.

'Tell you what. I feel bad about last night. It was pretty cheap, coming on to you like that. Why don't you come upstairs and have some iced tea. Then you run back to Bleecker and do whatever you do before a fight. Deal?'

Callum didn't like it. She could be as dirty as the rest. At the least, she knew about Paddy and Walsh pushing dope in the dungeon on the Upper West Side.

But he could get in her place, nose around. He was so paranoid he was probably wrong about the window. Could have been a curtain blowing in the breeze or a cloud throwing shade on the pane.

He said, 'Okay.'

She grinned and opened the door. They climbed the stairs in silence. She opened her apartment door and they stepped into a cramped hallway. Trinity bid him take his shoes off. The hall led to a small living space with a table, kitchenette and sofa. The TV was by the window looking over 95th. Wood flooring, a couple of prints from the MOMA. There was a bead curtain next to the kitchenette and a closed door on the other side. Another door to the right stood ajar. Callum glimpsed a bed inside.

'Is that where the magic happens?' he said pointing to the bead curtain.

'You wanna' see?'

Trinity walked past him and parted the curtain. She opened the door and he stepped through.

Walls painted dark purple. A leather padded table in the center of the room, restraints hanging from a wall. A leather cross against another. Some sex toys hanging next to it. A blind drawn over a small window. The whole room was no more than twenty feet across, twelve long.

Trinity hopped on the table.

'You can try something out if you want.'

'I need my energy for tonight.'

'True, that.'

He saw a collection of whips and floggers hanging by the cross, like those he'd seen in the dungeon on West 97th Street. He walked over and touched them.

'You like the toys?' said Trinity. She hopped off the table and joined him, ran her fingers down the leather thongs of a flogger and unhooked it from the wall.

'You can try this out on me, if you like.'

Callum said, 'I thought that wasn't your thing.'

'I never tried the receiving end. Maybe it's time I did.'

She had a sheen of sweat on her upper lip. The fine wisps of hair around her ears were wet and clung to her skin. Callum was aware of his t-shirt sticking to his back, the hot, heavy air in the room catching his throat.

'Where do these things come from?' he said. 'You can't shop for them in Macy's.'

Trinity hung the flogger around her neck.

'There are specialists make them. Some in this country. Some abroad.'

'How much do they cost?'

'Depends,' said Trinity. She walked back to the bench and sat. 'You can get synthetic ones, or cord, for twenty dollars or so. You want quality, the real good, handmade leather stuff? You can pay over a hundred.'

'And they make them here and abroad, huh?'

'All over the world.'

'Like those?' Callum nodded to a box in the corner. It had a skull-patterned cloth draped over the top that had shifted away from one corner and he could see the bound handles of floggers. The box looked full.

Trinity bent down over the box and pulled the cloth over. Callum saw a flash of something south of happy cross her face.

'Nah,' she said, 'this is just five-and-dime stock.'

'That box is full. Why do you need so many? Are they like a hypodermic you throw away after one use?'

'We sell them.' Trinity cocked her hip and put her arms across her chest. 'In the dungeon on the Upper West Side.'

'Doesn't that kinda' defeat the point? If people buy their own from there, why do they need to come to the dungeon in the first place? If they need one of the mistresses at the dungeon, why are they gonna' buy "five-and-dime" stuff to take home? That doesn't make sense.'

Trinity opened her mouth to speak when the phone rang.

'I gotta' take this,' she said and ushered him out of the room.

Back in the living area she answered the call and spoke in "yes" or "no" answers. Callum sat on the sofa. Trinity picked up the phone and walked across the room behind the TV to the window. She set the phone on the sill and her fingers played with the cord.

She hung up after a couple of minutes.

'I should go,' said Callum.

Trinity saw him to the door and said, 'See you at the fight.'

She watched him descend the first flight of stairs. He walked down the stoop on to 95th and looked at the spot where Sol Grundy was shot then turned for 3rd Avenue.

He thought about the box of floggers.

He reached, made connections: the heroin was coming in soaked in the leather tools of Trinity's trade. It made sense. David Chau, shot on the Hong Kong tram, had worked for a chemist involved in taxidermy. Callum followed the trail in his head – with the Triads using such a chemist they'd have knowledge of chemicals and treatments for tanning, just like Bobby Ho figured. Bobby heard talk of liquors on the phone taps, did his research and came up with fat liquor used for tanning leather. He, Milburn and O'Connell had checked out a fashion studio, BOJ, with a tanner had jumped ship: Kevin Zuk. Trinity said there were makers of bondage gear – toys, she had called it – abroad. Maybe in Hong Kong. Ruiz had surmised the drugs could be coating leather clothes or bags but maybe it was coating something else. The tanner in Hong Kong could soak the leather whips and bondage toys in heroin-laced fat liquor; the cargo would sail into New York; and a New York chemist – maybe Zuk – could separate the heroin from the fat liquors. Walsh and the Tongs would sell it on in the Five Boroughs. And Walsh had longshoremen connections at Red Hook.

Mattila and O'Connell needed to get onto Port Authority and customs to check for cargo ships carrying bondage gear or sex toys due to dock at Red Hook tomorrow night. Callum decided to try and call in again from a payphone at 86th Street subway station. He had reached the corner and started south for the station when a voice like peeling Velcro called out.

'Hey Burns, where the fuck are you goin' you sly-ass mother-fucker?'

Callum turned to find a glaring Jimmy Mulligan stood behind him, shoulders hunched and fists clenched like he was ready for a knockdown drag-out twelve-round bout right there on the sidewalk.

Chapter Twenty-nine

Ho, Mattila and Milburn were eating delivery noodles from a place a couple of blocks north of the Manhattan DEA building. Today the sit-down had an edge. Everyone was nervous about Callum's fight tonight and the shipment tomorrow at Red Hook.

Mattila knew a couple of missed calls had come in on Burke's designated number.

O'Connell sat cursing his goddamned dog. He finally persuaded Marcie to let Lily get a beagle and the kid's mutt had tread dirt from the garden into the house, almost sparking a domestic melt-down. Of course, he'd had to clean up the dirt. Of course, he'd been running late and Burke had called his cell when he was ten minutes away on the 495 with the soiled rag in the trunk from rubbing dirt off the kitchen floor. He tuned back into the conversation and realized the noodles tasted like straw this morning.

Bobby Ho was relating what he'd picked up from phone recordings when he got in early this morning. He had been working on transcripts all night, lost in his own world.

'There was a conversation between Charlie Lin and Freddie Wong. I could hear street sounds in the background. Two *brothers* are to reprimanded. They are small time and crossed paths last night with a candidate for membership of an affiliate business. The impression is they stepped out of line in some way. And they were interrupted by *low faan*.'

'Freddie Wong, huh? Flying Dragons business. And he mentioned police?' said Mattila.

Ho was pleased at the DEA Agent's improving grasp of slang. While *low faan* was a derogatory reference to whites in general, the Flying Dragons applied the term to cops, too.

'Yes,' said Ho. 'Lin chided Wong. Wong became angry and said his men didn't know the "guy was connected".'

'Burke is gonna' meet the Tong tonight at the fight. You don't think he's the candidate for affiliate membership? The "connected" guy? The affiliate could be the Walsh crew. Christ, you think they could be onto Burke?'

'No,' said Ho, 'The incident they discussed was out of town'. 'Freddie Wong was angry. He mentioned the east, a village, maybe Webster.'

O'Connell almost spat out his noodles.

'East?' he said. 'A village? East Village. Webster Hall's in the East Village. It was out of town, sure. Out of *China*town.'

He shoved his food aside.

'Ruiz was ghosting Burke at Webster last night.'

The men looked at one another. The call sounded like it was about Callum Burke. Mattila thought of the missed calls this morning.

He said, 'Burke must be alive if he called the designated numbers.'

O'Connell stood and said, 'Unless someone beat them out of him.'

They were silent for a moment, each building a picture in their heads they didn't want to see.

'Bobby and I will go to Chinatown,' said Milburn. 'Sammy Ong's funeral is today and there's a chance Walsh could attend. The Flying Dragons should be there at least: Callum might turn up somewhere.'

O'Connell said, 'I'll hit Chinatown, too. I can take west of Baxter, you two take east.'

Mattila said, 'I'll get some guys and check out the usual Walsh haunts. I'll call up Ruiz and Galinski, too.'

They all stood, O'Connell crossed himself and Niku Mattila downed his tea and walked out of the room.

*

'You're goin' to a funeral.'

That was what Jimmy Mulligan had said as he strode down 2nd Avenue with Callum. They took the subway in silence to Paddy's apartment on Bleecker. At the door of the building, Callum said, 'Hey, Jimmy, how'd you know I was up on east 95th?'

'I didn't. I was lookin' for Doolan's freak whore to see if she might know where you were. Fintan and Paddy and me been lookin' for you.'

Mulligan looked into Callum's eyes like he was reading a book.

'Let's go upstairs,' he said.

Callum thought of the bag in the tank on the roof and wished he had the solid weight of the gun in his hand.

Upstairs, Fintan Walsh sat in the small kitchen in a black suit. His face was slick with sweat, the ploughed side parting exposing pallid scalp flaked with dandruff. Walsh looked at Mulligan. Mulligan looked at Walsh. Walsh turned to the closed bedroom door and said, 'Paddy, the great white hope is here.'

Paddy came in the kitchen and snatched a lighter from the table then sparked up a Marlboro. The smoke hung thick in the small room. No one had looked at Callum since he walked in the door. Mulligan pushed past him and opened the refrigerator, took a quart of milk out and drank from the carton.

'How the fuck you live like this, Doolan?' he said. 'It's like the nineteenth century or some shit, you two sleepin' on top of each other in this shitbox.'

'It ain't exactly Five Points,' said Callum. He looked at Paddy. 'I thought you were working?'

Paddy busied himself with tapping ash in a mug.

'Job got cancelled,' he said.

Callum felt like he was watching the three men through a

309

window, like he wasn't there. They refused to look at him. The stilted talk was as though they didn't want him around until they came to terms with something he did.

His betrayal?

Did they know he was a cop?

It's as though you're dead to them, he thought.

Then Walsh said, 'Hey, Belfast, I got the venue for the fight. 66 Little West 12th Street. You ready to put that Boston fuck down?' He picked at a fingernail. 'Your head in the right place after that shit-show last night?'

Callum's pulse spiked.

'What shit-show?' he said.

'Those fuckin' Chinese,' said Walsh. 'Most times, those wily little slopes are smart as fuck. They got planning and patience, you know, without the wops fuckin' ego. But they fucked up last night, boyo.'

'You knew?'

'I found out this morning when one of them called me to apologize. Seems some low-ranking chink had a scam. A hot girl picks guys up in bars and clubs, she takes them outside and two goons in Halloween cop uniforms roll the mark. Word got back to the people who matter – the people you'll meet tonight – they picked you as a patsy last night, before real cops turned up and you walked away. Unlucky for the assholes tried to roll you, they chose my star turn on the fight card. Those dickheads are gonna' turn up in today's Kung Pao beef.'

'So, it was all a mistake?'

'Goddamned right. Just bad luck. Of all the Irish guys in all the world, huh?'

'Of all the guys,' said Callum. 'And you squared it?'

Mulligan said. 'What do you want, a written affidavit?'

'Hey, our boy got a right to be concerned,' said Walsh. 'Yeah, Christy, I squared it. The people we're goin' into business with are very cautious and last night was outta' their hands. See, they got this – what should I call it? – youth wing? Like a street gang do some of the heavy lifting for them. Those kids got their own scams and they just ran across you. Pure coincidence. 'Course, Paddy shouldna' had my boy out on the town before a fight.'

Callum nodded. In his head, he was spinning facts and assumptions like a bookie spun numbers at the track. How did Trinity know the girl in Webster had him down as a mark? Was she connected to The Flying Dragons? Had the girl not been able to communicate with the fake cops in time and tell them to leave him alone? It was too much. His nerves were cooked.

'I want you with me or one of the guys for the rest of the day,' said Walsh. 'You got star billing tonight, son. We ain't lettin' you out of our sight from now on.'

Callum reached for a smile. 'Alright,' he said. '66 Little West 12th.' He cleared his throat. 'So Jimmy said somethin' about a funeral.'

'That's right,' said Walsh. 'We're goin' to Chinatown. I brought a suit for you, it's on Paddy's bed. Put it on while I take a piss.'

'The john's at the end of the corridor past my bed,' said Callum.

'I know. I went when I got here. Been pissin' like a racehorse since I got up.'

*

The hearse gleamed in the sun, its bodywork a collage of Chinese characters in the reflected signage on Mott Street. A streamer was attached to either side, held by a procession of Hip Sing Tong members, foremost Mickey Chiu. Charlie Lin followed a couple of members behind. A portrait of Sammy Ong in benevolent repose, laid on a bed of flowers, sat on the roof gazing down on the people lining the route around Chinatown and back to the Hip Sing building.

The mourners wore sober suits, and sported mirror sunglasses and carefully calibrated expressions of reverence. The NYPD watched from the sidelines. Bail Bondsmen had gathered on Mulberry Street across from The Tombs detention complex and a delegation of two clerks from City Hall walked with the cortege in sober silence. Callum stood in front of a cheap souvenir store on Mott as the funeral procession approached, wedged between Mulligan on his left and Walsh on his right.

They had driven downtown and parked near the Manhattan Bridge. Walsh and Mulligan moaned about the Yankees and Red Sox, the O.J. soap opera, and the money Walsh had blown on a pay-per-view party for the Tyson vs. McNeely shit-show. They had walked to Chinatown either side of Callum, so close their arms brushed his, like guards steering the condemned man to the execution chamber. The first Chinese characters on storefronts sparked Hong Kong-flashbacks: the hot wet city smell, the burn of a high yellow sun trapped among tall shards of concrete, steel and glass. Then mental snapshots of Tara and Irene – and the panic that he might never see them again.

He felt the terror of alienation.

They know, he thought. Paddy won't look at me. They don't talk to me like before. Oh Jesus, they know.

A voice somewhere in his head whispered back, *Don't be an asshole. They're bad people, they don't do warm and welcoming. Keep it together.*

When they had found a spot on Mott Street he scanned the crowd. He had felt a terrible yearning to see O'Connell, or Milburn or Ruiz. But everywhere were Chinese. Good and bad, honest and sly. Some smoked or talked. Some stood with hunted-looking eyes and he thought how Chinatown was in some sense a micro city-state within the metropolis.

The hearse drew near.

'Who's in the coffin?' he said.

Walsh said, 'Sammy Ong, leader of the Hip Sing Tong.'

'*Former* leader,' said Callum.

Mulligan hissed, 'Show some fuckin' respect.'

Walsh said, 'We're here to see the great man off, and to be seen doin' it. Once that's done, we're gonna' meet the guy responsible for the idiots caused last night's little adventure for a personal apology.'

He looked at Callum sideways and nodded with a smug grin.

The hearse passed. Mickey Chiu gave Walsh a nod. City Hall gave him a wide berth. One of the cops from the Fifth Precinct gave him the finger when he scratched his nose across the street.

A man watched Callum under the awning of a chop house.

Tony Lau.

Callum's brain stalled and his limbs shut down. His innards seemed to liquefy.

Tony Lau, 14K Dragon Head. Here in New York. Callum couldn't put it together in his head. If it were a vision of Old Man Bamboo Zhao across the street he could put it down to undercover sweats. But Lau was something else. Lau was alive. Here. With a blood vendetta.

He saw Jimmy Mulligan stare at him, knew Mulligan saw his skull-eyes, his ashen face, his open mouth. An open book. Mulligan followed his gaze across the street. Callum looked at his own feet and back up again. The man under the awning was dapper, smoking a cigarette like it was Shanghai in the Thirties, fresh in a suit despite the early fall heat. He wasn't Tony Lau.

Shit, thought Callum, I'm really losing it.

'Alright, you're done,' said Walsh.

'*We're* done,' said Callum.

'What?'

'You mean *we're* done.'

'Yeah, sure.'

The crowd began to fracture into the narrow streets and

alleyways. Walsh cocked his head and they began walking toward Pell Street.

Are they gonna' give me to the Tong? thought Callum. Leave me for torture before a bullet in each eye?

He considered running, weighed his chances in the crowded street. He could probably slip Walsh and Mulligan but how many of the people milling around were Tong? How many were watching him, waiting their turn with a knife on the cop? Some seemed to stare, some avoided his eyes. One spat as he passed.

And there, up ahead on the corner of Pell, stood Tony Lau.

Or the same man as out front of the chop-house?

How many were there?

No, this was the real deal, the 14K Dragon Head. Lau nodded at him and smiled. Callum felt a pain in his chest. His bladder loosened as his guts went into freefall. He looked at Walsh.

'Where we goin'?'

His voice was thin with desperation.

'To get that apology then back to the car.'

'Why are we goin' this way?' Callum fought back the whine in his voice.

Mulligan said, 'It's the scenic route. What the fuck do you care?'

Callum looked at the corner again. The man had Lau's cheek-bones, Lau's calculating eyes and self-possession. But it wasn't him. They turned down Pell, Mulligan reciting the route to the car.

' ... Pell to Doyers to Bowery and back to the bridge. That okay with you, your fucking majesty?'

'You know,' said Callum, 'I don't wanna' piss these guys off before tonight. I don't need an apology. Let's just get back.'

'Hey,' hissed Walsh, 'you deserve an apology. I deserve an apology. These yellow bastards screw around with one of my men, even it's an accident – that ain't acceptable. This slope fucker's lucky I don't make him get on his fuckin' knees and beg.'

Callum searched for cops but they were all back on Mott. A large crowd was gathered further down the street where the hearse had stopped in front of the Hip Sing building. He, Walsh and Mulligan hooked right onto the narrow dogleg of Doyers Street. It was like a movie set, all three or four-floor walkups with eateries and Chinese stores on street-level. The sharp turn ahead gave the impression of a dead end. The street was small, enclosed, sealed off from the rest of the city. Callum knew there was at least one entrance to the labyrinthine Chinatown tunnels here. A young man stood smoking in front of a tea parlor. He nodded at Walsh and approached with another two youths who emerged from the parlor door.

Flying Dragons.

This is it, thought Callum. They're gonna' hand me over and I'll end up in those tunnels and never come out.

The lead youth had hair shaved close to the bone, a pencil mustache and a well-practiced sneer. He wore a short-sleeved shirt with a flame design over a white t-shirt and jeans. His companions were in similar clothes and smoked. One wore shades. The leader put his hand in his pocket and Callum got a glimpse of something like a switchblade handle.

He tensed. He could make a break and hope for the best but like the street, he was hemmed in. Mulligan seemed to press in on him. Walsh cleared his throat. The youths were a couple of yards away. Callum said a prayer in his head.

The man appeared on the left like he'd been waiting in the wings and this was his cue. He cut between Walsh and the youths, a diminutive Chinese in a polo shirt babbling in Cantonese and bowing in short bursts.

'What the fuck?' muttered Walsh.

'Fuck is this?' said Mulligan.

The lead youth looked confused. His companions backed up a step.

Everyone froze save the small Chinese man gesticulating and bowing and edging closer to the youths. His speech was garbled and he had his back to the Irish but Callum caught something about directions, and an offer of money.

'Let's go,' said Walsh.

He and Mulligan steered Callum to the curve toward The Bowery. Callum heard an angry roar from the youth and a confused yelling. They rounded the curve. As he, Walsh and Mulligan made for the Manhattan Bridge, he thought he heard the crackle of gunfire over the lament of a passing fire truck.

*

Officer Munn turned the corner onto Doyers Street after hearing angry shouts. He saw four Chinese, two on the ground and two struggling over a knife. The young men on the ground saw him and went stiff but the other two kept grabbing at each other clinging to the knife. One was a youth in some kind of fire-design shirt, the other a man in jeans and a polo shirt. Munn was vaguely aware of someone calling out in English behind him. The voice sounded like someone from a movie with that ripe British accent. Munn drew his Glock and yelled at the Chinese to stop fighting and put the fuckin' knife on the ground. They struggled more. He yelled again.

'Police! Put the weapon on the ground and step back!'

But the men were lost in their fight, the polo shirted man wheezing high pitched, almost moaning. The youth's face was red, eyes wild. He could have been tweaking. Munn was less than ten yards from the pair. The other two youths rolled onto their stomachs and spread their hands on the ground.

Munn took a step forward, gun held out far from his body like it was poisonous. He heard the British guy again behind him shout something about cops.

Munn screamed, 'Police! Put the fuckin' knife down now, dickheads!'

Polo shirt cocked his head, risked a look and saw Munn. He pivoted and tried to move the youth closer to Munn.

When Munn caught sight of the blood on the polo shirted man's hands and arms, some reflex kicked off in his brain. His balls retracted and his finger spasmed. The pop of the shots ricocheted around the street as three rounds hit polo shirt in the side, arm and neck. Another ripped into the fire-shirted youth's hip. The young man dropped like someone cut his strings. Polo shirt went down next to him and it was then Munn realized the blood had been because the polo shirted man had been gripping the knife by the blade, which had cut a deep gash in his hand. The last shot skipped off the street surface and blasted through a prone youth's left eye, drilling through his head and taking a chunk of brain, hair and skull out on exit.

The British voice exploded in Munn's left ear.

'Ho! Bobby! Get an ambulance, now!'

Officer Munn went for his radio. He felt a tight twisting in his stomach, like the Brit had reached inside and squeezed hard.

He'd killed a man, maybe three.

He vomited as an RMP pulled up by a store selling Buddhist funeral charms.

*

The scared man stood sweating outside the bar. He had been rooted to the spot for a full five minutes and knew sooner or later a curious drinker or suspicious bartender would push the filthy glass door open onto 8th Avenue and confront him.

The bar was a rough joint, known for serious drinkers, the kind who clock in at opening and drink through to the early hours. Some longshoremen supped a beer there at times, a few guys working Times Square theaters and peep shows. But the bar's reputation was built on that of its most famous patrons, the few of Fintan Walsh's crew who were still living, fighting and hustling in Hell's Kitchen.

The man took a breath. The Irish still had muscle, still had feet on the street. But muscle and numbers were no good without information and that was what he had to trade. That was what would give him enough money to get the hell out of New York, and out from under the bastards who'd put a fuckin' leash around his neck for way too long.

That was what would stop the Irish puttin' a bullet in his head and chopping him up for chum in Hudson Bay.

He swallowed hard and walked into the bar.

Chapter Thirty

Three hours to fight time. Callum sat beside Paddy in the cab of the truck smoking and rubbing his temples.

After Chinatown, Walsh and Mulligan had taken Callum to Woodside. Some peripheral guys from the crew had popped in and out of the café where they had coffee and wished Callum luck.

Callum had felt a twinge of relief in the Bleecker apartment when Walsh told him last night was some unintentional Chinese fuck-up. Was the Chinatown brush with the Flying Dragons kosher? Had the Dragons really been there to apologize for last night outside Webster Hall, and Walsh and Mulligan had panicked when some random local wandered in the middle of their scene? Who was the guy wandered in on the scene?

Paddy had turned up with the truck and a couple of errands.

'Shouldn't I, you know, do a little training and rest?' Callum had said.

Walsh had laughed. 'Tonight ain't a title bout and I sure as shit ain't Don King.' He took a cigarette from a pack of Pall Mall. 'I think you can manage a coupla' stops with Paddy.'

They made a run to an address in the north Bronx where Paddy told Callum to sit in the truck while he spoke to someone in a clapboard house on a quiet residential row. Thirty minutes later, they drove to a storage facility in Queens. Callum asked what they were doing.

'Business.'

Paddy had left Callum in the truck again. He had carried a long chest, like someone would put at the end of their bed, with another guy out of storage and loaded it in the back of the truck.

Now they were heading back to Manhattan.

Callum tried to figure whether Paddy had clammed up because he somehow knew Trinity had come onto him, or Walsh had told him to keep quiet because they cottoned on to the fact Callum was a rat or a cop. He'd had the wild idea of jumping from the truck but Paddy drove on large roads with heavy traffic.

And maybe they didn't know, thought Callum. Maybe they were playing things close because tonight was a big deal. Besides, the task force would be there at Little West 12th.

But the silence in the cab was driving him crazy, threatening to tip him over. He swallowed hard. Then he clenched his fists and let it burst out.

'What the fuck?'

Paddy flinched. 'Huh?'

'What is your fuckin' problem? You haven't said a word to me for hours. I ain't a dog – sit, Christy. Stay Christy. What's wrong, Paddy?'

Color rose in Paddy's cheeks. He glanced at Callum then stared at the road ahead.

'I saw you in Webster Hall,' he said. The truck sped up.

'Oh yeah?' said Callum, the bit between his teeth. 'What'd you see? You see your woman come on to me? You see her grab my hand, huh? That what you saw?'

'What I didn't see was you fightin' her off.'

'Jesus Christ, Paddy. What are we, in high school?'

'I need her, you dumb mick asshole.'

'You *need* her? So call Oprah. She came onto me, dickhead. And keep your fuckin' eyes on the road.'

Paddy took a left and sucked in a breath.

'Do you hear yourself?' he said. 'You walked in that room in that shit-box hotel, you were straight off the boat and Irish as a shot of Jameson's. Now you talk like an American, you're angry all the time. You want more and more and more.'

He slammed his palm on the wheel.

'You're using me!'

Callum said, his voice thin with spite, 'That's the New York food chain, *baby*.'

Paddy pulled up to a stop light. He turned to face Callum. Callum's arms went taut, his knuckles bone white in hard-knit fists. He waited for a move. But Doolan looked at him with bloodhound eyes and sagged. He took one hand off the wheel and ran it down over his face. It came away slick with sweat.

Paddy said, 'Who the fuck are you?'

It floored Callum harder than any punch. He stared, dumb. His arms went hollow, his chest too, and he felt his face burn.

He said, 'I'm Christy Burns, Paddy.'

It sounded weak. If he couldn't convince himself how could he make Paddy believe?

The stop light changed.

Paddy put the truck in gear.

He kept his eyes on the road and drove on in silence.

*

O'Connell stood with Mattila in a windowless broom-closet side-office in the DEA building. The air was thick with animosity and fear.

'Burke is out there alone with the worst of East and West and we got nothing?'

Niku Mattila had his arms crossed. His fingers were pressed pale against his arms.

'We got a cop in surgery in New York-Presbyterian. Your concern for Bobby Ho is touching.'

Poor Bobby, he thought. Way Milburn told it, they had spotted Callum wedged between Fintan Walsh and Jimmy Mulligan heading from the funeral procession onto Doyers Street. Bobby was so jumpy he looked like he was hooked up to electrodes. They saw the Irish approach a group of Flying Dragons. Bobby thought they were going to hit Burke. He panicked and took off with Milburn trailing behind. Bobby babbled some bullshit about being lost and looking for an address but he'd come on too strong, a little crazy, and a Dragon had pulled a knife. Then some cop came on the scene and pulled a gun. One Dragon was dead, one crippled and Bobby was in intensive care.

It hit Mattila hard.

O'Connell said, 'Let's focus on the cop who hasn't taken a bullet yet, huh? We just lost any ear on the Tong phones with Ho in the hospital. Who's on Walsh's line?'

Callous bastard, thought Mattila. But he knew that was the difference between himself and a street cop like O'Connell. O'Connell could keep it professional on The Job and reserve the best of himself for those that truly mattered in his life. Mattila hadn't developed that filter. He wasn't sure he wanted to.

He said, 'Galinski's on it now but we got nothing. Walsh isn't using his phones. Ruiz is sitting on Little West 12th Street but it's still a couple of hours until fight-time.'

'And Milburn's at Presbyterian with Ho.'

O'Connell wanted to lash out and crack some heads. With Burke in the wind the team was flying blind and he prayed Callum wasn't lying in a dumpster somewhere.

'I got some more news,' said Mattila. 'Results came back on the DNA analysis we took at the river, the bodies washed up we thought were Gabriel Muñoz and a lover.'

'We thought?'

'It isn't Muñoz.'

'So who is it?'

'No idea. We can't find a comparison. Looks like whoever they were, they were snatched at the Belleclaire – we got corroborating witness statements – and someone hit the wrong guy and a very unlucky young lady.'

O'Connell rubbed his face and let out a long, desperate sigh. Time to prioritize.

'So Muñoz is in the wind,' he said. 'We got more pressing problems. You know you gotta' pull Milburn from the hospital. We can't afford to lose bodies and Bobby Ho won't miss him right now.'

Mattila hung his head like it was too heavy and nodded.

'Niku,' said O'Connell.

Mattila stared at the sound of his first name.

'Yeah?'

'We need you. Wherever your head is right now, get back in the game. Okay?'

'Okay.' Mattila found a weak smile somewhere inside. 'Okay.'

'Is Ruiz doin' any good scoping the Meatpacking District?'

Mattila uncrossed his arms and stood with hands on his hips, the right atop his holstered Glock.

'We'll pull her,' he said. 'She can check the major sites from the investigation. Woodside, the Kitchen, the bondage place on the Upper West Side/ Trinity's apartment. She might get lucky and spot Burke, or run into Walsh or Mulligan and tail them to our man.'

'Sounds like a plan, Special Agent,' said O'Connell.

Mattila looked at him like he noticed something he hadn't seen before. Then he said okay once more, as if convincing himself, and made for the door.

*

Paddy pulled the truck up outside the New World office on Columbus Avenue. Callum thought of his first day there, the huddle of men by the ramp leading down to the box-room below street level, the foremen calling out to their crews. Now the office was closed, the box-room shut.

Fintan Walsh and Jimmy Mulligan strolled up and banged on the door of the truck with their fists.

Callum said, 'The gang's all here.'

Paddy looked away and opened the driver's door.

They clambered down from the cab and joined Walsh and Mulligan on the sidewalk.

'Where's Bill?' said Callum.

Mulligan said, 'Watching Fox back home. It's out of hours.'

'Shouldn't we be thinking of getting to the fight? I gotta' get my head ready.'

'All in good time, son,' said Walsh. 'All in good time.'

Mulligan produced a set of keys and stepped down to the box-room doors that opened out to create one large opening through which they could drag boxes and equipment. The ramp was stored inside and there was a drop of about a foot and a half below the sidewalk. As Mulligan opened the locks and swung the doors open there was a scuffling inside.

'Fuckin' rats,' he said. 'You know I read somewhere there are five times more rats than people in New York.'

Walsh sniffed. 'Don't get me started on the roaches. You know how much Combat we put down every spring? Makes no difference to the little bastards.'

Paddy and Jimmy unlocked the back of the truck then rolled up the door and clambered inside. They tossed aside blankets and dodged hanging straps then began shoving the chest toward the edge of the truck bay.

'So don't stand with your dick in your hand,' said Mulligan.

Callum moved to the back of the truck and took the weight of the chest. It was heavy. He held it on the lip of the truck bay until the other two jumped down then they carried it down the short drop from the sidewalk and into the box-room. It was early evening and those passing on the street paid no attention. The city's relentless grind continued.

They huddled around the chest in the box-room. Walsh flicked a switch and the lights came on. Mulligan closed the doors. Callum felt something cold creep through him.

'Alright,' said Walsh, 'let's get this over.' He sounded tired.

The floor had a large tarpaulin stretched across it. Callum had seen enough murder rooms not to like it.

Mulligan went to work on the chest. Callum stood next to Paddy. He was frozen out again, a bit player when he should have been down in the Meatpacking District ready to fight Bobby Cooper. The fight was a couple of hours away. Cooper would be in New York already. Walsh should be downtown playing host to the Chinese Tong. Something was wrong.

Mulligan opened the chest.

The creeping coldness dropped in Callum's center.

Gabriel Muñoz lay inside. One eye was closed over. His face was a palette of purples, sickly yellows and eggshell grays. His mouth was swollen like a baseball on one side, his lip split open. He coughed and gasped for air.

It took a couple of seconds for Callum to notice Mulligan had moved behind him. Paddy walked off to lean against a wall, his expression wretched.

Walsh took a clump of Muñoz's hair in his hand and pulled him into a rough sitting position. Muñoz groaned and his body moved all wrong. He looked like he had a broken arm.

'Alright, Gabriel,' said Walsh, 'take a look.'

He twisted Muñoz's head around. Callum felt the room tilt and contract, the walls moving in to crush him, narrowing until the only thing he could see was Gabriel Muñoz. The hooded open eye swept the room, seemed to struggle for focus, and locked on Callum. He tried to speak and spluttered.

God help me, I hope he chokes right here and now, thought Callum. I hope the bastard taps out like Old man Zhao back in Hong Kong.

Muñoz gagged and his ruined face creased in pain. The good eye shut and he seemed to doze off. Then he gasped and coughed and his voice came out like it was coming through a tinny radio.

'That's him. That's the cop.'

Walsh said, 'Which one?'

'The Irish one in the blue t-shirt. Callum Burke.'

Callum didn't hear the rest. His pulse went crazy and he felt like his skull was too tight for all the shit churning inside. He flashed images of Itsic talking about his Israeli tank as they scrubbed rooms in the Belleclaire. Luciana hanging back as they walked into Gabriel Muñoz's room. Reality cut through. The dismembered bodies by the river in the photos – the photos O'Connell had shown him of the corpses washed up on the Jersey shore: Itsic and Luciana. The witnesses, residents of the Belleclaire, probably high or hung over, got a couple of things right. They saw a swarthy man with blood on his face and a woman taken from Muñoz's room after shots were fired. They heard yelled Spanish. But the bloodied man and young woman weren't Gabriel Muñoz and a lover, they were workers cleaning the room. Itsic had a key because he needed access to clean. He must have taken a chance and slipped a couple of bills were lying around Muñoz's room into his pocket. It just so happened the bills were from the DEA's confidential informant trust fund. The Spanish the witnesses heard coming from the room had been Luciana screaming and pleading. The hotel owner had ID'd Muñoz to close the investigation on two illegal immigrant employees. No one reported Itsic and Luciana missing. They were just two immigrants missed only by people half a world away.

Callum nodded at Muñoz and said, 'Where'd you find him?'

'Asshole came to us,' said Walsh. 'Been hiding out ever since the Chinese shot his cousin out in Dumbo, and hit the wrong guy at the Belleclaire – not that we knew that part 'til today. He turns up at Reilly's Bar hours ago lookin' for me. Says he got information is worth enough to get him far away from the city and the D.E.-fuckin'-A. Information about a cop in our crew. Figured he'd make some money off your head and run.'

'Bastard,' said Callum.

'The boys held him until I was free. After Sammy Ong's funeral. He told us how he set you up to meet Paddy. Moron actually thought we'd let him go.'

Muñoz was prone in the chest again. No one had touched Callum. Mulligan stood back from him like he was infectious. Paddy lit up a smoke still leaning on the wall and sucked on the cigarette, nervous.

Were they all packing guns? Could Callum run? The door onto the street opened and a slight figure in a pair of tight black jeans and leather knee boots entered.

Trinity wore a white t-shirt and leather jacket on top, and a shit-eating grin on her face.

'Hey handsome,' she said.

Paddy snorted.

'She's here,' said Callum, 'so last night wasn't the Tong fuck-up you said back at Bleecker.'

Walsh shook his head.

'Oh, it was. Sure, Trinity here represents our new partners, but that was a screw-up last night.'

'I told you when I warned that skank off was sitting in your lap, *Callum*,' said Trinity, 'they were going to roll you for cash. They're Flying Dragons, kids working their own angles.' She burst out in a high-pitched giggle. 'Their spotter in Webster passed on your description to the guys in the cop-suits outside before anyone could find them and stop them.'

Walsh said, 'We only found out about you bein' a cop while you and Paddy was out in the truck today. When Paddy called into a place in north Bronx on an errand, we got word to him to bring you down here so we could talk. Chinatown today was what I said – an apology from the Chinese for steppin' out of line last night. Makes me look like an asshole now. It wasn't much later I found out about you.'

Walsh and Mulligan hauled the chest to the back of the box-room and left it next to a pile of dollies. Walsh kicked out at a scuffling sound near the tarpaulin behind some book boxes stacked next to the wall.

'Fuckin' rats.'

'You know it,' said Mulligan. 'Rats are always gonna' be around. When you find one, you gotta' break its fuckin' neck.'

He gave Callum a hard look. His eyes were small black pools. The strip lights overhead exposed the battlefield of broken blood vessels on his ruined nose. Callum thought of Dylan Acosta, Mulligan bristling at Callum challenging the Fields Of Athenry. He thought of Donal Morris, the casual savagery of his murder. He thought of men like Mulligan the world over, men like Fintan Walsh. He felt a prickle of rage on his back like hackles rising.

Fuck it, he thought.

'You thick plastic-paddy cunt.'

He saw the red hate spread across Mulligan's face and pushed harder.

'I drank with you, worked alongside you, laughed at you behind your back. When's the last time you got laid, Jimmy? Or are all the choirboys in the old neighborhood on to what a lecherous, sick cocksucker you really are?'

Walsh shot a look at Mulligan – *keep it calm.*

Callum said, 'You're just a dumb wannabe' Galwayman who comes from Hoboken, for fuck's sake. Your balls drop and you ever actually go to Ireland, they'll laugh you off the island for the useless waste of space you are.'

He laughed, warming to the task.

'Hey Fintan, you ever hear from that Dominican bombshell

you met out front of your gym? You know, the knockout with the Ferrari on Roosevelt.'

Walsh's eyes narrowed. A shadow drifted across his features like there was cloud overhead.

'That's right,' said Callum, 'Ferrari girl is a cop, asshole. You gave your direct line to the Chinese to a lady cop. You fucked your whole crew and the Tong because you couldn't keep it in your pants. You're a joke.'

The shot was a thunderclap in the closed room, making everyone jump except Walsh who went limp, folded at the knees and dropped on the tarpaulin with a soft sound. Blood pumped in a tight arc from an entry wound on the left side of his skull and Callum stared as Paddy Doolan walked over and put three more rounds in Walsh with Callum's funny gun.

Jimmy Mulligan said, 'Jesus!'

Callum said, 'Shit!'

Paddy must have got up this morning and followed Callum to the roof. Watched him smoke and hide the revolver in the water tank. Then grabbed it once Callum left.

Callum weighed his chances. Did someone hear the shots on the street outside? Those doors were thick like a bank vault, and if someone heard the bangs they'd be muffled: a passerby would think someone was dropping something heavy on a hard floor. Could he run? He'd never get through the doors onto the street from the box-room. But there was a connecting door just behind the boxes by the chest containing Gabriel Muñoz. It led to a short flight of steps to the office.

And if he made it what then? The office is locked. Columbus Avenue might as well be a million miles away.

Before he could act the door to the street opened and two men entered. They looked at the corpse of Fintan Walsh and closed the doors again.

'That's a prime shot with that piece of shit gun.'

It took him a second to realize the voice was Trinity's. She walked to Paddy's side and put a hand on his chest. Then she pulled a small Beretta 21 automatic handgun from a pocket in her leather jacket.

'You just swore, Trinity,' said Callum. 'Won't your clients be upset?'

He took a breath and reached.

'That how you shot Sol Grundy?'

Paddy gave him a look but Trinity smiled.

'Alright Sherlock, how you figure?'

He looked at Jimmy Mulligan. Mulligan gave him nothing – no rage, no shock. The others stood back.

Callum said, 'The cops who were on the scene said they didn't see anyone. The shooter was in a parked car in front of your building and shot Grundy from there, then ran up or down 95th Street behind other cars before the cops could reach the body. That takes someone small and agile. What are you, five-five?'

Trinity took her hand from Paddy's chest and stood with one hip cocked, the automatic hanging by her side in her right hand. 'Five-three. A hundred pounds, give or take.'

'You're pretty flexible, too, judging by what Paddy told me. You can contort yourself all ways.'

'So I could join a circus,' said Trinity.

'I'm guessing your friends backed your alibi that night were connected to this little enterprise somehow. And you're also a Triad enforcer.'

She laughed and let her mouth hang open for a couple of seconds then said, 'you must be high, Irish.'

'Your hand-signs,' said Callum. 'Last night when your fingers were all twisted up on the dancefloor. There were Chinese dancing nearby. You were giving Triad signs. It was quick but I caught it. It fit when you started trying to play me at your place this morning. The rest figures. The night we went to Bill's

Topless you didn't wanna' go near Chinatown with me around in case you were recognized. You pulled that woman off me in the club last night and whispered somethin' to scare the shit out of her.'

Trinity's smile fractured a little.

'You're crazy.'

'You got your hooks in Paddy too, huh? In all of these chumps, I'd say. Was that a Triad play? You were their liaison with Fintan and the crew? Their spy? I'd lay bets you were the shadow in the alcove when I went to the shooting gallery in Alphabet City. Probably the figure in the kitchen in the Mexican place where I met Walsh in Woodside to talk about the fight. That means you were with the shooters murdered Gabriel Muñoz's cousin under the Manhattan Bridge in Dumbo. You're probably their boss.'

Trinity looked at him like she'd discovered a new species.

Callum said, 'See, Jimmy, Paddy – I'm not NYPD. I'm Callum-fucking-Burke, a Hong Kong cop. I worked Triad cases for years and I can tell you right now, this cold-hearted bitch right here is a 429. An honest-to-God top-level Triad enforcer.'

Chapter Thirty-one

Oh no. No. No. No. No. No.

Oh Jesus, Momma, I'm sorry. I'm sorry I started with the drugs, I'm sorry I wasted my life. I'm sorry I ain't a better daddy for my children and a better man for Candice. I'm sorry God, Jesus and the Spirit. But I swear, you deliver me from this crazy white-boy shit and I'm gonna' change my life like you wouldn't believe, Lord Jesus.

Like you wouldn't motherfuckin' believe.

Johnny Johnson curled tighter behind the boxes and listened to Christy giving the psycho Asian bitch some major shit. His boy, Christy, was a cop! But some kinda' Hong Kong cop? 'Cept he wasn't Christy, he was Callum?

Johnny risked a peek around the edge of the flat cardboard boxes, stacked against the wall. The bad skin asshole with the Fred Flintsone hair was lying dead on the floor, a pool of dark blood around his head.

J.J. had thought the box-room was the perfect place to crash nights since Candice kicked him out. He knew he fucked up, staying out too late around the neighborhood, partying too hard. Now every morning he took a piss in the toilet out back of the office before he climbed into a truck for work and checked the top window of the john was left open. He always hit the john if his crew called back into New World between jobs, too, just to check.

Johnny was skinny and the heroin left him emaciated. It was nothing to go round back of the office at night, upend a crate against the wall, climb on top and haul himself through the open window.

He'd slept in the box-room a couple of times before he began pocketing some of the office stuff at night, stashing it outside and making sure he was out of the building again before Bill opened up in the morning. He sold the stash on and grabbed showers when he could in friend's places or the missions, or the Salvation Army. Recently he'd started shoving the flat book boxes through the window, too, although he didn't know how or where to sell them. He hid them behind the dumpster in the alley.

I don't keep quiet, they'll find my motherfuckin' body in the dumpster, he thought.

Oh please, oh please. Ohpleaseohpleaseohpleaseohpleaseoh please.

Just get me the fuck outta' here an I'll never touch the dope again. I'll go to Blessed Jubilee Baptist Church every Sunday mornin' and night, and I'll never touch the motherfuckin' dope again.

So help me God.

Chapter Thirty-two

Callum said, 'You gonna' let a chink bitch push you around, Jimmy?'

Jimmy Mulligan said, 'Way I see it, you might got a chink bitch of your own, if you're a Hong Kong cop.'

'Fact,' said Paddy, 'you probably got a little half-chink kid back there. Am I right? Maybe Trinity makes a phone call and gets acquainted.'

Callum felt like Mulligan, Paddy and Trinity had hooks in his skin and were pulling him in three directions at once. He played it, giving Mulligan a murderous stare. Let them think his family was in Hong Kong, keep them safe in Ohio.

'I think Paddy got the starter for ten,' said Trinity. 'You're easier to read than The Big Red Barn, Burke.'

He looked at the two men by the doors. What were they thinking? Was Mulligan in on this? How did he feel about Fintan Walsh's body on the floor attracting flies?

Callum asked.

'Did you know Paddy and Trinity were making a play, Jimmy? Did you know they were going to put a bullet in your friend?'

Mulligan hadn't looked at Walsh since Paddy gunned him down. Now he glanced at the corpse. His features seemed out of whack for a second. He cleared his throat.

'No,' he said. 'I didn't know this piece of shit and his freak-show girlfriend were making a play.'

'How about these two?' said Callum.

Mulligan nodded at the two men standing near the door to the street. 'I don't know who the fuck these monkeys are.'

Paddy said, 'They're with me. See, you're right, Christy,

Callum, whatever. Trinity shot Sol Grundy. But ol' Sol was a Russian Jew from Brighton Beach.'

He took out a pack of Marlboro and lit one.

'The Irish are finished. But the Russians are just getting' started. Turns out we did them a favor. Sol caused them some trouble a couple years back when his brother OD'd. "Just say no" style shit, you know? Once we explained the Grundy hit was ordered by the Irish to make way for Jimmy, once Trinity explained the bigger picture with the Chinese heroin comin' in, it was simple enough to broker a deal. The Columbians the Russians been dealin' with on and off for coke are a little too unstable. Seems the Chinese are a stronger bet.'

Mulligan said, his voice flat, 'You faggot piece of shit, Doolan.'

They looked at one another in silence. The two Russians began rolling Fintan Walsh's corpse in the tarpaulin.

Trinity walked closer to Callum.

'You know, Paddy really did like you. He got photos of you two on jobs for New World, drinkin' beer on the balcony, all that shit.'

Paddy had aged ten years in ten minutes.

She said, 'It's true. I am a Triad enforcer. Vietnamese/Chinese parents, born and raised in Brooklyn. I went to university in Hong Kong and never looked back. But though I'm not a Tong, there's plenty of crossover in my work with the Flying Dragons.'

She pointed her gun at Callum and made the sound of a shot like a kid playing at soldiers.

He tried not to flinch.

Trinity giggled and folded her arms.

'And my boss arrived in New York yesterday,' she said.

Callum saw him in his head. The angry man outside the Wan Chai whorehouse with the murderous glare and the hand signal that said, louder than any words, there was a vendetta at play.

'Tony Lau,' he said, 'is here?'

Trinity got serious.

335

She said, 'I took a couple of those photos from Paddy's apartment and showed them to him a couple hours ago. Just to give him a look at you and Paddy before the fight tonight got cancelled. He knows you, Callum Burke.'

Trinity walked to the chest containing Gabriel Muñoz. She pulled a pair of surgical gloves from her pocket, picked a box cutter up from the floor and went to work. Callum heard wet sounds, gurgling and a long sigh. Nightmare images of Dylan Acosta and Donal Morris clashed in his head. Trinity stepped back, peeled off the gloves and rolled them in a ball with the box cutter. She dropped them in the chest and lowered the lid.

'So, what now?' said Callum.

He guessed they weren't about to kill him and Mulligan here. Not now they'd rolled up the tarpaulin, and Trinity had said Lau knew about him. The Dragon Head would want to watch as he got his revenge.

'You get in back of the truck with Jimmy and our new comrades,' said Paddy. 'I'll drive with Trinity up front in the cab. Now put your hands out so the boys can tie you.'

'Where are we going?'

Paddy ignored him and looked at Trinity.

'It's the one with Margoyle's on the side, right?' he said.

She said, 'Yes.'

Once Callum and Mulligan's wrists were bound with packing tape, the Russians had them help carry the chest out to the truck, their hands underneath to hide the ties from passersby. It was awkward but they managed, aware of the guns in Paddy and Trinity's pockets. They clambered into the back of truck. The two Russians carried the tarpaulin with Walsh's body out to the truck. They hauled it in the back and clambered in. Paddy pulled the door down on its rollers.

As the truck pulled onto Columbus, Jimmy Mulligan began humming a tune.

Callum shook his head and smiled.

It was The Fields Of Athenry.

*

'We got nothing,' said Mattila.

'You been everywhere?' said O'Connell.

'Everywhere,' said Ruiz.

'And the Meatpacking District?' said Milburn.

'I already told you,' said Galinski. 'Nothing. It's dead.'

'He's blown. You know he's blown,' said O'Connell.

They stood in the DEA building. Mattila and O'Connell had been on the phones, sending in Walsh crew vehicle descriptions to RMPs and calling the One O-Eight, the precinct policing Fintan Walsh's corner of Woodside. Nothing.

They all knew Burke could be dead. They all worked hard not to believe it. They all started when the door opened.

A DEA Agent gestured for Mattila to step outside.

For a minute, O'Connell, Milburn, Ruiz and Galinski stared anywhere but at each other while Niku Mattila spoke on the other side of the door. Then Mattila threw the door wide and hooked a thumb over his shoulder.

'Someone called 911 from New World Movers,' he said. 'They saw someone get shot and three crazy white guys and a Chinese woman take two men away in a truck. Caller works at New World, name of Johnny Johnson. And one of the men these people took away was Christy Burns.'

O'Connell's stood to go and spilt coffee on his pants.

'Let's go,' he said.

He'd wash the goddamned pants himself.

*

337

The truck jolted and shook before they came to a stop.

Cobbles, thought Callum. Were they down in the Meatpacking District after all?

No, the drive had been too long. There had been an uninterrupted straight which could have been a bridge.

They waited while the engine died then heard the cab doors open and shut.

Tony Lau, thought Callum. It had been so long ago, in another lifetime.

The scent of disinfectant came back to him, the hot Hong Kong night like a wall on the other side of the whores' apartment block door. Lau standing in the street watching him as they loaded Stanley Bamboo Zhao into the ambulance covered with a sheet like a Halloween ghost. Lau giving the Triad hand sign for revenge. Callum jumped as the back of the truck rolled up with a metallic roar.

First he thought someone nuked New York. The truck was on cobbles in a post-apocalyptic wasteland of crumbling, derelict industrial buildings and deserted streets strewn with debris. The shell of a car sat by a dumpster on the corner.

They clambered out and walked, Trinity in front, Paddy and the Russians behind Callum and Mulligan. Callum tried to ease the pressure of the packing tape around his wrists. The Manhattan Bridge crossed above the street a couple of blocks ahead. The lights of lower Manhattan glittered across the East River.

We're in Dumbo, thought Callum, Brooklyn. Somewhere around here Anton Galinski traded shots with the killers of Gabriel Muñoz's cousin weeks back.

The street was lit by a sole lamp on the corner and the lights of the bridge ahead. Trinity crossed to a red brick monstrosity with four metal steps leading from the sidewalk to a metal door. Callum looked up and saw a faded mural two-floors high on the side with a diamond emblem. He read, *Margoyle's Tonic*.

'Can I have a drink?' he said.

'Spoken like a true Irishman,' said Paddy. 'A parting glass.' Something in his voice sounded broken.

One of the Russians said, 'Inside.'

They filed up the steps and into a large industrial space. Concrete pillars, sturdy wooden benches, bare walls lit by a couple of working strip-lights on the ceiling. A trough ran the length of one side of the room with taps set in the wall at intervals. Callum flashed Donal Morris in the butchers' and the sound of knives cutting through meat.

Tony Lau sat by the bench in a suit, legs crossed, coffee in a paper cup in one hand, a cigarette in the other, like a god awaiting his acolytes' worship. A small shrine was perched on the bench for the deity, Kwan Ti, beloved of Triads and police alike in Hong Kong. Lau was slimmer than Callum remembered, and the responsibilities of Dragon Head had etched a clutch of lines around his mouth. But his eyes blazed. When he took a drag on his cigarette his hand shook with rage.

Another be-suited Chinese man with a shock of spiked hair sat nearby. He shifted his hip on the chair like something was digging into his waist on his right side. Something like a handgun, thought Callum.

The Russians ushered Callum and Mulligan over to the Triad Dragon Head while Trinity stood back and offered a bow. Paddy walked over to a bench and leaned back with the funny gun revolver in his hand.

Callum and Lau looked at one another.

Time passed. Seconds, minutes. Years fell away like pages on a calendar.

Callum knew this man had been waiting to kill him and the emotions of the moment were threatening to overwhelm the

Dragon Head. The corners of Lau's mouth twitched. His nostrils were wide, his breaths deep and long. He set the coffee cup on the bench by his side.

Some coffee spilled.

He dropped the cigarette in the cup.

He spoke in deliberate, measured English, like he was addressing a child.

'So this is where you've been hiding you pathetic, Irish, cop sack of turtle shit.'

He put his hands in front of him in the aspect of prayer.

'In the United States of America. The new world.'

He stood and walked to within a couple of feet of Callum. His face seemed to melt, then reset in a terrible smile. He produced a photograph from his pocket of Callum and Paddy grinning on the fire escape back in Bleecker Street.

'When did you arrive in New York?' said Callum.

'Yesterday. And now that we've found each other I'm going to have my people cut you,' said Lau.

He trembled, his voice wavered.

'They will castrate you and feed your severed cock to you until you choke to fucking death, you *baak gwai* shit-eating motherfucker.'

Then he bowed and spat on the floor.

Chapter Thirty-three

The Russians left.

The spikey-haired man with Tony Lau lifted a cloth package from the under the bench and placed it on the floor and unrolled it.

Knives. Choppers. A short sword.

Paddy looked at the floor.

'Me and him still got business,' said Callum, pointing at Mulligan.

'My God,' said Lau, 'you sound like an American. Have you no pride?'

'This man wanted to fight me. What have you got to lose?'

Lau ignored him and knelt by the spread of blades on the floor.

'Two of you have guns. Maybe all of you,' said Callum. 'Me and Mulligan aren't going anywhere.'

Lau picked up a curved knife and turned it in his hands. A brilliant white flame of light ran along the steel blade.

'Come on,' said Callum. He heard the panic in his voice and fought to tamp it down. 'You get to watch us beat hell out of each other, then take your time with us after. It's just more pain and suffering for me.'

'No,' spat Lau. 'It is more time for you.'

Shit! thought Callum.

That was what he'd hoped for. Time. So long as he was alive he had a shot. He still needed to buy time for something – someone – to happen. If that meant toe-to-toe with Jimmy Mulligan, so be it.

He turned to Mulligan.

'Don't you want your shot? They'll kill you, too.' He turned to

Paddy. 'That the plan Paddy? You help cut us up then throw the trash bags in the river at the end of the street?'

Paddy looked away.

'Don't forget to rip the lungs out,' said Callum. 'Don't want us bobbing up around Hunters Point, right?'

'Fuck you!' said Paddy.

Callum called, 'Jimmy!'

He willed Mulligan to react. To say something. Anything. But the man had flat-lined when he needed a reaction.

'Hey, Jimmy!'

Mulligan's jaw worked like he was grinding his teeth.

Lau hissed, 'Shut up!'

'Ah, maybe you're right,' said Callum. 'Paddy, you gonna' take a shift after I'm gone?'

Paddy snapped, 'Can't you shut the fuck up, cop?'

'Take a shift fuckin' Jimmy's mother up the ass now I ain't gonna' be around anymore?'

Mulligan made a small, tight sound with his throat.

Callum laughed. 'You know why he sings the Fields Of Athenry, right? 'Cause his ma belts it out soprano while I'm puttin' her away wet.'

'Stop!' said Lau.

It was fast sound and motion. The scuffle of Mulligan's feet on the floor, the man's bulk barreling toward him. Callum's vision at a crazy cant as he took the impact, the hiss of air driven from his lungs. Yells in English and Cantonese. Callum staring at Mulligan's back then the wall then the ceiling. Taking pummeling blows on his side, his temple. They rolled on the floor in a tangle of limbs, all sharp knees and elbows with their wrists still tied. Mulligan drove his elbows into Callum's ribs. Callum threw his head at Mulligan and felt impact against cartilage and prayed he'd broken the fucker's nose. He rolled, got to his knees and felt crooked teeth take a chunk out of his arm.

They all went to ground with the shot. It roared in the empty space and kicked off the bare walls, then disappeared into the bowels of the building. Callum felt a hot stinging in his shoulder. He thought he was hit. He saw Trinity on the floor, a dark stain spreading across her t-shirt. She held a switchblade in her left hand. Her gun lay by her side. Then it didn't.

Paddy Doolan shoved it in his pocket and swept the room with the funny gun. Lau and the other Chinese, his hand on his right hip over his suit jacket, stared. Mulligan clambered to his feet and checked his busted nose.

Trinity made a small noise like escaping steam. Paddy, holding the gun, looked the most scared in the room.

'She's okay,' he said. 'She's okay. She's okay.'

'She's shot,' said Callum.

'In the arm.'

Callum stood slow. He looked at Trinity, her face matching the gray of the stone floor.

'She's shot above her left breast,' he said.

'So I missed her heart.'

'You could have shattered her clavicle. And there's shock to consider. She needs help.'

'She stabbed you in the shoulder. I thought she was gonna' kill you.'

Paddy winced like someone drove a blade into his gut. He held Trinity's gun in his left hand, Callum's funny gun revolver in the right.

'You really a cop?' he said. The hope in his voice that this was all a joke made him sound like a kid.

'Yeah.'

'Did you wear a wire? Fintan searched you.'

'The apartment was wired. Phone too.'

'I'm on tape?'

'You're on tape.'

Callum waited for the first round from the revolver. His shoulder felt like someone was lighting a fire inside. Would the bullet be worse? How long would it take to die? He wondered if Lau's man was really armed, would put Paddy down.

Paddy gestured from Trinity to the spikey-haired Chinese and Lau.

'Move her against the wall.'

The Chinese man looked to Lau. Lau nodded and the man dragged Trinity to the wall twenty-five feet away then propped her up. Her eyes were closed.

Paddy gestured for the spiky-haired man to leave her and stand next to Lau. The man obeyed with a look of pure murder.

'Both of youse,' said Paddy, pointing the revolver at Lau, 'take your jackets off. Mr Lau, pick up one of them knives. Cut their wrists free.'

Callum saw the rage in Lau's stare. The indignity of an American street thug ordering a Hong Kong Dragon Head around. Of an American shooting the Triad's spy, a top 14K enforcer at that. Trinity hadn't been Paddy's lover, thought Callum, she had been his handler, grooming him to stab Walsh in the back and go into business with the Triads and Tongs. Now he had turned on her.

Lau said, 'You will let them go?'

'No,' said Paddy, 'I'll let them beat shit out of each other. They're Irish. They got bad blood. They should have a shot at settlin' that before they die.'

'I cannot allow that. *I* have bad blood with that cocksucker, Burke. I have a *xie dou* vendetta that demands satisfaction.'

Paddy snorted. 'So get in line.'

Lau said, 'I am the Dragon Head of a Hong Kong Black Society that will make you very, very wealthy. I have hundreds of soldiers. The Tong will bend to me. And you would risk this for some small-minded notion of honor? That man – ' he pointed to Mulligan ' – is not even Irish. He's an American.'

The spiky-haired Chinese took off his jacket. Callum expected to see a snub-nosed revolver. Something easily hidden in a waistband.

No gun. Did he have an ankle holster or was he really unarmed?

'Cut their fucking wrists free,' said Paddy.

Lau barked an order in Cantonese to the spiky-haired man. Callum caught the man's name, Pineapple Wong. The man, Wong, chose a slim blade from the knives in the cloth bundle and walked to Jimmy Mulligan. He sliced through the tape. Then he cut Callum's bond with his head lowered, his thick shock of spiky hair inches from Callum's face. Callum smelled spice and sweat. When the tape snapped the man looked up, hate written across his features like a tabloid headline. He stepped away and placed the knife back on the cloth.

Lau pointed at Trinity and said, 'Mr. Doolan, if she dies, you owe me.'

'Alright,' said Paddy, 'you and your man take a seat by your statue.' He gestured to the small effigy of Kwan Ti. 'I got no love for Jimmy Mulligan, sure as shit not for a rat-bastard cop. Once this is done, you can torture and kill this fucker at your leisure.'

He moved to a bench and crossed his arms, the handguns still in his grip. Then he sighed and rolled his shoulders.

'Jimmy, cop, you got your fight. So have the fuck at it, boys.'

*

O'Connell's face was painted scarlet in the emergency vehicle lights.

'You're sure they were Russians?'

'No, I ain't fuckin' sure,' said Johnny Johnson. 'I been hiding behind cardboard while a man got killed. I'm scared white by the shit I seen and I ain't got well in a day. But I *think* Paddy said they was Russian.'

J.J. sat on the backboard of an ambulance on Columbus Avenue with a blanket over his shoulders sipping coffee from a paper cup. He kept spilling liquid on the ground because of his shaking hand. NYPD officers and DEA agents crowded in front of New World Movers and the block had been sealed off from foot and automobile traffic. O'Connell and Mattila crouched next to J.J.

Mattila said, 'Paddy is Paddy Doolan, right?'

'That's right.'

'After he shot Fintan Walsh.'

'Yeah.'

'Tell me about the girl again.'

'She was small but real mean, man. Looked like she was kinda' in charge, like she had Paddy by the balls, you know. Chinese or somethin'. A real cold-ass bitch.'

Mattila said, 'And they left with Callum Burke?'

'Callum Burke, Christy Burns: I don't know my own name after what I saw.'

Mattila imagined a bullet drilling into Burke's head with each heartbeat. He felt closer to losing it with each pulse.

'Listen, I need you to push through here Johnny. I know you might be hurting. I saw the track marks on your arms, but I need you to think for me.'

J.J. scowled.

'Motherfucking track marks? Man, fuck you! You don't know me!'

'Oh, I know you,' said Mattila, 'I've seen you everywhere. New York, Baltimore, Detroit and more.'

'Yo, get outta' my face, nigger!'

Mattila tipped over the edge. He stood and put his weight on his back foot. O'Connell saw him ready to launch and shoved up against the DEA agent.

'Agent Mattila,' he said, wedging an arm between Mattila and Johnny Johnson.

'You're the reason I do this job,' said Mattila, straining against O'Connell. 'You're the reason – '

J.J. dropped his coffee and said, 'You the problem, black, with your Uncle Tom cop shit! You probably pullin' for O.J. to go down!'

O'Connell said, 'That's enough.'

Mattila spattered Johnny Johnson with spittle as he hissed.

'A man could die here and you're whining about – '

'Mattila!'

'Niku!'

Mattila looked back at the sound of Ruiz's voice. She stood at O'Connell's shoulder. Her face was calm as Lady Liberty. He felt the anger drain from his face, felt heavy. He nodded.

'Give me a second, okay?' said Ruiz.

Mattila walked a few feet away with O'Connell. O'Connell glanced back at the ambulance.

Ruiz stood over J.J. Anton Galinski came over and stood by her side.

J.J. sniffed. 'So what, is this good cop/bad cop?'

Ruiz laughed. It sounded frantic and ugly to her ears. She fought to keep it together.

'If you think that guy – 'she cocked a thumb at Mattila ' – is bad, you haven't been around cops much.'

'I been around some.'

'He's just desperate. We all are because we want to save a man's life.'

'A cop's life. That's worth more, huh?'

Ruiz looked at her feet, set her hands on her hips. She saw Burke in her head on a street with blank eyes and blood on the asphalt like roots spreading to the sidewalk draining life away from his body. When she looked up again her eyes were bright and shining in the lights.

'Are you a father Johnny?

'Yeah.'

'Callum Burke was a father.'

'Is.'

'What?'

'Is a father. He ain't dead yet, what we know.'

Ruiz smiled at '*we*'.

'You're right. And we wanna' keep it that way.'

'Christy ... Callum ... is alright. A little uptight, sometimes, but he's alright.'

'So just work through a couple things again, okay?'

'Okay.'

They went through J.J.'s statement again. Ruiz fought back against the urge to rush and confuse Johnny Johnson, maybe miss some detail might give them a shot at finding Burke. She caught O'Connell tapping his watch.

She said, 'And when they left?'

'I told you, they was all goin' in the truck. Even Walsh's body and the guy in the chest.'

'And Doolan said something.'

'Paddy said a word sounded like *gargoyle*.'

Ruiz heard the plea in her voice. 'You're sure it was gargoyle? Like on a church?'

'No I ain't fuckin' sure but it's what I remember.'

She saw J.J. was pulling for Burke too. His hands dropped in his lap.

'What the fuck else sounds like that?' he said.

'*Margoyle's.*'

They both turned. Anton Galinski stood with a look on his face like he'd hit oil right there on Columbus Avenue.

348

'It's *Margoyle's*,' he said. 'When I was in Dumbo, before the shooting by the bridge, I passed an old building with a painted sign on the wall. It said, *Margoyle's Tonic*.'

'I think your boy's right,' said J.J., his eyes bright. 'Margoyle's.'

'It's thin,' said Ruiz.

'It's what we got,' said Galinski.

'You better get your boss over here,' said J.J. He rocked on the back of the ambulance, pointing at Mattila. 'Call Colin Powell or some shit, send in the motherfuckin' Marines.'

His eyes were wet.

Chapter Thirty-four

Jimmy Mulligan took off his shirt. He had almost ten years on Callum and a good ten pounds. His body was a block of solid power, his face like concrete. This was his comfort zone, the promise and execution of violence. Savagery was as breathing to the man.

Callum pulled his t-shirt over his head. The training and abstention had paid off. He was lean, the power in his forearms flexing the skin. His stomach was flat and hard, a single trench running from sternum to groin, packed muscle either side. But he was scared.

Cut the bullshit, he thought. Mulligan's nervous too.

But he saw the dead space in the man's eyes. Mulligan didn't seem to be feeling much of anything.

Trinity sat propped against the wall, eyes closed. Pineapple Wong and Tony Lau sat next to the shrine on the bench. Paddy now stood holding the guns.

He said, 'Lets go.'

Callum nodded at Mulligan. Mulligan spat.

They circled.

Fists up, thought Callum, simple feet. No probing yet. He willed Mulligan to take a shot. To get that first punch over with, break the seal of fear. Then Callum could get down to business.

Mulligan threw a jab. Knuckles cracked off Callum's arm. Callum went for a shoulder roll counter, threw the punch and took a freight train to his face, the bone under his right eye battered with Mulligan's left hook like someone hit him with a rock. He staggered back as Mulligan went to work on his body. He felt wrecking balls pounding his ribs, his kidneys. Callum closed his body up, went in tight on Mulligan and threw his head up. His crown cracked off Mulligan's jaw and he heard a grunt. He threw a couple of blind jabs, felt his fist hit sweat-slick meat and skin.

He backed off and saw Mulligan wipe a ribbon of blood from his lips to his chin. With luck, he thought, the bastard bit his tongue.

Callum's sides were throbbing with a dull ache. His face stung under his eye but he was okay. Okay enough that he prayed Mulligan wouldn't go for a big shot early. The bigger man was slower. If Mulligan threw a big punch, Paddy might expect Callum to see it coming and hit him with a heavy counter, maybe enough to put Mulligan down. Then Callum would have to go in hard and finish him.

What I need, thought Callum, is time. I need to prolong the fight.

It was a dangerous strategy. If Mulligan dropped him, it was over. If he put Mulligan down, it was over and Tony Lau would go to work on Callum. He had to buy time for someone out there to somehow find him.

Buy time for a bona fide miracle.

Some malicious asshole-voice in his head told him it was never going to happen. No one knew he was here. O'Connell and the rest were sitting in their cars eating doughnuts and monitoring dead wires on Little West 12th. He banished the doubt.

Best to work the jab, move. He had age, lightness and speed over Mulligan.

A straight right smashed into his temple. He threw his hands up and took a shot on his right arm then three battering rams on his body again. He gasped, threw a right hook out of rage and got lucky. His fist cracked off Mulligan's jaw below the ear and the bigger man's head snapped back hard. Mulligan went from sixty-to-twenty, legs sluggish, his big, thick head slow on his neck. Callum stayed away from punishing the face and went in on the body, worked some hard shots to Mulligan's flanks and backed off.

Then Callum hugged himself like his insides were on fire and he needed to breathe, and stole a look at Paddy. Paddy scratched his chin with the edge of the funny gun revolver's chambers. Did he know Callum was faking? Callum was hurting but he could take it – he was waiting for Mulligan to rally. When Callum turned back to Mulligan he saw a look in the man's eyes somewhere between burning hatred and cold self-possession.

Okay, thought Callum. Take it for a while then jab and move, punch on the defensive. Work Mulligan's body. Wear him down slow, control the fight.

He brought his elbows in to his sides as the freight train came roaring up to his body again. As Callum closed up tight Mulligan's body shot switched to an upper cut. Callum felt his jaw smash shut, his brain jolt hard.

His legs went and he dropped on the cold stone floor.

*

Goddamned traffic, thought O'Connell.

They drove in a convoy, O'Connell and Milburn in one car, Mattila, Ruiz and Galinski in another. Three DEA agents in a third bringing up the rear. An NYPD Emergency Service Unit would meet them when they turned off the Brooklyn Bridge in Dumbo for a tactical assault. The ESU were bringing their heavy truck and an REP, a metal cabin full of emergency gear mounted on a 4X4 pickup. Another ESU unit, Eight-truck team based at the Eighty-fourth Precinct near Brooklyn Bridge, would meet them for the hit.

The gridlock moved an inch. O'Connell wanted to hit the lights and part the waters but the car was a rented Buick like the other two, hired for what should have been the Meatpacking stakeout before the bust at the fight so no lights or sirens. They'd been so pumped to get to Burke they took off ahead of a blue-and-white escort. He slammed the steering wheel and cursed.

'Do you think he's dead?'

O'Connell turned at Milburn's reedy voice. Milburn was gazing at the bumper of the car in front.

'Burke's smart, he's got sharp instincts after months under-cover, and he's got two great reasons in Cleveland to fight all the way. He's alive.'

'The Triads don't stand on ceremony when it comes to murder.'

'He's alive. Shovel it up and swallow it, I ain't got time to carry you right now, Jim.'

O'Connell swore, edged the Buick onto the sidewalk and killed the engine. He jumped out and walked to Mattila's car behind. Mattila, in the front passenger seat, wound the window down.

'We gotta' ditch the cars,' said O'Connell.

'I called for patrols to get us through here.'

'It'll take them too long to reach us and we'll still be crawlin' until The Bowery at least.'

'You want to run?' Mattila looked sick.

'The subway is over there,' said O'Connell. 'We park up here, take the subway to Brooklyn Bridge.'

'Then what? The Bridge is over a mile long.'

'It's next to One Police Plaza. Radio now, have One PP get some cars ready to meet us with the ESU then we burn over the Bridge and Galinski finds the mural. Meet the second ESU team over there.'

Mattila nodded. He looked a little less wretched.

Ruiz jumped out as Mattila drove onto the sidewalk to let the third car know the plan. A taxi two cars back gave a blast of its horn. O'Connell pulled his shield out of his shirt and let it hang on his chest by its chain. A lady walking a Pekinese tutted and hustled past.

O'Connell patted the revolver on his hip and said, 'God bless the New York subway.'

*

Callum was on one knee, right hand on the floor, trying to find his balance and piece his head back together. Mulligan had hit him with the uppercut and he'd gone down then the psycho was on him like an attack dog. Callum had taken hard shots to his head, his face. The skin around his left eye felt tender and he figured he'd look like hamburger by the end of the fight. His head had cracked off the stone floor and he had a bite mark where Mulligan had chomped on his right ear. That was the point where someone had grabbed the crazy bastard and hauled him off.

He saw now it had been the spiky-haired Chinese. He stood yelling at Mulligan who was clenching his fists and shaking. No, not shaking – vibrating like he was packed tight with brutal energy and if he split at the seams the whole room would be engulfed in violence.

Paddy stood waving the guns and screaming at the Chinese to sit the fuck down, at Mulligan to get his shit together. Through the fog of his battering, Callum caught the idea that the Triad had panicked and didn't want Mulligan finishing Callum off. That honor should go to his Dragon Head, Tony Lau.

I'm on two feet now, thought Callum. Progress.

His head was clearing some and the nightmare carousel he was riding was slowing down. He was sore and busted all over, his knuckles were skinned, his lip split but nothing felt broken.

'Mr. Mulligan,' said Tony Lau.

The room went quiet at the quiet authority in the measured voice. Callum saw in Lau's small, cold eyes and controlled posture the true power of the man who commanded hundreds of criminals across Hong Kong, Asia and now New York City.

'Your opponent is on his feet again.'

Mulligan stood to his full height and took a deep lungful of air.

'I would ask,' said Lau, 'that in whatever punishment you exact on this cocksucker, you leave him alive and cognizant enough to suffer at my hands once you are finished. I want him aware when I finally cut his throat.'

'Sure,' said Paddy. 'Jimmy'll leave enough for you to play with, right Jimmy?'

Mulligan said, 'Go fuck your mother,' and moved in for another round.

*

They picked up the cars at One Police Plaza and a heavy truck from One-Truck Lower Manhattan ESU squad. The entrance to the Brooklyn Bridge had been cleared to let them through and they went in a convoy of three cars with the huge ESU heavy truck bringing up the rear. O'Connell and Mattila sat in the back seat of the lead car with two uniforms up front.

They were jacked, shifting on their seats. O'Connell wanted to grab the driver's seatback and scream at him to go faster, that a man's life was in the balance.

Traffic had been pulled to the left of the three Brooklyn-bound lanes on the bridge and they could keep the cars over forty-five or fifty. But the cops driving were nervous. It only took one asshole to pull out, to walk into the road, to open a door at the wrong time.

The asshole turned out to be almost at the off-ramp.

The first O'Connell knew, the cop driving was yelling. Then he swung the car right and O'Connell saw the taxi in the road ahead, the frantic uniforms waving for the idiot to stop, the blur of the guardrail as their car veered for the outer edge of the overpass. The driver turned into the skid and they felt a terrible stomach-lurch as they headed for the guardrail. The rooftops of downtown

Brooklyn sped toward them, the street a hundred feet below. Mattila grabbed for a hold next to O'Connell and snatched at his sleeve. They hit the rail and bounced off back into the middle of the two outer lanes. The following car with Ruiz and Galinski hit them in a crazy skid and they spun, both cars crumpling up front. Mattila yelled. O'Connell swore. They spun toward the guardrail again. The car seemed to tip upward and ride the rail. It was how O'Connell imagined a plane crash, the horror of no control as you plummet to the ground and wait for every bone in your body to break. But the car rode the rail for a couple of feet and settled on the outer lane. The ESU truck jackknifed and stopped.

They clambered out of the cars.

'My God,' said Mattila.

Their vehicle was dead. The second car had ended up on its side with a trail of broken glass behind in the center lane. Ruiz was hauling herself out the top with Galinski on the road waiting. Both had blood on their faces. Traffic sat bumper-to-bumper in the inner lane.

Uniformed cops swarmed the taxi, some with guns drawn, others with hands on holsters.

'Goddamn it!' yelled Galinski. 'We're so close if I walk to the edge I can practically see the fuckin' building.'

Mattila said, 'Everybody okay?'

Ruiz nodded. 'We run?' she said.

'We jump in there,' said O'Connell.

He pointed to the ESU truck, a hulking Ford the size of a garbage truck with the number One on the grill and metal platform on the front.

'We can ride with the team. Plough through this shit storm and get down there faster.'

Milburn ran up from the third car.

'Let's go,' said O'Connell. He nodded at Milburn. 'Our boy's waiting for the cavalry to arrive, Jim.'

Callum took a shot and felt a burning hot poker in his left side. He gasped. He threw a couple of desperate jabs. They kept Mulligan's head down but Callum's knuckles hit rock-hard skull and little else.

He stepped back and took a breath. His side burned but he could breathe and bear it. Maybe not a cracked rib after all. He raised his battered arms in defense and stepped in for some more punishment.

Body shots pounding his flanks, his gut like tenderized sirloin. Jabs snapped at his cheeks, his ears, a dull throb of pain building to a sense-dulling ache in his head. His knuckles were bruised and split from hitting Mulligan's thick head. Callum reckoned they were trading shots at a three to one ratio in Mulligan's favor. He was fading, knew it, felt the hope of a last minute reprieve – of survival – slip away. He felt his life ebb with each stamina-sapping punch he took.

He was going to die. No regrets for Irene or Tara or any of it: no space in his battered head for them now. He took another punch on his right ear and staggered back. His face was greasy with sweat and blood, both his and Mulligan's. He wiped his eyes with a forearm. They stung with sweat-salt.

'Shite,' he slurred like a drunk.

Mulligan stopped for a second and gave Callum a hard look. Mulligan's lip was split and swelling, there were a couple of cuts over his right eye, his nose was skewed to the left. But he wore it well like a mark of distinction. The bastard hummed the first bars of The Fields Of Athenry.

Callum tried for a whistle. His throat cracked. He cleared it and managed a fragile stab at Star Of The County Down.

Mulligan shook his head.

'You're fuckin' touched,' he said.

For a second it was just the two of them reaching through their pain and hate for something close to respect.

Callum broke it.

'And you're a wannabe, House Of Pain listenin' mother-fucker,' he said and went in upright.

He threw a combination with a power he didn't know he had left and watched Mulligan's head snap back with a right hook. It took a second. Mulligan seemed to freeze, his eyes flickering like he was changing channels in his head. Then Callum saw the man's legs buckle, saw the look of incomprehension on the busted face. Callum held back for a second. But he felt something huge and fierce and triumphal rise inside him and knew he couldn't help himself. It was meat to a lion, booze to a priest. He went in hard, wild haymakers smashing off Mulligan's head. The bigger man's face had the look of an animal when it knows it's tonight's dinner. Jimmy Mulligan went down.

Callum fell on him and started pounding. He pummeled skin puffed below an eye socket. A punch opened another split in Mulligan's lip. His split knuckles cracked off cheekbone. They were slathered in blood and sweat and Mulligan lay taking it, his arms on the floor.

He was done.

Somewhere deep in his head Callum thought, It's over.

Lau will take me, take his time.

'It's over.'

He heard a voice at his ear and felt arms grab him. The rage left him and he was lifted, turned, held close in a lover's embrace. Paddy Doolan's hand went to the back of his head. He felt the cold metal of the revolver's chambers on his cheek, the frame of the makeshift grip against his ear.

'You're okay,' said Paddy. 'You did good, Christy, you did good.'

Callum's memory slipped away to another place – a basement

with another beaten fighter on a hard floor. Dylan Costa babbling in Spanish. Fintan Walsh holding court on a cheap chair with a forty ounce of malt liquor. A lifetime ago. And Paddy whispering, *you did good.*

He swam back into the here and now. He could smell tobacco on Paddy's breath. He heard Lau speaking Cantonese to his man and a rustle of clothing. Tasted blood and salt in his mouth. He wanted to beg Paddy to save him. To protect him from Lau, not let the Triad go to work and cut him until he wasn't a man anymore and begging for death. But he couldn't form the words. He was too scared, too confused. Too damaged.

The crack of the shot seemed to come from far away and Paddy jerked like someone had yanked at a string around his arm. Paddy dropped the funny gun and looked at Callum as though he'd forgotten who he was.

Lau yelled, '*Diu!*' – *Fuck!*

Pineapple Wong screeched, '*Ngóh coeng!*' – *My gun!*

Callum looked at Trinity.

Wong's gun was in her hand.

Bastard, he thought. Must have slipped it to her when he dragged her over to the wall. She'd awoke and found a strength somewhere, raised her arm and fired on some killer instinct. Fired a shot into Paddy Doolan's shoulder. Paddy who stood staring at Callum with the small semi-automatic still in his left hand.

He turned to Trinity as Wong ran to her.

The gun still raised she seemed to jump as noise and fury erupted around her. Her face was there, then gone in a mask of crimson. Her arm dropped. Shouts echoed around the walls, sounds colliding in a mass of yelling. Callum charged Paddy, driving him back and down as black-clad men ran in. The semi-automatic clattered across the floor. He saw a couple of black body-bunker shields emblazoned with the word POLICE in

359

white letters. There were controlled volleys of shots and more shouts. Men in body armor and Fritz helmets. Paddy screaming with the pain in his shoulder, yells of *Police! Police!* Lau screeching in Cantonese.

Lau grabbing the semi-automatic.

Cops sighting H&K MP5s on the Triad Dragon Head. Callum yelling not to shoot.

Lau screaming and turning the gun on himself. Sudden, jarring quiet.

Radios whispering.

Everything in the balance. A Triad boss or nothing. Callum knew Lau would pull the trigger before he'd give the cops a 14K trophy as big as a Dragon Head. Before he'd risk letting some tiny detail slip in interrogation. Before he'd give Callum Burke the satisfaction of locking him up.

Crazy-silence. Cops staring, ESU men still aiming their MP5s. Lau crying.

The gun at his temple. In his mouth. His hands trembling.

Callum not breathing.

Lau slumping, the semi-automatic on the floor again. Unfired. The cops swarming him, securing him with plastic cuffs.

Then ghosts from a past life come to visit Callum: Mike O'Connell snapping, Niku Mattila shouting, Georgie Ruiz calling his name. James Milburn saying *Thank God!* over and over. American and Chinese voices clashing in the bare-walled space.

Callum on the floor, tangled in Paddy's limbs. Breathing, mainlining adrenaline.

Breathing hard.

Breathing.

Alive.

Chapter Thirty-five

The ship sat in dock at Red Hook.

Midtown across the East River spilled white Christmas lights in September on the dark water. Dylan Acosta could have been somewhere in the depths of the river, perhaps keeping company with Donal Morris. If so, they were among the last few of the Walsh crew victims to spend eternity in the black purgatory between Manhattan and Brooklyn. The devil was dead. Fintan Walsh lay in the morgue, his criminal empire gone with him.

There was no elation but a lot of pain for Callum Burke. He hurt everywhere. Some relief, maybe, but the job wasn't done. There would be further arrests, collating of evidence, interrogations and the slow grind of the RICO court case. A far cry from the chaos of last night in a deserted Brooklyn factory.

Paddy Doolan made it.

The spiky-haired Triad, named Pineapple Wong, didn't.

Trinity either.

Tony Lau was taken in an ESU truck to a guarded cell at Manhattan Correctional Center. The MCC hadn't seen so much security since Ramzi Yousef was swept into town earlier in the year.

Callum had stared at Tony Lau while the Hong Kong man lay on the concrete floor in Brooklyn. A delicate figure in captivity, surrounded by ESU officers in body armour with Glock Model 19s, Heckler & Koch MP5A3s and Ruger Mini-14s.

Lau had put a loaded gun in his own mouth, had put his finger on the trigger. Had been a hair's breadth from robbing the task force of its greatest trophy in the RICO case. A Triad Dragon Head. The man was ruthless and driven in his hatred of law enforcement and he didn't lack the nerve to blow his own brains out. But Lau had dropped the gun and slumped on his knees like a repentant sinner. The cops had kept Lau on the floor, patted him down, searched his pockets. And found the small Papal medal, the prayer card, the gold cross on a gossamer thin chain in the 14K leader's pocket.

Callum's mother and father had shared a devotion to God. Both held a rock-solid belief in the sanctity of life. His mother would not discuss suicide. His father called it a mortal sin. He never thought they would share a credence with Tony Lau but there it was. The Triad 14K Dragon Head couldn't pull the trigger, couldn't deny law enforcement their biggest game, because of his hidden Catholic faith.

Hypocritical bastard, thought Callum.

So the Triad Dragon was beheaded. But for how long? Rumors were hitting Hong Kong Police through CIs that 14K machinery was already in motion to place a Deputy Leader, a man named Tse, on the throne in Hong Kong.

All things passed; the world turned.

Now Callum stood on a raised platform at Red Hook watching the Customs officers, cops and Feds on the dock below. So many uniforms, so many lights, vehicles, holstered guns.

'I've never seen so many mustaches in one place,' he'd told O'Connell when they arrived.

From a core team of so few – himself, O'Connell, Milburn, Ho, Ruiz, Mattila, Galinski – the arrest of the Chinatown Tong element, seizure of Hong Kong heroin and dismantling of the remnants of the Walsh crew had become a city-wide concern. Callum's hunch had been right – the heroin had been soaked into leather floggers, bridles, a couple of corsets. Bondage gear some administrator with a hangover and an eye on the clock had got sloppy and written up as 'toys' in the cargo.

'Sex toys,' Galinski had said. 'No wonder we couldn't find any clothes or bags in the paperwork. It's all gimp couture.'

'You'd know,' Ruiz had said.

Tonight, more cops and DEA agents were at the MCC, not just to safeguard Tony Lau in his cell, but Jimmy Mulligan too. A special detail were also in place at New York-Presbyterian, half on Bobby Ho, half on Paddy Doolan.

Ho was still critical. His family were flying in from Hong Kong and Milburn had left his side only for the raid on Dumbo and some snatched sleep. Bobby might make it, they said. Might not. Callum didn't want to call it. He'd quit gambling.

Paddy Doolan was watching TV and eating take-out pizza. Only the best for the key witness in the RICO case to come.

Had Doolan turned against the Triad during the fight in the empty warehouse? That was the story and Paddy had his script down pat. It began with his betrayal by Trinity, how she had used him then tried to dump him for Callum the night before Walsh's killing.

'And when I saw you fightin' Jimmy,' Paddy had said, 'when I saw them chink bastards watching you suffer and bleed on the floor in Brooklyn? I knew it was all wrong, man. You're a cop, yeah, but you're an Irishman, Christy. Or whoever the fuck you really are. These fuckin' Asians feeding dope to Americans on our streets, I can't live with that.'

Prime bullshit but exactly what Niku Mattila wanted to hear. Paddy had already given them a location where they picked up the missing chemist, Kevin Zuk: an "empty" space two floors down from BOJ Garments in the building owned by Two-Six-Three Holdings, the subsidiary of Triad front company Phoenix Investments. Just the first of many promised nuggets of information Paddy picked up from Trinity during their time together. Doolan was angling for a deal and the DEA was going for it like a nun for gin. Mattila was going to get his case. Paddy would be the premier federal witness, Tony Lau the prize big game.

In a year or two, Doolan would be selling shoes in Nebraska

or some such under a new name, courtesy of the US Marshalls' WITSEC program. Irish organized crime in New York would virtually be a thing of the past. The Tong would take a serious hit, top members would go down, the heroin operation would collapse. For a while. The DEA had even opened a door to the Russians out in Brighton Beach.

'So how's the hero of the hour?' said Mike O'Connell.

He climbed the last step to the raised platform in the docks and offered Callum a cigarette then shook his head at the Hollywood production unfolding in Red Hook. The arc lights, the RMPs, the cowboys with shields hanging over t-shirts and Ithaca Model 37 shotguns. The pinprick lightshow backdrop across the river in Manhattan.

'Tip-top,' Callum said. He took a smoke and O'Connell lit him up.

O'Connell said, 'When this is done, you wanna' get a drink?'

'Sure. I been pissing blood all day, might as well mix it with a little booze.'

'I know this great bar on Canal Street, near the C Train station. Cheap, dark and seedy.'

'Just like your choice in women.'

'Fuck you. I don't go around getting' felt up by a homicidal dominatrix at night, asshole.'

Callum took a drag on the cigarette. The air was beginning to thin as the city slipped into fall. The pressure of the hot, wet summer had eased. Soon more of those electrical storms Paddy had promised him would move in as hurricanes strafed the east coast further south. He took in the majestic Chrysler Building, the Empire State lit red at its top, the fairy lights of the 59th Street Bridge spanning the black water. He couldn't imagine being anywhere else at that moment. And New York was a lot closer to Ohio – to Irene and Tara – than Hong Kong.

'That bar on Canal,' he said, 'I might've been there.'

'You just might. First night we met.'

'Tell you what, let's swing over by the hospital, look in on Bobby Ho, then go get those drinks.'

O'Connell looked at Mattila waving him over by an RMP.

'You got it,' he said. 'Only thing, I gotta' call my wife. Let her know not to wait up. You got some change I can use for a pay-phone?'

Callum looked away across the river and smiled.

'How much do you need?' he said.

O'Connell put his left hand in his pocket and stroked his chin with the right, looked at the ship at dock and the men swarming it like an attacking colony of ants, and cleared his throat. He checked his other pocket and sniffed.

'You got thirty cents?' he said.

Then he walked down to the madhouse spread out below.

THE END

Acknowledgments

Rat Island was a major undertaking for me. In writing the book I mined my memories and diary of much time spent in New York City back in 1995, where I knew some of the best, and a few of the worst, of The Big Apple's street life. I went back to the city in 2019 when writing this novel and found it much changed, but The Dublin House on West 79th hadn't and for that I (but not my liver) are grateful. Thanks to all the boys for making my visit such a good one.

Thanks, also, to the officers and sergeants on duty in the Fifth Precinct on a drizzly night in May who managed to spare a few minutes of their busy time for a chat when I wandered in the door unannounced.

Michael Matthews, writer and former police officer, was instrumental in making my research trip to New York so valuable and showed infinite patience in dealing with my emails – his book on policing in Detroit, *American Ruin*, is well worth a read. Huge thanks go to former NYPD detective Ira Greenberg, who put up with me bouncing between cafés in Manhattan when calling him; Vic Ferrari, writer and former NYPD detective, was gracious and helpful in replying to my emails querying some points of NYPD policy – his books on New York's Finest are recommended; and former NYPD detective Neil Nappi contributed hugely to the writing of this novel thanks to his generosity in giving so much of his time to sit down face-to-face and chat about his years in the narcotics division, and his memories of policing the streets of north Manhattan. All the authenticity within the pages of *Rat Island* is thanks to these men; all the inaccuracies are solely down to me: as are the wilder flights of fancy. However, having spoken to real cops, I can attest that truth really can be much stranger than fiction. I'll leave it to the reader to decide which is which in *Rat Island*.

Regarding the Triad practices and characters in the book, I found several non-fiction works to be of great help in research, none more so than *Warlords of Crime* by Gerald Posner. Gerald needs no introduction in the pantheon of American investigative journalism and I am grateful that, amazingly, he read my novel and gave it his own seal of approval.

Away from the US, in Gloucestershire, thanks go to Jon Pitman at Fight Factory and Andy Harris, a fighter and a gentleman, for talking about life as a boxer in and out of the ring.

Thanks, as always, to David Cameron for his opinions on early drafts. My editor, Humfrey Hunter has, once again, done a fantastic job and given freely of his limited time. Ollie Ray did a great job on the cover and put up with my fretting: thank you for making the book look so good. Also thanks to Claire McGowan, Gary Donnelly and David Peace, for taking the time to read my work. I hope to grab a beer with a couple of you when in London or Tokyo – my round. Finally, thank you as always, Tomoe and Hana for your love and support, and for such cool alternative cover ideas!

CPSIA information can be obtained
at www.ICGtesting.com
Printed in the USA
LVHW031137170721
692931LV00004B/613

9 781913 727086